DEATH MESSAGE

DEATH MESSAGE

Mark Billingham

Little, Brown

LITTLE, BROWN

First published in Great Britain in 2007 by Little, Brown
Reprinted 2007 (twice)

Copyright © Mark Billingham 2007

The moral right of the author has been asserted.

A CIP catalogue record for this book
is available from the British Library.

Hardback ISBN 978-0-316-73052-5
C Format ISBN 978-0-316-73054-9

Typeset in Plantin by M Rules
Printed and bound in Great Britain by
Clays Ltd, St Ives plc

Little, Brown
An imprint of
Little, Brown Book Group
100 Victoria Embankment
London EC4Y 0DY

An Hachette Livre UK Company

www.littlebrown.co.uk

For Claire, as they all are.

Revenge triumphs over death; love slights it.

FRANCIS BACON

PROLOGUE

He could tell they were coppers the second he clapped eyes on them, but it was something in how they stood, in that formal awkwardness and the way their features set themselves into an overtight expression of concern, that drilled a hole straight through to his guts; that sucked the breath from him as he dropped into the chair the female officer had advised him to take.

He drew spit up into his dry mouth and swallowed. Watched as the pair of them tried and failed to make themselves comfortable; as they cleared their throats and pulled their own chairs a little closer.

All three winced at the sound of it. The dreadful scrape and its echo.

They looked like they'd been dropped into the room against their will, like actors who had wandered on to a stage without knowing what play they were in, and he felt almost sorry for them as they exchanged glances, sensing the scream gathering strength low down inside him.

The officers introduced themselves. The man – the shorter of the two – went first, followed by his female colleague. Both of them took care to let him know their Christian names, like that would help.

'I'm sorry, Marcus, but we've got bad news.'

He didn't even take in the names, not really. Just stared at the heads, registering details that he sensed would stay with him for a long time after he'd left the room: a dirty collar; the delicate map of veins on a drinker's nose; dark roots coming through a dye-job.

'Angie,' he said. 'It's Angie, isn't it?'

'I'm sorry.'

'Tell me.'

'There was an accident.'

'Bad one . . .'

'The car didn't stop, I'm afraid.'

And, as he watched their mouths forming the words, a single, banal thought rose above the noise in his head, like a distant voice just audible above the hiss of a badly tuned radio.

That's why they sent a woman. Because they're supposed to be more sensitive. Or maybe they think there's less chance I'll break down, get hysterical, whatever . . .

'Tell me about this car,' he said.

The male officer nodded, like he'd come prepared for this kind of request; was happier to be dealing with the technical details. 'We think it jumped the lights and the driver couldn't brake in time for the zebra crossing. Over the limit, like as not. We didn't get much of a description at the time, but we were able to get a paint sample.'

'From Angie's body?'

The copper nodded slowly, took another good-sized breath. 'We found it burned out the next morning a few miles away. Joy-riders . . .'

It was sticky inside the room, and he could smell the recent redecoration. He thought about sleeping, and of waking up from a nightmare in clinging sheets.

'Who's looking after Robbie?' He was staring at the male copper when he asked the question. Peter something-or-other. He watched the officer's eyes slide away from his own, and felt something tear in his chest.

'I'm sorry,' the woman said. 'Your son was with Miss Georgiou at the time of the accident. The vehicle struck them both.'

'They were both pronounced dead at the scene.' The male officer's hands had been clutched tightly together. Now he loosened the grip and began to spin his wedding ring around his finger. 'It wasn't drawn out, you know?'

He stared at the copper's thumb and forefinger working, shivering as his veins began to freeze and splinter under his skin. He felt the blood turning black and powdery, whispering beneath his tattoos and his yellowing flesh, like the blood of something that had been dead for a very long time.

'OK, then,' the female officer said, meaning: Thank Christ for that. Now can we get the hell out of here?

He nodded, meaning: Yes, and thanks, and please fuck off before I smash my head into your face, or the wall, or the floor.

Walking back towards the door, where the warder was waiting, it was as though each one of his senses were suddenly working flat out; heightened in a momentary rush, before everything began to shut down.

Cracks in the painted brick gaped like crevasses, and he was tempted to push his fingers inside. He felt the material of his jeans, coarse against his legs as he walked. And, from across the room, the whispers of the two police officers came to him easily – deafening above the sound of his own feet and the noise of the water streaming through the radiators.

'When's he get out?'

'A couple of weeks, I think.'

'Well, at least he won't have to wear handcuffs to the funerals . . .'

PART ONE

'SEND'

ONE

Tom Thorne wasn't convinced that the old woman had the ace she was so obviously representing. He wasn't fooled for a minute by the sweet-old-lady smile and the spectacles; by the candyfloss hair or the cute tartan handbag. He didn't believe the square-jawed type in the tux either, whose bluff he'd successfully called a couple of hands earlier. He put the guy on a pair of tens at most.

Thorne raised fifteen dollars. The ace *he* was holding gave him top pair, but with three hearts on the board, he wanted to scare off anyone who might possibly be chasing the flush.

The guy in the tux folded, quickly followed by the bald bloke in the loud shirt who'd spent the entire game chomping on a fat cigar.

Now it was just Thorne and the old woman. She took her time, but eventually laid down her cards and let him take the twenty-five dollars in the pot.

This was the joy and the frustration of online poker. Though the players were real enough, the graphics of the characters around the table never changed. For all Thorne knew, the old woman – who rejoiced in the username Top Bluffa – was in fact a dough-faced adolescent in the American Midwest.

Thorne, who for the purposes of Internet gambling was known as The Kard Kop, had been logging on to Poker-pro.com for a few months. It was just a harmless bit of fun, no more. He'd seen enough of its victims to know that gambling could take away everything you had as efficiently as a smack habit, and that there were many thousands around the country for whom its availability online only sped up that process. For him, it was a relaxing way of winding down at the end of a shift, no more than that. Or, like tonight, killing time while he was waiting for Louise to call.

He glanced at his watch and was amazed to see that he'd been playing for two and a half hours.

Flicking his eyes to the bottom of the screen, he saw that he was forty dollars up for the evening. Two hundred and seventy-five dollars ahead overall. There was no arguing with that, and he reckoned that even if he lost some money now and again, it would still be less than he'd get through in the same amount of time in the Royal Oak.

Thorne got up and walked across to the music system. He ejected the Laura Cantrell CD he'd been listening to and began looking for a suitable replacement, deciding that he'd give it another half-hour; forty-five minutes maybe, until two o'clock. Then he'd call it a night.

He'd been involved with DI Louise Porter since the end of May; since the end of a case they'd worked on together, when Thorne had been seconded to her team on the Kidnap Investigation Unit. The Mullen case had cost a number of lives, some lost and many more shattered beyond repair. Thorne and Louise were as surprised as anyone that they had forged something positive out of the carnage, and even more so that, five months down the line, it was showing no obvious sign of running out of steam.

Thorne took out a Waylon Jennings compilation. He slid the disc into his player, nodded along with the guitar at the opening of 'Only Daddy That'll Walk The Line'.

It was tricky for two police officers working on different units to spend too much time together anyway, but Louise firmly believed that not being in each other's pockets helped keep things fresh. She had her own small flat in Pimlico – a decent enough trek by Tube or car from Thorne's even smaller one in Kentish Town – and though they usually spent at least two or three nights a week together in one place or the other, Louise said that the distance was enough to stave off any anxiety that might otherwise creep in. Any worries about losing independence or becoming over-familiar. Or even just getting bored.

Thorne had been prone to all those anxieties at one time or another, but he had still told Louise that perhaps she was worrying a little too much. A couple of months into it, they'd been drinking coffee at the Bengal Lancer and their discussion about domestic arrangements had been starting to sound like a squad briefing. Thorne had leaned across the table and touched her fingers, and said that they should just try to relax and enjoy themselves. That taking things a day at a time couldn't hurt.

'That's a typical "bloke's" attitude,' Louise had said.

'What?'

'The "just relax" shit. *You* know.'

Thorne had grinned, feigned ignorance.

'I'm always amazed at the way men can barely spare five minutes to talk about a relationship, but can happily spend all day putting a CD collection into alphabetical order . . .'

Thorne certainly knew that Krauss came before Kristofferson. But he also knew that he felt as good about everything, as happy, as he had since his father had died two and a half years before.

As Waylon Jennings – filed between The Jayhawks and George Jones – began to sing 'The Taker', Thorne returned to the computer and sat down to play a few more hands. He could feel Elvis mooching around beneath the table, nosing into his shins in the hope of a late snack, or a ridiculously early breakfast.

Thorne was searching for the Go-Cat and contemplating king–ten in the hole when his mobile rang.

'I'm sorry,' Louise said. 'I'm only just leaving.'

The Kidnap Investigation Unit, along with others in Specialist Operations, was housed at Scotland Yard. It was another reassuringly good distance from where Thorne's homicide team was based at the Peel Centre in Hendon, but at this time of night, it was probably no more than twenty minutes' drive from Kentish Town.

'I'll put the kettle on,' Thorne said. There was a pause, during which he could hear Louise exchanging mumbled pleasantries with officers on security duty, as she made her way out and down towards the underground car park.

'I think I'm going to go straight home tonight,' she said, eventually.

'Oh, OK.'

'I'm knackered.'

'That's fine.'

'Let's do it tomorrow night.'

'*I'll* still be doing it tonight,' Thorne said. 'Just looks like I'll be doing it on my own.'

She laughed; a dirty cackle. Her breathing was heavy and Thorne could picture her walking quickly, eager to get to her car and home. 'I should have called earlier,' she said, 'but you know what it's like. Have you been waiting up long?'

'It's not a problem.' And it wasn't. They'd both been working ludicrous hours of late, and there had been plenty of these late night/early morning conversations.

'How was your day?'

'Up and down.' As ever, Thorne was working on half a dozen different murders, each at a different stage, somewhere between a body that was still cooling and a court case that was starting to warm up: a woman whose husband had flipped, bludgeoning her and her mother to death with an empty vodka bottle; an Asian teenager suffocated by an uncle in what looked suspiciously like an 'honour' killing; a young Turkish man, murdered in a pub car park. 'What about you?' Thorne asked.

'A bundle of laughs,' Louise said. 'I had a fabulous afternoon, trying to convince a major crack dealer – who doesn't want to press charges against another major crack dealer – that he didn't hold himself hostage for a week and chop off three of his own fingers.'

'How did that go?'

'Apparently, he accidentally locked himself in a shed, decided to do a spot of DIY to pass the time and got careless with an electric saw.'

'Don't go jumping to any conclusions,' Thorne said. 'Has he got an honest face?' Another big laugh. He heard the slight echo and realised she'd gone underground.

'You sound tired,' Louise said.

'I'm fine.'

'What have you been up to?'

'Not a lot. I watched some shitty film . . . caught up on a bit of paperwork.'

'OK.' The call was starting to break up as the signal went. Thorne heard the squawk as she unlocked her car with the remote. 'So, tomorrow night then, for definite?'

'If I'm not washing my hair,' Thorne said.

'I'll call you during the day.'

Thorne glanced at the computer screen as 'fourth street' was dealt. Saw that, with one card still to come, his king–ten had turned into an open-ended straight draw. 'Drive safely . . .'

He walked into the kitchen to make tea, apologised to Elvis for forgetting her food and flicked on the kettle on his way to the fridge. He was reaching up for a mug when he heard the beeps of the message tone from his phone.

He knew it would be from Louise, was smiling as he pressed SHOW, and the text itself only widened the smile into a grin.

I know you're playing poker. XXX

He was still trying to think up a funny comeback when the tone sounded again.

This time the message was not from Louise Porter.

It was a multimedia message, with a photograph attached. The picture was poorly defined, shot from close up and low down, and it wasn't until Thorne had held the phone eighteen inches away for a few seconds and angled it correctly that he could see exactly what it was. That he finally realised what he was looking at.

The man's face filled the small screen, pasty and distorted.

A clump of dark hair curled across the only visible cheek. The mouth hung open, its lips flecked with white and a sliver of tongue just visible inside. Chins bulged, one above the other; each black-and-silver stubbled, with a thin red line delineating the two. The single eye in shot was closed. Thorne could not be sure if the marks that ran across the brow and on to the forehead were from the camera lens or not.

He jabbed at the handset to retrieve the details of the message. Scrolled past the time and date, searching for the identity of the sender. There was no name listed, but he pressed the call button twice to dial the phone number that was shown.

Got a dead line.

He went back to the picture and stared, feeling the pulse quicken at the side of his neck. Feeling that familiar, dreadful tickle, the *buzz*, building further round, at the nape. When it came to a lot of things, there were times when Thorne couldn't see what was staring him in the face; but this, for better or worse, was his area of expertise. Accountants were good with numbers, and Tom Thorne knew a dead man when he saw one.

He angled the screen again, moved the handset closer to the lamp on the desk, the poker game forgotten. He stared at the dark patch below the man's ear that was certainly not hair. At the red line where it had run into the crack of his double chin.

Blood was not definitive, of course, but Thorne knew what the odds were. He knew that most people didn't go around taking pictures of friends and relatives that had been struck by falling masonry or accidentally tumbled down the stairs.

He knew that he was looking at a murder victim.

TWO

'Have you any idea how many forms would have to be filled in?'

'OK, so just take something out of petty cash. I presume we *have* some petty cash?'

'Yes, and that would be even more bloody forms.' Russell Brigstocke took off his glasses and pinched the bridge of his nose between thumb and forefinger.

Thorne held up his hands, conceding defeat, unwilling to heap any more misery on to his DCI's shoulders. 'Whatever. I'll pay for it. Can't hurt to have a spare anyway, right?'

His original enquiry had been innocent enough . . .

It was immediately obvious that Thorne would need to hand over his phone to see what information could be extracted from it, and like almost anyone else who had come to depend on the damn thing far too much, the thought of being without a mobile for any length of time had filled him with horror. He had stared down at the handset on Brigstocke's desk as if he were saying goodbye to a cherished pet for the last time.

'You could always hang on to the phone,' Brigstocke had said. 'Just let them have the SIM card.'

'What's the point? All my numbers are on the card anyway.'

'You don't know how to swap them over?'

'What do *you* think?'

It was obvious to both of them that they didn't have too much time to mess about. 'Look, just get one of those prepay things,' Brigstocke had said. 'Set up a divert and you won't miss any calls.'

'How much are they?'

'I don't know, not a lot.'

'So will the department pay for it?'

It had seemed like a fair question . . .

Brigstocke replaced his glasses and pushed fingers through his thick, black hair. He reached for Thorne's handset. 'Now, if we've finally sorted out your problematic phone situation . . .'

'I'd like to see you cope without one,' Thorne said.

Brigstocke ignored the jibe, stared down once again at the picture on the Nokia's small screen.

Thorne eased off his heavy leather jacket, turned to drape it across the back of his chair. It had been freezing when he'd stepped out of his flat an hour and a half earlier, but he'd begun to sweat after ten minutes inside Becke House, where most of the windows were painted shut and all the thermostats seemed permanently set to 'Saharan'. Outside, wind sang against the glass. November was just getting into its stride, brisk and short-tempered, and from Brigstocke's office Thorne could see leaves swirling furiously on the flat roofs of the buildings opposite.

'It's probably just someone pissing about,' Brigstocke said.

Thorne had tried to tell himself the same thing since the picture had first arrived. He was no more convinced hearing it from someone else. 'It's not a wax dummy,' he said.

'Maybe a picture from one of those freaky websites? There's all manner of strange shit out there.'

'Maybe. There's got to be some point to it, though.'

'Wrong number?'

'Bit of a coincidence, if it is,' Thorne said. 'Like a plumber getting sent a picture of a broken stopcock by mistake.'

Brigstocke held the phone close to his face, tipping it just a fraction to catch the light and talking as much to himself as to Thorne. 'The blood hasn't dried,' he said. 'We have to presume he's not been dead very long.'

Thorne was still thinking about coincidence. It had played its part in more than a few cases down the years and he never dismissed it easily. But already, he sensed that something organised was at work.

'This isn't random, Russell. It's a message.'

Brigstocke laid the phone down gently, almost as though it would be disrespectful to the as-yet unidentified dead man to do otherwise. He knew that Thorne's instincts were spectacularly wrong as often as they were right, but he also knew that arguing with them was a short cut to a stress headache, with a stomach ulcer waiting down the road. He certainly didn't see what harm it would do to give Thorne his head on this one. 'We'll get this to the tech boys, see what they can do about isolating the picture. I'll put someone on to the phone company.'

'Can we get Dave Holland to do it?'

'I'm sure he'll happily tear himself away from the Imlach paperwork.'

Darren Anthony Imlach. The man about to stand trial, accused of killing his wife and mother-in-law with a vodka bottle. He had been christened 'The Smirnoff Killer' by those red-tops that still had a nipple count in double figures.

'Dave's good at getting stuff out of people in a hurry, you know? Might save on a few hours' form-filling.'

'Sounds good to me,' Brigstocke said. He tapped the phone with his index finger. 'Why don't you see if there's any sign of a body we can put this face to?'

Thorne was already on his feet, reaching for his jacket. 'I'm going to log on to the bulletin right now.'

'Did Kitson talk to you about the Sedat case?'

Thorne turned at the door. 'I haven't seen her yet.'

'Well, she'll fill you in, but we found a knife. Dumped in a bin across the road from the Queen's Arms.'

'Prints?'

'Haven't heard, but I'm not holding my breath. It was covered in fag-ash and cider and shit. Bits of sodding kebab . . .'

'Maybe now's a good time to let the S&O boys come in.'

'They can fuck off,' Brigstocke said.

The Serious and Organised Crime Unit were convinced that the murder of Deniz Sedat three days earlier was in some way linked to the victim's involvement with a Turkish crime gang. Sedat, found bleeding to death by his girlfriend outside a pub in Finsbury Park, was not a major player by any means. But his name had come up during more than one investigation into north London's thriving heroin distribution industry, and the team from S&O had been quick to start throwing their weight around.

'Getting *seriously* fucking territorial,' Brigstocke had muttered the day before. 'Well, two can play at that stupid game . . .'

Thorne had had dealings with both S&O and some of the Turkish crime gangs that they were up against. There were good reasons – *personal* reasons – why he would prefer not to get close to either of them again. That said, it was to the DCI's credit that he refused to be bullied, and Thorne knew his boss well enough to be sure it was not a pissing contest. He was one of those coppers, just as Thorne was, for whom a murder was something to be solved, as opposed to something that lay on the desk and threatened to fuck up clearance rates. Three weeks into an inquiry that was stone cold and Brigstocke could be as miserable as anybody else, but once he caught a case, he knew that there were those, dead and alive, to whom he owed the best efforts of his team.

Now, Thorne was starting to believe that he had his own victim to work for. One to whom his attention had specifically, had *purposely*, been drawn and on whose behalf he must do whatever he could.

For now, he'd try not to think too much about the killer; about the man or woman he could only presume had sent him the message.

18

Right now, he knew no more than that the man in the picture was dead.

All Thorne had to do was find him.

Officers from the various Homicide Assessment Teams on call during the 11 p.m. to 7 a.m. shift would have faxed in preliminary reports to a central contact desk at Scotland Yard. In turn, those on duty there issued a daily bulletin to which anyone within the Specialist Crime Directorate had access. The report outlined all unexplained deaths – or injuries inflicted that looked to be life-threatening – offences involving firearms, rapes, high-risk missing persons or critical incidents that had been picked up overnight from anywhere within the M25 area.

Name and address of victim, when available, and brief details of the incident. Cause of death, if evident. Officer in charge of the case where one had been assigned.

At a spare desk in the open-plan Incident Room, Thorne logged on, called up the email and read through such details as were available of those murders caught the night before. The record for a single night – terrorist atrocities notwithstanding – was eleven; one night a couple of years earlier, when, on top of two domestics and a pub brawl, guns were fired at a house-party in Ealing, a flat was torched in Harlesden, and a gang on the hunt for crack money had sliced up the entire staff of a minicab office in Stockwell.

Predictably, many had been quick to point out that if the Met really was, as its motto boldly claimed, 'Working for a safer London', then it clearly wasn't working hard enough, though there were plenty of people, Tom Thorne included, working their arses off in the weeks following that particular evening.

He scanned the bulletin.

Three bodies was above average for a Tuesday night.

He was looking for 'dark hair', 'head injury' – anything that might match the picture on his phone. The only entry that came close described the murder of a barman in the West End: a white man attacked on his way home and battered to death with half a brick in an alley behind Holborn station.

Thorne dismissed it. The victim was described as being in his mid-twenties, and though death could do strange things to the freshest of faces, he knew that the man he was looking for was older than that.

He could hear DS Samir Karim and DC Andy Stone working at a desk behind him; although 'working' in this instance meant talking about the WPC at Colindale nick that Stone had finally persuaded to come out for a drink. Thorne logged out of the bulletin, spoke without turning round. 'It's obviously a positive discrimination thing.'

'What is?' Stone asked.

'Colindale. Taking on these blind WPCs.'

Karim was still laughing when he and Stone arrived at Thorne's shoulder.

'Heard about your secret admirer,' Stone said. 'Most people just send flowers.'

Karim began to straighten papers on the desk. 'It'll probably turn out to be nothing.'

'Right, you get sent all sorts of shit on your phone these days. I get loads of unsolicited stuff every week. Upgrades, ringtones, whatever. Games . . .'

Thorne looked up at Stone, spoke as though the DC were as terminally stupid as his comment had made him appear. 'And do many of these come with pictures of corpses attached?'

'I'm just saying.'

Karim and Stone stood rocking on their heels, like third-rate cabaret performers who had forgotten whose turn it was to speak next. They made for an unlikely-looking double-act: Stone, tall, dark and well tailored; Karim, silver-haired and thickset beneath a badly fitting jacket, like a PE teacher togged up for parents' evening. Thorne had time for them both, although Karim, in his capacity as office manager, could be an old woman when he wanted to be, and Stone was not the most conscientious of coppers. A year or so earlier, a young trainee detective with whom he was partnered had been stabbed to death. Though no blame had been formally attributed, there were some who thought that guilt was the least that Andy Stone should have suffered.

'Can't you two find somebody else to annoy?' Thorne said.

Once they'd drifted away, he walked through the narrow corridor that encircled the Incident Room and into the small, ill-appointed office he shared with DI Yvonne Kitson. He spent ten minutes filing assorted memos and newsletters under 'W' for 'Wastepaper Basket' and flicked distractedly through the most recent copy of *The Job*, looking for pictures of anyone he knew.

He was staring at a photo of Detective Sergeant Dave Holland receiving a trophy at some sort of Met sports event when the man himself appeared in the doorway. Incredulous, Thorne quickly finished reading the short article while Holland walked across and took the chair behind Kitson's desk.

'*Table-tennis?*' Thorne said, waving the magazine.

Holland shrugged, unable to keep a smile from his face in response to the grin that was plastered across Thorne's. 'Fastest ball game in the world,' he said.

'No it isn't.'

Holland waited.

'*Jai alai*,' Thorne said.

'Jai *what?*'

'Also called pelota, with recorded speeds of up to one hundred and eighty miles an hour. A golf ball's quicker as well. A hundred and seventy-odd off the tee.'

'The fact that you know this shit is deeply scary,' Holland said.

'The old man.'

Holland nodded, getting it.

Thorne's father had become obsessed with trivia – with lists, and quizzes about lists – in the months leading up to his death. These had become increasingly bizarre and his desire to talk about them more passionate, as the Alzheimer's had torn and tangled more of the circuits in his brain; had come to define him.

The world's fastest ball games. Top five celebrity suicides. Heaviest internal organs. All manner of random rubbish . . .

Jim Thorne. Killed when flames had torn through his home while he slept. A simple house-fire that any loving son – any son who had taken the necessary time and trouble – should have known was an accident waiting to happen.

Or perhaps something else entirely.

A murder, orchestrated as a message to Thorne himself, altogether more direct than the one preoccupying him at that moment.

One or the other. Toss a coin. Wide awake and sweating in the early hours, Thorne could never decide which was easier to live with.

' *Jai alai*,' Holland said. 'I'll remember that.'

'How's it going with the phone companies?' Thorne sounded hopeful, but knew that unless the man they were dealing with was particularly dim, the hope would be dashed pretty bloody quickly.

'It's a T-Mobile number,' Holland said.

'Prepay, right?'

'Right. They traced the number to an unregistered pay-as-you-go handset, which the user would have dumped as soon as he'd sent you the picture. Or maybe he's kept the handset and just chucked away the SIM card.'

Either way, there was probably nothing further to be gained in that direction. As the market for mobile phones had expanded and diversified, tracking their use had become an ever-more problematic line of investigation. Prepay SIMs and top-up cards could be picked up almost anywhere; people bought handsets with built-in call packages from vending machines; and even those phones registered to a specific company could be unlocked for ten pounds at stalls on any street market. Provided those employing the phones for criminal purposes took the most basic precautions, it was rarely the technology itself that got them nicked.

The only way it *could* work against them was in the tracing of cell-sites – the location of the masts that provided the signal used to make a call in the first place. Once a cell-site had been pinpointed, it could narrow down the area from where the call was made to half a dozen streets, and if the same sites were used repeatedly, suspects might be more easily tracked down, or eliminated from enquiries. It was a time-consuming business, however, as well as expensive.

When Thorne asked the question, Holland explained that, on this occasion, the DCI had refused to authorise a cell-site request. Thorne's response was predictably blunt, but he could hardly argue. With the phone companies charging anywhere up to a thousand pounds to process and provide the information, he knew he'd need more than the *picture* of a corpse as leverage.

'What about where he bought it?' Thorne asked. If they could trace the handset to a particular area, or even a specific store, their man might have been caught somewhere on CCTV. If mobile phones were making life trickier, the closed-circuit television camera was quickly becoming the copper's best friend. As a citizen of the most observed nation in Europe, with one camera to every fourteen people, the average Londoner was captured on video up to three hundred times a day.

'It's a Carphone Warehouse phone,' Holland said.

'Is that good news?'

'Take a guess. According to this geeky DC at the Telephone Unit, their merchandise can never be traced further than the warehouse it was shipped out from. If our man had got it somewhere else, we might have been in with a shout, but all the retailers have different ways of keeping records.'

'Fuck . . .'

'I reckon he just landed on his feet in terms of where he bought his kit. I don't see how he could have *known* any of that. Not unless he works for a phone company, or he's one of the anoraks I've spent all morning talking to.'

'Thanks, Dave.'

'I'll keep trying,' Holland said. 'We might get lucky.'

Thorne nodded, but was already thinking about other things. About the *nature* of the message he'd been sent. He knew what it was, but not what it meant.

23

Was it a warning? An invitation? A challenge?

Thinking that, if the powers-that-be ever wanted to change that motto of theirs, he had the perfect replacement. One that gave a far more accurate picture of the job. Thorne imagined the scrap of headed notepaper on the desk in front of him with that tired, blue logo erased from the top. Pictured a future where all Metropolitan Police promotional material came emblazoned with a new catchphrase.

We might get lucky.

THREE

'Everyone's got one of these.' The shop assistant pressed the gleaming sliver into Thorne's palm. 'You see the celebs with 'em in *Heat* and *Loaded* and all the papers. We got some in black, but the silver one's wicked . . .'

The phone was not much bigger than a credit card. Thorne stared down at the tiny keys, thinking that his fat, stubby fingers would be punching three of them at a time whenever he tried to press a button. 'I think I need something chunkier,' he said. 'Something that's actually going to make a noise if it falls out of my pocket.'

The salesman, whose name-tag identified him as Parv, was a moon-faced Asian kid with spiky hair. He rubbed at a pot belly through a polo shirt that was a couple of sizes too small for him and embroidered with the shop's logo. 'OK, what about a G3? These are bigger because of the keyboards, right? You can do all your email, browse the Internet, whatever.' The kid started to nod knowingly when he thought he saw something approaching genuine interest in his customer's face. 'Oh yeah, high-speed access. Plus you got your live video streaming, your one-to-one video calling, whatever.'

'I don't know anyone else who's got one,' Thorne said.

'So?'

'So who am I going to have a one-to-one video call with?'

Parv considered it. 'OK, this is a pretty basic phone,' he said, reaching for another handset and passing it over. 'Nothing flashy. You got your WAP, your Bluetooth, a voice recorder, a 1.3-megapixel camera – or a 1.5 with a better zoom on the flip-top model – and a built-in MP3 player.'

'Sounds good,' Thorne said. 'Does it send and receive calls?'

Parv stroked his belly again, and did his best to smile, though his eyes made it clear he thought he was dealing with a customer who might produce an automatic weapon from his jacket, or maybe get his cock out at any moment.

'It's just to have as a spare, really.' Thorne was looking around, helpless. 'I don't need any of the flashy shit.'

'Sorry.' The kid took back the handset and began scanning the shop for another customer. 'Everything comes with . . . *some* shit.'

It sounded to Thorne like the second fantastic motto he'd heard so far that day. Maybe he should get off the force and start a company selling greetings cards with realistic messages.

'Let me know if you need any more help,' Parv said, sounding almost like he meant it.

Thorne couldn't help but feel guilty at being the black hole into which the kid had poured his considerable knowledge and enthusiasm. Quickly assuring him that he *would* buy something, but had just a few more questions, Thorne took a step back towards the display of G3 handsets and asked if it was possible to play online poker by phone.

It was four-fifteen, over an hour past the end of his shift and already starting to get dark. The clocks had gone back the week before and, as always, there had been the usual complaints from those trumpeting the trauma of seasonal affective disorder. Thorne was less than sympathetic. Glancing up from his desk, he decided that the darkness certainly improved the view from his window. Besides, who needed

SAD, when ten minutes on the phone with a tiny-cocked jobsworth could depress even the happiest of souls so effectively?

It had taken Thorne a little over an hour to set up and register his new phone; now all that remained was to divert calls to his newly issued prepay number. Unfortunately, the mobile from which he needed to activate the divert had already been couriered to a properly equipped laboratory so that the photograph could be examined in detail. Thorne had put a call through to Newlands Park, the technical facilities base in Sidcup that handled image manipulation, audio/visual enhancement and other such tasks beyond the wit of those who could barely programme a VCR.

'It's easy enough,' Thorne had said. 'I've got the manual in front of me and I could talk you through it in ten seconds. I just don't want to miss any calls, you know . . .'

'Really, you don't need to talk me through it.' The technician had been unable, or hadn't bothered trying, to keep the sarcasm out of his voice. His name was Dawson, and Thorne immediately pictured bad skin and overlarge ears, a tie with egg stains and a vast collection of porn. 'I can't make changes to the settings, d'you see?'

'Sorry, no.'

'The phone has been submitted to us as evidence.'

'No, it hasn't,' Thorne had said. 'The *picture* is the evidence.'

'And the picture is on the phone. I can't tamper with the phone.'

'It's just setting up a simple divert on my personal calls. How's that tampering?'

'All I'm permitted to do is extract and enlarge the photograph, which is what we've been requested to do. I've got it in writing.'

'I'm sure you have, but this is just about common sense, right? If I get sent a videotape with footage of a murder on it, and I watch it, it doesn't mean I can't change the settings on my video recorder, does it?'

'We're not talking about what *you* do,' Dawson had said. 'There are set procedures here.'

Thorne's favourite word. It could only get worse from this point.

'We have to remain sensitive to the integrity of evidence.' It had sounded like Dawson was reading from a printed card. 'We need to be aware of any forensic issues.'

'There aren't any forensic issues,' Thorne had said. He had done his best to sound joky, but it was a tall order. 'It's *my* phone. It's not like you'll be smudging the killer's fingerprints, is it?'

There had been a pause. 'All I'm permitted to do—'

'This is fucking ridiculous.'

'Bad language isn't going to help anybody.'

It had helped Thorne immensely. 'Who else can I speak to?' Waiting for an answer, he had pictured Dawson leaning casually against a workbench, with a Rubik's cube and an erection.

'I'm guessing that your senior officer needs to make an official request to my shift manager.'

'It's a very thin line,' Thorne had said.

'What is?'

'Between loving your job and bending over while it fucks you up the arse . . .'

Thorne had only given Brigstocke the edited highlights of the conversation when he'd spoken to him. Though his new phone still hadn't rung yet, he presumed that the DCI had got straight on to Dawson's boss to authorise the divert, and Thorne sat trying to choose one of several dozen equally irritating ringtones while he waited.

'Don't use any of those hip-hop ones,' Kitson said. 'People will think you're having a mid-life crisis.'

Thorne looked up. He hadn't heard her come in.

'You can download them now, you know,' she said. 'You could get some Hank Williams, or Johnny Cash.'

'"Ringtone of Fire",' Thorne suggested. He watched as his fellow DI ordered her desk and scribbled something on a piece of paper. When she said his new phone looked flash, he passed it across to her and explained the hassle he'd gone through buying it, while she scrolled through some of its features. Though Kitson had heard the jungle-drum version of the photo-on-the-phone story, Thorne talked her through the true sequence of events: the message in the early hours; the picture of a dead man.

'It's the same as when people show you their holiday snaps,' Kitson said.

'Like a souvenir, you mean?'

'Only up to a point. They're really saying: "Look how well off and wonderful we are. Look at where we've been."'

'You think he's bragging?' Thorne said. He blinked, saw the black inside the open mouth, the wet mess behind the ear. Spoke as much to himself as to Kitson: '"Look what I've done" . . .'

She nodded, handing back the phone. 'I still don't see why you needed to get this. Why didn't they just send the SIM card to the lab?'

'Don't ask me.' Thorne did not want to explain that he hadn't known how to swap over his contact numbers. Or the fact that he was rather enjoying his tasty new phone.

'You could have got a prepay SIM card and put it in your old handset.'

Thorne shrugged, stared down at the phone. 'Yeah, well, I'll know next time.'

'Anything from the lab yet?'

'Nothing useful,' Thorne said. 'Tell me about this knife.'

It was, according to Kitson, a bog-standard, six-inch kitchen knife, fished from a litter bin in a park opposite the pub where Deniz Sedat had been stabbed to death. The council street-cleaner who'd found it, having seen enough episodes of *CSI* to know about such things, had put his hand inside a plastic bag before picking it up and carrying it carefully along to Finsbury Park police station.

Thorne told Kitson he didn't watch a lot of cop shows. She said he wasn't missing much, but at least they were good for something. He asked her if she thought they'd found the murder weapon.

'It looked like there was blood smeared on the blade.'

'Brigstocke told me there was all sorts of shit on it,' Thorne said. 'You sure it wasn't chilli sauce?'

'Size of the blade fits with the fatal stab wound, according to Hendricks.'

'What does he know? Useless Mancunian twat . . .'

Kitson grinned.

Phil Hendricks was the pathologist attached to Team 3 at the Area West Murder Squad. He was also Tom Thorne's closest friend, or the closest thing to it.

'I'd be surprised if S&O are quite as excited as they were,' Thorne said. 'Does the average East European hitman, or whoever they've got pegged for this, usually chuck his weapon in the nearest litter bin?'

Kitson still had a pen in her hand, but from where Thorne was sitting, it looked like she was doodling. 'Well, they don't normally use knives, so fuck knows.'

'Knives, guns . . . dead is dead.'

'Right, and it was certainly quick,' Kitson said. 'Professional, you know? How long was Sedat out of his girlfriend's sight? One minute, two?'

Harika Kemal had announced that she'd needed to visit the ladies' as the two of them were leaving the Queen's Arms. Sedat had reached for his cigarettes and said he'd wait for her in the car park. Harika told the police afterwards that she'd gone outside a couple of minutes later and found Sedat dying on the floor. Kitson had seen the horror in the girl's eyes as she'd made her statement; could only imagine her feelings at seeing her boyfriend slumped against the front wheel of a car, leaking blood into the dirt and gasping for air, like a fish in an angler's fist.

'Yeah, certainly quick,' Thorne said. 'Dispassionate.'

Kitson jabbed the air with her ballpoint. 'Nice and clean. Straight through the heart.' She leaned back in her chair, dropped the pen on the desk and let out a long breath. 'Fuck, I could murder a cigarette.'

'Since when?' Thorne had given up years before, but still got pangs every now and then. Holland had recently started smoking, much to his girlfriend's disgust. Maybe nicotine-stained was becoming the new black.

'Just a couple in the evening, you know? With a glass of wine or a cup of coffee, whatever.'

It sounded good. Thorne looked at the clock. 'Let's piss off, shall we?'

They talked as they gathered up their things, Kitson rooting in her bag for car keys, Thorne shoving papers into a tatty brown briefcase he'd found in the bottom of his father's wardrobe.

Kitson turned off the lights. 'Well, whether hitmen use knives or throw them into bins afterwards, they don't tend to leave a lot of fingerprints, so we'll know soon enough . . .'

The Homicide offices were on the third floor of Becke House. Thorne and Kitson gave the lift a minute, then decided to walk. The communal areas had recently undergone a modest upgrade, which had included carpeting the stairs. The smell, which lingered three weeks on, reminded Thorne of moving house, sometime when he was a kid: cardboard boxes, and his dad bringing home takeaways.

It also made him feel a little apprehensive.

'What have you got on tonight, then?'

He wondered if it was carpet beneath the head of the dead man in the picture. It had been impossible to tell. Maybe when they enhanced the photo . . .

'Tom?'

Thorne turned, stared until Kitson repeated her question. 'Just stopping in,' he said, after a moment. 'You?'

'The usual madness,' Kitson said, sounding a little envious of Thorne's empty schedule. 'Actually, even madder than that. My eldest has GCSEs coming up, so things are a bit tense.'

'I bet.' They turned on to the final flight. Kitson rarely spoke about life at home and Thorne felt vaguely honoured.

'It's hard for him,' Kitson said. 'You know? It's a lot to cope with at that age. They don't know how to handle the pressure.'

'How old is he?'

'Fifteen.'

Thorne grimaced. 'I'm three times that, near enough.' He leaned his

31

shoulder against the door. The cold slapped him in the face as he stepped out into the car park. 'I wish some bugger would tell *me* how to handle it.'

At the flat, Thorne had grated cheese into a bowl of tomato soup and stared at his new phone, willing it to ring. Finally, it had, twice in quick succession. Now Thorne was sitting in his living room, watching the two callers drink his lager and cheerfully take the piss out of him.

It was a continuation of a discussion that had been going on for the last week, since Halloween, when Thorne had voiced his considerable antipathy towards the practice of 'trick or treating'.

'It's a paedophile's dream,' he said now. 'An endless parade of kids knocking on the door.'

Phil Hendricks took a slurp of Sainsbury's own-brand lager. 'That's bollocks. You're just tight, and you can't be arsed to get any sweeties in.'

'It's a stupid bloody Americanism. *We* never used to do it . . .'

'You're such a miserable git,' Louise said.

'Most of them don't even make any effort. They don't dress up or anything.'

'They're *kids* . . .'

'It's just an excuse for ASBO fodder to chuck fireworks and stick dog-shit through old people's letterboxes.'

'I think Louise is right,' Hendricks said. 'You're tight *and* miserable.'

Thorne got up to fetch more beer from the kitchen. Hendricks was perched next to Louise on the sofa, and Thorne leaned in close as he walked past. As always, the pathologist was dressed in black, with the usual array of metalwork through eyebrow, nose, lip, cheek and tongue. 'You just like it because you don't need to wear a mask,' Thorne said.

Hendricks gave him the finger. 'Homophobe!'

Louise laughed and knocked over her beer can. She scrambled to pick it up but there wasn't too much left in it anyway.

Walking back into the living room, Thorne was struck, as always, by how alike Hendricks and Louise were. They were both thirty-four, which, to their endless glee, gave them ten years on Thorne. Each was dark-haired and skinny, though Hendricks' hair was shaved rather than short, and Louise had far fewer piercings. Save for the differences in their accents, they might have been mistaken for brother and sister.

Thorne handed each of them a fresh can.

The two had become friends very quickly, gone out together to gay bars and clubs, and sometimes, watching them together, Thorne felt envious in a way he didn't care to spend too long analysing. When he and Louise had first started seeing one another, he'd been slightly annoyed that Hendricks *hadn't* seemed overly threatened; especially as Thorne, on occasion, had found himself to be more than a little jealous of Hendricks' boyfriends. As it happened, the three of them had spent a good deal of the last few months together; Hendricks having split from his long-term lover around the same time that Thorne and Louise had hooked up. The break-up had been over children: Hendricks was desperate to be a father and was now searching for a partner who shared his enthusiasm. More than once, he and Louise had joked about how she might help him out; about cutting Thorne out of the picture altogether.

'Come on, Lou,' Hendricks had said. 'You'd be far better off with me. I've got decent taste in clothes, music, everything.'

'Yeah, OK. Why not?'

'I mean, obviously we won't actually *do* anything. There's ways and means. Besides, I don't think you'd be missing much, sex-wise.'

'I can't argue with that.'

Hendricks had hugged Louise and leered at Thorne. 'Right, that's sorted. Me and your girlfriend are buggering off to get creative with a turkey-baster . . .'

Tonight, they drank a good deal more and emptied the cupboard of every available snack. They watched some TV and talked about football, and facelifts, and the tumour Hendricks had found inside the stomach of a middle-aged woman which had turned out to be a long-unborn twin.

The usual stuff.

Around eleven-thirty, Hendricks phoned for a cab back to his flat in Deptford and, while they waited, they talked about the photograph some more. They'd discussed it earlier, in three separate phone conversations: Thorne and Louise; Louise and Hendricks; Hendricks and Thorne. Then they'd spoken about it when each had arrived at the flat, and again when the three of them were finally together. It was always just a question of when they'd get back to it.

'Until you find a body, it's just a picture,' Hendricks said.

'You didn't see it.'

'So what?'

'You should listen,' Louise said. She put a hand on Thorne's arm, nodded in Hendricks' direction. 'He's spot on. It's just a photograph. You might never find a body.'

'What am I supposed to do, then?'

'Forget it.'

'Like I said to Phil . . .'

'No, I *haven't* seen it, but I know what death looks like. Come on, Tom, we all do.'

Thorne knew she was right, but couldn't shake the unease. It was like a draught he kept walking through. 'It feels like it's mine, though . . . It *is* mine.' He hunched his shoulders, the chill at them again, bracing himself as Louise leaned in against him. 'It was sent to me.'

Hendricks nodded slowly. His eyes flicked momentarily to Louise, then dropped to his watch. He stepped across to the window, pulled back the curtain and peered out on to the street.

'The cab firm said to give it ten minutes,' Thorne said.

They all moved into the hall and stood a little awkwardly around the front door. Though Thorne had spent the better part of twenty-four hours trying to avoid it, he suddenly felt the question hanging there between them; could feel the weight and the heat of it. Certain as nausea.

Hendricks was as good a person as anyone else to voice it.

'Why you?' he asked.

After Hendricks had gone, Thorne and Louise didn't take too long to get into bed, but nothing that came afterwards was any more than half-hearted. Tiredness, beer or something else altogether had dampened the desire, and warmth or simple proximity had been enough for both of them.

'I don't think you're a miserable git,' Louise said, just before she turned over.

Later, Thorne lay awake in the dark, fighting hard to silence the shrill, insistent, 'Why?' Until, in the end, it became like a car alarm to which you grew accustomed. It was not exactly a comfort, but he knew there was every chance that the answer would present itself before he'd had to spend too long worrying about the question.

With Louise snoring quietly next to him, he thought about something he'd said earlier. When Kitson had asked him why he hadn't just handed over the SIM and kept his handset.

He'd said it casually then, without thinking.

'*Well, I'll know next time.*'

He'd done a lot of walking at night. During the last few months, anyway.

It was partly because he *could*, obviously; because the novelty had still not worn off. The flat wasn't small, not by a long stretch, but anywhere started to close in after a week or two; and it felt nice to get out. He didn't care a whole lot about the rain or the wind. It was just weather, and all of it was good.

Tonight it was cold and dry as he walked quickly along the main road, past the shuttered-up shops and the all-night garages. He turned into a side street, letting his hand rest against the spanner in his coat pocket as he moved towards a group of teenagers on the corner.

He'd walked just to kill time at first; to get through the endless hours without sleep. He was still managing no more than a couple of hours each night, three at the most, in fifteen- or twenty-minute bursts. He didn't think he'd managed more than that since that morning they'd been in to see him.

The second time his life had been turned upside down.

Funny how both times everything had changed, had turned to shit, he'd been sitting there with people who were waving warrant cards at him . . .

Over the weeks he'd covered most of west London. He'd spent long nights walking up to Shepherd's Bush and then along the Uxbridge Road through Acton and Ealing. He'd gone south, around Gunnersbury Park, then turned towards Chiswick, watching the cars rush both ways above him along the M4. He'd walked back towards Hammersmith, zigzagging through the smaller streets and coming out just shy of the bridge, where the river bowed, a mile or two from where the flat lay in the shadow of the flyover; a hospital on one side of it, a cemetery on the other.

The teenagers at the end of the street paid him no real attention. Maybe there was a look about him.

There certainly had been at one time.

He'd got used to it now, doing this instead of sleeping. He *enjoyed* it. The walking helped him think things through, and though there were plenty of times in the day when he felt completely wiped out, it was like his body was adjusting; compensating, or whatever the word was. He remembered reading somewhere that Napoleon and Churchill and Margaret Thatcher had all made do with a couple of hours' kip each night. It was obviously all about how you approached things when you were awake. Maybe you could get away with it, as long as you had a purpose.

He turned for home. Headed down Goldhawk Road towards Stamford Brook Tube station.

He'd write to her again when he got back.

He'd make a coffee and turn on the radio, then he'd sit down at the crappy little table in the corner and bang out another letter. Tell her how everything was going. Two, maybe three pages if it came easy, and when he'd finished he'd put it with the others; wrapped up in elastic bands, in the drawer that he'd stuffed full of handsets and SIM cards.

Then he'd take out another phone, and sit there, and wait for the sun to come up.

FOUR

Dawson might have been a sanctimonious little shit, but there was no faulting him and his colleagues when it came to speed. Before the morning's first cup of coffee had gone cold, Thorne was sitting at a computer in the Incident Room, looking at a high-resolution JPEG of the photograph that had been sent to his phone.

It *was* carpet beneath the dead man's head.

'He'll never get that mess out of the shag-pile,' Stone had said, waving around his own hard copy of the picture. 'I don't think there's a Stain Devil for blood, is there?'

Kitson took the photo from him, looked at it for a few seconds, then laid it down. 'Stain Devil number four. But if it's this poor bastard's carpet, I really don't think he's going to give a toss . . .'

Thorne was using one hand to move the cursor across the image, tracing a line around the ragged patch of red, while the other pressed a phone to his ear. He'd emailed the picture straight across to St George's Hospital, where Phil Hendricks supplemented the pittance the Met paid him by teaching three days a week.

Hendricks had called him straight back. 'It's still just a picture,' he said.

Thorne waited a few seconds. 'Well?'

'I'm not exactly sure what it is you want.'

'An opinion, maybe. *Expertise*. I'm probably wasting my time . . .'

'It might be a high-resolution image, but the photo itself is still pretty low quality. Not enough megapixels, mate.'

'You sound like that kid in the phone shop.'

Hendricks was right, though. The image remained undefined, and even the magic worked by the boffins at Newlands Park had yielded little in the way of useful information: the body lay on a carpet; the hair was perhaps greyer than it had first appeared; what had looked on the phone's tiny screen like a patch of shadow at the neck was probably the edge of a tattoo, poking from below the line of the dead man's collar.

'So nothing that's going to help me, then?' Thorne asked, letting the cursor rest on the single visible eye. 'Blood not giving you any clues? Bullet wound, blunt instrument, what?'

'I'm not a fucking miracle worker,' Hendricks said. 'Arterial blood is brighter, and there's certainly enough of it, but it's impossible to tell from this. Like I said . . .'

'Megapixels, right.'

'I need to see the body. I'll tell you how many sugars he had in his tea if you let me have a look at him in the flesh. Or what's left of it.'

Thereafter, the chat was more or less idle: Arsenal's recent lack of form; a vague arrangement to meet up for a drink later on. There was only one more reference to the picture and to the questions it posed. Hendricks sounded as serious as he had on Thorne's doorstep the night before; letting him know that, megapixels aside, one thing about the photograph had been clear enough. 'If it helps, I can see now why you'd want to know,' he said.

When he'd hung up, Thorne sat around and let the clock run for a while. Aimless, he watched as Karim worked at the whiteboard that dominated one wall of the Incident Room: scribbling, erasing, updating the map of each outstanding murder where there was any change to be made. He listened as Andy Stone tried in vain to milk more laughs from his 'blood on the carpet' routine, and as Yvonne Kitson

39

pestered the lab for news on the knife that might have killed Deniz Sedat.

He didn't catch everything that was said. The previous night's lack of sleep had been gaining on him since six-thirty that morning – when he'd trudged towards the bathroom, dragging off a sweaty T-shirt, Louise still dead to the world – and four hours later Thorne was already feeling like he'd done a hard day's graft. Even as he looked up and grunted his response to Brigstocke, he was wondering if he might have nodded off at the desk for a few seconds.

'When did you last check the bulletin?' the DCI asked.

'About an hour and a half ago . . .'

Brigstocke waved a piece of paper in front of him. 'This came in just after nine.' When Thorne reached up for it, Brigstocke snatched the sheet away and read, enjoying himself: 'Raymond Tucker. 32 Halifax Road, Enfield. Found by his mother around seven this morning. Victim appears to have died from massive head trauma . . . Signs of forced entry at rear of premises . . . Blah, blah, blah-di-blah.' He paused for effect. 'Sound good to you?'

'Sounds *possible*.'

Thorne moved for the paper again and this time Brigstocke let him have it. He carried on talking as Thorne read through the brief report. 'A team out of Barking caught it, so I called up the chief super over there, got the DCI's name, and faxed the picture across fifteen minutes ago.'

Thorne stared up, waited, but not for long. 'Come on, Russell, fuck's sake . . .'

'The man from Del Monte . . . he say "yes".'

Thorne stood and started to move, Brigstocke following, towards his office. 'I'll ask Hendricks to meet us at the crime scene.'

'I should skip that for now,' Brigstocke said, 'and get down to Hornsey Mortuary. When the DCI rang back about the photo, he said they'd be bringing the body out in the next half-hour or so.'

Thorne nodded and pushed through the door, the tiredness shaken off and left for dead. He was already at his desk, leaving a message on

Hendricks' machine, when Brigstocke, en route to his own office further up the corridor, stopped in the doorway.

'When I spoke to the DCI, he also told me the body had been there for a while.' Brigstocke paused for a second or two, until he was sure Thorne understood the implications. 'Over a week, he reckoned.'

The pictures in Thorne's head were less than lovely. 'I bet that carpet's fucked,' he said.

By the time Karim was at the whiteboard again, marking out a new column in lines of black felt-tip and taping up the dead man's picture below Tom Thorne's name, Thorne and Holland were already in the car.

Raymond Anthony Tucker had died two days shy of his fifty-second birthday. He'd run a small second-hand car dealership in Chingford, which had hardly catered to the top end of the market, but was nevertheless a notch or two above the cut-and-shut merchants working out of yards in the dodgier parts of Tottenham and King's Cross. His body had been discovered by his mother, who lived a couple of streets away. Despite the fact that her son was a reasonably successful small-businessman, old enough to have his own grandchildren, she'd still popped in to collect his dirty washing once a week or so.

This information had been fed to Thorne and Holland by phone, as they had driven towards Enfield. Thorne had decided that, despite what Brigstocke had said, it would be a good idea for someone from the team to get themselves on site as quickly as possible. He'd dropped Holland off at 32, Halifax Road, told him to get in there and make his presence felt, and said that he'd try to get back to pick him up after the post-mortem. Then he'd pushed on towards Hornsey, hoping that it would prove to be worth the effort.

The arm of the Specialist Crime Directorate that handled murder cases was divided into three areas, with those bodies turning up in the London Borough of Enfield being dealt with by one of the teams from Homicide East. It would be Russell Brigstocke's job to liaise with the DCI on whichever team had caught the Tucker case. In turn, each

41

would speak to his chief superintendent, who would then pass the final decision on to the commander. *He* would weigh up the relative merits of each team – or toss a coin, depending on how many meetings he had on that day – and allocate a senior investigating officer to the case.

All working *together* for a safer London . . .

The mortuary was located two floors below Hornsey Coroner's Court. As if the place were not spooky enough, proceedings were routinely disturbed by the guttural rumble of Piccadilly Line trains on their way to and from Bounds Green station. On arrival, it hadn't taken Thorne long to see that the team from Homicide East would not be putting up much of a fight for possession of the case. He'd listened to his opposite number bitch about his workload. He'd watched him smoke a cigarette to the filter in half a dozen desperate drags, and decided that these boys were not exactly gagging to get after Raymond Tucker's killer.

'Help yourself,' DI Steve Brimson had said. 'I can't remember what my missus looks like as it is.'

The part of Thorne that relished a decent scrap had felt rather disappointed.

Convoluted as it could be, there was at least a method for the allocation of officers among the Homicide Squad. No such system existed to decide who might have the honour of slicing up the corpse. As quickly as Thorne had read the lie of the land, Phil Hendricks had marked down the Coroner-appointed pathologist as someone rather less keen on any accommodation. He'd read it in the man's handshake; in the widening of the eyes when they'd first encountered the spike through Hendricks' eyebrow and the stud through his tongue. So, Hendricks too had been forced to stand and observe while the body of Raymond Tucker – such as was left of it – had been opened and gone through as dispassionately as luggage in a customs hall.

Thorne had seen countless post-mortems, many conducted by Hendricks himself, but they'd never been part of the same audience before. Glancing across at Hendricks, standing between himself and

Steve Brimson, he'd wondered how involved his friend was getting with the procedure. He'd caught the occasional scowl and an involuntary twitch of the fingers. He'd been curious as to how far Hendricks had been mentally deconstructing his colleague's work while he watched; critiquing the other man's delicacy when weighing a liver, or his technique with a bone-saw.

'He wasn't too bad,' Hendricks said. 'But he's clearly not in my league when it comes to good looks. You know, basic sex-appeal.'

They were sitting in a greasy spoon a few minutes' walk from the mortuary. It was the sort of place that served a fried breakfast all day every day, but hungry as he was, Thorne couldn't quite manage a full English this soon after a post-mortem. He'd settled for scrambled eggs on toast, while Hendricks tucked into a sausage sandwich.

'What about cause of death?' Thorne asked.

'Fuck all to disagree with. Blunt trauma to the brain, massive internal bleed . . . occipital artery just about shredded. He would have died pretty quickly: first couple of blows would have done it. Now, you can call me Sherlock Holmes, but I reckon that bloodstained lump-hammer they found in Tucker's flat might have had something to do with it.'

'I'll bear that in mind,' Thorne said.

A waitress stepped up to clear the plates. She'd clearly been earwigging as she'd worked at the next table and Hendricks had caught it. 'It's a new TV show we're writing,' he said. 'A maverick, gay pathologist. You know, usual stuff: fuzzy black-and-white bits, half a dozen serial killers every episode.'

The waitress pulled a face, as though she'd caught a whiff of something and couldn't decide if she liked it or not. 'Well, don't have that bloke who used to be in *EastEnders*. I can't stand him.'

They watched her leave, one of them enjoying the way her backside moved beneath a tight black skirt considerably more than the other.

'It's an odd one this, though,' Hendricks said.

'They're always odd.'

Hendricks grunted his agreement. He stuffed what was left of his sandwich into his mouth and took a healthy slurp of tea. It always surprised Thorne that someone whose hands could move with such poise and dexterity ate like a half-starved docker.

'Go on then,' Thorne said. 'Why is this one so strange?'

'Killer can't make his mind up.'

Thorne pushed a finger round the rim of his cup. Waited.

'Five, six blows with that hammer. Decent ones, you know? Not that people are usually tentative when it comes to bludgeoning someone to death . . .'

'Not as a rule.'

'I'd probably call it "frenzied" if I was pushed in a witness box.'

'But . . .?'

'But then there's this whole picture business. He smashes Tucker's head in; then, while he's stood there covered in blood – and he would have been *covered* – he calmly takes out his mobile phone and starts snapping away. Cool as you like.'

'Maybe he took his time,' Thorne said. 'Went and cleaned himself up a bit. Composed himself.'

'Maybe. Where he *definitely* took his time was in sending the picture to you. I reckon Tucker was dead nine or ten days when his poor old mum walked in and got the shock of her life. So, whoever killed him waited over a week before sending you that message. That's pretty bloody relaxed, I'd say.'

Thorne had already worked it out; had come to the same conclusion when Brigstocke had told him that Tucker's body had lain undiscovered for a while.

'So, what the fuck is he?' Hendricks downed the last of his tea. 'Ordered or disordered.'

Thorne had come across a few who were both. He knew that they were the worst kind. The hardest to catch. 'You can pay for the grub,' he said. 'Seeing as how you've cheered me up so much.'

'I'll tell you something else for nothing.'

'Do you have to?'

'I think there's more to our victim than meets the eye.'

44

'You're really on form today,' Thorne said.

'I'm telling you.'

'You should stop doing so much cutting and *watch* more of it. You don't miss a bloody trick.' But once Hendricks had told him what he meant, Thorne could not find much to argue with in his friend's assessment.

They settled up and walked out into what remained of a grey afternoon. For a minute or two, heading towards the car, Thorne was back in the mortuary suite. Watching as the pathologist moved around the slab. The Home Counties monotone raised above the noise of the Tube trains, his commentary echoing off the tiled walls.

Thorne stared at the body again, his eyes moving down from the sunken cheeks and the spots of dried blood caught on lashes and stubble. He saw the intricate designs in blue and green and red. The pictures inked across the chest that disappeared from view as the flaps of skin over the ribs were peeled back and laid aside. Hendricks said he'd seen similar designs on a body before, but nothing as impressive as these: the large outline of a snarling dog's head on one shoulder; the panther that stretched along an arm; the ornate cross and grinning skull.

Hendricks had a point.

Raymond Tucker had a few more tattoos than the average used-car salesman.

Once a body had been removed from a crime scene, the atmosphere changed. Eight hours since the discovery of Raymond Tucker and, in a first-floor flat that was already starting to smell an awful lot better, the scene-of-crime officers had done most of what would be necessary on the first day. Now there were just a few stragglers working the scene, cleaning up: the video and stills cameramen; the woman working as exhibits officer; a couple of fingerprint guys. Many SOCOs – who thought it sounded a little more glamorous – insisted on being called crime scene examiners these days.

To Thorne's mind, 'glamour' in such circumstances was a relative term.

One day into it and, like a well-drilled unit of white-suited locusts, the team, whatever it chose to call itself, had completed the majority of the front-line forensics. Though a few were still moving around with that distinctive, all-too-evocative rustle, Thorne and Holland were at least spared the plastic bodysuits and bootees.

'Small mercies,' Holland said.

They were standing with their backs to the window, the dying light kept at bay by large black screens and the room illuminated by a pair of powerful arc lights. The furniture was modern: smoked glass and chrome; built-in bookshelves and halogen spots; a three-seater sofa covered in dark brown leather and light brown blood.

Thorne dug out some chewing gum from his jacket pocket. 'Not a lot of mercy shown in here . . .'

The body had been removed from its final position between the sofa and the fireplace, and it was clear that the dead man had not fallen at the first blow. Aside from the blood, spattered in scratches across the sofa cushions, there were patterns in the other direction, thrown against the glass front of a tropical fish tank and, lower down, finely sprayed across a large wooden bowl filled with smooth stones, black and grey.

A passing SOCO/CSE followed Thorne's eyeline. He nodded towards the rectangle of bare boards where the carpet beneath the body had been cut away and removed. 'Central heating was cranked up, so he probably started leaking like a bastard after less than a week,' the officer said. 'Almost as much of him in the carpet as there was anywhere else. Gone right through.' He pointed, keen as mustard. 'Look, can you see?'

Thorne and Holland did, and could. The caramel-coloured blotch on the dusty boards was like damp behind a cistern.

'Are you sure you want this one?' Holland asked.

'Already got it,' Thorne said. 'Brigstocke called when I was on the way over from Hornsey.' He talked Holland through the PM, focusing on the headlines, finishing on Hendricks' notions of what constituted a standard number of tattoos on an average used-car salesman.

Holland was unconvinced. 'Hendricks has got a few more tattoos than your average pathologist.' He counted them off, pointing to the appropriate point on his body as he did so. 'That Arsenal thing on his neck. The Celtic band or whatever you call it on his wrist. That weird symbol on his shoulder. There's probably a couple more that only his very good friends have ever clapped eyes on.'

'I wouldn't know,' Thorne said. He stared hard at a SOCO working near by, a smart-arse he'd come across before who'd glanced over with something like a smirk.

They walked into Tucker's kitchen. There was washing-up stacked next to the sink and the sheen of Luminol across the work surfaces. On their way out through the hallway they casually stepped over a finger-print specialist working on a stretch of flaking skirting board.

'Maybe it means something,' Holland said. 'That he waited before sending you that picture.'

'Maybe it just slipped his mind.' Thorne took the stairs two at a time. 'You know what it's like. You batter someone to death, take their photo, forget all about it . . .'

'It might be significant, you know? Something about the day he chose.'

'What? His birthday?' Thorne turned to Holland, palms raised. 'First Monday in the month? Let's not forget how close it was to November the fifth. Maybe this bloke's got a thing about bonfires.'

'I was only thinking aloud.'

Thorne stopped at the door and took a breath. 'Sorry, mate.' There had been more anger than upset in Holland's tone, but Thorne still felt like a twat for being snappy. 'Maybe he's just another fucking mental-ist, Dave. You know?'

Outside, Thorne stopped to talk to the video cameraman who was packing away his equipment, while Holland reached for cigarettes. A young couple with a pushchair appeared from between two unit vehicles and marched up to the crime scene tape.

The man leaned across and shouted to Thorne: 'What are you filming?'

Holland opened his mouth, but Thorne beat him to it. 'It's a new TV show about a maverick, gay pathologist.' He put a hand on Holland's shoulder, as if to introduce the star of the show. 'You know the sort of thing. Fuzzy black-and-white bits, half a dozen serial killers in every episode . . .'

The clocks going back seemed to have brought the rush hour forward, and the North Circular was already starting to snarl up as Thorne nosed the car towards Finchley.

'Things seem to be going well with DI Porter,' Holland said. 'It's a few months now, isn't it?'

Thorne searched Holland's face, but saw only honest curiosity. 'Five, give or take a week. That's a long time for me.'

'It's good . . .'

Thorne wasn't about to argue. 'How's Chloe?'

Holland grinned. His daughter had turned three years old a couple of months earlier. 'Can't shut her up,' he said. 'Coming out with all sorts of weird shit. Stuff she's picking up at nursery, whatever. She's going a couple of days a week now. I told you that, didn't I?'

It was the first Thorne had heard of it, but he nodded anyway.

'Sophie's trying to do some work part time, you know? That'll be good for everyone, I reckon.'

'Right . . .'

Holland had been nodding while he spoke. He carried on after he'd turned to look out of the window, as though he were trying to convince himself.

'Definitely,' Thorne said.

It was natural that he hadn't seen quite so much of Holland outside the Job since Chloe had come along. But even when they spent time together at work, Thorne thought that he and Holland weren't connecting in a way that perhaps they once had. He could see that his colleague – was he a *colleague* now, as opposed to a friend? – had a lot more on his plate since being made up to sergeant the year before, but Thorne wondered if it didn't also have something to do with the more subtle demands of a family. With the grinding drive to become the sort of police officer Holland had once professed to despise: the head-down and shut-the-fuck-up kind of copper his father had been. The copper that sometimes, when he'd upset one too many of the wrong people, Thorne wished he had it in himself to be.

Pulling away from the lights at Henley's Corner, something beneath the BMW's bonnet began to complain, and as Thorne wondered just how hard the complaint was going to hit his wallet, the jokes began. However uncertain things might be, however far they shifted, there would always be Holland's shtick about the car: the fact that it was yellow and almost as old as he was, and that Thorne could have bought a new one for what it cost him in repairs every year.

And it was all fair enough.

Coppers solved crimes or they didn't. They laid down their lives to protect others and they shot innocent men for looking swarthy in the wrong place at the wrong time. But smart or stupid, honest or bent, they all took the piss. Took it, and had it taken.

And you didn't need a psychology degree to figure out why.

Some were better at it than others. The likes of Andy Stone had a drawer stuffed with photocopies of colleagues' warrant cards, so that when and if the time came, they could place embarrassing personal ads on their behalf in the back pages of *The Job* and *Metropolitan Life*. Bogus lonely-hearts stuff and requests for mail-order brides. When Samir Karim had split up with his wife a few years before, an ad had appeared the following week with his contact details offering: 'Double bed for sale. Hardly used.'

Karim had laughed along with the rest of them, obviously.

'*Vorsprung, durch* . . . utterly fucked,' Holland said, getting into his stride.

Thorne steered the car slowly through the mess of traffic at the Brent Cross flyover, then turned north towards Hendon, waiting until Holland had hit him with his best shots.

'Say what you like.' Thorne stroked the steering wheel theatrically. 'Still my baby.'

'Listen to yourself,' Holland said. 'It's a clapped-out piece of German scrap. It's not Herbie . . .'

Thorne sighed and stared ahead, refusing to dignify the comment with a response. The blocks of single-storey warehouses and furniture superstores crawled by along the length of the A406: Carpet Express; Kingdom of Leather; Staples. His eye was caught by the Carphone Warehouse logo across a set of grey, metal shutters, and it suddenly struck Thorne that the reason for the killer's delay in sending the photograph might have been altogether simpler yet more bizarre.

'Fritz, maybe . . .' Holland said.

Was it possible that, after committing the murder, the killer had kept a watch on Tucker's flat? On seeing that the body was going undiscovered, had he simply decided to give the police a helping hand?

Ordered or disordered?

Perhaps he wanted someone to go to the trouble of finding out . . .

Next to him, Holland was saying something about a running joke that ran a damn sight better than the car did, but Thorne was already elsewhere. Thinking that the dead were never decorous. That death itself was rarely dignified, whether you were tottering towards collapse on a mixed ward or rotting into a carpet. But that for the most unfortunate, what was left could barely even be called 'remains'.

Thinking that, when people talked about leaving something of themselves behind, they usually meant more than just a stain on a floorboard.

FIVE

Back at Becke House, the news was mixed. But then, life itself was perfectly capable of taking the piss . . .

From Kitson, the familiar two-steps-forward-three-steps-back routine. The blood on the knife retrieved from the litter bin had been identified as belonging to Deniz Sedat. They had also managed to pull a decent set of prints from the handle. Sadly, though, these failed to match with any held on record.

From Karim, a predictably frustrating technical update. With a cell-site search having been formally authorised by Brigstocke, T-Mobile had been in touch to acknowledge the request. And again later, to say that they would give it their highest priority, as soon as their virus-riddled computer system was up and running again.

Thorne retreated to his office, but five minutes later Andy Stone was babbling at him from the doorway.

'There's a DCI from S&O on the phone.'

'And?'

'And he's been calling every fifteen minutes since lunchtime trying to get hold of the guvnor.'

Thorne hadn't seen Brigstocke since his return from the mortuary. 'Where is he?'

'No idea, some meeting. Anyway, I think this bloke's had enough, because now he's just asking to speak to the appropriate DI.'

'Kitson's looking after the Sedat case,' Thorne said.

'I don't think it's the Sedat case he wants to talk about . . .'

Thorne was curious, but he was also exhausted, and with more than enough to occupy his mind at that moment. He shook his head. 'He'll call back.'

'He's waiting for me to put him through.'

'Tell him you couldn't find me.'

'He won't be happy . . .'

Thorne stared until Stone backed, muttering, into the corridor. He began to wonder if he'd inadvertently activated some kind of shit magnet, and when the phone on his desk began to ring a minute later, he just stared at it for a few seconds. Thought about sneaking down to the canteen for tea and a piece of cake, sorting out that weaselly little fucker Stone later on . . .

'Your guvnor's been ducking me all day. You're not trying to piss me about as well, are you, Tom?'

There'd been laughter, of a sort, as he'd asked the question, but it was clear enough from DCI Keith Bannard's tone that he wasn't joking. Thorne presumed it was rhetorical anyway, being more of a threat than a genuine enquiry.

'I think DCI Brigstocke's been stuck in meetings most of the day, sir,' he said. 'Have you got his mobile number?'

'I've rung three times. Twice he's dropped the call and now he's turned the phone off.'

Thorne guessed Brigstocke had got wind that S&O were on his case, presuming, as Thorne had done, that they were still trying to muscle in on the Sedat case. 'Shall I take a message? I suppose you've already left one on his office voicemail?'

'Tell me about your dead car salesman,' Bannard said.

'*Tucker?*' Suddenly, Thorne had a lot more to occupy his mind.

'Tucker. Raymond, Anthony.' There was gravel in the voice, giving an edge to what would otherwise have been a gentle West Country burr. *Get off my land, or I'll rip your lungs out . . .*

'Tell you *what*?' Thorne said.

There was a sigh and a sniff. 'Right. Silly buggers, is it?'

'I'm not trying to be difficult . . .'

'No?'

'I just don't have much more than you could easily get off the bulletin, you know? So, I don't think I can really be a lot of help.' There was a soft knock, and Thorne looked up to see one of the civilian office assistants staring in through the window in the door. She formed her fingers into a 'T' and held them up to the glass. Thorne shook his head.

'I know a lot about Ray Tucker and his mates,' Bannard said. 'Fuck of a lot, matter of fact. It's just this very recent stuff I'm a bit woolly on . . . the getting his head caved in and what have you.' He laughed again, and let out a short volley of coughs, which caused Thorne momentarily to pull the phone away from his ear. 'The "dead in his front room" stuff, see? It's just about getting up to speed really, keeping on top of things. So, anything you can tell me will almost certainly be useful. Fair enough, DI Thorne?'

Thorne duly told Bannard what had come to light that day. He told him about the state of the body when it was discovered, the likely murder weapon and the preliminary results of the PM, sensing, even as he did so, that he wasn't telling the man anything he didn't know already.

The only thing he neglected to mention – for no very good reason he could put his finger on – was that he'd been sent a picture of the dead man two days before.

'"Ray Tucker and his mates", you said?' Thorne heard Bannard take a drink of something on the other end of the line.

'For fifteen years, Tucker, better known to us and his *close* friends as "Rat", was a leading member of the "Black Dogs". They're one of the bigger biker gangs, OK? Swallowed up two or three other mobs over

53

the years and nobody's quite sure how many members there are now, but thirty-five or forty, easy. They're dotted around, but we've got most of them based up towards the edge of north London and Hertfordshire these days.'

Thorne had heard the name. 'Hell's Angels, right?'

'Absolutely not. Business rivals, as a matter of fact, but they all work along the same lines: a strict hierarchy, members sworn to secrecy, the wearing of club colours and what have you.'

'And I'm guessing most of the time, when they meet up, it's got fuck all to do with motorbikes.'

'Not a great deal, no.'

'What is it, dope?'

'Dope, cocaine, ecstasy, whatever. They work with affiliated gangs in Europe, bring the stuff in from Holland and Scandinavia. We think they've just started moving into the heroin business.'

'Not beating up mods on Brighton seafront any more, then?'

'There's still plenty of violence,' Bannard said. 'Plenty. They move around, expand into new areas, whatever, and the turf wars can get seriously tasty. Mind you, they've gone beyond machetes and bike chains. We found rocket launchers and assault rifles in a Black Dogs lock-up last year.' He paused, as though he were making sure that the seriousness, the *scale*, of what he was describing was sinking in.

'That explains the tattoos,' Thorne said.

'Sorry?'

Thorne told him about the conversations he'd had with Hendricks and Holland. Bannard listened, then described one tattoo in particular, a pair of entwined daggers, but Thorne couldn't recall seeing it.

'It's usually a small one, but it'll be there somewhere,' Bannard said. 'Go back and have a look. That's a "kill" symbol. Most gangs have got them, a special patch or a tattoo, and they have to be earned . . .'

Another seemingly significant pause. Thorne bit. 'So, what . . .? You reckon that whoever smashed Tucker's head in has just earned one of his own?'

54

'It's possible. Maybe Rat got on the wrong side of somebody.'

'I've seen him,' Thorne said, 'and I think it's safe to assume he pissed off *someone*.'

The S&O man's laugh seemed genuine this time, but just when they seemed to be getting along, Thorne spoiled it by asking if there was a specific reason why Bannard had called in the first place.

The throat was cleared and the voice sharpened. 'Obviously, Tucker was someone of interest to us, so his murder is hardly something we can ignore. Letting you know would seem to be a good idea, don't you think? Would be a *courtesy*, that's all.'

It sounded very reasonable. 'So you wouldn't be trying to stake a claim or anything like that?' Thorne asked. 'Same as you're doing with the Deniz Sedat murder.'

'Nobody's stepping on anyone else's toes here.'

'I understand that, sir.'

'Good.'

'But surely you can understand people thinking that you were letting someone else do the donkey work, you know? So you could come in at the last minute like the heavy mob.'

'The case you mentioned isn't one of mine. And you're being seriously fucking cheeky, Inspector.'

It was Thorne's turn to leave the significant pause. 'Sir.'

'Now, you've been helpful, so let's not fall out, but there's just one more thing. I wonder if you could tell me why the Tucker murder was taken away from the team at Homicide East that originally caught it, and allocated to you?'

Thorne heard nothing he liked in the seemingly innocent enquiry. He could make out Bannard's enjoyment at having caught him out in the lie-by-omission. And there was no mistaking the relish with which his superior demonstrated just how well connected he was in every sense of the word. He couldn't remember when he'd last felt so outmanoeuvred by another copper. So outclassed.

With no choice, Thorne finally told Bannard about the message from Raymond Tucker's killer: the photo that had started everything. Gave another answer which he was sure Keith Bannard had already known when he was asking the question.

'How did that go?' Kitson asked.

'Do you mean the phone conversation with Serious and Organised, or the bollocking I've just given Andy Stone for putting the fucker's call through?'

'Well, I'm guessing the second part was more enjoyable, but I meant the phone call.'

They were standing in the corner of the Incident Room, behind Karim's desk, where a collection of mugs and a stone-age kettle sat on top of a small fridge. Thorne reached for the sugar. There were dried brown lumps in the bowl and caked on to the teaspoon. He turned around and let anyone within earshot know that the next person to stir their tea and then get sugar without wiping the spoon first would be rocketing straight to the top of his shit list.

'That good, was it?' Kitson said. 'Your phone call?'

Thorne smiled and played it down. He didn't let Kitson know the extent to which he'd been stitched up. Or how, despite the fact that the conversation with Bannard had ended casually enough, he'd hung up feeling well and truly dismissed.

'He seemed OK,' Thorne said. 'Fancied himself a bit, but you know what they're like.'

Kitson was relieved the call had not turned out to concern the Sedat case. She wondered aloud if S&O would be backing off from her inquiry, now that the knife had turned up where it had.

'They will if they've got any bloody sense.' Thorne took the milk from the fridge. Gave it a sniff. 'I still don't see it as a gangland thing.'

'Shame about those prints,' Kitson said.

'Never mind. Maybe whoever knifed Sedat left his name and address in a different bin.'

They drank their teas. Nodded hellos to faces from one of the other teams settling in on a new shift. 'Well, at least you know a lot more about your body in Enfield now,' Kitson said.

Thorne nodded, reminding himself that he needed to call Hendricks; let him know he'd been right about the tattoos.

'Sounds like *that* might well be a gangland thing.'

Thorne groaned across his mug: 'I sincerely hope not.'

'Yeah, I know what you mean.' Kitson dug around in her handbag for a compact. 'It really helps if you give a toss, doesn't it?' She strolled away towards the toilets, leaving Thorne wondering whether Brigstocke or Chief Superintendent Trevor Jesmond would still talk about an 'innocent victim' if there was a press conference. Deciding that he'd give it another hour, two at the most, then head home.

He walked slowly back towards his office, thinking that he'd need to find out a little more about the Black Dogs and how they operated. He passed the board with Tucker's picture on it, and felt himself starting to smile. Even though the gloom was gathering strength outside the window, and the day behind him felt like something he'd hacked his way through, he was strangely cheered by the notion of a heavily tat-tooed, vicious member of an outlaw biker gang with a mum who still washed his underpants.

He'd never really worked out why there was any need for security at a hospital. Obviously, there were drugs knocking about, but they kept them locked up, didn't they? He knew there were nutters who tried to nick babies, so he could understand them being careful on maternity wards, and it made sense to keep an eye on anywhere they had infec-tious diseases, but apart from that he couldn't see what it was they were so worried about.

As it went, the place where they were looking after Ricky Hodson was hardly Fort Knox.

The Abbey was a large, private hospital in Bushey, and the Beaumont building sat between banks of trees on the edge of its fifteen well-tended acres. There were a dozen rooms on the first floor. There were commanding views across a car park from one side or rolling fields from the other, depending on how high a premium you'd paid on your health insurance.

He smiled as he walked into reception; said something funny about how cold it was. He received a smile in return and was buzzed through into the lobby. Waiting for the lift, he looked at himself in the highly polished doors. He lowered his hood and pushed a hand through his hair. Took a deep breath.

The place didn't even *smell* like a hospital.

When he walked into Hodson's room, it didn't surprise him that he wasn't looking out over the car park. Not that he could see a lot: the fields were grey under the charcoal sky, and he could just make out lights a long way in the distance. He thought it might be Watford or Rickmansworth.

There was a noise from the bed.

Hodson was watching MTV. On a television fixed high up in the corner of the room, some rap star or other was showing the cameras around his house. There was a pool table with gold-coloured baize and a plasma screen ten feet across.

He walked around the bed, took the remote from the small table and turned off the television.

It wasn't exactly recognition in Hodson's eyes, he couldn't say that, but there was curiosity, certainly. Drugged up to the eyeballs as he was, it was hard to make out exactly what he said. '*What?*' Or '*who?*' maybe. Definitely a question.

He held up the plastic bag he was carrying. Laid it down gently on the edge of the bed and began to delve inside.

'Here you go,' he said.

When he'd first seen what had happened, he'd been afraid that the accident was going to do the job for him. He'd written one of his letters, telling her just how furious and frustrated he was. But once it became clear that the situation was improving, that Hodson's condition wasn't life-threatening, he began to think that it might have done him an enormous favour. Now, looking at the state Ricky Hodson had been left in, he knew that he'd been spot on.

There were wires running all over the shop; machines either side of the bed with bags hanging off them. There were dressings along both of Hodson's arms where he'd taken the skin off and a brace around his neck. He'd punctured a lung, apparently, as well as shattering his hip and pelvis, and one leg had been smashed up so badly that he'd been lucky to keep it, by all accounts.

'Jesus, Ricky. What a mess.'

Hodson's eyes were moving back and forth quickly now. A beam of panic cutting through the fog of sedation; allowing out a few sputtered words, slurred and hoarse. 'You're in the wrong room, mate . . .'

He took out a sorry-looking bunch of grapes and held them up for inspection. Then went back into the bag and produced a paperback book. He put them both on the table then reached across to rub the back of his hand across Hodson's unmarked face. It rasped against the man's stubble.

'At least you were wearing a helmet,' he said.

He took the rag from his pocket and pushed it quickly into Hodson's mouth, forcing his head down into the pillow. He winced as his fingers caught on the teeth, before bringing the bag around and slipping it over Hodson's head. He gathered up the plastic, wrapped the handles around his fingers and squeezed, tightening his hands below the jaw to get a decent seal.

The metal bed-head rattled, but not for very long.

He watched as the thin, crappy plastic was sucked in, as it wrapped and crinkled around the nose. He waited until it slowed, then turned his eyes to the window; looked out at the distant lights, his hands still clamped tight above the neck-brace.

It was probably Watford . . .

He turned back again and leaned in, as the bag slapped gently one last time against Ricky Hodson's face. 'That black ice is a bastard, eh?'

Thorne had been leaving messages for Louise since early afternoon, but she hadn't called back until he'd been on his way home.

He'd told her that he'd had an 'interesting' day. Said he'd give her the gory details later if she fancied it, that he'd be happy to get over to her place. Louise had confirmed she wouldn't be working horrendously late, but that she really ought to get an early night, if that was OK. She'd said she would call him if she changed her mind; if she found herself utterly unable to get through the night without him. Thorne had told her he'd be waiting for the call.

The Bengal Lancer had been about to close, but, as a favoured customer, the manager was happy to let Thorne sit at the bar with a couple of the waiters and work his way through a plate of onion bhajis and lamb tikka while the cleaners carried on around him. It did the trick. When he'd walked in, Thorne was still pissed off with Louise, but two pints of Kingfisher and a few off-colour stories had put him in a far better mood by the time he got home, just before ten-thirty.

He fed Elvis, stuck some washing in and caught the end of *Wednesday Night Football* on Sky. He was about to log on to Poker-pro when he noticed that he'd got email. Hendricks had clearly not had the busiest of days and had spent far too much of it thinking up names for their new 'gay pathologist' drama. In his email he'd suggested *Poof-Mortem* and *Mincing in the Morgue* before deciding that perhaps they could spin off into a talk-show format in a mortuary-style location, with a working title of *On the Slab with Kinky Phil*.

Thorne decided that, for a while at least, this was more fun than gambling. He sat and thought, scribbling notes on a piece of paper normally reserved for assessments of rival poker players. Then he fired off an email to Hendricks, proposing *Stiffies!* and *Queer Eye for the Slab Guy*. But he couldn't come up with anything he liked better than *Is That Rigor Mortis, or Are You Just Pleased to See Me?*

Waiting to see if Hendricks would come back with anything, Thorne remembered his phone. His original handset had been sent back from Newlands Park that lunchtime and was now sitting, sealed inside its Jiffy bag, on the table by the front door.

Thorne fetched scissors from the kitchen and cut into the parcel while keeping one eye on a potentially dirty film on Channel Five and racking his brain for more comedy titles. He decided, as he worked, that this was male multitasking at its most advanced. That the tight-arsed jobsworth at Newlands Park was clearly trying to get his own back, having wrapped up the phone in several layers of impenetrable plastic packaging.

It took him almost ten minutes to dig out the Nokia. Then ten more to retrieve the battery and the SIM, each of which had been mummified separately. By the time Thorne finally put everything together, the film had finished and he'd used up all the swear words he knew.

He switched on the phone. Watched as the signal and battery indicators appeared. He looked at the screen for ten seconds . . . fifteen, then laid the handset down and went back to the computer.

The moment he sat down, the tone sounded, and the phone began to vibrate on the table. Calls were being diverted through to his new phone, but you couldn't divert text and MMS.

He had a message waiting.

SIX

Mid-morning, Thursday, and for the second time that week Brigstocke sat staring at Tom Thorne's mobile phone. He tapped at the screen. 'Is that some sort of wire on the right-hand side?'

Thorne walked around the desk, leaned down and looked over Brigstocke's shoulder. He stared at the picture which had arrived the night before. There was no blood this time, no signs of violence. To the casual observer, the man on the screen might even have looked asleep; a notion reinforced by the fact that his head was resting on a white pillow.

But Thorne was no casual observer.

He looked hard at the light, wavy line that snaked down one edge of the picture and almost touched the dead man's face at the bottom of the screen. 'It's clear,' Thorne said. 'Like a tube, or a cable . . .'

Brigstocke stared then shook his head, defeated. 'Let's see what they can do at Newlands Park.'

Holland peered in at the glass and pushed the door open at the signal from Thorne. He announced that T-Mobile had finally come back with details on the original message: the call had been made via a mast on top of an office block in Acton.

In the Incident Room and beyond, the team was working flat out. As of a few hours previously, when Thorne had received the second photograph, the inquiry had been substantially upgraded. Officers moved across from other cases – including the Sedat murder, and several being worked by other teams – had already established that this latest message had been sent from another prepay handset, this time on the Orange network. A request for cell-site intelligence had been lodged overnight and steps were being taken to locate where the phone had been purchased. Providing they were able to pinpoint the retail outlet, and based on an average turnover of stock, this could mean wading through a month's worth of CCTV footage or more. It might provide evidence that could be useful if they ever got an offender into a courtroom, but it was highly unlikely to help in catching them. Like much else that the team were busy knuckling down to, it was like collecting pieces of a jigsaw puzzle, with no idea what the finished picture was supposed to look like.

'How quickly can Orange get us the cell-site?'

Holland looked pleased with himself. 'I lied and told them T-Mobile had really pulled the stops out for us,' he said. 'Reckon a bit of healthy competition might do us a favour.'

Thorne and Holland walked out together and were passing Andy Stone's desk as the DC came off the phone and collared them. 'Bin-bag can't see us this morning.'

'You'll need to talk English,' Thorne said.

'Martin Cowans.' Stone held up a printout, with a number of arrests detailed beneath a fetchingly menacing photograph. 'Black Dogs' top dog, but he prefers to be known as "Bin-bag", for some reason. You told me to call and let him know we wanted a word.'

'So what's keeping Bin-bag so busy this morning?' Holland asked.

'A mate of his has died unexpectedly, so he said. He's got stuff to arrange.'

Thorne looked at Stone.

'Tucker getting the big biker funeral, is he?' Holland asked. 'Coffin on the back of a Harley. Motörhead as he slides through the curtains . . .'

'That's the thing,' Stone said. 'I thought he was talking about Tucker as well . . . but he wasn't. Some other mate of his died last night in hospital. He says he needs to get over there apparently, sort—'

'Call him back,' Thorne said, already turning. 'Find out which hospital he's on about and get a crime scene unit over there on the hurry-up.' He carried on barking instructions as he marched out: 'Call Phil Hendricks and get him down there. Make sure the hospital know we're coming, then tell Cowans to stay exactly where he is. After we've paid our respects to his friend, we can all get together for a chat . . .'

Putting things together as he went, Thorne fought the urge to run all the way back to Brigstocke's office.

A death in hospital, a certain *kind* of death, would not have shown up on the daily bulletin. This time, the man responsible had not waited to let him know what he'd done.

Thorne opened the door and marched straight over to Brigstocke's desk. He jabbed at the screen of his phone, traced a finger down the mysterious line on the photograph.

'It's the tube from a hospital drip.'

The majority of heroin coming into the UK was still controlled by the Turkish mafia based in and around the Green Lanes area, but for the previous few years their position had been challenged by Asian gangs, many of which operated from the heart of the Sikh community in Southall. If, as Bannard had suggested, the Black Dogs were expanding into heroin smuggling, it put their leader's decision to live just off Southall Broadway somewhere between provocative and plain idiotic.

Martin Cowans clearly saw things rather differently. 'I'll live where the fuck I like,' he said. The way Cowans' lips twisted as he spoke told Thorne all he needed to know about the man's racial politics.

It was hardly a revelation.

Nor was the fact that Cowans extended his precious freedom of choice to those he welcomed into his home, and that no police were on his guest-list. The Black Dogs' president had agreed to meet instead at the club's HQ in Rayner's Lane, a few miles north of where he lived. The 'clubhouse' consisted of two ordinary end-of-terrace houses in a quiet side street, which looked as though they had been knocked through into one without the benefit of professional building advice. One half of the ground floor was crowded with mattresses and motorcycle parts. The other housed a tiny kitchen, living room and a purpose-built bar area complete with pool table, dartboard and beer pumps connected to metal barrels.

'Nice,' Thorne had said, as he and Holland had been given the tour.

Unusually furnished as its interior was, the outside of the building gave less away, if you didn't count the bikes lined up in what was left of the front garden. There were enough clues, though: the reinforced steel doors; the blacked-out windows; the security cameras mounted high on the pebble-dash at front and side.

'What do your neighbours make of this place?' Holland asked.

Cowans flicked ash on to a scarred grey carpet. 'Ask any of them. They'll tell you we're no trouble.'

'I bet they will,' Thorne said.

They were gathered in the living room: Holland and Thorne on tatty, high-backed chairs that looked as though they'd come from a doctor's waiting room; Cowans and two of his friends sprawled across a selection of armchairs and settees in scorched corduroy, velour, or torn and dirty vinyl.

The room stank of stale beer and motor oil.

'Listen, I don't know if anyone's given any thought to Ray Tucker's tropical fish,' Holland said. 'What's going to happen to them, I mean. Obviously he might have left them to someone, and this is just a sug-gestion.' He pointed. 'But the tank would look lovely against that wall . . .'

All three bikers were dressed as might have been expected. The uni-form was compulsory on club premises. Thorne knew that the patches they wore on the backs of their leathers, or denim jackets – the club's colours – were hugely important to them. He understood that they were not to be abused, and that the wearing of patches to which a biker was not entitled would be dealt with severely. He'd read of gang members being dragged from their bikes, having their colours cut off with Stanley knives, without anyone first bothering to remove the jacket.

Cowans, who only ever answered to his nickname, was pushing fifty. He was stick-thin, but with a gut on him; long hair was tied back and silvering, while his thick beard hadn't quite turned the same colour. His younger colleagues had introduced themselves quite politely as 'Gazza' and 'Ugly Bob'. Gazza was stocky, with a beard that tended towards bum-fluff, while Bob was shaven-headed and sported a thick moustache. Thorne knew that men looking not unlike Bob hung out in some of the clubs Phil Hendricks frequented, but he decided to keep that to himself.

There was much that Thorne might have found almost comical, if he hadn't known exactly what these men were capable of. If he hadn't been wondering which of them had entwined daggers tattooed on some secret patch of pale flesh. He nodded towards Gazza and Ugly Bob. 'What are you two, then? Road captains? Sergeants-at-arms?'

They said nothing.

Thorne turned to Cowans. 'And Ray Tucker was vice-president, wasn't he?'

'I'm not going to talk to you about individual members of this club,' Cowans said. 'But I'm pleased that you've done some homework.'

'Oh yes.' Thorne took a piece of paper from his pocket, brandished it proudly. 'Printed out your rules and regulations as well. Nice website, by the way.'

'Music's a bit shit,' Holland said.

Thorne looked down at the list laid out in a dramatic, Gothic typeface: the club rules and the respective fines for any breach; the cost of patches; the guidelines for general behaviour. 'Five pounds a week subs,' he said. 'That's fairly steep.'

'You get a lot for your money,' Cowans said.

'How many of you are there? Twenty-five, thirty? Hundred and fifty quid a week doesn't pay for this lot.' Thorne looked around. 'I'm betting there's no mortgage on this place, right?'

'You'd need to talk to the club's accountant.'

Thorne nodded, like he was grateful for the suggestion. 'So what about Ricky Hodson, then? Was he high up on the club ladder?'

'Hoddo was a member of this club for fifteen years. That's it.'

'Tucker dead, now Hodson. You must be wondering what's going on.' Cowans and his mates didn't look like they were wondering about a great deal. 'He was murdered. That *has* sunk in, right? Whatever the hospital might have said first thing, I can promise you that. There were no marks on him – well, nothing he didn't get coming off his bike – so my guess is suffocation, but he's on his way across to the morgue as we speak, so we'll know soon enough.'

Cowans shook his head, smiled as if he admired the effort Thorne was putting in. They were words he'd spoken many times before, but the voice didn't sound quite as casual as he wanted it to. 'I won't talk about members of this club. I won't talk about any outstanding or open cases or comment on any suggestion of criminal activity. I will not make a statement . . .'

Thorne squinted at his piece of paper in mock confusion. 'I didn't see anything in the rules about not talking to the police.'

Now Cowans' smile was less forced. 'Right. Because we're not morons, and we don't want to get done for conspiracy.'

Thorne looked across at Gazza and Ugly Bob. Neither of them seemed particularly sharp, but Thorne knew very well that in any organised crime gang, in any unit, having one person who wasn't stupid was usually enough.

'So it's an *unofficial* rule, is it?' Holland asked.

Cowans gave him a hard stare. Scratched at his crotch. 'It's more of a philosophy.'

'Well, it seems a bit pointless,' Thorne said. 'Us coming all this way for a chat, I mean, if you aren't going to talk to us.'

'Nobody invited you,' Gazza piped up.

'Maybe *you* not talking is a good idea,' Holland said.

Cowans seemed to find Holland's rebuke funny. 'Look, I'm perfectly happy to chat. I just won't *say* anything.' He turned to Ugly Bob. 'Go and chase up that fucking tea, will you?'

Bob sloped out, ash dropping on to his chest from the roll-up that had been clamped beneath his moustache since they'd sat down.

'Very nice memorial section on the website by the way,' Thorne said. 'Some touching tributes.'

If Cowans was narked by the sarcasm, he didn't show it. 'This is a family, and members stay members, even if they're gone. The Dogs don't forget anyone.'

'A lot of them have gone over the years,' Holland said. 'Surely they didn't all come off their bikes?'

Cowans shook his head. 'Like I said. Happy to chat . . .'

'Can you tell us about the history of the club, then?'

'It's all on the website.'

'How long have you been club president?'

'Six years.'

'Right.' Holland took the chance to show that he had done some homework as well. 'You took over from Simon Tipper.'

'"Tips" . . .'

'Whatever . . .'

At that point Ugly Bob kicked the door open and came in with three mugs of tea. A woman walked in behind him with three more and a packet of biscuits. She was fortyish and pale, with bleached blond hair and a crop top that did her no favours. She handed mugs to Thorne and Holland and then took her own over to the sofa, settling on the arm next to Cowans. Thorne saw that she was wearing slightly different colours to the others: a 'property' patch given to those 'old ladies' of club members lucky enough to be afforded the honour.

'This Mrs Bin-bag, is it?' Thorne asked.

The woman tore at the packet of biscuits with her teeth. Gave Thorne the finger without looking up.

'Nice picture of Tips on the memorial page,' Thorne said. 'What happened to him?'

Cowans took a handful of biscuits from the woman. 'Well, that's a matter of public record, isn't it? Some burglar knifed him while he was

68

turning Tips' place over. All done and dusted quick enough by your lot. Arsehole got banged up. That's it.'

'What about the ones that weren't done and dusted? The ones that didn't die on their bikes and weren't tragically killed disturbing burglars. You sorted those out yourself, right?'

Cowans dunked and drank.

'Don't be like that,' Holland said. 'See how nice this is – a cup of tea and a natter?'

'Come on, I presume you don't have an "armourer" for nothing,' Thorne said. 'I know that scores have to be settled.'

Holland began to pick up on cues. 'Tucker and Hodson. There's two for a start.'

'Mind you, it's a fair bet that whoever killed them was settling some scores of their own.'

'And obviously you've got no idea at all who that might be.'

'Can't be too many candidates though, surely?'

'Another biker gang?' Holland addressed the questions to Thorne. 'Some local business that doesn't like the competition?'

'Come on, Bin-bag,' Thorne said. 'Who's going to pay for Rat and Hoddo?'

Thorne could only presume that Cowans was opening his mouth to refuse to answer their questions when his old lady beat him to the punch.

'Some cunt'll pay for it, sooner or later.' She looked like she was enjoying herself. 'We've got long memories and—'

Cowans reached over, expressionless, and took hold of his girlfriend's wrist. She sucked in a breath through her teeth and, as she stared right back at Thorne, he watched her struggling not to show any of the pain or anger.

There wasn't too much more chat after that.

Thorne turned at the door as though he'd forgotten something, and stabbed a finger at the Black Dogs' rules. 'This is a strange one,' he said. '"Members found to be injecting drugs will be subject to the severest punishment, and may be expelled from the club."' He looked at Cowans, thought about what Bannard had told him. 'Now, bearing in mind that other gangs involved in heroin smuggling are the most likely people to be pissed off with you lot right now, I was wondering: is *that* a philosophy as well? Or are you just being ironic?'

He screwed up the piece of paper and tossed it towards the bikers. Gazza swore, and swatted it away, while Cowans just smiled and reached into his tea; fished out bits of biscuit with dirty fingers.

'I didn't think it would be too long before we were talking again,' Bannard said.

Thorne turned from the phone and pulled a face at Holland; long-suffering and scornful. 'Why's that then?'

'Well, now there's *two* dead bikers. Changes things a bit.'

'I need to pick your brains about the Black Dogs,' Thorne said.

'There's no other reason why you'd be calling.'

'You OK with that?'

'Why wouldn't I be? We're not trying to step on anyone's toes.'

'Yeah, you said.'

'We're happy to let you run with this one.'

Despite the nonsensical corporate language and the West Country accent, the 'we' still managed to sound faintly ominous. 'But you're still keeping an eye on things?'

'Oh shit, yes.' Bannard coughed out a laugh. 'There's something major kicking off, obviously, and we'd be fucking idiots if we weren't seriously interested.'

'Course.'

'But it would also be pretty stupid to come in over the top of you, when you've got such a . . . *connection* to the case, don't you reckon?'

Thorne mumbled a 'yes', thinking: Will you let me know if you find out what it is?

'So, I take it you've been to see Bin-bag and got fuck all?'

'Tea and biscuits.'

'He must have liked you.'

Bannard promised to send Thorne a file on the Black Dogs. Said it would give a much better picture of their recent history and set-up than could be found on any website; intelligence that might point Thorne and his team towards whoever was cheerfully picking off senior members of the club.

Thorne was suitably grateful, and equally pissed off at having to be. He asked how far back the file went. He'd started to wonder to what extent the club's activities in the last few years were connected with a change of hierarchy, and what Bannard knew about the death of the Black Dogs' former leader.

'Probably no more than you,' Bannard said. 'The Tipper murder was before I came on board. We've got all the details on file.'

'It might be interesting to have a look.'

'Are you out and about?'

Thorne said that he was. He didn't bother to mention that he and Holland were sitting in a car fifty yards from the Black Dogs' clubhouse, but Bannard was the sort of copper who made him paranoid enough to think he didn't have to.

'I'll dig out the name of the original SIO and get back to you,' Bannard said. 'If you really think it's worth it, you're probably far better off talking to them.'

The Airwave system, rolled out across the Met over the previous two years, had become the bane of many coppers' lives; more specifically the built-in GPS, which enabled those in the control room to pinpoint the location of any officer, if they so chose. There were times, however, when the combined phone/radio/data transmitter came into its own. When Bannard proved as good as his word and called back ten minutes later with a name, Thorne was able to make direct contact immediately.

DCI Sharon Lilley worked on an anti-terrorism unit based at Paddington Green station. Pleasantly enough, she told Thorne that the rest of her day was a bastard. But, if he fancied it, he was welcome to sit in on an important debriefing session after work.

Thorne had cracked tougher codes. He asked her what she would be drinking.

71

SEVEN

He had seen his fair share of the capital's stranger sights, most of them predictably situated at the ghoulish end of the spectrum. But on a Sunday morning a couple of months before, Thorne had stumbled upon what had to be among the most bizarre spectacles the city had to offer.

Now, hurrying past St John's Church to meet Sharon Lilley, it was the smell of it he remembered more than anything else. If new carpets took him back to his childhood, perhaps he was destined for ever to associate churches with the stench of fresh horse-shit.

The last time he'd seen the place – the immense, ornate windows glittering from its Gothic façade – there had been upwards of a hundred horses gathered on its forecourt: shire horses and Shetland ponies; nags and thoroughbreds pulling carts, carriages and traps. Men, women and children in every conceivable type of outlandish equestrian outfit had paraded on horseback past a fully regaled minister. The priest – who, not to be outdone, was sitting happily astride a mount of his own – had proceeded to bless each and every animal, having first found out a little about them from their owners.

'What's his name? Squirrel? God be with you, Squirrel . . .'

Thorne and Louise had stood and watched in happy amazement. They'd asked a fellow spectator and established that the event was called Horsemen's Sunday and that it took place every year. They'd enjoyed the bacon rolls and coffee that were laid on; listened as a small jazz band had provided the soundtrack. Then they'd wandered away, agreeing that whatever darkness London hid, or had visited upon it, any city where you could walk round a corner and see a frocked-up vicar on horseback was still a pretty good place to be.

The pub Sharon Lilley had suggested was more run-of-the-mill. A stone's throw from St John's church, on the north side of Hyde Park, the Duke of Kendal was a small place, busy enough at six-thirty on a Thursday for a dozen or so punters to be sitting at the wooden tables outside, hunched over their drinks in coats and scarves.

Inside it was noisy, the chat almost, but not quite, drowning out an old Meat Loaf single. As Thorne walked towards a woman he thought might be Sharon Lilley, he passed a blackboard with a decent-looking Thai menu and decided that he might order something later, if the conversation went on a while. The woman saw him coming. She held up an almost empty wine glass and nodded. When Thorne pushed his way through to the bar, he was horrified to see that it was already decked out with tinsel and plastic holly.

'This isn't a coppers' pub, then?' Thorne said, handing Lilley her drink.

'What gave it away?'

'Oh, I don't know. The fact that there's an atmosphere. People enjoying themselves. That kind of thing.'

Lilley smiled, touched her glass to Thorne's. 'Place is pretty perfect, as it goes,' she said. 'It's only five minutes from the station, but that's just far enough to put off the serious pissheads. The ones who can't be arsed to walk more than twenty-five yards to get a drink.'

The accent was pure Essex, but Lilley was a long way from the comic stereotype: she was sharp and funny, the cynicism just the right side of miserable. Her dark hair was scraped back, emphasising a face that was puffy, but if she was a little heavyset, her expression said that

73

she really didn't give a toss. Crucially, she couldn't have been more than thirty-five, which told Thorne something more important. To have led a murder team in her late twenties meant that she was good at what she did, or good at playing the game. Or, best of all, both.

'I was still a DI at the time,' she said. 'But my DCI was happy to step back and let me run the Tipper enquiry.' Thorne raised his eyebrows. It wasn't unheard of, but it was still rare for an inspector to be SIO on a major murder case. 'I had my eye on moving up to chief inspector.' Lilley smiled, remembering. 'It's important to see how you handle yourself, isn't it? Try the shoes on for size.'

'Never fancied them myself,' Thorne said.

They talked for a while about her present job; about how Antiterror had seemed a cushy enough unit when she'd first joined a few years before. There had been some scaling down as IRA activity on the mainland had fallen away. But, of course, everything had changed on 11 September; had been ratcheted up still further after the London bombings of July 2005.

Thorne told her how relieved he was that she hadn't said '9/11' or '7/7'. How he hated the numerical shorthand that had crept in to so much conversation. Lilley happily revealed herself to be a kindred spirit. She said that anyone who said '24/7' was deserving of a slap. 'Same as twats who talk about "windows" in their diaries or order drinks by asking if they can "get" a beer.'

She went to the bar. Asked if she could *have* another glass of wine and a pint of Guinness . . .

'Simon Tipper started up the Black Dogs in the early nineties,' she said. 'He was president until he got carved up by a bloke called Marcus Brooks in his front room. July 2000.' She sipped her drink, thinking back. 'The place was a mess. Blood and papers and shit everywhere. Brooks was really turning the place over when Tipper came home and caught him.'

'That the story?'

'Well, it wasn't *Brooks'* story, but I reckon that was how it happened.'

'How did you get him?'

'He was too fucking cool for his own good. He tears the place apart, cuts Tipper up for good measure, then sits down and has a drink. We got a nice set of prints off a glass behind the settee, and we already had Brooks on record for all sorts of things.'

Thorne froze, the glass halfway to his mouth. Lilley's description of events had rung a bell with him, and he was suddenly thinking about something Hendricks had said:

'He smashes Tucker's head in; then, while he's stood there covered in blood . . . he calmly takes out his mobile phone and starts snapping away. Cool as you like.'

Thorne took a drink. 'So, all nice and easy for you then?'

'Well, like I say, it wasn't what Brooks said happened. He reckoned he was "told" to rob the place, and when he got there someone had done the job for him. Said Tipper was already dead when he walked in.'

'Told to rob the place by who?'

Lilley grinned, like it was something that had kept her sporadically entertained for a long time. 'Brooks always claimed he'd been fitted up by two coppers. Told us they'd threatened to put him and his girlfriend away unless he did them a favour.'

Thorne had heard similar tales a hundred times. 'Right, but he couldn't tell you who they were?'

'Oh yes, he could. He kept on telling us. Gave us their names, details of meetings, the lot.'

Thorne waited.

'Well, it was bollocks, obviously. We looked into it and basically DI "Jennings" and DC "Squire" didn't exist. Not in the Met, anyway. We *did* find a copper called Jennings, but he was doling out traffic tickets in North Yorkshire somewhere . . .'

They were jammed together on one side of a small table, in a corner next to the cigarette machine. Thorne watched as an attractive blonde struggled to find the right coins while jabbering into her mobile. He got a filthy look and turned back to his pint.

'Is any of this shit helping?' Lilley asked.

Thorne told her about the murders of Raymond Tucker and Ricky Hodson. Seeing no reason not to, he told her that he'd been sent pictures of both dead men. He answered Lilley's question without waiting for it to be asked. 'No, I haven't the faintest fucking idea why,' he said.

The blonde was still on the phone. Now she was trying to extract a cigarette from the packet using her teeth.

'Tell me about Brooks,' Thorne said. 'You said his prints were on record.'

'Marcus had been a bad lad, no two ways about it. He was your typical south London tearaway, sort of kid who would've been drowning in ASBOs today, know what I mean? He does a couple of years in the army, buys himself out and ends up doing odds and sods for one or two of the nastier local firms. Deliveries, some security work, whatever. Nothing too heavy himself, as far as we could tell, but he was *useful*, you know?'

'Hard man?'

'If he needed to be, definitely. Then, round about '95, '96, Marcus meets this girl, has a kid and changes careers. I don't mean he becomes an accountant or a brain surgeon or anything, but he walks away from the organised end of things – from anything that's going to get him in serious trouble – and him and this girl start working for themselves. Some sort of burglary scam they worked together. He'd been doing that, keeping his head down, until he showed up in Simon Tipper's house and went mental.'

'Ever find the knife?'

'No, but we had the prints on the glass, so we never needed to.'

'You said Brooks was never into anything too heavy himself. Just working on the fringes, right?' Lilley hummed agreement. 'Stabbing someone to death sounds a bit out of character.'

She acknowledged the thought with a look then dismissed it with another. 'People like Brooks are always going to fuck up. Maybe they get carried away when they're just supposed to be threatening someone. A routine job goes tits up and they panic. Whatever. I wouldn't have put him down as someone who could lose it that easily, but this shit happens all the time, right?' She closed her eyes as she drank, then widened them, leaning towards him. 'Come on, are you telling me you're still surprised by *anything*?'

Thorne looked at Lilley's fingers curled around the stem of her glass. He noticed that the nails were chewed beyond the quick. 'How long did he get?'

'Well, here's where Mr Brooks *did* surprise me. Once he'd stopped banging on about these fictitious coppers that had stitched him up, he was offered the chance to come up with some *real* information. He certainly knew stuff about all sorts of characters and, if he'd given the Organised Crime Unit something, we might have been able to make the Tipper murder look a bit more like self-defence. Get the charge knocked down to manslaughter, whatever. But he wouldn't go for it.'

Thorne could see the sense in refusing to grass. 'He gets a few years more, maybe, but if he's kept his mouth shut, he's not watching his back every minute he's in there.'

'I suppose,' Lilley said. 'He was put away for eleven years in the end. Did six.'

'He's *out*?'

'Released five months ago.'

For a second, Thorne had the urge to reach up and scratch at the tickle of excitement crawling beneath his collar. He was pleased that he'd read Lilley right; impressed that the woman had kept such close tabs on someone she'd put away so many years before. He told her as much.

She laughed. 'Listen, I'm not saying there aren't one or two I keep a close eye on. And I'm chuffed that you think I'm so . . . diligent, or whatever. But I wouldn't have had a fucking clue when Marcus Brooks was getting out of prison if someone else hadn't asked me about him earlier in the year.'

'Who?'

'Bethnal Green CID got in touch in June, when Brooks' girlfriend and kid were killed in a hit and run.'

'Christ.'

77

'Yeah, nasty . . .'

'Hang on.' Thorne held up a finger. Did the maths. 'This would have been right around the time Brooks came out, surely?'

'A fortnight before. A couple of the local boys went to see him inside, to deliver the death message. Can't have been an easy one.'

'Hit and run?'

'Car jumped the lights, went into them on a zebra crossing. On their bloody doorstep, more or less.'

'Did they get the driver?' Thorne asked.

'They got the car, burned out.'

'No possibility it was deliberate?'

'It was joy-riders,' Lilley said. She stared, like she was trying to work out what he might be thinking. 'Pissed up . . .'

She was probably right, but Thorne was remembering Bin-bag's old lady, the look on her face, a couple of hours before.

'*We've got long memories.*'

'Even if it *was* an accident, maybe Brooks thought it was something else.' Thorne was talking low and fast. 'What if he decided the Black Dogs had killed his girlfriend and his kid as revenge for Tipper?'

'Six years on?'

'No better time to do it, is there? Just when Brooks is about to be released, when he thinks he's getting his life back.'

'So, he comes out of prison and starts to even things up?'

'Tucker, then Hodson . . .'

Lilley frowned and emptied her glass. 'I don't know,' she said. 'It's a thought . . .'

The music seemed to have been turned up. Meat Loaf had long since given way to Coldplay, or an equally miserable soundalike. Thorne listened, letting things settle. He had a fair idea of what grief and rage could drive someone to do, but still, he wondered if he wasn't looking too hard for something. 'Square-peg thinking,' Jesmond had once called it.

They talked for another few minutes, then Thorne said he should be getting off. He reached for his coat, but Lilley said she was staying put for a while. Thorne offered to get her another drink as a thank you, but she waved him away. He watched her reaching for her purse and wondered if she had anyone to get home to; if there was a way of asking if she fancied something to eat without it sounding like a come-on.

Lilley squeezed out from behind the table. 'I tell you what, though,' she said, 'it doesn't make a fat lot of difference if it was the Black Dogs who killed Marcus Brooks' girlfriend or not.' She smoothed down her skirt. 'If they didn't want revenge then, they certainly will now.'

It was past nine-thirty, and Thorne was starving by the time he reached Louise's place in Pimlico. She went into the kitchen, defrosted some bread to make a sandwich. 'You should have eaten something in the pub with this DCI,' she said. 'What was his name, anyway?'

'Sharon.'

Louise stuck her head round the kitchen door.

'Jealous?' Thorne asked.

'Do you want this sodding sandwich or not?'

Thorne ate while Louise filled him in on her day. Her kidnapped drug dealer was still refusing to admit that anyone had kidnapped him. She told Thorne that she envied his job; that at least murder victims couldn't pretend they weren't dead. Thorne told her she should be grateful to escape the paperwork.

He talked about his meeting.

He told Louise all about the Black Dogs, asked her what she thought about the timing of the accident that had killed Marcus Brooks' family. He tried, and failed, to convince her that Sharon Lilley was a leggy blonde who'd taken an instant fancy to him.

The conversation was punctuated by the sound of fireworks going off in nearby streets. It was another of Thorne's pet peeves: the fact that firework night now appeared to last from Halloween through to mid-November. The noise seemed to bother him a little more every year and, sitting and wincing in his girlfriend's living room, he didn't like the thought of Elvis freaking out back at home.

And it was another smell he hated.

He'd left the car at the Peel Centre, and walking from the Tube to Louise's flat the air had been thick with it: the acrid, sulphuric smell of gunpowder. The same tang as had bitten at the back of his throat one morning two decades earlier, when he and another DC had walked into a large, brightly lit kitchen and seen their first murder victims: the wife and her mother; the weapon still lying beside the man who had killed them both, before turning the gun on himself.

Remember, remember, the fifth of November . . .

To Thorne, Bonfire Night always smelled of blood and shotguns. And tasted of whatever had started to rise into the throat of a young DC.

They watched the local news at ten o'clock. There was an update on the hunt for the killer of Deniz Sedat: a Turkish community leader was saying how disappointing it was that no progress had been made, despite the discovery of the murder weapon. There was no mention of the Raymond Tucker or Ricky Hodson killings.

'How old was the kid?' Louise asked later.

'Ten,' Thorne said. 'Ten-year-old boy.'

They were together on the sofa. Louise nursed a cup of tea, pulled stockinged feet up beneath her. 'You'd be destroyed,' she said.

Thorne turned his attention from the television. 'What?'

'Getting that sort of news. *Then.*'

'Or any time . . .'

'What you said before, though, you know? About the moment when he should be getting his life back.' She shifted position, slid one of her feet beneath Thorne's leg. 'Whatever this bloke might have done in the past, that's a shitty thing to happen. You've been thinking about nothing but coming out for months, right? Getting back to your girlfriend and your kid. Having that to look forward to might be the only thing that gets you through your sentence.'

'In which case, having it taken away from you sounds like a fairly decent motive.'

'Like a *fucking* decent motive.'

Thorne couldn't be certain that Louise's enthusiasm for his theory was completely subjective. But the support felt good.

'We both know that some of these people are toerags,' she said. 'The sort who are just waiting to get out and do whatever it was they did all over again. But some just want to do their time and get back to their families. There's plenty that just want to stay safe and . . . uncorrupted.'

'*Plenty?*'

'All right, then. *Some.*'

Louise's words meant all the more, because Thorne knew that she was no bleeding heart. She was someone who preferred to give the benefit of the doubt, but if it was taken and pissed away, she would be hard as nails second time around. He really started to believe that Marcus Brooks could be the sort of prisoner she was describing; the sort on whom a death message – especially one delivered when it was – would have wreaked unimaginable havoc. 'Six years out of an eleven stretch,' he said. 'He can't have got himself into too much trouble inside.'

'Which says a lot, because he'd have been, what? Cat B? That's a high-security prison, with some serious company.'

'Parole boards look at what prisoners are coming out to, right?'

'Absolutely. Brownie points for solid family units . . .'

'Christ, if we're right about this—'

'What do you mean "we"?' Louise said. 'I'm just agreeing with you in the hope of getting a shag later.'

Thorne's smile died quickly, as he began to reflect on what would be as cold an act of revenge as he had ever come across. 'If *I'm* right about this, and the Black Dogs wanted Brooks to suffer for killing their old president, they certainly picked their moment. They waited until just the right time, when they could really fuck up his life.'

'Or the *wrong* time,' Louise said. 'And the wrong bloke. Because they're getting it back in spades now, aren't they?' She got up and took the plates and mugs through to the kitchen; shouted back to Thorne over the noise as she loaded them into the dishwasher. 'Even if it is

81

Brooks,' she said, 'we still don't know what this photo business is all about. Why he's sending them to you, I mean . . .'

But before Louise had even finished speaking, Thorne suddenly felt as though he might know; could feel a dreadful possibility rushing towards him. What had Louise said before? '*That's a high-security prison, with some serious company . . .*'

He got up and grabbed his phone; dialled the number that Sharon Lilley had given him as he was leaving the pub.

He could hear the music in the background, the chat of her fellow-drinkers, when Lilley eventually picked up. He wasn't hugely surprised that she was still where he'd left her.

'It's Tom Thorne. Listen, I'm sorry for calling so late.'

'Lucky you caught me,' she said, slowly. 'I was about to head home.'

'Just one quick question.' Something began to jump in Thorne's stomach. He took a deep breath and asked which prison Marcus Brooks had been released from.

Got the answer he didn't want to hear.

And then, Thorne *knew*.

Baby,

I'll probably keep this one short, because I'm so wiped out, and even though I know I won't sleep for very long, I'll have to get up and out. I need to walk when I wake up, to keep moving. If I just lie there, things that I don't want to think about for too long get in my head, and I'm afraid they might stick, and I can't stand it.

Actually, the walking has been brilliant. You probably think that sounds stupid, or like I'm taking the piss, because of how much I used to hate it. You couldn't even get me to walk to the bus stop, remember? It's weird, but it makes me less tired, not more. I can't explain it. It sharpens me up, you know? Like the exercise did when I was inside. I just go for miles every night, don't matter where, and when I get back here, things are a bit clearer. It isn't like I might forget what I'm going to do or anything, but it helps me focus.

It reminds me why I'm doing this. Why I don't really care about anything except doing it.

Last night, after I sorted Hodson out, I walked towards these lights I could see out of the window. Across fields and a motorway. I know they were just houses and cars and whatever, so don't think I'm going totally mental, but while I was walking in the dark, up to my knees in mud and shit and Christ knows what, it felt like I was getting closer to you and Robbie. Like you were both waiting in the lights somewhere.

I had to stop myself running in the end.

Like I said, mental. I'm even grinning about it a bit myself now, because I could hear you pissing yourself while I was writing it!!

Kiss him for me, will you?

I'm sending kisses and all sorts of other stuff to you as well,
COURSE I AM. I'll write again soon, tomorrow maybe, but now
I've got to at least try and get my head down. I'm so fucking tired.

Sleep well, angel.
X

EIGHT

The last time Thorne had seen Stuart Nicklin had been across a crowded courtroom at the Old Bailey, when he had spoken from the witness box at his trial. But the last time he had been this close to him, Thorne had been screaming and spattered in blood. A school playground in Harrow. A man dead at Thorne's feet and a woman, a police officer, dying a few yards away while he could do nothing. 'Congratulations on being alive,' Nicklin had said to him, smiling. 'Being alive's the easy bit though, isn't it? It's *feeling* alive that's the hard part.'

Thorne had reacted then, lashed out, and watched Stuart Nicklin spitting out the wreckage of teeth and long strings of blood as he was finally seized and led away.

The smile growing broader as he went.

That winter had been mild, and terrible. Nicklin had killed at least four people himself – three young women and an old man – and been directly responsible for as many deaths again. One of them, a man named Martin Palmer, had murdered two women at his behest; killings he had carried out simply because he had been easy to manipulate, and too terrified of his tormentor not to.

Nicklin had learned early that fear was the most powerful weapon of all. He wielded it as skilfully as any butcher used a blade and with as much deadly force as the police marksman who had finally gunned down Palmer in that school playground, five years before.

It had been a little under two hours on the train to Evesham, then a fifteen-minute cab ride from the station to the prison. Thorne hadn't eaten anything the whole way, and now, staring at Nicklin's wide, rejuvenated smile, he was happy to put the feeling in his stomach down to hunger.

'I feel like I should be sitting in a swivel chair,' Nicklin said. 'Stroking a white cat or something.'

'This'll have to do.'

'I was expecting you sooner, if I'm honest.'

'I only got the first picture four days ago.'

'Oh, I take that back then. Sorry.'

'I should think so.'

Nicklin nodded, pleased with himself. 'I told Marcus you were the right man for the job . . .'

HMP Long Lartin in Worcestershire housed around six hundred of the country's most dangerous adult prisoners. Stuart Nicklin certainly fitted into that category. Thorne would never forget the face of a boy named Charlie Garner. A child forced to watch while his mother had been strangled; to sit alone for two days with her body, starving and dirty and howling.

Thorne looked at Nicklin, seated across from him behind a shiny, battered table. He was wearing jeans and training shoes. A dark blue bib over a light grey sweatshirt.

Not a monster, certainly.

However those readers of the *Daily Mail* and others of a similar persuasion chose to label the likes of Stuart Nicklin, however the word seemed the only one fitting to describe what they had done, Thorne found it hard to believe that such offenders were naturally *evil*. The description suggested that others were naturally *good*. This was a concept Thorne found equally tricky to grasp. And it introduced a religious connotation into the discussion which made him hugely uncomfortable.

Nicklin was a man, not a monster . . .

'You had lunch?' Nicklin asked. Thorne shook his head. 'Very good today.' He patted his belly. 'Piling on the pounds, of course, but I'm hardly the type to work out all day, am I?'

A man Thorne would be happy to see die in prison.

In the pub the night before, Lilley had talked about there being a couple of those she'd put away on whom she'd always keep a watchful eye. Observe their progress through the system. It was the same for Thorne, and Nicklin was top of that mercifully short list.

'Why is he sending the pictures to me?'

Nicklin pretended to be taken aback. 'Bloody hell. You don't want to waste any time, do you?' The voice was quieter than the one Thorne remembered, and coarser. He presumed that Nicklin, like many prisoners, was smoking heavily. 'On a promise later on?'

'You're not as fascinating as you think you are,' Thorne said. 'And I get bored very easily. Why am I getting the pictures?'

Nicklin raised a hand to his face, brushed delicately at the side of his nose for a few seconds. 'That was a favour to me,' he said.

Thorne tried hard to show nothing. 'Why does Marcus Brooks owe you any favours?'

'I suppose you could say that I took him under my wing.'

'I bet you did.'

'Showed him the ropes when he got here.'

Thorne had already checked. Like many prisoners, Brooks had been moved around. He'd spent time in Wandsworth and Birmingham before arriving at Long Lartin towards the end of the previous year. 'Was that all you showed him?'

'No point. I could see Marcus wasn't interested in anything like that.'

'Which probably made it even more exciting, right?'

'Where are you dredging this stuff up from?' Nicklin asked.

At the time of his arrest five years before, Nicklin had been married for several years, but he'd lived a number of lives under assumed names, and had worked, during one of them, as a rent boy in the West End. Thorne had no idea if Nicklin had a conventional sexuality of any sort; only that he would fuck anyone, in any way necessary, to gain power over them.

'We were close,' Nicklin said. 'Friends.'

'This is all very heartwarming . . .'

'I was around to dole out the odd piece of advice when he came in here, and he did the occasional good turn for me. There's always someone wants to have a go at the local nutter, you know? Marcus helped me out once or twice.'

'I thought you could look after yourself,' Thorne said. 'I heard about that poor bastard in Belmarsh.' Thorne had been sent a full report when, two years previously, Nicklin had left a fellow inmate brain-dead after calmly but forcefully jamming a sharpened spoon into his ear.

Nicklin beamed. 'I'm touched that you've been taking an interest.'

'Well,' Thorne said, 'I *worry*. We all do. Me and the families of the men and women you killed. Charlie Garner's grandparents. We like to be double sure you're still where we think you are. That you haven't got creative with the bed-sheets or a bottle of smuggled painkillers.'

Nicklin's expression didn't waver. 'Seriously, I'm touched. And it's good, you know, that the pair of us have been keeping an eye on each other.'

Thorne felt the colour rising. '*What?*'

Nicklin waved the question aside, as though he preferred to delay such prosaic push and shove for a little longer. 'You've not changed much, I don't think.' He pointed at the straight scar that ran along Thorne's chin. 'This is new. And there's a lot more grey in the hair. Looking pretty good, though.'

Thorne could not say the same thing. He didn't know if the baldness had been Nicklin's choice, but the creased and pitted head only emphasised a weight gain far greater than might normally have been expected from an extended diet of prison food. If his teeth were looking better, the other features had sunk into the jaundiced flesh of his face. A rash of tiny whiteheads was clustered just inside one nostril. There was dry skin along the lines of both lips. But the eyes were warm still, and seductive.

'What did you mean?' Thorne asked. 'When you said Brooks was doing you a favour.'

The Legal Visits Area was little more than a large corridor with a series of interview booths running off it. Each had a thick, Perspex wall at the front, so that the prisoner could remain 'in sight and out of hearing' of the prison officers on patrol, with CCTV cameras angled in such a way that any documentation could not be seen. On either side, inmates were meeting with solicitors or probation officers, and muffled voices, raised as often as not, bled through the flimsy partitions that separated one booth from the next. For a few seconds before he spoke, Nicklin gazed around as if he'd never been there before. As though he were suddenly amazed at the dirty fingermarks on the glass, at the drabness of the pale yellow walls and the MDF. 'You do know about his girlfriend and the kid?' he said. 'The reason why this is happening?'

Thorne nodded.

'Right, well, you can imagine how fired up he was then. A fortnight before he was due to get out. He went through that whole fucking hippy-dippy range of shit you're supposed to go through when you lose someone: guilt, denial, rage, acceptance, whatever. Only he went through them fast, and he never quite got to the nice toasty part at the end. Marcus was just left with the rage, and it did him a power of good. It made him able to deal with what had happened, to make decisions. It *reconfigured* him.'

'Why was he so sure it was the Black Dogs who were responsible?'

'Someone in here passed the word. I don't know who, but those fuckers made certain he got the message.' Nicklin widened his eyes. 'They wanted him in pain, and he was. He still is, I know that much. But now, so are they. All he talked about before he got released was how much he was going to make them suffer in return. We talked about it a lot.'

'You must have fucking loved that,' Thorne said. 'Someone else you could send out there and encourage to kill.'

'I did nothing, I swear. Marcus didn't need any encouragement. I just made the odd . . . suggestion.'

'The pictures?'

'I asked if he'd mind sending you the messages.'

Thorne leaned forward, but Nicklin did not back away an inch from him in return. 'Where did you get my number?'

Nicklin puffed out his cheeks. 'For someone who clearly has a brain, you can be as thick as shit sometimes. And careless.'

Thorne's mind was racing through scenarios. He knew Nicklin was good with computers, and must have had access to them inside. Had he been hacking into phone records? If he could get *them* . . .

'Three things.' Nicklin raised his fingers one at a time. 'Shop around for your utilities. Try to keep that overdraft under control a bit. And stop eating so many takeaways, or I swear you'll end up as porky as I am.'

Thorne took a few seconds to get it, then almost laughed, despite the horrendous possibilities. 'You've had someone going through my bin?'

'A friend of mine who lives in your neck of the woods pops by now and again to rummage around for me. Has done for quite some time.' He paused, gave a wry smile. 'I think I know you pretty well now, and I do mean above and beyond what brand of washing-up liquid you use.'

'And you don't think I'm going to do anything about this?'

'I think you might buy a shredder.' Nicklin said. 'But if you mean do anything to me, I'm not sure it's going to make an awful lot of difference to my sentence.'

Thorne knew he was right. Nicklin had been able to attack the inmate in Belmarsh safe in the knowledge that any extension to his sentence would have been purely cosmetic. It was what could make lifers, *real* lifers, such dangerous prisoners. 'Why wait until now?' Thorne asked.

'I had no way to use the information. None that I would have been satisfied with, anyway. I did think about having some fun with your credit cards, but seriously, what am I going to do? Ring you up in the middle of the night and breathe down the phone at you? Doing this is a lot more interesting, has a lot more possibilities, and I need that in here. The drama classes just aren't doing it for me, you know?'

'I don't see why Brooks would agree to sending photos of these people he's killed to a copper. A little risky, I would have said.'

'I told you, he's doing me a favour and there's really not a lot of risk.'

'You reckon? If it wasn't for the photos, we wouldn't even know who he is. And every crime scene gets us closer to him.'

Nicklin shrugged. 'Most murder victims show up eventually. They bob to the surface, or a dog starts digging, or some neighbour with a big nose sniffs them out. Since when has getting a sneak preview actually helped you *catch* anyone?'

It was a fair point. 'And there was I thinking this was all about you being helpful.'

'Fuck, no. I just want you frustrated.' Nicklin grew more animated as he continued; searched for Thorne's eyes with his own. 'I want you involved in this because I know how much you care. You probably care a little less about dead bikers than you do about little old ladies, but you care enough to get caught up in it. I like the idea of that. I just fancied walking around in here, thinking about you going quietly barmy, while the bodies kept piling up on your queer mate's chopping board.'

Thorne had not bothered to take off his jacket. He leaned back on the chair and forced his hands down into the pockets; let them tighten into fists when they were out of sight. 'What's your friend's plan?'

'I've no idea.'

'How long is he going to carry on with this?'

'Until he feels like they've paid enough, I would have thought. Or until *he's* had enough. Whichever comes first.'

'Can you contact him?'

'No.' Nicklin looked at Thorne, unblinking. Said it again.

'I don't believe you,' Thorne said.

Nicklin seemed mildly disappointed. 'Listen, there's really no point lying when you're in here. It's like tidying up, or caring what you look like. It's actually a relief not to have to bother.'

'If Brooks decides to get in touch—'

'He won't,' Nicklin said. 'He's moving on.' He sighed and nodded when he saw that Thorne was about to press the point. 'But if he does, I'll be sure to give him your best.'

Thorne pushed back his chair.

'Never know your luck.' Nicklin scratched lazily at his neck, fingers curled against the stubble. 'You might get the chance to do it yourself.'

Seeing that Thorne had left his chair, a prison officer stepped towards the door. Nicklin stood too, turned and leaned back against the table. 'It's not the same for me as it is for Marcus,' he said. 'I don't hate you, not at all, and I don't give two fucks about revenge. You do know that, don't you?'

Thorne kept on walking. 'I don't care.'

Nicklin clearly found this hilarious. 'Course you do,' he said.

Brooks raised the handset, checked the small screen and pressed the button to shoot. Marvelling still at how much this technology had come on in the time he'd been inside. Back when he'd gone down, as far as he could remember, people had just been starting to use their phones to do other things than make calls. But Christ, he could hardly believe the stuff that could be done now, the extent to which these gadgets had come to dominate people's lives six years later.

Celebrations. Accidents. Disasters.

It didn't seem to matter what the occasion was, punters would be reaching for their Nokias and Motorolas and Samsungs, and chances were the camera would be used before loved ones were called. Wrong place, right time, right place, whatever. Funny or plain disgusting. All of it captured, saved to an inbox, and sold to Sky or the *Sun* or whoever else stumped up the cash and was desperate to share some on-the-spot footage with the world. Where else could you get pictures of poor fuckers picking their way through smoke-filled Tube trains, or staggering, blackened and bleeding like stuck pigs, from the wreckage of a bus?

There was no denying, it was seriously handy.

He'd seen that stuff on TV when he was in Long Lartin; had discussed it with Nicklin. Marking out dead time on the landing; putting the world to rights in his cell or Nicklin's. They'd talked about all sorts of shit like that, whatever was on the front page, until the news had come about Angie and Robbie and he'd had more important things to worry about.

The man was on the move, so he moved with him. Slowly, on the other side of the road. Keeping his subject in shot, staying that little way behind so he'd have time to lower the phone if the man turned round.

A year or two before, there'd been a lot of bollocks talked about the craze for 'happy slapping': kids filming strangers' reactions when they attacked them, then passing the footage around like they were swapping football cards. Nicklin had thought it was funny, had got quite worked up when the papers made such a fuss about it. He'd asked why the fuck anyone was surprised. I mean, you couldn't uninvent this stuff, could you? Everyone used their phones in the same weird ways, he'd said. Coppers and perverts, and all sorts. So why not schoolkids, who hadn't made their minds up yet which way they were likely to go?

Brooks thought about what he was doing. Wasn't it just a more extreme version of happy slapping? He wondered if maybe that's where Nicklin had got the idea from.

A young black girl coming towards him slowed down and turned to see what Brooks was pointing his phone at. She looked across the street, then back at him, and carried on walking, not seeing a whole lot to get worked up about.

Brooks smiled at the girl, then continued filming, using his thumb to zoom in as far as he could go.

He was worked up enough for both of them.

Thorne had bought himself lunch at the station, eaten it while he was waiting for the train back to Paddington. Soggy pizza and piss-poor

93

coffee. Replacing one bad taste for another. Thinking about Stuart Nicklin while he ate; the prisoner still laughing when the warder had put a hand in the small of his back to guide him from the room.

Brigstocke called before the train had pulled out of the station. 'Where've you been?'

'Long Lartin.'

'Who the fuck's in Long Lartin? Never mind—'

'I've got lots to tell you.'

'It'll have to wait,' Brigstocke said. 'We've got a likely-looking match on a print from the Tucker scene.'

'I'm listening.'

'Bloke was done for murder six years ago.'

The train wasn't busy. There were only three other people in the entire carriage. Opposite and just ahead of Thorne, a man lay sprawled across two seats, his feet pulled up, his head dropping slowly on to his chest, before being jerked back up with a grunt, only to drop again fifteen seconds later. Life or alcohol. Thorne wasn't sure which, but the man had obviously had too much of one or the other.

'I'm chasing the results from Hodson's room in the hospital,' Brigstocke said. 'Be nice to get a positive ID at both scenes, but I think we may have got our man . . .'

'Marcus Brooks,' Thorne said. He let it hang for a few moments, enjoying the sound of the DCI's amazement crackling down the line. 'Go on, tell me I'm the best.'

'Who the *fuck* were you seeing in Long Lartin?' There was a short pause, then Brigstocke remembered. 'Oh . . .'

'It's why I'm getting the messages.'

'Let's hear it.'

So, Thorne told Brigstocke what Nicklin had told him: about why Marcus Brooks was on a killing spree, about his relationship with the prison's most notorious inmate, and why photos of his victims had ended up in Thorne's inbox.

'How do you feel about it?' Brigstocke asked, when Thorne had finished.

'What?'

'Nicklin. The stuff he says he knows, the personal stuff.'

'I don't know what you mean, "feel about it",' Thorne said, ducking the question. Killing it.

Thorne told Brigstocke he'd be back at Becke House by about five, that they could go over things in more detail then, decide on which way to go over the next few days. Brigstocke told Thorne that he'd see him later. Said, 'You know *exactly* what I meant by "feel about it".'

When the train began to pull away, Thorne realised that he wasn't facing the direction of travel. He'd been distracted, hadn't been paying attention when he'd sat down, and although it wasn't a big thing with him, he'd always face forward, given the choice.

He got up and changed seats.

When she'd asked, on a trip down to Brighton, he'd told Louise that sitting the other way made him feel slightly sick. He'd been unwilling to admit that, in truth, he found it disconcerting. It made no real sense, he knew that. Even now, having moved, he didn't have any sort of view beyond the toilets at the end of the carriage. But he told himself that it wasn't a literal thing, anyway. It was stupid, but it was simple enough.

He was happier sitting this way; facing forward. He felt as though he could see what was coming.

NINE

Thorne could sense it within seconds of coming through the door: the change of atmosphere in the Incident Room. Before he'd had a chance to ask anyone what had happened, he saw that it was still happening. The man and woman walking down the corridor that ringed the Incident Room answered his question with a look, glancing in at Thorne and the rest of the team as they passed on their way to the lift. A moment of something like defiance before their eyes slid away from his own.

These were the sorts of coppers who had become so used to the reaction their presence triggered that most of them decided to get their retaliation in first. They were those who, whatever their nickname might have been, no longer cared if anyone could hear them coming.

Rubber-heelers . . .

Whether it was the expansion of the Police and Criminal Evidence Act, the Stephen Lawrence inquiry, or something altogether more insidious, the Directorate of Professional Standards had grown into a branch of the Met as complex and overstretched as any other. It had Internal Investigation Commands based in every one of the four Met areas, each one handling every sort of basic complaint or allegation against police officers, from simple ineptitude upwards. Other DPS units, including an Anti-Corruption Group and an Intelligence Team, handled more specialist enquiries, and were engaged where accusations of murder or other major offences were involved.

As someone who had fallen foul of the DPS enough times to wonder if he merited some sort of loyalty card, Thorne had made up his mind long ago. There were good ones and bad ones, of course there were, but they all needed the sticks extracting from their arses. That whole 'taking the piss' thing tended not to apply to the upstanding men and women of the DPS.

Samir Karim appeared at Thorne's shoulder. They moved to the door together and stood, watching the two DPS officers step into the lift.

'What's going on?' Thorne asked.

'Someone's fucked.'

'Who?'

Karim shrugged, nudged him. 'Well, if *you* don't know . . .'

Thorne turned to see Brigstocke stalking from his office, and for the second time in as many minutes his question was answered by the look on a colleague's face. Without any signal, the pair of them drifted away from one another as Brigstocke entered. Thorne watched as the DCI walked across to the fridge behind Karim's desk and casually flicked on the kettle. Then he rejoined Karim in front of the whiteboard, looked across to where they'd last seen the DPS pair.

He kept his voice low. 'Where were they from?'

'Just local, by the look of them,' Karim said.

Thorne nodded. The four north-west teams were based five minutes' walk away at Colindale station. 'Working late, aren't they?'

Karim smirked. 'It's *very* important work, Tom.'

'Probably just something stupid.'

That was more than likely. One recent complaint had concerned an officer who'd arrested a man twice, each time mistaking him for an elder brother who had been sent to prison six months earlier. Thorne knew a sergeant on one of the other murder squads who had been questioned by the DPS following the apprehension by an armed unit of a man whose only crime had been sleeping with the sergeant's girl-friend.

'Yeah, probably,' Karim said. 'I'll call a couple of mates at Colindale, see what I can find out.'

Thorne sauntered across to where Brigstocke stood, pressing his hand against the kettle every few seconds, impatient for it to boil.

'Cracking news about those prints,' Thorne said. 'Looks like we got him from two directions at once.' Brigstocke squatted to take milk from the fridge. Poured a splash into a mug. 'And sorry for stealing your moment of glory when you called, but I couldn't resist.'

'Not a problem,' Brigstocke said.

'I needed some light relief, I think. After a morning with Stuart Nicklin, you know?'

Brigstocke nodded, pouring in the hot water. He turned away, began mashing the tea-bag against the side of the mug with a teaspoon.

'Are you OK, Russell?'

'Why shouldn't I be?'

'I'm around if you fancy a pint later on, have a natter or whatever.'

'Not sure I know what you mean.'

'Must be catching,' Thorne said, smiling. 'Didn't I come out with much the same crap on the train?'

Brigstocke looked around, his eyes moving beyond Thorne and catching those of several others turning quickly back to desktops. Gazes shifting to nothing or dropping down to shoes. He tried, but could summon only the weakest of bedside smiles. 'I think I'll get some tea in the canteen,' he said.

Thorne watched Brigstocke go and heard the volume of conversation climb as soon as he'd left the room. Coppers were rarely short of opinions, and they gossiped almost as much as they took the piss.

He picked up the tea Brigstocke had left untouched and carried it through to his office. Yvonne Kitson was busy trying to type too quickly; swearing and stabbing at the delete key every time she made a mistake. 'Our visitors gone?' she asked.

Thorne nodded, blew on to his tea. 'They didn't stop in here, then?'

Kitson looked up. 'I'm clean as a whistle, mate,' she said.

'Goes without saying.'

'There was that wanker from Vice I punched in the knackers when he grabbed my arse at Andy Stone's birthday party, but I don't think he'll have told anybody . . .'

Thorne laughed and, looking across at Kitson frowning over her keyboard, decided that she was looking pretty good. A couple of years before, her life – private and professional – had almost fallen apart after an affair with a senior officer. These days, although the Job still mattered, she seemed to care about the *career* much less, and to Thorne's eye, it suited her. She'd traded in the harsh lines of the designer business suits for outfits that were a little softer. The blunt bob had become shaggy, and the face it framed belonged to someone who knew she didn't need to try so hard.

There had never been a hint of anything between himself and Yvonne Kitson, but Thorne had guiltily entertained an impure thought or two when the occasion demanded it. He would never mention this to Louise, of course. Or to anyone else he worked with, come to that.

'Heard you had fun with Stuart Nicklin this morning,' Kitson said suddenly.

'"Fun" is probably too strong a word.'

'Did the trick, though. Things are really moving on this.' She nodded towards his desk. 'We've got the cell-site details on the second message and the PM report came in while you were away. Both in your in-tray.'

'Oh.' Thorne reached across for the files.

'You don't seem overly chuffed about it.'

'I'm ecstatic, you know me.' He began turning pages. 'But I always think it's slightly weird when a killer isn't trying awfully hard not to get caught. You know?'

'I wouldn't mind a few more like that,' Kitson said.

Thorne saw that the second call had been made via a cell-site within half a mile of the Abbey Hospital. Brooks had almost certainly sent the message as soon as he'd taken the picture; within minutes of killing Ricky Hodson. He glanced through the post-mortem report, not surprised to see that Hodson had died as a result of suffocation. They had, after all, found the murder weapon lying next to the bed, the inside of the plastic bag still slick with the victim's hot breath and spittle. Armed as he now was with an accurate time of death, Thorne was keen to see what the pathologist's estimate had been. He flicked forward to it and decided he would take great delight in telling Phil Hendricks he'd been half an hour out.

'Where are we on Sedat?'

'I'm getting pissed about, to be honest,' Kitson said. 'First they prioritise your case, so mine goes on the back burner. Then, as soon as this Turkish councillor or whoever he is starts moaning on the local news, they expect me to jump. I don't know whether I'm coming or fucking going.'

'Like a fart in a colander,' Thorne said. 'That's what my old man used to say.' Kitson chuckled. 'It'll sort itself out, Yvonne.'

'We *did* get a call.' She stood and moved around her desk, picking at a stray thread on the sleeve of her jacket. 'Some woman rang the Incident Room. Went on about knowing who'd killed Deniz, like she really knew him. She got hysterical in the end and hung up. Scared or upset, I'm not sure which. Both, maybe.'

'Genuine, you reckon?'

'I don't know. Yeah, I think so.'

'Maybe she'll call back.'

'Maybe I'll get bumped off it again if your bloke decides to do any more bikers in . . .'

Karim's face appeared at the window in the door and Thorne waved him inside. 'No details,' he said. 'Just Regulation Nines is all I know.'

'More than one?' Thorne said.

Karim nodded slowly.

A Regulation Nine notice was the initial paperwork issued to any officer under investigation. It outlined the details of the allegation and notified the subject that paperwork was being seized and that he or she had the right to reply. For anybody served one, a Reg Nine signalled the start of proceedings, however trivial or otherwise the complaint against them had been.

It was their first sniff of the shit they were in.

100

'Who else?' Kitson asked.

Karim looked towards Thorne. 'Well it's usually him, so fucked if I know . . .'

Thorne started slightly at the noise: his phone's message tone sounding from inside his jacket. He reached for it, leaving Kitson and Karim to turn away and carry on their conversation.

The message display itself was blank, as usual.

He scrolled down to look at what was attached.

After a few moments, he became aware that Kitson and Karim were saying nothing. That they were watching, stock-still, as he stared at the movement on the screen. As soon as it had finished he looked up, answering their unspoken question with a small nod, before pushing himself away from the desk.

Heading out of the door . . .

The canteen was on the same floor, on the opposite side of the building to the offices. Thorne could smell it within thirty seconds, was bearing down on Russell Brigstocke's table a minute later.

If Brigstocke looked less than delighted to see him, one glance at what Thorne was holding, at the expression on his face as he marched across the linoleum, changed his outlook instantly.

'Fuck . . .'

Thorne dropped in next to him, slid the phone across and pressed the button. 'This one's alive,' he said. 'At least he *was*.'

Brigstocke watched the fifteen-second clip, barely breathing. When it was finished he said, 'Play it again.' And after watching a second time: 'It's another one we won't need to send to Newlands Park.'

Thorne took a second. 'I'm not with you.'

'I know who this is,' Brigstocke said. 'Because I worked with him.' One hand reached for his tea, and with the other he pushed the phone back along the table, looking suddenly pale and tired. 'He's a copper.'

TEN

Detective Inspector Paul Skinner stared down at the screen and chewed slowly on his top lip as he watched himself: walking along the street; stopping briefly to stare into a shop window; turning at one point and looking directly towards the camera. When the short video clip finished, frozen on a blurry shot of himself and a female passer-by, Skinner sucked his teeth and handed the phone back to Thorne.

'Fucking weird, that is.'

Skinner, Thorne and Holland were standing in the large, dimly lit kitchen of a Victorian semi-detached house in Stoke Newington. It was a lively enough location: Clissold Park on the doorstep; a busy market on Church Street at the weekends. Once popular with dissenters and radicals, this area of north London retained a multi-ethnic, Bohemian feel, in the village at least; easygoing, peaceful. But Skinner's house was no more than a few streets from where, in 1967, Reggie Kray had murdered Jack 'The Hat' McVitie, skewering him repeatedly with a carving knife. And not a million miles away from where, nearly forty years later, someone had done much the same thing to Deniz Sedat.

Skinner's wife put her head around the door; asked again if Thorne

102

or Holland would like anything to drink. Skinner said no on their behalf and sat back down at an orangey pine table.

He pointed to Thorne's mobile phone. 'That was yesterday.'

'When?' Holland said.

'I'd nipped out to get a sandwich, same as usual. Half twelve, quarter to one, something like that.' He pointed again. 'That's a hundred yards from my nick . . .'

Skinner was based at Albany Street station in Camden, on a borough public protection unit. It was a nice cushy number, the sort of job that most coppers would kill to get, towards the end of their thirty years in. Checking to see that the occasional sex offender was where they should be was about as stressful as it got. Meetings and beanbag sessions, as much tea and biscuits as you could handle, and no likelihood of anything eating into your weekends. Plenty of free time to garden or golf. Or to see how much beer you could get down your neck, which seemed to be the way Paul Skinner preferred to pass his Saturday mornings.

A can of bitter and the sports pages of the *Daily Star* were both open on the table in front of him. As he had known in advance that Thorne and Holland were coming, Paul Skinner was clearly not too bothered what sort of an impression he gave.

He was somewhere in his mid-fifties. An open-necked white shirt hung off a frame that was slight but still muscled. His sandy-coloured hair was thinning but just about doing its job, and the eyes were bright behind steel-rimmed specs.

'So, Marcus Brooks still not ringing any bells?' Thorne asked.

Skinner had a habit of licking his lips all the time, as though they were dry and sore, or he was contemplating taking a bite out of someone. He licked them again before taking a quick swig of beer. 'Not even slightly,' he said. The accent was pure south London; the voice gruff enough to go with it. 'And I've got a decent memory for names, so . . .'

'What about the Black Dogs?'

'Bikers, right?' Thorne nodded. 'Nasty fuckers, I've heard.'

'You've never had any dealings with them?'

'I know people who have.' Skinner looked from Thorne to Holland. 'This bloke Brooks. One of them, is he?'

Thorne explained the part Marcus Brooks had once played in the history of the Black Dogs motorcycle club. His time in prison and the unsolved deaths of his family. The part he was playing now.

'Jesus . . . you never know how people are going to react, do you? Something like that happens, tips them over the edge.'

'Right,' Holland pushed himself away from the worktop and leaned against the opposite wall. 'And now he's taking pictures of you.'

Skinner licked his lips, stared down through the hole in the top of his beer can.

'We need to find out why,' Thorne said.

'Like I said, the name means bugger all, but I think I remember that original case, as it goes.'

'July 2000 . . .'

'Yeah. Geezer getting done by a burglar, sounds familiar. I think I was just starting on the Flying Squad at the time, but I had a few mates on Organised Crime, you know? This was not long after I moved across from the old AMIP East, which was where I knew your guvnor from.' He turned to look at Holland; explained himself as though he were talking to a wet-behind-the-ears trainee. 'AMIP. Area Major Incident Pool. "Homicide East", as it is now.'

Holland could see that Thorne was smirking and had to look away. 'Cheers . . .'

'Change the names of fucking everything,' Skinner said. 'Every ten minutes.'

'You don't have any connection with the officers who investigated the Tipper murder?' Thorne asked.

'Not that I can think of.'

'You don't know Sharon Lilley?'

Skinner shook his head; emptied his can. 'Not surprised Russell Brigstocke made DCI, though. He was a decent bloke.'

'Still is,' Thorne said.

'Can lick all the right arses if he has to, mind you. Knows the game.'

Thorne would normally have agreed, but he remembered Brigstocke's face the day before, after his session with the DPS. 'Listen, you might not know Marcus Brooks,' he said, 'or at least not know *how* you know him . . .'

'I *don't* know him.'

Thorne held up his hands, said, 'Right, whatever,' but he was keen to move this along. They'd explained about the picture messages when they'd called the night before, gone through it again when they'd first arrived, but Skinner did not seem to have grasped the seriousness of the situation. It was as though he'd been shown a clip of somebody else. 'The bad news is that he seems to know you.'

'And that's not good for anyone's health,' Holland added. 'The people whose photos we get sent have definitely looked better.'

Skinner thought about it. 'Why is Brooks sending *you* these messages, anyway?'

'He was in prison with someone I put away,' Thorne said. 'Someone who thought it might be fun to get me involved.'

'Well, maybe that's what the connection is to me.'

'Sorry?'

'Like that, through a third party.'

'It's possible . . .'

'Maybe I put a friend of his away some time. One of his family.'

'Maybe.' Thorne thought it was unlikely. And he knew that Skinner thought it was unlikely, too. While they were talking long shots, Thorne decided to chance his arm. 'I don't suppose the names Jennings and Squire mean anything, do they? Coppers.'

Skinner looked blank. 'I've met a lot of coppers.' He shrugged. 'I had a skipper called Jenner, when I worked in Kennington . . .'

'Doesn't matter,' Thorne said. 'We'll check into that third-party thing, but in the meantime, if you think of anything . . .' Skinner nodded, pushing himself up and stepping around Holland to get to the fridge. 'Obviously we'll be putting a watch on the house, clearing some time off with your DCI.'

Skinner shut the fridge door. There was another beer in his hand. 'Will you fuck,' he said. 'I can watch out for myself and I certainly don't need time off. I think I'm safe enough at work, don't you?'

'Brooks killed his second victim in a busy hospital,' Holland said.

'Yeah, well, he's not going to walk into a police station, is he? However fucked up he is.'

Thorne could see little point in arguing. Whatever needed to be done would happen. He moved to let Skinner back to his chair and threw a look at Holland. 'We'd better get out of your way,' he said.

That seemed to be fine with Skinner. He began flicking through the back pages of his newspaper. 'What are you, Arsenal?'

'Spurs,' Thorne said. 'Yourself?'

'Millwall, tragically. I'll be there this afternoon, watching us get stuffed.'

'Character building, though,' Holland said. 'Right?'

'Christ.' Skinner popped the ring-pull on his can. Sucked froth from around its rim. 'How much fucking character does one man need?'

Turning from the doorstep – Skinner watching them all the way and his wife peeking, somewhat nervously around him, from further back down the hall – Thorne and Holland were all but flattened by a big man barrelling across the front garden.

Holland held up a hand. 'Easy, mate.'

The man stopped but stood his ground, waiting for Holland to move aside and let him past.

Thorne could smell the Job on him.

Skinner stepped down on to the path, made the introductions. Richard Rawlings was an old mate, he said. A fellow masochist who was off to the New Den with him to see Millwall destroy the beautiful game.

'That's nice,' Thorne said. 'And he just happened to pop in four hours before kick-off, did he?'

'I don't see as it's your business,' Rawlings said.

Skinner smiled at Thorne and shrugged. 'You know how it goes,' he said. 'Always good to have a bit of moral support when a couple of lads like you come knocking and you're not sure what's happening.'

Thorne smiled back. 'What is it you're not sure about, exactly?' When Skinner's answer was not forthcoming, Thorne turned his attention to the new man. 'Should have got here half an hour ago. We're just leaving, I'm afraid. I'm sure your friend will fill you in.'

Rawlings grinned and stuck a cigarette in his mouth. He had a large head, bad skin. A well-tended gut hanging over the top of his grey tracksuit bottoms. He moved, none too politely, past Thorne and Holland, jabbing a thumb towards the main road while the other worked at a lighter. 'Traffic's fucked all along Green Lanes,' he said. He nodded to Skinner. 'Sorry, mate . . .'

As Thorne and Holland moved away, Thorne was aware of Rawlings sauntering into the house to be warmly greeted by Skinner's wife. And of Skinner's eyes on his back, as Holland opened the gate and they stepped on to the street.

Holland had picked Thorne up first thing. They'd eaten bacon sandwiches on the drive from Kentish Town and found a parking space in the street next to Skinner's. Now, the wind was picking up as they walked back to Holland's car. Newly fallen leaves skittering across the pavement, and older ones gathered into a slick, mud-coloured mulch in gutters and against walls.

'What did you make of Skinner?' Holland asked.

'I think, bearing in mind what we told him, he made a very good job of not looking shit scared.'

'Maybe he wasn't.'

'Well, he's a fucking idiot then.'

'What about his boyfriend?'

'Like he said. "Moral support".'

'Bollocks.' Holland stepped to one side, let a woman with a buggy walk between them. 'We went round to tell him to look out for himself. Maybe save the twat's life. What's he need back-up for?'

Thorne had to admit it was a fair question. Skinner hadn't struck him as the type who would need his hand holding. Rawlings had been spiky all right, but the plain fact was that you didn't have to be DPS to put the wind up other police officers. Or to put backs up. Whatever the situation, coppers were never happy being on the receiving end.

Holland took out his car keys as they approached a red Astra that still looked brand new. 'He wasn't keen on having any protection, was he?'

'Sort it out with Brigstocke when you get back,' Thorne said. 'Skinner might have a point about being OK at work, but we should get someone at the house tonight and over the weekend.'

'So where are you going?'

Thorne walked around to the passenger door, rubbed theatrically at a dirty spot on the car's roof. 'More fun and games, mate. Can you drop me off at Paddington?'

'Eh?'

'It's on the way back, more or less, isn't it?'

'Not really.'

'Cheers, Dave.'

It hadn't taken him too long to find them.

They'd said enough, back when they were setting him up, for Brooks to work out that they were based in north-west London, so he'd had somewhere to start. Even after all his years out of the game, he'd still got enough contacts with high-level firms to get a decent list of coppers' pubs in the area: Camden, Golders Green, Edgware, Muswell Hill . . .

He'd done a fair amount of drinking. He'd chatted to landlords and bar staff; to regulars with their own tankards behind the bar and warrant cards in their jacket pockets. He'd poked around and asked questions; leaned across bars to get a closer look at the photos of customers pinned up among the optics and the dry-roasted nuts.

The faces imprinted on his memory would be a bit older now, he knew that, so he'd tried to age up the descriptions. Although he'd been given a few names, none was mentioned more than once. He took to telling people that his dad had been a custody skipper at a number of different stations – Kentish Town, Swiss Cottage, Holborn. Said that cancer was getting a grip on the poor old sod, and that he'd thought, you know, it would be a nice idea to get all his old man's mates together while he still had the chance.

They'd loved all that, the sentimental twats. Getting teary over their lager-tops and throwing ideas at him. Several people had offered to help, to pitch in and maybe raise a few quid. Then somebody had suggested *The Job*; told him that it might be a good way to trace his dad's old muckers and that the paper was archived online . . .

It had only taken a couple of days after that. Hour after hour poring over pages on the Internet, until he'd finally seen a face he recognised; one that he would never forget. Posing like a prat, outside a station with French detectives who'd come across from Paris on some exchange scheme. He wouldn't forget that headline in a hurry either: THE GENDARME OF THE LAW.

Now he had a name, a *real* one, and from then on it was a piece of piss. He'd rung around stations. Asked for him by name until he got a hit. Then all he'd had to do was watch, and wait; feeling fairly sure that once he'd started keeping tabs on one, the other fucker would turn up sooner or later.

Jennings and Squire.

He'd written to Angie the day it had all come together. It felt like it was serious then; that he was really going to go through with it. It had been one thing sitting in his cell, burning with it, making plans. But then, *seeing* them, the bastards responsible for everything, he'd known he would have to do exactly what he'd been fantasising about. So he'd written and explained what he had in mind.

And asked for her blessing.

Now he needed to get on. These were the ones that mattered. The bikers had it coming, no question, but there were others who shared the blame. No, who shouldered *most* of it. The ones who'd taken Angie and Robbie away to begin with; the ones who'd put him inside.

He trotted down the steps at Hammersmith Tube station. Half an hour on the Piccadilly Line to Finsbury Park, then he'd walk from there. He'd already scouted the place out, sorted himself a way in.

He drifted down on the escalator, wondering what Detective Inspector Tom Thorne was making of it all; asking himself why he was even bothering to do what Nicklin had asked.

The shit with the phones and the pictures.

Because he'd said he would, end of story. There wasn't too much he believed in, but not grassing and paying your debts were what made you staunch, and people had always been able to count on him. Nicklin was a twisted fucker, no question, and not the sort he'd normally have anything to do with. But things changed in prison. The slate tended to get wiped clean once you were inside. Favours mattered. Small kindnesses mounted up, little things, and the bloke had been all right with him, so it had seemed a simple enough favour to grant in return. Nicklin had a way of making people do him favours, do the things he wanted. Some of the screws even.

Besides which, Brooks didn't really care; certainly not about the likes of Thorne. Coppers hadn't been his favourite people, even before any of this had happened, and sympathy was something he knew he would never feel again.

He dug in his pocket for the change to buy a newspaper, thinking about paying back what was owed. And about how you couldn't let down the people who counted on you, even after they'd gone.

ELEVEN

'It suits you, sitting there,' Nicklin said. 'You look . . . comfortable.'

'Meaning?'

'Five years ago. You'd like to have been the one sitting where the judge was, wouldn't you? Putting me away . . .'

They were seated in the Adjudications Room on Long Lartin's Segregation Unit. There were no legal visits on a Saturday, and normally a request for any kind of visit at such short notice would have been denied. But Thorne had explained the situation to everyone necessary; had sucked up shamelessly to the prison's police liaison officer; and had finally managed to wangle a session with Stuart Nicklin, albeit in somewhat unusual surroundings.

The room was, in essence, a miniature court.

Here was where all the prison's internal disciplinary matters were settled and punishments meted out when necessary. The room was high-ceilinged and windowless. Dark furniture on a thick blue carpet; a gold pattern snaking around its edge below the wood-panelled walls. Thorne was sitting at the centre of a T-shaped table where the governor, or more often his deputy, would preside. There was a metal water jug and glasses on a tray. There were rows of notebooks and pencils.

'I think the judge made a pretty good job of it,' Thorne said.

Nicklin stared at him from ten feet away, at the tail end of the 'T'. 'But how many times do they fuck up? How often does all your hard work count for nothing? It must really hurt to see people like me get off because someone gets the procedure wrong. To watch some overpaid legal team arguing that their client isn't mentally competent to stand trial, when you know they're as sane as you are.'

'I wouldn't go quite that far,' Thorne said. 'Certainly not in your case. Besides which, you didn't get away with it.'

'Can't blame a bloke for trying though, can you?'

Nicklin was right, of course. On those occasions when months, maybe years, of graft came to nothing in the face of ineptitude, or when the law proved itself to be more of an arsehole than an ass, it hurt like hell. Thorne's major fear, five years before, had been that the issue of mental competence would override all others. That Nicklin would escape sentence and spend the rest of his life as patient rather than prisoner.

Among many other things, Nicklin was a conman; an individual who could be powerfully persuasive, one whose influence had driven others to kill for no other reason than it had made him feel good. But, thankfully, the jury had seen through the 'mad not bad' sham. Or if not, they had decided that killing because the voices in your head told you to made you no more deserving of a fluffy pillow and paper slippers than anyone else. Made you no better than the killer who did it because of greed or racial hatred, or because someone had looked at his girlfriend.

'Why does Marcus Brooks want to kill a police officer?' The question Thorne had come here to ask.

'Why not?'

Thorne poured himself a glass of water.

'Oh, right,' Nicklin said. 'Sorry.' He straightened in his chair, mock-sombre. 'All very serious now, is it? Could I just ask first: why is the life of a police officer any more important than any other? Than a little old lady's or a child's. Or mine.'

112

'Now you're just being ridiculous.'

'I'm right though, aren't I? I bet things have really gone into top gear, now it's about a copper. I bet things are frantic.'

'Did you tell Brooks to do it?'

'I never tell anyone to do anything.'

'Course not.'

'I talk to people, that's all.' Nicklin looked up at the ceiling. 'Invite them to weigh up their options.'

'Right,' Thorne said. 'Until they start believing the ideas you've put in their heads are their own.' He remembered a superintendent telling him once that this was the essence, the *trick*, of good leadership. Thorne knew that the man sitting opposite him had no shortage of ideas. A dark tangle of them; barbed and brilliant.

He took a deep breath and blinked away the face of Charlie Garner.

'Tell me why I should help you.' Nicklin scratched at the surface of the table. 'Why should I tell you anything other than how far you can stick your questions up your arse?'

'Because this is what you wanted all along, isn't it? To get me involved enough that I'd come here looking for help. Well, I'm involved.'

Nicklin smiled. 'Twice in two days.'

'I understand about the bikers—'

'Friend of yours, is he? This police officer?'

'No.'

'I'm relieved to hear it. Wouldn't want you knocking around with too many bad apples.'

'You saying he's bent?'

'Look, Marcus is hardly what you'd call a model citizen,' Nicklin said. 'Most decent people wouldn't want him living next door, you know? But he didn't murder anybody.' He grinned. 'He's making up for it now, though, obviously.'

'Come on, how many people in here claim to be innocent?'

'Plenty. But not for six years, and not to each other.' Nicklin leaned forward, his head only inches above the table. 'You get to know people intimately in here. You know when to look away from someone and when to let someone in on a confidence. After a while you can tell who's had a shit just from the smell drifting along the landing. And like I said, eventually the bright ones realise there's no point lying.'

Thorne took a sip of water. It was tepid; tasted metallic, old. 'They went through all this when he was arrested: the story that he was fitted up.'

'They didn't look hard enough,' Nicklin said. 'Nobody believed him. But even if they had, they would have presumed that the two "police officers" were bogus – members of a rival gang or whatever.' Despite the thick carpets and the panelling, there was the slightest of echoes: the low wheeze of Nicklin's voice rising up from the polished surface of the table towards the elaborate cornicing and the ceiling rose. 'Nobody considered it seriously enough to come to the more obvious conclusion.'

Thorne didn't need it spelling out: nobody could play the part of a bent copper better than a bent copper.

Nicklin could see that Thorne had got it. 'Hardly the most fiendish of plans, was it? They just gave false names. I don't know if they had fake warrant cards, or if Marcus even bothered to ask. Doesn't really matter now, does it?'

'It's starting to matter to quite a lot of people,' Thorne said.

If Nicklin was right, then clearly Marcus Brooks would not have held just the Black Dogs responsible for the death of his family. He would also have blamed the people who got him sent to jail in the first place; those whose actions had ensured that his girlfriend and son would one day become targets. That he would not be around to look after them when it happened.

Thorne could understand why Brooks thought these men had to die. 'I don't suppose you know the names of these two men? Their real ones, I mean.'

Nicklin shook his head. 'Marcus didn't know their real names six months ago. I'm guessing he does now, though.'

114

Jennings and Squire. Thorne wondered which one Paul Skinner had been.

'"Want to kill",' Nicklin said suddenly. 'You said "*want* to kill a police officer". So I gather that Marcus hasn't got round to it yet.'

'Well, you know, seeing as he gave us advance warning, we thought we might try to do something about it.'

'I wouldn't bother.'

'Who the fuck are you to get on his high horse about who deserves to live and die?'

'That's not what I meant,' Nicklin said. 'But as you bring it up, you can't tell me you care *quite* as much about a bent copper as you do about a nice, dull, honest one, can you?'

Thorne said nothing.

'*I wouldn't bother* . . . because unless you've got this fucker locked up safe and sound in one of his own cells, Marcus *is* going to kill him.'

'Thanks. We'll bear that in mind.'

Whatever was on Thorne's face, whether he was visibly holding his anger in check or being nakedly sarcastic, Nicklin seemed to enjoy every reaction he provoked. 'I'm not saying he's any kind of lethal weapon or whatever. He's not a fucking ninja . . .'

'That's a relief.'

'But he won't give up. It's very simple. You'll be in a world of trouble unless you appreciate that.'

Thorne was already starting to, but he let Nicklin continue. Looked past him, staring at the prints on the white wall beyond. Washed-out landscapes and hunting scenes.

'I've seen every sort of gate fever in the last few years,' Nicklin said. 'Blokes going mental, starting to lose it when that magical release date appears for the first time on their Page Three calendar. Getting hyper. Doing something silly, a few of them, and blowing it at the last minute. But Marcus just looked . . . *lighter*, you know? Like he'd slipped off some sodden, shitty overcoat, so he could go running out of here that little bit quicker. Then those coppers turned up with their best bad-news faces on, and it was like something cracked open inside him. Let the bad blood out. Everything he'd spent six years looking forward to was gone, and you could see the poison spread.' Nicklin gestured as he spoke, splaying his waxy fingers. 'It was in his face, in the way he spoke, strung a sentence together . . . everything. When he finally walked out of here, he went just as quickly, but there was something very dark slopping about in his head.'

'Something you stirred up.'

'It *drove* him,' Nicklin said. 'And I can't believe that you don't understand exactly what that must be like. I know that if someone did that to you, if they took away someone you loved, you'd want to hurt them. More, probably . . .'

Thorne looked up. Nicklin was staring at him; something intense, *joyful* in his eyes, and Thorne had to ask himself if this was more than just free character analysis. Could Nicklin really *know* such things? About what had happened to Thorne's father.

Might have happened . . .

There had been moments earlier, just one or two, when Thorne had looked at the man across the table; when he had asked himself, in the absence of any prison officer and in the light of what he knew Stuart Nicklin to be capable of, if he should be concerned for his safety. Now, as he felt his own reservoir of bad blood start to leak, cold into his veins, he knew that Nicklin was the one who should be afraid.

'Your friend,' Thorne said. 'The one who goes through my rubbish whenever he fancies it. Tell him it's finished, OK?' Nicklin held the stare. 'Tell him that if I as much as see a rat nosing round my bins, I'm going to presume it's him in disguise. That I'm going to find him and fuck him up. Make sure he gets that message.'

Nicklin gave a small salute.

Thorne pointed. 'And *you* need to do some forgetting. Whatever you know . . . numbers, dates, names. Anything about me, or anyone close to me, just let it go.'

Nicklin shook his head. 'As it happens, I've almost forgotten your girlfriend's address already. The number, I mean. But I'm sure the street name will go as well, eventually.' He jabbed at his temple. 'Maybe my mind's going, same as your old man's did. I'm having some trouble remembering the last two digits of Auntie Eileen's phone number as well, so I don't think you need to worry.'

Thorne could feel the dark blood starting to rush, singing beneath the skin. 'You need to forget it all,' he said.

'It's such a shame . . .'

'Really, you do. Because even if you spend the rest of your life inside, whether or not you think you've got fuck all left to lose, trying to use any of this stuff would not be clever.'

Nicklin chuckled, but he suddenly looked tired. 'Well, you were as good as your word in that playground.' He grinned, showing Thorne his false teeth. 'As good as your threat, I should say. But those were exceptional circumstances, weren't they? I'm not sure you'd be up to it this time.'

Thorne leaned back, folded his arms. 'Just take a good, long look, and remember me sitting in this chair.'

But Nicklin was already pushing his arms along the tabletop. He leaned down slowly and turned his head to lay his face on top of them. From where Thorne was sitting, he could see several small, irregular patches, dark against the baby-pink of Nicklin's bald head. Purplish blots or lesions, like wine stains, on his scalp.

Paul Skinner steadied himself against the worktop and tried to stop the can rattling against the glasses as he poured out the beer. He stopped and took a deep breath, fought the urge to vomit.

He'd been telling himself that the sweat was a result of being frantically busy all day, but it was sounding less convincing by the minute. Not that he hadn't been tearing around like a blue-arsed fly. He'd spent the best part of two hours persuading his wife what a nice idea it would be for her to take the kids across to her mum's for the weekend. He'd helped them pack, loaded up the car and waved them off. Once they'd gone, he'd continued to charge around; aimlessly, he knew, but he couldn't stop. He refused just to sit and wait for whatever was coming.

The sweat had begun to prickle the moment those two Murder Squad twats had stepped across his doorstep, and it had been pouring from him, thick and sticky, ever since. It wasn't the same as sweat on a hot day, or after a kickabout in the garden with the kids. He'd smelled fear on plenty of people in his time, but his own sweat was richer and more rank, worse than anything he'd caught coming at him across a cell or over an interview-room table.

The stink of his own terror made him gag.

He dropped the two empty cans into the bin and told himself that things were sorting themselves out. He'd made the call as soon as Annie and the kids were out of the way, and it had calmed him down a little. He'd been told to relax, to try not to panic; that there was nothing to get worked up about. They'd been in this sort of mess before, hadn't they? *No*, not *this* kind, he'd tried to say, and it's not like it's *you* on that fucking video clip, is it? But in the end, after some arguing, he'd been as reassured as he could have hoped for.

There had been trouble over the years, of course. That was the risk when you went the way they'd chosen to go, he knew that. A couple of colleagues had got nosey once or twice. The rubber-heelers had sniffed around on occasion, too, but to no avail. And when it came to those on the other side of the fence, there were always one or two toerags who tried to have it both ways: happy to hand over cash to get you onside, then trying to be clever and putting the squeeze on once they thought they owned you; when they thought they'd got enough to put you away.

Arseholes like Simon Tipper. Top Black Dog and stupid, greedy, dead bastard. Which was where Marcus Brooks had come into all this in the first place . . .

Skinner carried the beers back into the sitting room, cursing as he tripped and banged his head against the edge of the door. He pushed himself up on to one knee, moaning and puffing; rubbed at his head and at the spilled beer that was soaking into his trouser leg. He looked up at the familiar figure standing above him; saw the blood that seemed to be painted on to his hand, that was dripping on to the carpet, and realised that he hadn't tripped at all.

118

That he hadn't banged his head.

The room grew suddenly hot and bright, the whiteness screaming inside his skull, and his tongue was heavy in his mouth as he tried to speak. 'Do we really need to do this?'

And, gasping for breath, the smell grew richer still: the bite of urine, the coppery smack of his own blood.

'Yes, we *really* do.'

But the words never reached Skinner's ears. They were lost in the grunt of effort as the hammer was brought down a second time.

Down to the last four in a no-limit tournament, playing as the 'old lady', Thorne called a ten-dollar raise with a king–queen suited, and sat back to see what Number1Razr made of it. He looked at the chair that was occupied, as always, by the huge, bald man in the Hawaiian shirt; chewing on his cigar, ready for anything. Thorne couldn't help but be reminded of Nicklin. The figure looked as full of himself and was equally difficult to read. The major difference was that the cartoon looked a damn sight healthier.

Number1Razr lived up to his name, and when Thorne missed out on the flop completely, he got out of the hand while the going was good.

By the time his train had reached Paddington there was no point going back to the office, so he'd filled Brigstocke in over the phone. Since the call, he'd tried to convince himself that he'd simply misread the DCI's mood, but there was no doubting the strangeness of his boss's reaction when Thorne had suggested that Skinner was one of a pair of corrupt officers being targeted by Marcus Brooks. There had been a weariness in the long silence before Brigstocke had spoken: 'This is based on what you've been told by a convicted serial killer, is it?'

'He's got no reason to bullshit me.'

'He doesn't need a reason.'

'It makes a lot of sense,' Thorne had said.

Another pause. Then: 'Let's talk about it tomorrow.'

He'd as good as told Thorne to sleep on it. That Skinner was tucked up, safe and sound, with officers outside his house. He'd said there was nothing they could usefully be doing that night anyway, and even if the accusations being thrown around by reliable chaps like Stuart Nicklin were true, it wouldn't make much difference in terms of trying to stop him being murdered, if that was all the same to Thorne.

Thorne had let it go. He knew very well that Brigstocke had plenty on his mind; knew even better there would be no point asking if he wanted to share any of it.

He folded a low pair when Number1Razr went all-in and was called by The Big Slick, playing as the cool black guy in the snazzy waistcoat.

Thorne had lost count of the times he'd been swayed by Brigstocke's opinion; when his judgement in doing so had proved to be spot on. But this time the DCI's lack of enthusiasm had done nothing to lessen Thorne's conviction that Nicklin, and by association Brooks himself, had been telling the truth . . .

At the table, Slick showed a pair of tens, and even though he'd hit a third, he was put out of the game by Razr's low flush. Thorne watched as a message appeared on the site's dialogue box: *Bye Nigga!*

Thorne didn't know if he was outraged in spite of or because of the absurdity in racially abusing a cartoon. Either way, he made the decision that he was going to put Number1Razr out of the game if it took him all night.

They each folded their next three hands early. Then, with a decent-sized pot already built up and with two cards still to come, Thorne found himself sitting on 8–9, with 10–jack–queen on the board. He should probably have slow-played it, but couldn't resist making a big bet and typing out a message to go with it: *Come on then, you racist fuck* . . .

Number1Razr took the bait and went all-in. Thorne called immediately. When the hole cards were revealed, Thorne saw the ace–king which gave his opponent the higher straight, and with the final two cards of no further help, he crashed out of the tournament in third place.

Later, getting ready for bed, he realised that he'd probably been stupid. He knew well enough that players deliberately wound each other up in the hope that someone at the table might start to bet rashly; might go 'on tilt', as poker parlance put it.

Fifty dollars down on the night, it had been an expensive lesson to learn, but Thorne didn't much care. He'd loved every minute of it and was still buzzing an hour later, wide awake.

He enjoyed the game anyway, but having someone to go after had made it even better.

Baby,

I don't know how far I walked tonight and I don't suppose it matters. But I swear I don't know how I kept putting one leg in front of the other, because it feels like my head's full of dirty cotton wool. I know I said I was enjoying it, and it's better than rotting in the flat, but all I could think about tonight was sleep. How much I want it, and how much I'm dreading it. Knowing that when I do get off, it won't last long, that I'll be up again feeling like shit in a couple of hours.

I think that, maybe, there's dreams I don't remember. Worse than the normal ones, I mean. So fucking terrible that something, some survival instinct or whatever, knocks me out of them and wakes me up before anything really bad happens. God knows what they'd be, though. The ones I can remember are shitty enough. Stuff about you and Robbie, about what happened. Or worse, when nothing's happened at all and everything's just fine, just the way it was. But then I remember, in the dream I remember, and when I wake up it's like I've only just found out, you know? Like I'm back at Long Lartin, listening to those coppers all over again, every word kicking the shit out of me.

Talking of which . . .

One of them's dead. One of the two from before, I mean, when I got sent down. But there's other stuff going on now, other people involved. Things are happening that are bugger all to do with me, and I don't really feel like I'm in control of this any more. Not to worry, the details don't matter. You were never that big on the nuts and bolts of stuff anyway, not unless there was a handbag or shoes involved!

I'm not going to stop, though. I just wanted to tell you that. However fucked up or strange things get, I'm going to finish it. And yes, I do remember the shelves I never got round to putting up, and the bathroom that stayed half-tiled for over a year, so I know damn well you'll be having a good laugh about me finishing anything.

That's fine, I don't care. As long as I can see you laughing . . .

Right, time to try and sleep again. I'll go through the cupboard full of pills I've got and see if there are any I haven't tried. Maybe I should mix up a sodding cocktail.

Give the boy a squeeze for me. And all sorts for yourself, baby.

Marcus XX

TWELVE

Camden Market was one of the capital's top tourist attractions; the fourth-biggest retailer in the country, according to some sources, with up to one hundred thousand people descending on the place every weekend. Making his way slowly up from Mornington Crescent station towards Camden Lock, Thorne had decided that he'd been held up or jostled by twice that many.

Well, there *were* only forty-two shopping days left until Christmas.

He had scowled, weaving through the mêlée, leading with his shoulder. 'I told you this would be mad.'

'Shut it, Grandad . . .'

Louise had suggested the trip a day or two before, saying it had been years since she'd been. Then Hendricks had got wind of the idea and it had rapidly turned into an outing. The three of them had met for breakfast at a café near the Tube station, and there was talk of walking up to Primrose Hill later on, or of splashing out at Marine Ices when they got shopped out.

At the very least, it should have been distracting.

Pushing his way through a sea of black leather and multicoloured hair extensions ought to have allowed Thorne some time away from thinking about Marcus Brooks. Wondering why there were so many people, relative to the huge amount of quirky pottery and faux-antique tat; moaning about the fact that cleaning up after the market each week was like painting the Forth Bridge; grumbling, sweating in spite of the drizzle, feeling too old to be anywhere near the place. All of that should have taken Thorne's mind off dead bikers and bent coppers for at least an hour or two.

After the first half-hour, though, Thorne suggested they split up, so that he could browse through the second-hand CDs in the Stables, look for a couple of Cash albums he only possessed on vinyl. In reality, it was because, alone, he could focus more easily on the case: on Brooks and the drive for revenge that Nicklin had stoked up and described with such relish; on Skinner and his partner; on the slow and terrible chain of events that they had begun six years earlier.

He could think about a woman and her child being mown down on a zebra crossing. About men who lived by rules and believed in a reckoning.

About a whirlwind being reaped . . .

When he caught up with Louise and Hendricks, who were drinking coffee on a crowded pavement, it was only to let them know he'd decided to go into work, even though he was booked out for the day, with a DI from another team covering for him.

Louise wasn't happy about it. She pointed out that the case would not fall apart without him. He said that she'd do the same thing if she had to.

'Yeah, if I *had* to,' she said.

Hendricks raised his hands. 'Uh-oh! Domestic . . .'

Louise threw him a look, in no mood to let it drop.

'You two can stay,' Thorne said.

'Can we? Thanks a lot.'

'I haven't got time for this.'

'No, you'd better get a move on,' Louise said. 'They'll all just be standing around, wondering what to do until you get there.'

Thorne looked to Hendricks for support, for a 'bloody women' raise of the eyebrows that might diffuse the situation, but his friend stared resolutely into his coffee cup. Thorne turned back to Louise. 'We said we wouldn't do this.'

'That was when I thought you were "dedicated" or whatever,' Louise said. 'That you just liked the job.' She pressed a hand to her chest. '*I* like the job, but I'm not a nutter about it . . .'

Walking back as quickly as he could towards the Tube station, Thorne swore at more than one person for not getting out of his way fast enough. He seethed at being described as a 'nutter', shaking his head and muttering to himself, and cursing anyone with the temerity to be sharing his pavement.

Queuing at the ticket barrier, he was approached by an overweight individual with neatly combed blond hair and a warm smile.

'Do you want to live for ever?'

'Sounds all right,' Thorne said.

The man thrust a leaflet at him. 'You need to let Jesus into your life.'

'There's always a fucking catch,' Thorne said.

As she watched Thorne disappear into the crowd, Louise felt a twinge of guilt cut through her anger – remembering that the case had rather found him, that there had probably been times when she had been equally driven – but the guilt cooled rapidly into resentment at having lost her temper. At being made to feel guilty.

She'd been irritable all day – since Thorne had announced that there would be *three* of them going out together. She loved Hendricks to bits, how could she not? But she'd been hoping that she and Thorne could enjoy a Sunday without company. Joint days off were few and far between, and she could count on one hand the number of times they'd spent one on their own. She'd hoped that they could relax for a few hours; that they might get the chance to talk about a few things.

There were so many things they'd never discussed . . .

She turned to Hendricks, pulled a face. 'Tosser . . .'

Hendricks lowered his head, then looked up at her, doe-eyed and batting his lashes. He had the voice off to a T: posh and wistful,

126

Princess Diana with piercings: 'The thing is . . . there were three of us in that relationship, and, you know . . . it was a bit *crowded*. Me, him and the Metropolitan Police . . .'

Louise smiled, just a bit. 'It's not the job.'

Hendricks shrugged, like it was none of his business. They finished their coffees. 'So, what shall we do?'

Louise wanted to go home. She wanted to spend some time on her own, to let her resentment breathe. To bloom or burn itself out. She wanted to climb into jogging bottoms and kick around in her nice, warm flat for the rest of the day, until she knew whether she should cling on to this relationship or think about cutting her losses.

'Lou?'

She reached for her bag. 'I think we should carry on shopping. Buy a few things we don't need. Then we should both treat ourselves to enormous, fuck-off ice creams.'

The hunt for Marcus Brooks was up and running . . .

With Nicklin's information backed up by fingerprint matches from both murder scenes, the team and all resources at its command were now focused in the same direction. The cell-site intelligence on the sending of the Skinner video indicated that the call had been made from a site near Shepherd's Bush Green.

'It's no more than a mile east of Acton, where the first message was sent from,' Samir Karim said. 'We know the Hodson message was sent straight away, from the hospital, but maybe these other two came from somewhere closer to home.'

'Maybe . . .'

'We need a few more calls, that's all.' Karim handed over the blown-up section of the *A–Z*, with the relevant cell-sites marked in red. As things stood, the area to which Marcus Brooks may or may not have a connection was no more than two dots on a map. It wasn't a great deal to go on.

Paper had been passing across Thorne's desk since he had walked through the door: printouts, statements, diagrams; authorisation documents;

memos and maps. Sheaf upon sheaf, building a comprehensive picture of where Marcus Brooks was not. Of what he had done in the few months before he'd started killing anyone. Details of the last known address: the house he'd shared with Angela Georgiou and their son Robert, now empty and locked up. An inventory from the company which had been storing all of the furniture for the last three months; the rental paid a year in advance, the bill settled in cash. Statements from Brooks' parole officer and from local social services, verifying that he had reported each week as required; had been signing on, seeking work and claiming housing benefit until three months before, when he'd slipped off the system. From his parents, now living in Wales, confirming that telephone contact had stopped around the same time. Requisitions for the usual records and searches: credit and store cards, DVLA, voters' register, National Insurance . . .

'He'll slip up,' Thorne said.

Karim's nod was hopeful at best. 'He's been pretty clever so far, though, with all the phone business. I think he's learned a fair amount about flying below the radar, you know?'

Thorne was coming to the same conclusion. This was stuff that a career criminal like Brooks would have started picking up early in life, and prison was the best finishing school there was.

He would have learned a lot from the likes of Stuart Nicklin.

'He's got to be living on something, though.'

'Cash,' Karim said.

'Where's he getting it from?' Thorne rifled impatiently through piles of paper for Brooks' bank and credit-card statements, none of which showed much in the way of funds.

'Well, he might have had some stashed away, but let's presume he hadn't, that he needed to get some.' Karim slid a plastic wallet containing a CD across the desk. Thorne looked at the printed label, took out the disk and pushed it into the computer's drive as Karim continued: 'We got some names from S&O. Pulled in a snout from one of the firms Brooks used to do some driving for in the mid-nineties.' The image appeared on the screen: time-coded, black-and-white footage from the fixed camera in a typical interview room. Karim pointed to the man sitting at a table, opposite himself and Andy Stone. 'This bloke's been giving your new mate Bannard bits and pieces for years.'

'Looks like a charmer,' Thorne said. 'Where's this?'

Karim jerked a thumb towards the window. 'Colindale. Me and Andy had a chat with him first thing.' He leaned over and moved the mouse, taking the footage forward until he reached the section of the interview he wanted. 'Here we go . . .'

Thorne turned up the volume. The interviewee, a skinny old sort with leathery chops and eyes like black beads, had plenty to say for himself. He spat his words out in a reedy voice laced with Glaswegian; leaned through the smoke that rose from a cigarette.

'Plenty of people owe Brooks, you know? It's not a secret that he could've made a deal when they did him for that murder. That he was offered a year or two off his sentence in return for a wee chat, and he told them where to stick it.'

Stone had been unable to resist. 'Unlike you, you mean?'

The man had ignored the dig. 'These are people he could easily have gone to for money when he came out. People who remembered that he kept his mouth shut when he didnae have to. They'd have been more than happy to help him out.' The man took a deep drag on his cigarette, then looked up, well aware where the camera was, blowing out smoke through a smile. 'They'll be queuing up to do him a favour now. Considering some of the arseholes he's getting rid of . . .'

'I don't think Brooks needs a bank,' Karim said, stopping the playback.

Brigstocke entered without knocking, and Karim quickly got the message that there were other things he could be doing.

'Thanks, Sam,' Thorne said, as the door closed.

Brigstocke leaned against Kitson's desk. 'How's it going?'

Thorne straightened the papers on his desk. 'Well, it looks like Brooks was as good as gold while he was setting all this up, then he just dropped out of sight. He's not making it easy for us . . . well, other than helping us identify his victims, obviously. His *potential* victims. But you know, we'll get there . . .'

Brigstocke nodded. 'Why "potential", suddenly? Why do you think he's started sending videos? Sending us pictures *before* he kills them?'

'A psychiatrist would probably say he wants us to stop him.'

'What do you say?'

'I think he's just fucking us around.'

Brigstocke nodded, like he was thinking about it. 'I was really just asking how you were, by the way.'

'Sorry?'

'When I asked how you were doing. It's possible to talk about something other than the job for five minutes.'

Thorne laughed. 'Have you been talking to Louise?'

Not getting it, Brigstocke smiled anyway, and Thorne could see that he was in a better mood than he had been since the DPS had come calling. But still, there was no invitation to reciprocate and ask how Brigstocke was doing. Or to enquire as to the nature of the Regulation Nine he had been served.

Thorne had known Russell Brigstocke for years. Had met his wife and kids, had eaten at their house. It suddenly didn't seem to count for very much.

'Right.' Brigstocke dragged round a chair. 'This Skinner business. These allegations . . .' Thorne waited. 'I just think we need to be careful. Prison testimony can be iffy at the best of times.'

'I know—'

'Remember what sort of a headcase we're dealing with here.'

'I'm hardly likely to forget,' Thorne said. 'But everything Nicklin told me made sense. It may turn out to be nothing, but Marcus Brooks certainly thinks Skinner and somebody else set him up for murder six years ago. He's sure enough to want them dead for it, so, even if he's wrong, it's got to be worth looking into.'

Brigstocke took off his glasses, yanked out a corner of his shirt and rubbed at the lenses. 'I *know* Paul Skinner, Tom.'

Thorne blinked. He watched as Brigstocke tucked in his shirt and replaced his glasses, wondering what he meant.

I know him well enough to be sure that he isn't bent?

I know him and right now it would be hugely embarrassing for me if he *did* turn out to be bent?

I know him, so do me a favour and drop it . . .

Thorne decided it was as good a time as any for grasping nettles. 'Has this got anything to do with the DPS coming in to see you on Friday?'

It might have been the fact that the lenses had just been cleaned, but Brigstocke's eyes seemed to brighten behind them. He sat up straighter. His voice was low and dangerous. 'Why the fuck should it?'

'Russell . . .'

'And why would you think *for one minute* that it would?'

Thorne could do little but bluster and bluff and try to limit the damage. He said that it was a perfectly innocent question, that he'd been worried by Brigstocke's mood, and there was really nothing more to it. That he was there if Brigstocke wanted to talk about anything, anything at all.

'You should go whichever way you want on this,' Brigstocke said eventually. 'You're the one getting these messages. You were drawn into this, and I suppose you're giving the case a certain . . . impetus. As far as Skinner goes . . .' He trailed off, his head dropping, fingers picking at what might have been a loose thread on his trouser leg.

For a few minutes after that, they proved Brigstocke's point and talked about something other than the case, the awkwardness dissipating slightly over the first few laughs. A story about a mutual ex-colleague; kids; a recent episode of *The Bill*. Thorne dug out the copy of *The Job* he'd stashed and they shared a joke at the expense of Holland and his table-tennis trophy.

It finished on about the best terms Thorne could have hoped for. But when Brigstocke was leaving, Thorne stopped him at the door. 'I'm still not sure what you're telling me, Russell.'

Brigstocke sounded resigned as much as anything else. 'When has me telling you anything ever made the slightest bit of fucking difference?'

★

Not wanting to spend too long thinking about it – worrying about friendship and favours and the sickly smell of burning bridges – Thorne didn't wait more than a couple of minutes after Brigstocke had left before putting in the call to Albany Street police station.

He put on his most efficient voice, and tried not to laugh as he asked to be put through to Human Resources. He chatted for a minute or two with the civilian administrative officer. He gave his name and warrant-card details, a fax number and email address, then asked for the Personal Information Management System record on Detective Inspector Paul Skinner. He paid a visit to the canteen while the admin officer accessed the PIMS file. The information he'd requested was spewing from the fax machine in the Incident Room before he'd finished his coffee.

Thorne cast an eye across the pages.

Three sheets detailing every posting held by Paul Skinner in nearly thirty years as a police officer: dates and locations; contributions to significant operations; courses attended and qualifications gained. When he had spoken to Thorne the previous morning, Skinner's memory had not let him down: he had been a DS on the Flying Squad at the time of Marcus Brooks' arrest for murder in 2000. He had worked on a variety of borough units prior to that, as well as with the AMIP East Murder Squad, and he had subsequently spent time on a stolen vehicle unit in addition to three years as part of a team attached to the Drugs Squad, concentrating on European trafficking.

There were no suspensions and Skinner had never been the subject of any complaint. He had, by contrast, received two commendations, including one for bravery during the arrest of a notorious armed robbery firm.

Thorne was interested to see that Skinner had twice passed what the DPS called 'integrity tests'. These could range from the absurdly simple – a tempting quantity of cash or drugs left in an abandoned vehicle – to more complex set-ups involving dozens of officers over a period of months. Most of the time, unless the subject failed, they would never even know they'd been tested at all. Though the Anti-Corruption

Group tried to be as inventive as possible, the received wisdom was that a bent copper clever enough to get away with it for a while could spot an integrity test a mile away.

To his knowledge, Thorne had never been tested, and he couldn't say with certainty that he'd pass when they finally got around to him. With a pint or two inside him, he'd tell anyone who gave a toss that they were testing for the wrong thing: it wasn't about pocketing a few quid if it came your way; it was a question of lines, always had been. Where you drew yours, relative to where the fuckers you were after drew theirs. Whether those lines grew closer together as experience chipped away at you. And whether you stepped across it for the right reasons, with your eyes open, or drifted to the wrong side without even knowing it.

He read through the report once more, his frustration growing with every page. Brooks had been set up by two officers, so in order for this information to be of any use, Thorne would need to cross-reference it with a PIMS report on somebody else. He was fairly certain that Skinner would have worked at some point with Richard Rawlings; and he knew he'd worked with Russell Brigstocke for that matter. But at this point, it was all useless information. Over such a long and varied career, Skinner would have worked closely with hundreds of officers and, even if Thorne *did* have likely names, he quickly realised that he would gain nothing definitive. The man with whom Skinner had set up Brooks needn't have been a close colleague. He could just as easily have been someone who drank in the same pub. Someone Skinner had met at a party. Someone he had played table-tennis with . . .

Thorne let out a long, slow breath.

He had to presume that this unknown man, *both men*, were dangerous. They had framed Marcus Brooks for murder, but Skinner and his partner-in-crime may have done considerably worse than that.

Somebody had killed Simon Tipper, after all.

The longer Thorne stared at the information in front of him, the more pointless it became. He had no real idea where to attack it from;

what else he would need to make the task easier. There were days when he felt ill equipped to deal with regular police work, but he couldn't even begin to think like a DPS officer. He was not sure if he should feel frustrated or relieved.

When Yvonne Kitson strolled in, Thorne pushed the PIMS report to one side.

'Thought you were booked out,' she said.

'Couldn't keep away.'

A nod, like she knew what he meant. 'My other half's got his mates round to watch the rugby, and the kids are being little bastards at the moment. What's your excuse?'

'Louise is working. You know.'

'How's it going?'

Thorne remembered the exchange with Brigstocke an hour or so before. With the exception of that conversation, and Thorne's request for Paul Skinner's records, Kitson knew as much about the Brooks investigation as he did. So he presumed she wasn't asking about the case; that her enquiry was more personal.

'It's good,' he said. He wondered if Louise was still pissed off with him. Still *as* pissed off with him. 'It's great . . .'

Kitson seemed pleased.

Thorne watched her sort through some papers on her desk and begin reading. 'They still got you riding two horses with one arse?'

She looked up, sour-faced suddenly. 'This is the only chance I've had to even think about the Sedat murder in days.'

'And?'

'I think I should've stayed at home.'

'Your mystery woman not called back?'

'We've blagged five minutes on Tuesday night's *Crimewatch*,' Kitson said. 'See what we can do to persuade her.'

'You doing it yourself?'

'They couldn't get anyone else.'

'Well, providing there's no football on, and they're not repeating *Animal Hospital* or *Watercolour Challenge*, I'll be watching . . .'

For an hour or so, they swapped *Crimewatch* stories, their own and other people's. They moaned about the perpetually tanned presenter: the nauseating simper as he told viewers to 'sleep tight'; the reminder that their chances of becoming a victim of violent crime were minuscule. Kitson said she'd like to drag the smug bugger round the Incident Room; maybe take him to a post-mortem and watch *that* take the colour off his face.

Thorne thought a good hard slap would do the job just as well.

The day dimmed quickly outside: Hendon a glinting patchwork beyond the glass, and headlights brightening on the cars that crept away from Brent Cross or north towards the M1. But Thorne could not summon up the energy to head home. To call Louise and continue the argument. By the end of the day, he and Kitson had decided to grab an early dinner, and they were tossing up between the Royal Oak and the nearest Chinese when Thorne got a call from the main security gate to say that he had a visitor.

Brian could be an arsehole in the wrong mood, and he wouldn't let Tony Blair in without seeing an ID, but he'd watched every kind of copper from cadet to commander pass under his barrier, and he could usually be relied on when it came to a thumbnail sketch.

'He's DPS,' Brian said.

'Oh, great. You sure?'

'Twenty quid says he's from the Dark Side.'

Thorne knew better than to take the bet. 'From Colindale, you reckon?'

'Nah, he's not local. His overcoat was too nice.'

'You're wasted on the gate, Brian.'

'He says he'll wait for you at reception . . .'

'We're popular suddenly,' Kitson said, when Thorne hung up. 'Maybe it's the same lot who were in here the other day with the DCI.'

Thorne told her that Brian hadn't thought so. 'He's keen though, whoever he is. Five o'clock on a Sunday.'

'Somebody else as job-pissed as we are. Or with nobody who wants to spend a Sunday with him.'

Thorne said he'd be as quick as he could. He grabbed his coat and told Kitson to pick somewhere they could eat when he got back.

He took the stairs, the smell of the new carpet assaulting him again, taking him back to that uncertain moment somewhere in his childhood.

Adding to the apprehension.

Talking to police officers, ordinary citizens would often be overcome with feelings of guilt, however innocuous the reason for the conversation. It was much the same for the police officers themselves when talking to those representing the Directorate of Professional Standards.

Racking his brain, Thorne trudged towards the ground floor of Becke House. Wondering exactly what it was that he had done.

THIRTEEN

They walked in the dark, across the parade square, through the HGV testing area and slowly around the track that bordered the athletics arena.

'This seemed a hell of a lot bigger when I was a cadet.'

'When was that?' Thorne asked.

'I left here eighteen years ago.'

It didn't tell Thorne precisely how old Detective Sergeant Adrian Nunn was, but it reinforced his initial impression that he was somewhere in his late thirties.

'You?' Nunn asked.

'A *lot* longer . . .'

Five minutes before, in those few moments between stepping into the reception area at Becke House and shaking hands, Thorne's assessment of his visitor had been much the same as his friend's at the gate.

Neither of them had lost their touch.

The Anti-Corruption Group dealt only with the most serious crimes involving Met officers, and Nunn's introduction of himself as one of their dread number meant that this was no simple disciplinary matter. He wasn't there because some idiot had filed an iffy expenses claim. Someone had fucked up on a grand scale; shaking hands, Thorne could only pray that it wasn't him.

Whatever the reason for his visit, Nunn *did* seem to be smiling an awful lot.

'I thought it would be best to wait down here.' He'd walked towards the door; an invitation to follow him outside. 'People tend to jump to conclusions. Start imagining all sorts.'

'It wouldn't be anything they haven't imagined before,' Thorne had said. Watching Nunn step outside, he'd seen that Brian had been right about the coat as well.

'It's all a lot different now though, right?'

They were standing beneath one of the orange lamps on the edge of the running track. 'I suppose,' Thorne said. There was still a cadet school based at the Peel Centre, but there seemed to be fewer of them around these days, and the dormitories in which recruits had once slept were now the self same offices in Becke House from which Thorne and his team operated.

However, as Nunn continued, Thorne understood that he was talking about more fundamental changes. It wasn't about the abolition of height and vision requirements, or because the training period was shorter, and it wasn't just a question of judgement being clouded by nostalgia. Anyone with half a brain cell could see that the quality of personnel coming into the force had fallen. Maybe there was a need to increase recruitment, to get bodies on the street faster. Whatever the reason, the perception among many serving officers was that, these days, any idiot could become a copper.

'That's pretty damning,' Thorne said. 'Especially coming from some of the people I've worked with over the years.'

'It trickles down though, right? The drop in standards.'

'Well, it's hardly going to trickle *up*.'

'CSOs,' Nunn said. 'Fucking Plastic Plod . . .' Nunn muttered in measured, unaccented tones about Community Support Officers being no more than coppers who couldn't cut it. About the commissioner's policy of increasing their numbers in the capital being brought into horrifying perspective. 'It's an accident waiting to happen,' he said.

Thorne quickly marked Nunn down as the type who had plenty to say for himself. The sort who would write meticulously drafted letters to *The Job* and *Metropolitan Life*. Who ate, drank and slept the Police Service. Like Kitson had said: 'Job-pissed'. Whatever Nunn wanted with him, Thorne decided this was probably bad news.

They carried on walking. Nunn was a six-footer, several inches taller than Thorne, and well built. He had American teeth, and had made the best of thinning hair by cutting it brutally short, with what was left no more than dark stubble against the scalp. The coat, grey and elegantly tailored, reached almost to his ankles and moved around his legs with each long stride. He told Thorne that several of those with whom he'd once been a cadet were now working within the DPS; that it was a branch of the Met that many were keen to be a part of.

Thorne knew the chat was merely a precursor to conversation of a trickier kind, and he was happy to cut to the chase. 'Listen, I was about to go and get something to eat,' he said.

'Is that an invitation?' Nunn asked.

'What was it you wanted?'

Nunn stopped. He stared over Thorne's shoulder long enough for Thorne to turn around; to see whatever it was that Nunn found so interesting. On the far side of the track, a lone recruit was tearing down the straight. He slowed at the hundred-metre mark, then stopped. The breath drifted back from him, caught in the glow from the orange lamps, as he rested, his hands braced against his knees. Just watching made Thorne feel tired, and he thrust his hands deep into the pockets of his leather jacket.

'What's your interest in Paul Skinner?'

Thorne turned back. 'Bloody hell, that was quick work.'

'We've got a flag on the PIMS system. Lets us know if anyone's taking a look.'

'Where are you based?'

'Jubilee House, Putney.'

'Well, that's at least an hour away, even with no traffic, so you must have left the minute your "flag" came up.'

'I finished my tea first.'

'This must be important.'

'Sundays are slow,' Nunn said. 'Not a lot else on.'

'Same here.'

'So, tell me about Skinner.'

They looked at each other. The fact that Thorne was the senior officer meant nothing. When the DPS was involved, rank went out of the window. A DC could interview a commander as aggressively as he or she liked; and, unless they were supremely confident and well connected, a wise commander would answer all their questions.

'I'm investigating a series of murders,' Thorne said. 'Skinner's been targeted by my prime suspect.'

'Your prime suspect's name?'

Another look; another pause. 'Marcus Brooks. And if you're that interested in Skinner, I'm guessing the name's probably familiar to you.'

Nunn's face showed nothing. 'So, you thought information in Skinner's PIMS record would be helpful to your murder investigation?'

'Yes.'

'Was it?'

'Not hugely, to be honest.' Thorne carried on quickly, before Nunn had a chance to ask anything else. 'Look, I'm guessing this is a oneway street. That I don't get to ask why you're interested in Skinner.'

'You can ask, by all means.'

'OK, then. Why?'

Nunn showed a great many of his American teeth. 'Paul Skinner is an officer that my team has been . . . monitoring for some time.'

'As in months? Years?'

More teeth. 'Some time.'

'In which case, you're probably *monitoring* at least one other officer with whom Skinner's involved, right?' Nunn held up his hands; now they were straying into 'need to know' territory. Thorne pressed on. 'This is information that would be helpful to my investigation. This other man is somebody my prime suspect will almost certainly be taking a pop at next.'

'I can't,' Nunn said.

'"Can't" as in "not allowed" or "can't" as in "don't know"?'

'"Can't" as in "can't".'

'So, you tell me sod all, and possibly endanger the life of another officer. Meantime, I carry on trying to catch a killer, with no help whatsoever from you, while your team maintains an "active interest" in my case. That about right?'

'Close enough.'

'Then you step in when it's done and dusted and help yourself to the bits that'll do you any good.'

'Look, none of this is my decision. But everything's done for a very good reason.'

'Well, you've got competition, mate. I don't suppose you know Keith Bannard, do you? A DCI in Serious and Organised . . .'

Nunn was shaking his head before Thorne had finished speaking.

'Doesn't matter,' Thorne said. 'Just someone else who's "interested" in my case. Someone else who's happy to sit back, while me and all the other mugs on the Murder Squad work our arses off. Tell you the truth, I've never worked on anything in which so many different people were so *desperately* interested. It must be the most fascinating case of my entire fucking career . . .'

Thorne's phone rang, and he turned away to answer it. The runner had come a little closer; was jogging slowly towards them. He grabbed at his feet, pulling them up towards the small of his back as he ran. Considering that his fellow-cadets were almost certainly making nuisances of themselves in The Oak, Thorne guessed he was either hugely keen or had made very few friends.

It was Brigstocke calling: 'We're in big fucking trouble.'

'I'm listening.'

'Skinner's dead.'

Thorne felt something jump against his ribs and instinctively stepped further away from Adrian Nunn. '*What?* How the fuck—?'

'Right now, you know as much as I do.'

Thorne started slightly when Nunn's phone rang behind him; turned to see the DPS man walking away to take his own call.

'I don't understand. We had men on Skinner's house.'

'I know. Do you not think I fucking *know?*'

'Who found the body?'

Thorne could hear the anger, the tension in Brigstocke's silence. In the background there were raised voices; none he recognised, the words indecipherable as they were shouted one over another. He listened to the fractured breathing that told him Brigstocke was on the move; heard him tell someone to wait.

The runner jogged past a few feet away.

'Russell?'

'Just get over there, Tom.'

Thorne hung up and turned. It was clear from the look on the face of the man marching towards him that they had been having much the same conversation.

'We might as well take the one car,' Nunn said.

FOURTEEN

It always amazed him. How death drew a crowd.

Though it was obviously less of a novelty for him than it was for most people, Thorne still found the fascination strange. It wasn't as though any of them were actually going to see anything. The men in the shiny suits like the ones off the telly weren't suddenly going to come trotting out and carry the body across. They weren't going to pull back the sheet and invite everyone to take a good look, maybe fire off a few quick snaps for friends and neighbours.

And yet, there they were.

While those in the adjacent streets of Stoke Newington laid out school uniforms, ironed shirts for the morning or just drank tea and grew miserable as Sunday fizzled out, a few lucky punters were outside, making their own entertainment. Thorne pushed his way through them: the cluster of gawpers fragmenting for just a moment; one or two exchanging snippets of whispered guesswork as they came back together; as a pissed-off uniform raised the tape for Thorne to duck under.

'Shouldn't this lot be indoors watching *Antiques Roadshow*?' the copper asked.

Thorne pressed on towards the house, heard a child somewhere behind him asking if he was the man who'd come to chop up the dead body . . .

There was as much of a gathering inside, and at the back of the house. Inside, it was as though there were at least two teams of SOCOs working the scene; investigators squeezing past one another in the narrow hallway that ran between the kitchen and the living room, where Paul Skinner's body had been found. In the first few minutes Thorne spoke to three different photographers and video cameramen and, approaching the body, he half expected to see Phil Hendricks battling it out with rival pathologists for prime position.

Hendricks looked up from his Dictaphone. 'Head smashed in, I'd guess with a hammer, much the same as the first victim. Dead at least twenty-four hours. And you need to call your girlfriend.'

'Still pissed off?'

Leaning to one side, Hendricks pointed to what was left of Skinner's head. 'What do you think?'

'You crack me up,' Thorne said, stony-faced.

Hendricks grinned, pleased with himself. 'OK, she's probably happier than our friend with the hammer, but then she did eat a *lot* of ice-cream. I'm not an expert, obviously, but isn't that supposed to be a major giveaway?'

'I'll ring later on, if I get a chance . . .'

Thorne pushed on towards the back of the house, stepped through sliding patio doors on to a small paved area: a round table, umbrella and chairs; a rotary washing-line; a grime-covered barbecue on wheels.

There was barely room to move.

The patio was heaving with the overspill from the crime scene and more besides: ambulancemen and a mortuary crew, waiting until they were needed; a CSI or two catching their breath, or using it to smoke a crafty fag; a woman dispensing tea and coffee from catering-sized flasks.

But the majority were in the Job.

A few in uniform, but most wearing whatever they'd had on when

144

the call had come through: Sunday best on one or two; jeans and puffa jackets; black tie on the poor bugger who had been dragged from a charity dinner. They stood around, muttering to one another in awkward groups of two and three. Like guests at an unconventional barbecue party.

Thorne's team were all there, obviously, and he saw several officers from others on the same unit. He also recognised DS Richard Rawlings, with a group he guessed were from Albany Street. Nunn had joined a couple of officers he seemed to know well. And there was no shortage of brass: Trevor Jesmond was one of two chief superintendents; making the rounds, doing his level best to smile when he caught the eye of the area commander.

There were more coppers than Thorne had clapped eyes on at any crime scene he'd ever attended.

Especially if you included the dead one.

Eventually Thorne managed to grab Russell Brigstocke and guide him towards a corner of the patio. The light from a pair of carriage lamps attached to the back wall made the DCI's face look even paler than it had been earlier in the day.

'Skinner told you he didn't want protection, didn't he?' Brigstocke said. 'Was adamant about it, according to Holland.'

'He wasn't hugely keen, no,' Thorne said. With so many experts around, he was not surprised that the process of covering arses had already begun.

'Right. And actually, we got protection officers in position pretty quickly, all things considered.'

'You don't need to convince me, Russell.'

'The wife's screaming blue murder, saying we should have done more, but I think we did all we could.'

A uniformed officer brought them both teas in Styrofoam cups.

Skinner's body had been discovered by the very men put outside his house, front and back, to protect him. Anne Skinner, alarmed at not being able to raise her husband on the phone, had called one of his mates at Albany Street. He'd got hold of someone at Homicide and, a few calls later, the protection officers were kicking in the front door.

'Brooks must have got inside some time between your visit and the surveillance team being put in place late afternoon.'

'Maybe he was watching the house,' Thorne said.

Brigstocke nodded towards the cordoned-off area around the back door. 'Easy enough for him to get in,' he said. 'Broke a window and reached inside.' He looked as though he wanted to spit out something bitter. 'You'd have thought a fucking copper would have known better.'

'Any prints?'

'Plenty, apparently.'

They drank their tea, and Brigstocke filled Thorne in on a few more unpleasant details. Looking around as they talked, Thorne caught Rawlings looking his way more than once; and Nunn drawing a colleague's attention to him before turning back to mutter something.

When Brigstocke was beckoned by the smallest of nods from Jesmond, he walked slowly back towards the house, like a man on his way into an oncologist's office.

A little later, Thorne caught up with Hendricks when the pathologist came out to get coffee.

'Your man's on a roll,' Hendricks said. 'That's three bodies in a week. He's paying for my holiday.'

Thorne stared towards the back door and spoke as much to himself as to his friend: 'They didn't find the murder weapon.'

'Sorry?'

'He took it with him this time.'

'So, he's being careful.'

'He's left prints at every murder scene, left the weapon behind every time. It's a bit bloody late to start being careful, isn't it?'

'Judging by how much force he used on that poor bastard's head, he's not exactly thinking rationally.'

'He's cool. That's what you said.'

Hendricks shrugged. 'Maybe I should stick to what's going on inside dead people.'

Thorne let out a long, slow breath. Watched it drift up into the fug of blue-grey cigarette smoke that had formed above the patio. He noticed that several empty cups had been tossed into the narrow flower beds around its edge. Something else for the widow to complain about. 'You're probably right,' he said, eventually.

'What are you thinking?'

'You don't want to know.'

'Please yourself.'

'I'm not sure *I* want to know.' Over Hendricks' shoulder, Thorne saw Rawlings moving past people, making his way, grim-faced, in their direction. He glanced back at Hendricks. 'This should be fun.'

Hendricks saw what was coming and stepped away, suddenly fascinated by a hover-mower leaning against the fence.

'Rawlings.' Thorne had been prepared for some hostility as he proffered a hand, but saw that Skinner's friend was fighting back tears as much as the urge to punch somebody.

'I can't decide,' Rawlings said. 'I don't know whether I'd rather have ten minutes alone in an interview room with the cunt who did this or fifteen with the cunt who organised the fucking protection.'

'It's a tough one.'

'It's OK, I know it wasn't your call.' He turned and stared blackly towards the corner where Trevor Jesmond and the area commander were deep in conversation. 'The fuckers with the pips tell the likes of us what to do, right?'

Thorne said nothing.

'Knew him ten fucking years. More. Only worked together for a couple of months, but we really hit it off, you know? Don't know if it was the football or something else, but we clicked.'

'Where was that?'

'What?'

'You and Paul working together.'

'Flying Squad, late nineties. I was just moving on and he was getting his feet under the table. Like a fucking lifetime ago now . . .'

Thorne nodded sympathetically; watched as Rawlings looked back towards the house again, as he muttered 'cunts' and gave the damp-course a kick. He couldn't help thinking that Rawlings swore too much and wondered if he might be one of those coppers who was equally excessive when it came to sentiment; to *showing* it at moments like this. The righteous anger at the death of a fallen comrade; a great mate, a good copper; 'just let me get hold of the bastard' . . . all that cobblers.

He remembered seeing Rawlings stroll into Skinner's house thirty-six hours before, being greeted warmly by the wife. It had crossed Thorne's nasty, suspicious mind for a moment or two then, that it wasn't just Millwall FC that Rawlings and his friend had in common.

'What happened yesterday morning?' Thorne asked. 'After we saw you.'

'Come again?'

'Did you stay long?'

Rawlings took a second, then smiled sadly. 'Paul was all over the place, in a right old fucking state. Trying to persuade Annie to take the kids and piss off to her mum's. She started kicking up a fuss and Paul was shouting the odds, so I thought I'd best make myself scarce. I couldn't have been there more than half an hour, forty-five minutes, after you left. He said he'd bell me later, after the game. We'd usually talk about the match on the phone if we weren't watching it together, you know? But he never did . . .'

Thorne nodded. He and his father had done the same thing until the Alzheimer's had got too bad. Before social niceties had gone out of the window, and the old man had begun to swear almost as much as Richard Rawlings. 'So did you go?' Thorne asked. Rawlings blinked, not understanding. 'The game?'

Rawlings shook his head. 'Listened to it on the radio in the end. Bleeding Doncaster equalised in the last fucking minute . . .'

The crowd at the front had dispersed by the time the body was brought out just before ten-thirty. The area commander and the DCIs were a picture of solemn outrage, while Nunn and his DPS cronies pulled the right faces, even if they knew rather more about Paul Skinner than most people. Rawlings stood with his head bowed and his fists clenched. A couple of the boys in Met Police baseball caps took them off as the stretcher went past.

Once the mortuary van was on its way, Thorne took his final chance to speak to Hendricks, who immediately asked if he had called Louise yet. Thorne admitted that he hadn't, neglecting to add that it would probably be better for both of them if they didn't talk until the following day.

'Shouldn't go to bed on an argument,' Hendricks said.

'She could always call *me* . . .'

Brigstocke came quickly down the path towards them, a look on his face when he caught Thorne's eye that said 'private'. Thorne passed the message on to Hendricks, who was happy enough to leave them to it. He said that he'd phone mid-morning with the PM results, try to provide the team with a more accurate time of death.

'He was dead by full time,' Thorne said. 'If that's any help.'

Brigstocke watched Hendricks move away, then stepped closer to Thorne. 'They've authorised live listening.'

It wasn't a phrase Thorne had heard often, but he knew what it meant – that it was a serious step. 'Who's the subject?' Brigstocke stared at him like it was a stupid question, and Thorne realised that it *was*, a second after he'd asked it. 'Me. Right?'

Since the Regulation of Investigatory Powers Act, intelligence gathering had changed as radically as anything else. RIPA had laid down strict guidelines about such things as unlawful interception and monitoring of transmissions, with heavy penalties for those in breach of them. Thorne knew well enough that, when it was deemed necessary – when there was 'imminent threat to life', for example – such things went on. But the public, and indeed the majority of police officers, remained unaware of the covert technical support unit, on call to any branch of the Met, that installed the bugs and then listened in. The unit that gathered information which was totally inadmissible as evidence but would be given to those working on the case to use as they saw fit.

A unit, like a handful of others, that existed but didn't exist.

Thorne wasn't a suspect, and, crucially, would be giving his consent to such 'intrusive surveillance'. But there were others whose privacy would be compromised, whose consent would never be sought, and Brigstocke was at pains to point out that the operation would therefore remain extremely sensitive. He told Thorne that so much as mentioning it to anyone outside the senior command structure could result in a prison sentence. 'You OK with that?'

'Yeah, I suppose.' The thought of prison was enough to give anyone pause for thought, but Thorne was as worried about how much his life, its details, its *ordinariness*, would become a mundane aspect of someone else's day at work. He winced at the idea of sweaty coppers wearing headphones, pissing themselves as Louise called him a nutter.

It was only a small step up from someone going through your rubbish.

'What are we talking about?' he asked.

'Home, office and mobile phones,' Brigstocke said. 'You still have that pay-as-you-go?'

'Yeah, but I've only just bought it, haven't I? There's no way Nicklin could have given Brooks that number.'

Brigstocke nodded. 'Well, that's good. At least you'll have *some* privacy. They'll do email as well, obviously. And intercept the post.'

'Can't I open my own sodding *post*?'

'I don't think so.'

Thorne's eyes widened with sarcasm. 'I promise I'll pass on anything from the murderer. Anything that isn't a final demand or a pizza menu.'

'It doesn't work like that, Tom.'

Thorne sighed, shook his head. 'Whatever.'

'We need this sorted,' Brigstocke said. He looked towards the phalanx of police officers, and beyond, at the house of the one that was on his way to the mortuary. 'Things have got very bloody serious now . . .'

Later, Thorne would reflect on the perfection of the timing, and wonder if Marcus Brooks had been watching them at that moment. Staring down from the window of a nearby house.

The tone sounded from his jacket pocket just as Brigstocke was out of earshot. He thought the message might be from Louise. When he saw that it wasn't, saw the unidentified number appear, he scrolled down quickly; wondered whose picture he would be looking at this time.

There was no photograph. Just a simple text message: *He was dead when I got there.*

Brooks. Telling Thorne the same thing he'd told Sharon Lilley all those years before.

Not hoping for anything, Thorne dialled the number from which the message had come. He tensed when it rang and almost shouted out loud when the call was answered.

'Marcus . . .?'

There was just the faintest breath, and the sound of distant traffic for a few seconds before the connection was broken. As Thorne thrust the phone back into his pocket, he turned to look at the house and suddenly understood something.

He was dead when I got there.

Brooks hadn't been describing the murder for which he'd been arrested in 2000. He'd meant this one. The message was about Skinner.

Looking back later, when arrests had been made and bodies buried, and regret had been fuelled by cheap lager, Thorne would be unable to put his finger on exactly why he did what he did next.

It was nothing specific . . .

Stupidity, instinct, a tendency towards self-destruction . . . because the fuckers weren't going to let him open his own letters. Whatever the reason, Thorne watched Nunn, Rawlings, Brigstocke and the rest moving slowly towards their cars, and he was no longer sure he could trust *anyone*. The copper who, together with Paul Skinner, had set up Marcus Brooks for a murder he may well have committed himself had got away with so much for so long. He was obviously very accomplished when it came to covering his tracks.

Thorne at least had to consider the possibility that the man might be closer than he realised.

There were long stares at the roadside now; nods exchanged between the ranks. There were promises made and a deal of gung-ho back-slapping. These people shared this terrible loss equally and were bound together by a determination to nail whoever had murdered one of their own. A copper's death seemed to count for so much, relatively. Seemed, on the surface at least, to mean more than that of a biker, or those of a young mother and her child. Was the suffering of Paul Skinner's family really any worse than that of Ray Tucker's or Ricky Hodson's? Or of Marcus Brooks?

If a copper's death was so important, then catching a copper who was also a killer should carry equal weight, shouldn't it?

Thorne looked at them, fired-up and full of it. And knew that, standing where he was at that moment, he was not one of them.

That was when he made the decision.

He knew he didn't have much time: Brooks might well be disposing of the SIM card at that precise moment. He had probably done so already. For the best, Thorne thought. It was a fucking insane idea anyway . . .

He couldn't use his usual mobile; they'd be checking it. And the new one, the *safe* one, was back at his flat . . .

Hendricks was just climbing into his old, silver Renault estate, when Thorne all but pulled him out, on to the pavement. 'I need to borrow your phone.'

'What?'

Thorne snapped his fingers, fought the urge to reach into Hendricks' pockets and search for it. 'Just give it here, Phil . . .'

He walked away fast up the street, navigating through the phone's menu as he went. His hand trembled a little as he keyed in the text, then the eleven digits of his unmonitored, pay-as-you-go phone number. Then he leaned against a low wall and entered the number Brooks had called from.

He pressed 'SEND' and waited. Watched as the graphic of an envelope span across the screen and the words appeared: *Message sent.*

Almost breathless, Thorne stabbed at the keypad, dialling the number once more.

He got a dead line.

PART TWO

'SHOW'

Jennings had led him into the pub where Squire was already waiting, then gone off to get the drinks in.

He toyed with getting bolshie, maybe asking to see warrant cards, but there was really no need. He knew the Old Bill when he saw them, and these two had the look. Had the chat.

It was lunchtime and there weren't too many other customers about. They sat around a large wooden table next to the gents' toilets; the smell of piss and bleach-blocks wafting out whenever the door was opened. Jennings came back with beers for himself and his mate, water for him; tossed a couple of bags of peanuts across, and they got down to it.

'Keeping busy, Marcus?'

'You know . . .'

'Yeah, *course* we know. Nice little racket you and your old woman have got going.'

It *was* nice, had been working out a treat, as a matter of fact. He'd been looking for something ever since he'd got out of the game. Had tried and failed to hold down any number of ordinary jobs, but he wasn't cut out for life on the up and up. Then Angie had started doing some cleaning work, making a decent job of it, doing more houses on word of mouth and what have you. Bigger houses, where people were that much better off and didn't seem bothered about the cleaner having a set of keys; letting herself in while the owners were out having long lunches and getting their nails done.

It had been Angie's idea and it had worked out right from the off.

Once she was in there, trusted enough, and knowing all the family's comings and goings, he'd turn the place over. Go in with the keys, put a window through when he was finished, maybe kick a back door in or whatever to make it look kosher. Usually Angie would leave a few weeks afterwards, start in a new area, although there were a couple of houses he'd robbed where she was still cleaning. Because she liked the people, and the money was so bloody good . . .

'Very nice,' Jennings said. He licked his lips. 'Sweet as you like and, you know, I'd hate to be the one to fuck it up for you. But I *will*.'

Squire threw a fistful of peanuts into his fat mouth. 'You've got a job to do, and so have we.'

'Livings to make.'

'Not sure how good Angie's going to look after a few months in Holloway.'

'Tasty enough for most of the slags in there, mind you . . .'

He wasn't stupid. He'd come across plenty of coppers like these two before, when he was working with other people. The sort who'd tip you the wink about a raid; come in and help themselves to a bundle of twenties when a take was being divvied up.

'How much are we talking?' he asked.

Squire finished the nuts, wiped his palms against his jeans. 'It's not about money. We just need a favour.'

'Something up your street,' Jennings said.

'Be a real shame if things went tits-up for you now. Especially with a kid and all that.'

Then they explained about the job, Jennings getting excited and licking his lips all the bloody time, some kind of nervous habit; Squire leaning across the table, quieter and scarier. They told him where the house was, when the owner was likely to be out; that they just needed him to go in there and grab whatever paperwork he could find.

He asked them whose place it was and they told him that he didn't need to know. That it was just a favour. That they really didn't like to ask, but they hoped he might see his way clear. They gave him a phone number and told him to think about it, and that was about the lot.

He didn't have a great deal to think about, and a week later he was stepping across broken glass into a darkened kitchen. The place smelled strange. Oily. The house wasn't overlooked from the back and they'd assured him that the man of the house would be away, so he wasn't too worried about being seen or making a lot of noise.

He turned on the light. Stared at the stripped-down engine on the kitchen table . . .

Then he heard voices, and was about to head straight out the way he'd come in when the music told him there was a television on somewhere. It still wasn't right: the place should have been empty. He'd only done somewhere that was occupied once before, and he wasn't thrilled about doing it again. But it wasn't like he had a lot of choice.

Even then, creeping towards the front, there was no way of knowing there was anything wrong. There was no sign of a struggle until he slowly opened the door to the lounge, where they'd told him all the papers would be.

That was when he started to panic.

There was blood, just fucking *everywhere*. The armchair was on its back, and there was crap scattered about, and the bloke who wasn't supposed to be there at all was dead as mutton. Lying on his face in front of *Coronation Street*. The back of his head all wet and shapeless.

He didn't see any papers; guessed that whoever had done the bloke in had taken them. He didn't see an empty glass on the floor behind the settee. But then he didn't see too much of anything; he was far more bothered about getting the hell out of there.

In retrospect, it was probably thick of him, but he didn't grasp it all straight away. Quite how dodgy it was. He tried calling the number they'd given him, but couldn't get hold of Jennings and Squire. It was only later, after he'd been nicked and they brought in the glass with his prints on, that it finally clicked. Then he saw just how seriously he'd been stitched up.

The glass he'd been drinking water from in the pub . . .

Brooks was amazed how much of the detail he could still remember from that night: what was on the television; the design on the back of the dead man's leather jacket; the material of the armchair and the blood on one of its castors. It was odd, because the idea of revenge had faded during the years he'd spent inside. At first he'd been obsessed with it, with making them pay for fitting him up, but eventually he'd let it go. There had been other things to think about. Angie and Rob. Stuff that made him feel better.

The two men who'd taken six years of his life had as good as got away with it. But then the Black Dogs had gone after his family. And now, all bets were off.

Jennings and Squire. One down and one to go. But there were others he needed to settle up with first, and as he walked back towards the flat, he remembered the piece of paper and the number that he'd scribbled; the message he'd been sent by the man who by all accounts should be trying to catch him.

He'd thought a fair bit about Thorne, asking himself why Nicklin should have had such a thing about him. He was a bloke to be taken seriously, that's what Nicklin had said. Had to be, if he'd managed to put Nicklin away.

Now the copper they'd lined up to be on the receiving end was sending messages of his own. Like an invitation.

Exhausted, he watched the sky beginning to turn pink beyond Hammersmith Bridge, and wondered what the hell Tom Thorne was up to.

FIFTEEN

'There's one by us, lit up like sodding Disneyland. Big, fuck-off sleigh on the garage roof and a flashing Santa climbing up a ladder on the outside of the house.'

'Some people actually take their kids. Get out of their cars to look at this shit.'

'The electric bills must be a fortune.'

'Have you noticed that the more of this tat anyone's got, the cheaper the fucking house is?'

Halfway through November, and already Christmas was giving the team plenty of things to get worked up about. Plenty to take minds off the job for a minute or two, when the work was frustrating.

The chain of days, and deaths.

Stone looked up from his desk, saw Tom Thorne at the photocopier, and shouted across: 'Tipped your dustmen yet this year?'

Big laughs all round.

A few years before, Thorne had handed over a tenner to men in fluorescent tabards and woolly hats, knocking on his door and wishing him 'Merry Christmas from your dustmen.' When Thorne had discovered that they weren't in fact his or anyone else's dustmen, he'd stormed into work, blood boiling. Told anybody who would listen about the scam and how he'd uncovered it, as though he'd pieced together the Jack the Ripper killings.

'You can't exactly ask for a fucking ID, can you? And you can pick up one of those fluorescent jackets *anywhere* . . .'

His indignation had only increased the hilarity of his colleagues.

'Bit early for that one, isn't it?' Thorne said, lifting the lid of the copier and gathering his papers.

Karim grinned. 'I don't know. I reckon once they switch on the lights in town we should be allowed to start taking the piss.'

That suggestion met with general approval, and when, a minute or two later, Stone started whistling 'My Old Man's a Dustman', there was scattered applause to go with the laughter. Thorne smiled, but found himself heading out of the Incident Room shortly afterwards.

Tuesday morning, thirty-six hours since they'd gathered as a team, as a *force*, at the scene of Paul Skinner's murder, and Thorne was finding it hard to see too much humour in anything. Along with everyone else, he'd thrown himself into the work, but that hadn't proved an especially helpful distraction. Brooks was still making a good job of keeping himself hidden, and their best bet – until such time as he popped up on some credit-card check or CCTV camera – remained the cell-sites.

Another message might help; might narrow down his location from several square miles of west London to a few streets in which to concentrate their efforts.

Another message like the one Thorne had chosen to keep to himself.

He had taken a step which might open up a channel of communication between himself and a man who had killed at least twice. The implications of his actions were growing more terrible as time passed, but it was too late to do anything about it. He couldn't go back and admit what he'd done. Try to explain why he'd done it.

Killed at least twice . . .

If Brooks *hadn't* killed Skinner, then who had? The same man who had killed Simon Tipper? The same *police officer*?

Ever since he'd sent the text to Brooks, the repercussions had begun to gather at the back of his mind. Elbowing their way forward and crowding out the good stuff. Fucking up any moment when he began to look forward to something; any encounter that should have been pleasant.

Louise had finally called the morning before. Early, when he was still thick-headed, when what had happened at Skinner's place had seemed, for a few precious seconds, like a dream that was refusing to fade.

'You're not a nutter.'

'Thank you.'

'You sound like shit, though. Were you on the piss last night?'

It felt like it. Except that he could remember exactly what he'd been doing. 'I wish,' he said.

'We going to see each other later?'

'Can I call you in a bit?'

'Oh, OK.'

'I'm just on my way out the door.'

He'd been standing in the kitchen wearing nothing but underpants, waiting for the kettle to boil; on his way nowhere. His only thought had been to keep the conversation short. He could hardly say, 'This phone's being monitored, so for Christ's sake don't say anything embarrassing. Anything that might drop me in the shit . . .'

He'd decided that he'd tell her later on, in person.

Not that he would tell her everything.

As it was, Louise had been the one to cry off the previous evening, when the wife of an Albanian gangster had been hauled into a car outside Waitrose just before the end of the day.

Now, in his office, Thorne thought about Louise; about the look on her face when she stared at him and unhooked her bra. He decided that was definitely something worth looking forward to. And that unless Marcus Brooks decided to step up his game and slaughtered the Mayor, the Commissioner and their families, he *was* going to see her, and that look, later.

The look on Marcus Brooks' face was harder to read. For the umpteenth time, Thorne opened the file on his desk and stared down at the man who'd received the shocking message that had started it all – the death message – five months before. Who had come out of prison, made his plans and begun sending messages of his own.

The hair was dark, short. The eyes were darker; 'brown', according to the information printed below the picture. This was all that Thorne could tell for certain. It wasn't just the blank expression that might equally have been masking simple boredom or murderous fury. Or that the picture itself was six years old, and that prison, as Thorne had seen only too well with Nicklin, could change a person's appearance as radically as any surgery.

Thorne was simply unable to get a handle on who Marcus Brooks was, and his picture did not tell the whole story. Common sense told him he was dealing with a man who knew how to take care of himself; who might watch a man die and not blink. But the man Nicklin had described, the man Thorne had heard in the silence down a phone line, had also been destroyed by grief. Had been hollowed out by it.

He thought that most faces gave it all away. Was sure that almost anyone presented with a photograph of *him* would not have needed more than one quick look. Would say: *Copper. Lives alone. Doesn't mix too well with others.*

But Marcus Brooks' picture was a lot less revealing. Thorne could only hope that if and when it came to it, he could look into the man's eyes and understand what they were telling him. Lives, his own included, had depended on a lot less.

Meantime, try as he might, he couldn't see the person behind the picture.

It was like looking at one of the cartoons around his online poker table.

DS Adrian Nunn had called earlier in the day for a quick chat. He'd moaned about his workload, about caps on overtime, and had asked Thorne what time his shift was ending.

When Thorne walked out of Becke House a little after six, Nunn was waiting for him. He was wearing his Gestapo coat again.

'Tube or car?' Nunn asked.

'I'm on the Tube.'

Nunn fell into step with him. 'Suits me. I can get the Northern Line straight down to Embankment. District from there all the way to Putney.'

'Going back to work?'

'No, but I only live round the corner from the office. It's pretty handy.'

'That's still a three-hour round trip,' Thorne said. 'I'm guessing you want more than just a quick chat. Mind you, you wanted more than that when you rang, didn't you?'

They walked quickly through drizzle up Aerodrome Road, and left towards the Tube station. Past Colindale Park and the British Newspaper Library. Thorne had used the place several times, trawling through the back copies and the microfiche in search of some crucial piece of information. He'd always ended up spending longer in there than he'd needed. Losing himself in stories and pictures that had no relevance to the case he was working; enjoying the feel of the crisp, yellowing pages of the old editions. Pre-Page Three. When Spurs had a team, and celebrities were famous for *doing* something.

'I just wanted to stress that everything we talked about the other day remains confidential,' Nunn said.

'Go on then.'

Nunn smiled, but only with his mouth.

'It seems a bit bloody odd,' Thorne said, 'that you should be so adamant about it. Considering Skinner's dead, I mean.'

'Nothing's changed.'

'Try telling that to Mrs Skinner.'

'Things don't just stop, that's all I'm saying.'

'"T"s to cross and "i"s to dot, right?'

'Little things like whether Mrs Skinner gets her husband's police pension if it turns out there would have been sufficient evidence to press charges against him.'

Thorne almost laughed for the first time in a day or more. 'Is that what this is all about?'

'I'm just making a point. This has got to run its course.'

'Look, I know you lot love all this cloak-and-dagger shit,' Thorne said. 'But the fact that Skinner may not have been completely kosher has probably got quite a lot to do with why he's dead. Why several people are dead. So it's not like we can keep this a secret. I've already spoken to my DCI about it. It's part of our case.'

Nunn looked up at the information board; thinking about it. 'As long as you really try to keep out of our way,' he said.

They didn't have to wait long for a southbound train, and Thorne was grateful. Standing on the platform was conducive to nothing more than small talk and he was fresh out of it. The train was more or less empty: they had a carriage to themselves. It was surprisingly hot once the doors had shut and they were moving, and Nunn stood to take off his coat; folded it across his knees.

'Is that really true?' Thorne asked. 'That nothing's changed?' He was desperate to know exactly what Nunn had meant. Was the status of the investigation still active for such prosaic reasons as Nunn had suggested, or was there something else going on? Were they actively pursuing a second officer?

'Nothing substantial,' Nunn said.

'Well, thanks for sorting that one out for me.' Thorne wondered if DPS recruits did courses in remaining amicably non-committal. If they shared classroom space with politicians and certain women he'd been involved with. 'Good result, or bad?' he asked.

'What?'

'Skinner being murdered.'

'Hang on a minute . . .'

'I'm serious. We both know Skinner was as bent as a nine-bob note, even though nobody's come out and said it, so what do the powers-that-be make of his getting knocked off? Are they happy enough to be rid of a corrupt officer without having to go to the trouble of actually doing it themselves? Saves embarrassment, I would have thought.'

166

'Nobody's *embarrassed.*'

'And what about you? You've lost the chance to nick him. Don't you feel a bit . . . robbed?'

'More than a bit,' Nunn said, enjoying how much his answer took Thorne aback. 'That's a shock, right? Don't you think that getting shot of a seriously corrupt officer is every bit as rewarding as catching a killer, or a gang of armed robbers, or nicking a drug dealer? I've done all those things, and I can promise you that it is. Every bit.'

Thorne could only shrug, but he wasn't sure he believed Nunn. At least, he wasn't certain *he* would feel the same way; would get the same satisfaction from nabbing a bent copper as he would from catching a murderer.

Until he remembered they could be one and the same thing.

There wasn't too much conversation from then on. People joined the train at Brent Cross and Golders Green, and it was full by the time they pulled away from Hampstead. Thorne and Nunn had been raising their voices to be heard above the noise of the train, but with passengers sitting around and standing above them, lurching as the train rocked and juddered, neither man was very keen to talk any more.

'This is me,' Thorne said as the train approached Camden.

Nunn had been sitting on the flap of Thorne's jacket, shifted slightly to let him stand up. 'You know where I am if anything else comes up.'

'Right. Same here, for what it's worth.'

Nunn looked at his watch. 'I don't suppose you fancy a quick drink?'

The invitation seemed genuine enough and it took Thorne completely by surprise. He looked at his own watch while he thought about what to say, but Nunn's expression as he'd asked the question had revealed a thumbnail snap of the man that he hadn't expected to see. That was sad, for all manner of reasons.

Copper. Lives alone. Doesn't mix too well with others . . .

'Sounds like a great idea,' Thorne said. 'But my girlfriend's cooking me dinner . . .'

★

The Bengal Lancer's home delivery was as reliable as always, and the two of them made short work of rogan gosht and chicken tikka, with mutter paneer and a sag bhaji, pilau rice and nan bread. Thorne fetched two more bottles of Kingfisher from the fridge, then carried the plates out to the kitchen.

He shouted through to the living room: 'I meant to say, about my mobile . . .'

Louise called back, asked him to say it again. His words had been lost in noise from the TV as she flicked through the channels.

Thorne came to the doorway and Louise turned down the volume. 'Just about my mobile,' he said. 'It's nothing important, but you need to call me on the prepay phone from now on.'

'I thought you had your old Nokia back.'

'I do, but that line is being . . . *monitored*. You know, in case Brooks sends another message, in case he decides to call, whatever. So best if you use the prepay. You've got the number, right?'

She told him that she had. He said he could go to prison for what he'd just told her. She promised to visit.

'You think he might, then? Get in touch again?'

'God knows.'

'I presume they've set up a trace on it, right? Silly fucker rings, you've got him. Simple as that.'

'Yeah, be nice,' Thorne said. He drifted back into the kitchen and Louise turned the sound back up on the TV. He finished loading the dishwasher then leaned back against the draining board. From where he was standing he could see her in the living room. She had found some cable channel showing eighties music videos and began humming along with an old Depeche Mode track.

Thorne glanced over at his leather jacket, hung across the back of a kitchen chair. His Nokia was in one of the inside pockets; the prepay phone was in the other. He'd programmed distinctive ringtones into each, so there would be no confusion.

He polished off his beer and started an argument with himself.

He'd been straight with Louise about the phone being monitored

168

when she didn't strictly need to know, hadn't he? So, maybe that excused his not telling her about the message he'd sent to Marcus Brooks. Or went some way towards excusing it, at least. Wasn't she better off not knowing about it? Not being involved? Not getting dragged through the steaming trail of shit he was busy creating?

He knew she wouldn't buy that for a minute.

It came from the same well-worn bag of tricks as, 'I didn't tell you I was sleeping with someone else because I knew you'd be upset, and I didn't want to hurt you'. Thorne knew, deep down, that it had more to do with cowardice than it did with compassion. That the lie by omission was usually worse in the long run than the terrible truth.

He still wasn't going to tell her, though. Not if he could avoid it . . .

When Thorne went back into the living room, they made themselves comfortable. They sat together on the floor in front of the sofa; broke up the last of the poppadoms and watched Yvonne Kitson do her turn on *Crimewatch*.

In a five-minute round-up slot at the end of the programme, Kitson fronted an appeal for more information about the murder of Deniz Sedat. Wearing a well-chosen, charcoal business suit, she said that the incident had 'shocked a community' and urged anyone with information to get in touch. Assured them that calls would be treated in confidence. She finished with a special plea to the young woman who had called once already; who had seemed eager to tell them something and whom they were extremely keen to talk to again.

'Knowing that *lovely* part of north London as I do,' Louise said afterwards, 'I think it would take more than some gangster getting knifed to shock anybody.'

Thorne smiled. 'We can't let anyone know that though, can we?'

With millions lavished each year on improving the city's image, it wasn't clever to highlight those places where policing came close to warfare. The Olympic Games were only a few years away and already there were jokes. About how well Great Britain would do in the shooting this time round, and the marathon runners straying into parts of Hackney and Tottenham and never being seen again.

Louise began searching through the channels again. 'She came across well, I thought. Kitson,' she said.

Thorne shrugged, like he hadn't really thought about it.

Louise and Yvonne had got on well enough when they'd met; for the few weeks when they'd been working together. But Thorne had sensed a problem developing since, had heard it in Louise's tone just then, when she was seemingly being complimentary. He'd suggested to her, *once*, that she might be jealous, and she'd bitten his head off, told him not to flatter himself. He hadn't been sure what she'd meant. Was he flattering himself to think that Kitson would be interested? Or that Louise would give a shit? He certainly wasn't going to push his luck by asking.

'Is there anything else on?' Louise asked. Thorne leaned over and snatched *Time Out* from the low table in the window. 'Anything worth staying out of bed for?'

Thorne flicked through to the TV pages. There were Champions League highlights on ITV after the news. They were showing *The Usual Suspects*, which he never missed, on Channel Four. There was late-night poker on at least three different cable stations.

'Absolutely fuck all,' he said.

There was very little light. Barely enough to see faces thirty feet away, and he couldn't move too much for fear of making a noise. This was hardly going to be winning any Oscars.

He only had fifteen seconds to play with anyway. But he did what he could to make the clip more interesting: started on the canal and moved across until he had the bloke in the middle of the picture; until he had both of them. 'Developing the shot', that's what it was called.

He lowered the phone, looked at the woman on her knees. His big hands on the top of her head. The grunting and the sucking noises.

There was plenty to develop to . . .

Him and Angie hadn't been big on the cinema before; just once or twice probably, before Robbie'd come along. But he'd seen a lot of films over the years inside, got quite a taste for them. Once a week on the big screen and DVDs from the prison library. Nothing like this, of course, they wouldn't allow that, but there'd been the occasional flash of tit to get excited about now and again. Plenty of prison movies, obviously; they were fond of showing those to wind everybody up. *Stir Crazy*, *Escape from Alcatraz*, he'd seen all of them more than once. *The Shawshank Redemption* when the screws really wanted to take the piss . . .

He tried to shift his leg an inch or two, could hear something moving in the long grass behind him. It was uncomfortable, crouching in the shadows to keep out of sight, but it wasn't like he'd planned it this way. He'd had no idea where the fucker was going when he'd started following him. What he'd got planned for the evening.

He'd followed the big van past Southall Park, along the Broadway and down along the route of the canal between the school and the retail park. He'd slowed and turned in when he'd seen the van do the same. Watched the girl walk up to the window and realised that the driver had known exactly what he was looking for.

And what he wanted for his money . . .

Brooks had got what he needed. Invisible behind a row of recycling bins, he put the phone away. Disgusted with the man leaning back against the dirty, wet wall. Disgusted with himself for being excited.

He watched as the man pushed; the tom's ponytail swinging as her head moved back and forth. Remembering the feeling – Christ . . . *trying* to remember it, years ago – when Angie had done the same thing to him.

Closed his eyes, but could remember only that he would never touch her again. Feel her again.

He took one more good look at the man's face. Then he lowered his head, and waited for them to finish.

They lay in the dark afterwards, Thorne pressed up against her, sucking in mouthfuls of hair. The breath coming back. They'd finished with Louise on top, and when he'd told her he was coming, she'd pushed herself down in an effort to hold him inside her. He'd rolled from beneath her in the nick of time and she'd groaned and dropped on to her side.

'I thought it wasn't safe,' he said finally.

'No.'

'So, why . . .?'

She grabbed his hand, pulled his arm tighter around her waist.

'Do you *want* to get pregnant?'

'No. Just at that moment, you know? I wanted you to stay inside me.'

A cat – Thorne couldn't be sure that it was Elvis – was yowling in the garden. The old lady who lived upstairs had some TV quiz show on stupidly loud.

'I should probably wear something next time.'

'What, like a fireman's helmet and wellies?'

'A condom.'

She snorted. 'Yes, I *know*. It just makes me laugh to hear you say it. That you find some things hard to say. You're weird.'

'*I'm* weird?'

They both laughed and rolled over together. Thorne brought his knees up as Louise curled against him. Her breath was on his back and he could feel her eyelashes against his shoulder when she blinked.

He listened to the applause from the television upstairs. And when it had been switched off, he lay there thinking: I don't know this woman at all.

Remember that time I missed Robbie's birthday party? The last one before I went inside, the one in the burger place. I know you will, because we had a steaming row about it. You telling me that Robbie was in tears and me shouting all the more because I felt like such an arsehole about it. I'd been doing some stupid favour for Wayne. Poxy driving job down on the coast. Waiting around, wondering what I was involved in and thinking about Robbie running around with his mates and trying his new football shirt on.

It was a favour I owed the bloke, that was the thing.

Thing about it is, I know sometimes people have taken the piss, made me look like a right mug, whatever, but I've always tried to be as good as my word, to be reliable. You say you'll do something, you do it. You understand that, don't you, Ange?

Same as this business with Nicklin. Liking someone, not liking them's got fuck all to do with it. When someone does you a favour, you owe them and, whatever else, I've always settled my debts. Simple as that.

From what Nicklin told me inside, I reckon this bloke Thorne is pretty much the same. The sort who follows things through, you know? He'll feel as if he owes something to these fuckers, to their nearest and dearest at any rate. That's exactly what Nicklin wants, if you ask me. Thorne won't leave it alone, he'll get right deep into it. Once he's made a promise he'll keep it, or at least he'll try to keep it, and I've always respected that.

I've not learned much. I know, fuck all probably. Except how important it is to know you're doing the right thing, even if it doesn't always feel like it.

Funny fucking pair, the two of us. Me and this copper. Sitting here, filling up these pages, trying to work things out in this poky shithole, I can't help wondering what he thinks about what I'm doing. I don't really care, but all the same, it's on my mind.

Which one of us is going to end up looking like a mug.

Maybe both of us . . .

SIXTEEN

The sun was just coming up, and Thorne scraped a thin crust of frost from his windscreen with the edge of a CD case. The trees on his road – he had no idea what sort they were – were completely bare, and all had been severely cut back for the winter. Looking along the pavement, there was an almost perfect line of them. Bleached and stumpy in the half-light.

The message had woken him half an hour before. The tone he'd set up on the prepay handset.

He'd stood there in his dressing-gown, the cat pushing at his shins, and watched the clip. If he hadn't recognised the man, he might have thought he'd been sent some random snippet of amateur porno. But dark and fuzzy as the image was, there was no mistaking the face; the punter being serviced by a woman who was almost certainly a hooker and was definitely not the man's wife.

Not Mrs Bin-bag.

Thorne had stared at his other phone, at the mobile that was being monitored, and waited anxiously to see if the message would be sent to that handset too. He had given it a couple of minutes: felt colder and more uncertain with every few seconds that passed.

Louise had staggered through, pulling on a robe and asking who his message had been from.

'Some fucking upgrade offer . . .'

'What?'

'Do I want an upgrade?'

She mumbled something, still half asleep, then turned and walked back into the bedroom.

Brigstocke had sounded only barely more awake when he'd answered the phone. 'Fucking hell, Tom . . .'

'How much surveillance have we got on Martin Cowans?'

'What? Er . . . there's an officer at his home address.'

'What about the clubhouse?'

'Can't we do this later?'

Thorne had heard a woman's voice; a muffled question as a hand was placed over the mouthpiece; children shouting somewhere. The Brigstockes had three kids to get ready for school every morning. 'Russell?'

'Yeah, there's someone at the clubhouse. And I think S&O have got people on the place as well.'

'How many?'

'Fucked if I know. Nobody's breaking into there though, are they? You said it was like Fort Knox.'

'We thought we'd got Skinner's place covered, remember?'

Brigstocke was wide awake now, and irritated. 'We'll talk about this at work, OK? I've got a meeting at nine . . .'

Thorne tossed the CD case back into the boot and climbed into the car. He had already started the engine, giving the BMW's ancient heating system a chance to take the chill off, but the steering wheel was still freezing to the touch and he couldn't be arsed to go back inside for his gloves. He looked at his watch; it was a good time to be driving. All being well he'd get in before seven-thirty.

Pulling the car round into a three-point turn, his eye was caught by movement above him, and he glanced at the tree opposite; at a fat, wet pigeon, perched awkwardly, halfway up. Its movements –

176

the umbrella-shakes of its feathers – made it seem as if it were shivering.

Cold and pissed off; naked as the tree.

He didn't quite have the place to himself, but for half an hour or so he was able to sit in relative peace and quiet. To eat toast and drink tea, and worry about the health and safety of a drug dealing, heavily tattooed gangster. To reflect on a course of action that meant he was the only one who knew Martin Cowans was in immediate danger.

To wonder if it was the stupidest thing he'd ever done.

It was a tough chart to top . . .

From his window, he watched officer after officer coming through the Peel Centre gates. Some he knew well; some he didn't know from Adam; others he'd no more than smiled at when they'd passed on the stairs or in the canteen. Somewhere, there was a police officer who, in league with a friend or colleague, had killed a gang leader and sent an innocent man to prison for it. And who, six years later, according to Marcus Brooks, had battered his partner in crime to death rather than risk seeing their criminal history exposed.

Thorne wanted to find that man. Wanted him every bit as much as he wanted Marcus Brooks.

'Bright and early, Tom,' Karim said, marching straight across to the kettle. He held up the teabags, asking if Thorne was ready for another.

Thorne nodded. 'Plenty of fucking worms to catch.'

He wasn't the only one making an early start. Richard Rawlings was on the phone before Thorne had finished his second mug of tea.

'Any news?'

'The PM confirms that the cause of death was blunt trauma to the head, and puts the time of death somewhere between three and five on Saturday afternoon.'

'You know that's not what I meant.'

'I'm not sure what else I can tell you,' Thorne said.

'Any news about Brooks? Any *progress* . . .?'

Nobody had spoken officially to Rawlings about Marcus Brooks, but Thorne was not surprised that he knew the name of their prime suspect. He could have found out through any number of sources: jungle drums; friends or friends of friends on the squad. Or even Skinner himself, who had probably told him all about the video clip he'd been shown, and what it meant.

And there was another possibility: a simple explanation for Rawlings knowing all about Marcus Brooks; for knowing more about the case than anybody else.

'Is there anything *you* can tell *us*?' Thorne said.

There was a pause. 'Such as?'

'Such as why Marcus Brooks, or anyone else, would want to smash your friend's head in with a hammer.'

'No fucking idea.'

'That's your first "fucking" of the conversation. I'm pleased you're making an effort.'

Thorne was surprised to hear Rawlings laughing. 'Well, I like to start off slowly, build up during the day, you know?'

Afterwards, Thorne failed to return several messages: one from Keith Bannard, the DCI from S&O: another from a CPS clerk, wanting to talk about a bloodstained training shoe that had 'gone walkabout' from an evidence locker; and a rambling message from his Auntie Eileen, who never got round to saying why she was calling. Thorne guessed she wanted to have the 'What are you doing at Christmas?' conversation.

He heard someone outside the door telling Kitson how good she'd been on TV the previous night. When she came in, Thorne added his own congratulations.

'Anything?'

'A few people ringing in to say they saw someone dropping something into the litter bin that could have been a knife, but I don't think that gets us very far. The woman hasn't called back.'

'There's time yet.'

Kitson was something of a closet football fan and they talked about the previous night's European results. Arsenal were now at the bottom of their group having lost at home to Hamburg. Thorne hadn't had a chance to talk to Hendricks yet, who he knew would be devastated.

'Did you see the highlights?' Kitson asked.

'Better things to do,' Thorne said.

He walked around to Colindale station; waited for Brigstocke to emerge from his meeting with the borough commander.

'Sorry I called so early.'

'Why the sudden urgency?' Brigstocke asked.

'No urgency. I just thought we should cover our arses.'

'Like I said on the phone, I think they're covered.'

'It's understandable that we're focusing on the Skinner killing,' Thorne said. 'But there's no reason to presume that Brooks has finished with the Black Dogs.'

'We're not presuming anything.'

'That he shouldn't want to hit them again.'

'No, you're right.'

'You said there are people on the home address *and* the clubhouse?'

They walked into the station's reception area, and out. Began to walk back across to Becke House. The sky was a grey wash, but here and there were glimpses of sun, like streaks of milky flesh seen through thin and frayed material.

Brigstocke smiled as he buttoned his overcoat. 'It's good to know you're taking the welfare of the city's biker gangs so seriously.'

'I understand some of them do a lot of work for charity,' Thorne said.

They crossed the road in front of a Met minivan which had just turned out of the main gates. The driver leaned on his horn and, recognising him as someone he knew, Thorne gave him a friendly finger.

Brigstocke was taller, with a longer stride, but had to jog a step or two to match Thorne's pace. 'Slow down, for fuck's sake.'

'I'm too bloody cold to dawdle,' Thorne lied.

They showed their passes at the Driving School entrance as it was closer, and walked towards Becke House, which rose, less than majestically, brown and grey on the other side of the parade square. They passed the gym, and Brigstocke put a hand on Thorne's arm. 'Listen, I wanted to say sorry.'

'For what?'

'For being a twat.'

'Which particular time?'

Brigstocke looked at the floor as they walked. 'You know there's been something going on.'

'The Dark Side, you mean?'

'Right. I don't want to go into it, OK?'

Thorne had raised it three days before with Nunn. As they'd driven hell for leather towards Skinner's house, Thorne had asked the DPS man what he knew about an investigation into his own team; about the Regulation Nines that appeared to be flying about in Russell Brigstocke's Incident Room. Nunn had been as forthcoming as usual. He said that it was an Internal Investigation Command matter, that his was a separate department, that he couldn't comment in any case. Seeing no point in another 'couldn't' meaning 'don't want to' conversation, Thorne had let it drop.

But he still wanted to know; now more than ever.

'I told you before,' Thorne said. '*If* you want to talk about it . . .'

'Cheers.'

'We can go and get hammered somewhere. Sit and slag the fuckers off.'

Brigstocke nodded. 'It's tempting, but I just wanted to explain why I've been walking around with a face like a smacked arse, that's all.'

'I couldn't tell the difference,' Thorne said.

They walked into Becke House and straight into a waiting lift. They rode up in silence, each staring ahead at his own reflection in the steel doors. Stepping out on the third floor, Thorne made straight for the Incident Room, watching Brigstocke head the other way along the corridor and close his office door.

He loitered for a minute, then went to find Holland. 'How busy are you?'

'Up to my tits in phone-company correspondence and CCTV requisition orders,' Holland said. 'Have you got a better offer?'

Ten minutes later they were arguing about which CD to listen to as Thorne drove towards Southall.

SEVENTEEN

A quick glance at the Police National Computer had revealed not only a couple of fines for shoplifting and a suspended sentence for possession of a Class A drug, but the rather more surprising fact that Martin Cowans' 'old lady' was actually a nice posh girl called Philippa. That she'd been brought up in Guildford and privately educated.

'How the fuck should I know where he is?'

Standing on the doorstep of Martin Cowans' semi, Thorne couldn't help but admire the degree to which the young woman doing the shouting had reinvented herself. There was no hint of anything remotely genteel; not the slightest trace of a 'Pimm's and ponies' accent.

'And why would I tell you? Even if I did fucking know?'

Thorne wondered if her parents had ever met their prospective son-in-law. He imagined two jaws dropping and the hasty redrafting of wills.

'Have you called him on his mobile?' Holland asked.

Bin-bag's girlfriend almost smiled, but caught herself in time. She took the cigarette from her mouth and flicked it past Holland's shoulder on to the path. 'Call him your-fucking-selves,' she said. She tightened the dressing-gown across her black T-shirt. 'I'm going back to bed.'

'Thanks for your help, Pippa,' Thorne said.

Her eyes widened, furious for just a second before she slammed the door.

Holland left a beat, cleared his throat. 'Have we got his mobile number?'

Thorne shrugged. 'I haven't seen it listed anywhere. He didn't give us a business card, did he?'

'Maybe your mate at S&O's got it.'

Thorne owed Keith Bannard a call anyway. He fished out the number as they were walking back towards the patrol car parked opposite the house. He got Bannard's voicemail and left a message.

Coming off the back of twelve hours in the front seat of a Ford Focus, the uniformed officer on surveillance had been a tad surly when Thorne and Holland had first arrived. He seemed cheerier now, having obviously enjoyed watching them get Cowans' front door slammed in their faces.

'Silly bitch,' he said. 'Probably just pissed off because he didn't come home all night.'

Thorne felt a bubble of panic rise and burst in his stomach. 'When did you last see him?'

'He'd already gone out by the time I came on last night. He stays out quite a lot, mind you. Crashes round at other bikers' places, one of the lads was saying.'

Holland looked at Thorne. 'We've got people watching all the known addresses for Black Dogs members. Shouldn't be too hard to track him down.'

The officer in the car grinned, tossed his newspaper into the back seat. 'I reckon he's got a couple of other women on the go, an' all.'

'Jammy sod,' Holland said.

Thinking about the video clip he'd seen a few hours earlier, Thorne wondered how many of those women Martin Cowans had to pay for.

Kitson carried the cassette player through to her office and closed the door. She'd listened to the most recent batch of calls in the Incident

Room, leaning close to the speaker to hear above the chatter; had jabbed at the buttons, pressed REWIND, and listened again to one call in particular.

One that was exciting and confusing in equal measure.

In her office, she played the tape again, studying the transcript of the call as she listened. It was no more than twenty seconds long. Then she went back out and helped herself to the headphones from Andy Stone's iPod, came back and listened one more time, to make sure.

The voice had sounded familiar to Kitson immediately, but not because she'd heard it when the woman had called before. That first time, when she had obviously rung from a mobile on the street, the voice had been competing with the noise of traffic. The words had been muffled; hesitant and choked with nerves.

This time, there was only the sound of her voice. This time, the woman had been braver. Clearer.

'I know who killed Deniz.'

And Kitson recognised the voice. The woman had still not been quite brave enough to mention a name, and Kitson could not be sure she was telling the truth. But she knew for certain who the caller was.

From Cowans' house they drove up on to the main drag and east along the Broadway. The traffic moved slowly through the densely populated half-mile of Asian shops and markets – the Punjabi Bazaar, Rita's Samosa Centre, the Sikh Bridal Gallery – before they turned into a small road that ran alongside the canal and parked just below the bridge.

Thorne got out and walked back up to lean on a low wall a dozen or so feet above the water. To his right, razor-wire coiled along the top of a fence separating the towpath from a huge B&Q warehouse, its windows dull and its red metal siding streaked brown with dirt and rust.

Holland took a pack of ten Marlboro Lights from his pocket. He pushed at the wrapping with a fingernail for a few seconds, then put it back. 'What are we doing here?'

It was a perfectly fair question, and Thorne could do no better than duck it. 'Would you rather be back at the office filling those forms in?'

Dotted along the edge of the black water, overflowing rubbish bags hung from fence-posts every twenty feet or so. The banks were littered with cans and plastic bottles, but Thorne was amazed to see, concentrated in one small spot next to the water, upwards of two dozen swans, gathered as if for a meeting. Most were all white, but a number had darker bills and feathers, seemingly covered in dust. The grass around them was thick with small, white feathers.

It was the sort of surprise that Thorne enjoyed. That London provided now and again.

'One of them went for me when I was a kid,' Holland said. 'Vicious fuckers.'

Thorne moved a few feet along the wall, towards the warehouse. There was a track down to a small area of accessible wasteland, canal-side of the huge metal skips and stacks of wooden pallets. Twenty feet further on, the scrub became the car park of a squat, grey pub; a sign below the flag of St George advertised 'Food and Live Premiership Football'.

He replayed the video in his head.

It was here, or somewhere very like here, that Brooks had hidden, to film Martin Cowans' sordid encounter. Had he followed them? Maybe Brooks had set up Cowans in advance, had paid the hooker himself. Thorne tried to remember the fuzzy image of the man with the woman kneeling in front of him; to picture the outlines of the buildings just visible against the black sky behind them. He stared around in the vain hope of seeing something familiar.

'Are we looking for something?' Holland asked.

Thorne saw only a distant gasometer, and, emerging from a house in the terrace below them, an Asian woman waving a stick, sending a clump of pigeons rising from her front garden.

He wasn't sure what he would have done if he *had* recognised something.

'What's that?' Holland asked, pointing.

Thorne looked down and saw something football-sized and almost round in the water. It bobbed against the black brick, catching the light. 'It's a coconut,' he said. 'Wrapped in plastic.'

'Come again?'

'Some of the local Hindus chuck them in during religious festivals, as a sacrifice. It's the closest they can get to a sacred river.'

'The Grand Union Canal?'

'Well, in theory, the coconuts can float all the way out to sea. Maybe find their way into the Ganges one day.'

'That's fucking ridiculous. They'll be washed up in Southend, if they're lucky.'

'It's just a gesture, Dave.'

Holland shook his head, carried on staring. 'Is it even possible?'

'Nothing wrong with being optimistic,' Thorne said.

Especially when it was just about all you had left . . .

They wandered for a few minutes along the main road, resisting the temptation of the food on offer at the pub, and opting instead for lunch at a Burger King. Thorne felt a twinge of altogether more manageable guilt as they carried Whoppers, fries and onion rings to a table near the window and tucked in.

'Sophie still smelling the fags on you?' Thorne asked.

Holland nodded, grunting through a mouthful of food, but Thorne could see a wariness around his eyes at the mention of his girlfriend's name. She had never been Thorne's biggest fan. He couldn't remember ever falling out with her, had not even met her that many times, but she had some idea that he was the sort of copper she never wanted Holland to turn into. Whatever she might think of him, it was clear to Thorne that the woman only had Holland's best interests at heart. And that she was a pretty good judge of character.

'I bet the baby keeps her busy.'

'Chloe's *three*,' Holland said.

'You know what I mean.'

Holland looked like he hadn't the faintest idea. He went to the toilet, and stopped at the counter on his way back to get them both tea.

'Christ, you'll be thinking about schools any minute.'

186

'Already started, mate.'

'Anywhere decent round your place?'

'Sophie wants to get out of London.' Holland looked down, stirred his tea.

'OK.' Thorne wondered how long that idea had been floating around; if it was more than just an idea. 'You not keen?'

Holland shrugged, certainly not keen on talking about it.

'Well, hopefully she's less pissed off with me these days,' Thorne said. Holland was about to reply, but Thorne stopped him. 'It's fine, I know what she thinks. It doesn't matter.'

'Why "these days"?'

'Well, I'm not leading you into quite so much trouble.' Holland's face darkened a little, so Thorne tried to lighten things, beckoning with a finger across the table. 'Not luring you towards the shadows . . .'

They said nothing else until they got up to leave, when Holland stood waiting for Thorne to get his jacket on, and said: 'What makes you think you were leading me *anywhere*?'

With no further news of any sort, Thorne was tense and jumpy by the end of the day. Unaware of quite how much he needed a drink until it was suggested. He happily joined Stone, Holland and Karim on their way across to The Oak, but when Kitson caught up with him in the pub's car park he let the others go on ahead.

'Where've you been all day?' she asked.

'Trying to stay invisible,' Thorne said. 'Why are you so horribly full of yourself?'

'My mystery woman called again.'

'Told you she would.'

'And she's not a mystery any more . . .'

'Go on then.'

'Harika Kemal.'

Thorne took a second. 'Sedat's *girlfriend*? The one who was in the toilet?' Kitson nodded. Thorne twisted his face into a parody of confusion.

'Fuck knows,' Kitson said. 'I'm bringing her in for a chat tomorrow and we'll find out.'

'Sounds like something to celebrate, though.'

'God, yes.' They walked towards the entrance. 'What about you?'

'Let's stick with good news . . .'

Inside, The Oak was busy for a midweek evening with the noisiest and smokiest pockets indicating the presence of the men and women from the Peel Centre and Colindale, the majority of the pub's regular clientele. The 'traditional' atmosphere and drab decor had remained unchanged for as long as Thorne could remember, thanks to a land-lord who now understood that his customers' tastes did not run far beyond beer and simple pub grub. He had occasionally tried to ring the changes, but usually with little success. A quiz night had ended in a brawl. Two weeks earlier there had been a karaoke evening in the back bar, but two rat-arsed constables caterwauling their way through 'I Fought the Law' had forced several of the most hardened drinkers to make an early night of it.

Thorne and Kitson got in their drinks and joined Holland and the others. They congratulated Kitson on the break in her case, wished her luck with her interview, but nobody raised a glass just yet. That would have to wait until she'd made an arrest.

'What's it been, then?' Kitson said. 'Four, five days, since the last message from Brooks?'

Thorne took a healthy gulp of beer. 'Five. The Skinner clip.'

'That might be the lot. He's got a couple of the bikers, a copper he thinks is responsible for fitting him up. Maybe he's called it a day.'

'Maybe . . .'

'How much revenge can anyone want?'

'Depends how much they've suffered.'

'It's not going to bring back his girlfriend, is it? Or his kid.'

'Imagine they were your kids,' Thorne said.

When Brigstocke arrived, the group shuffled around the table to make room, and began to let off steam. They joked about a recent court case which had seen a man prosecuted, having taken payment from a mentally disturbed woman in return for promising to kill her, and then failing to honour the contract.

Karim said it was a waste of money, that somebody in the CPS needed shooting. Stone wondered, while they were on the subject, how much it was costing to play nursemaid to a bunch of 'hairy-arsed drug dealers'. Holland said that if they really wanted to talk about waste, they should do something about the time and energy he'd had to spend over the past two days filling in mandates and fucking requisition forms. That it was small wonder they weren't solving more cases . . .

Stone raised his glass. 'Here's your answer, matey. They've done research proving that alcohol – in moderation, *obviously* – can help you think more clearly. I swear. They should just let us all have a drink or two during the day.' There was laughter, a couple of small cheers from around the table. 'I'm telling you . . . stick a beer barrel in the Incident Room, a few optics by the coffee machine, and watch the clear-up rates go through the fucking roof.'

Next to him, Thorne felt Kitson jump when Brigstocke banged his glass down on the table. 'Don't talk like a cunt, Andy. Fuck's sake . . .'

Everyone watched, dumbstruck, as Brigstocke stood up and stalked away towards the bar. Stone sniggered awkwardly, Karim raised his eyebrows at Holland, and the others shrugged or stared into their drinks.

Thorne got up to follow Brigstocke, but thought better of it halfway there, and made for the exit instead. Outside, in the doorway, he used his prepay phone to call Louise. Told her he was having just the one more, and that he wouldn't be back too late.

The bell had rung half an hour earlier to clear out the civilians, and Thorne had decided that one more drink couldn't hurt. He guessed Louise would be in bed now anyway; hoped she wouldn't think he was avoiding her, after what had happened the night before.

Was he avoiding her?

Kitson had left well before last orders. She wanted to say goodnight to her kids, and sort out the next day's interview with Harika Kemal. Brigstocke was ensconced in a corner with Stone. Thorne hoped everything was OK, but the conversation looked pretty animated. He had drunk three pints of Guinness but had taken them slowly, in halves. He knew he'd be OK to drive home.

He heard his mobile ringing, reached for his jacket, dug around, but missed the call. He was looking at the details when it rang again in his hand: Bannard.

'You got Cowans' mobile number for me?' Thorne asked.

'I don't think that phone's working any more,' Bannard said. 'It got a bit wet . . .'

Thorne listened, and when the call was finished, he walked across to the bar. Holland was already there, reaching for a fresh pint. 'They found Martin Cowans,' he said. 'Pulled him out of the canal, a few miles up from where we were this morning.'

'Fuck.' Holland pushed himself away from the bar. 'Are we on?'

Thorne was already turning for the door. 'Poor sod didn't even make it as far as the coconuts,' he said.

Hello babe,

Am I in trouble? I feel guilty enough . . .

I could always tell, the second I'd walked through the door, when I'd pissed you off about something. You had that look, you know? The one that told me I was in the shit, but wanted me to start guessing exactly what it was I'd done wrong.

Seriously, I do feel strange about last night, about what I felt, watching that twisted little fucker. What he was getting. It sounds like something you'd hear someone say in one of those soap operas you always had on, but afterwards, I felt dirty for what I'd been thinking. Really fucking hated myself . . . still feel like I let you down.

Like it was disrespectful, I don't know, to your memory, or something.

I don't think you'd really believe that. I reckon you'd probably think there was something wrong with me if I hadn't been turned on watching that. That maybe I'd gone queer in prison or whatever.

Anyway, while it was happening, it was only ever you I was thinking about.

It's always you . . .

Walked a long way again tonight, seven or eight miles maybe, thinking all this crap through and trying to work out what to write. I suppose what's odd is that I can feel you and Robbie with me, which is fucking fantastic, but there's things I don't want you to see. Stuff that's . . . not fit, you know?

And I feel bad because you do see it, and there's that thing in your

191

voice when you don't approve, like when I'd had a few too many. I can hear you trying to explain to Robbie about me, about some of the things I'm doing.

And then there's other times, the worst times, when what I've got of you is nowhere near enough. When all I can think of is how much better everything could be, if we could just have a few more minutes. Half a fucking hour.

Like knowing, if you were there to hold me, that I might be able to sleep.

I'll take what there is, don't get me wrong. Why wouldn't I? Having you there how you are, feeling you there, is the best thing I've got, and I know I'd be totally lost without it.

There'd be less of me left than you . . .

Gone round the houses same as usual, I know, but forgive me?

Marcus xxx

EIGHTEEN

The area bordering the canal towards Greenford was somewhat different to the one Thorne and Holland had seen earlier. The towpath was cleaner and wider; designated, according to a sign, as part of something called the Hillingdon Trail. On one side, the bank sloped up to a row of sleek, modern houses. Thorne could see residents behind many of the full-length windows, standing in dressing-gowns and staring down on the action at the waterside below.

It was a complicated set-up: lights, noise, a tent around the body. With the added pleasures for those working of muck and drizzle.

From a manning point of view, the timing presented certain 'logistical dilemmas'. The Homicide Assessment Team had been and gone, having passed the job to the on-call Murder Team. As part of an ongoing investigation, however, it was now being handed back to Russell Brigstocke's MIT, several of whom had had to sober up very bloody quickly.

'Coffee's good,' Holland had said. 'But a body does it quicker every time . . .'

This particular body had been spotted a couple of hours earlier, but had only been out of the water fifteen minutes or so by the time

Thorne arrived. It had been wedged in tight between the bank and a narrowboat which was moored in front of the houses. Nothing could be done until the owner had been traced and the boat moved so that the body could be extracted.

Now it was laid out on the towpath, brown water running off the plastic sheeting beneath it.

Hendricks was already busy, as were a team of frustrated SOCOs, doing their best to preserve a scene that was compromised at best; the slimy bank dotted with cigarette ends and dog-shit, and the towpath a muddy confusion of footprints.

DCI Keith Bannard stared down the length of the canal, then turned and looked in the other direction. 'Your man can't have killed him too far away,' he said, after he'd introduced himself.

Thorne had been right to think that the S&O man's accent belied something grittier. He was tall and shithouse-solid. He had a shock of greying, curly hair, with more sprouting from the neck of his white shirt. His face was weathered and fleshy, with watery eyes that all but disappeared when he smiled.

'Doesn't seem bothered about hiding the bodies, does he?' Bannard continued. 'So we can assume he dumped Cowans more or less where he killed him.'

'Sounds reasonable.'

'So, what the fuck was Bin-bag doing by the canal? Night-fishing?'

Thorne said nothing.

Whistling something to himself, Bannard started to stroll away down the towpath. Thorne followed. They walked for fifty yards or so and stopped under a low bridge. The banks and the water were black where they weren't lit by orange lights fixed to the walls on either side.

'Very artistic,' Bannard said. He nodded towards a bizarre, three-dimensional mural on the far wall: a heron, a line of ducks, starfish and leaping rabbits, all created from pieces of coloured glass and shards of pottery.

Thorne presumed it was there for the benefit of those whose narrowboats passed beneath the bridge. Guessed it had also given the kids something nice to look at while they'd been spraying their graffiti tags on every spare inch of wall around it.

'Well, I've had a good chat with your guvnor.'

'That's nice,' Thorne said.

Bannard looked happy. 'I think we can safely say none of this is gang-related, so I can probably get out of your way now.'

'Whatever you think.'

'That's right. Try not to let on how delighted you are.'

'Doing you a favour this, I would have thought.'

'A few less arseholes like Martin Cowans does everyone a favour, don't you reckon? But I can't see it doing a lot for my workload, if that's what you mean.'

Their voices echoed under the bridge. As Bannard spoke, he illustrated his words with elaborate gestures, and Thorne had trouble keeping his eyes off the man's hands. They were enormous. His own had been virtually lost inside one of Bannard's when they'd met over the body.

'Will that be it for the Black Dogs, then?' Thorne asked.

Bannard shook his head. 'Shouldn't think so.'

'Three of the longest-serving members gone. That must shake things up, surely?'

'They'll reorganise, bring other members through the ranks. There'll be a new leadership sorted by tomorrow afternoon.'

'Same as happened when Cowans took over from Simon Tipper.'

'Right.'

They stopped, hearing movement on the far side of the water, stared into one of the pools of shadow opposite, but could see nothing. 'Who might have wanted Simon Tipper out of the way six years ago?'

Bannard was about to light a cigarette. He stared across at Thorne for a few seconds; sounded almost amused when he finally replied. 'Tipper was killed by Marcus Brooks, when he caught him turning his house over. That's what the woman who nicked him told you, right? Lilley?'

'That's what she told me.'

Bannard lit his cigarette. 'Which, as far as I'm aware, is why all this shit's happening in the first place. Yes?'

'Hypothetically, then,' Thorne said. 'Who would have been happy about it?'

'Christ, *hypothetically* it could have been anyone. One of the other biker gangs, most likely. One of his own lot who didn't think he was getting a fair shake. Someone whose bike he'd borrowed without asking. A bloke whose girlfriend he'd shafted . . .'

'The Black Dogs? The other gangs? Many of them have coppers on the payroll?'

Bannard grinned, hissed smoke through his teeth. 'You doing a spot of DPS work on the side, Inspector?'

Thorne dropped his voice, mock-conspiratorial. 'Every little helps, doesn't it?'

'Listen, all these gangs try to buy themselves an edge,' Bannard said. 'Unless they're stupid, they know it's a good investment, long term.' He started to whistle again; louder this time, enjoying the echo. He took two fast drags on his cigarette, then flicked it into the water.

Back at the crime scene, the body was being prepared for removal to the mortuary, and Brigstocke was already talking about how they'd be proceeding, and how quickly, the next morning. They would conduct a house-to-house, early, before any of the residents had left for work. All members of the Black Dogs who may have seen or spoken to the victim would also be interviewed, to piece together a picture of Martin Cowans' movements. They'd request footage from the two CCTV cameras mounted on lamp-posts near by.

Thorne listened, and knew it was all a perfectly proper and well-thought-out waste of time.

With what he knew, he considered other things they might do if he had not painted himself, and the whole investigation, into a dark corner. They could try to trace the hooker. It couldn't be that difficult. She might have spotted something, and was almost certainly the last person, bar Marcus Brooks, to have seen Martin Cowans alive.

But that wouldn't happen – couldn't – not while Thorne kept his information to himself.

He kept on telling himself it didn't matter. They knew who the killer was, after all. The details might matter later, but right now, knowing exactly how Brooks had gone about this latest murder wasn't likely to help catch him.

'We're concentrating on the Premiership this year anyway. Champions League doesn't matter.'

Thorne turned round. 'You're gutted. Admit it.'

'We'll put all our effort into stuffing you lot when we come to your place in a fortnight,' Hendricks said.

They watched as the body was carried past.

'Time of death would be good,' Thorne said.

'I'd like to get naked with Justin Timberlake, but, you know . . .'

'Approximately?'

Hendricks watched the stretcher-bearers trying to keep the body level as they struggled up the grass bank. 'He'd been in the water a good while. Plenty of bloating. Twenty-four hours, I reckon; maybe a bit more.'

'So, late last night?'

'Probably some time yesterday evening.'

Thorne knew that the worry had been for himself, for his own career, rather than for the man who had authorised the murders of a young woman and her son. But all the same, he felt the anxiety lift in a rush: Cowans had been dead by the time he'd received the message. There was nothing Thorne could have done to save him.

'That any use to you?' Hendricks asked.

'Yeah, thanks.' But the relief was short-lived. There had been no pattern to the sending of the messages: Brooks had waited over a week before sending the image of Tucker; but he had sent the picture of Hodson from the hospital moments after he'd killed him; then the clip of Skinner had arrived the day before his murder. Brooks would probably do it differently next time, too, and Thorne knew that he might not be so lucky.

Andy Stone jogged across to join them, looking thoroughly pleased with himself. 'Well, at least we know Cowans wasn't killed by a woman,' he said.

Thorne could see, by Stone's expression, that it was a set-up. He raised his eyebrows at Hendricks. 'Yeah, go on then . . .'

Stone threw it away nicely. 'Well, when was the last time any woman you know took out a bin-bag?'

It was a good joke, and got an appropriate response. Thorne laughed harder than he might have done normally, seizing on the chance.

It was a straightforward journey back, west to Hanger Lane, straight into town along the A40. He would cut down through Knightsbridge and Belgravia to Louise's place in Pimlico. With Holland needing to get home to Elephant and Castle, no more than ten minutes further on at this hour, Thorne offered to drop him off first.

The roads were almost deserted and the rain had stopped. Watching for the cameras, easing off when he needed to, Thorne drove quickly past Ealing golf course and the Hoover factory. He turned the radio down, spoke as if it were the middle of a conversation they'd been having. 'Brooks was just unlucky. He was an ideal candidate when it came to setting someone up for Tipper's murder. The fall-guy.'

'For Skinner?'

'For Skinner, almost certainly, and whoever his mate is: "Jennings" or "Squire". Why did they want Tipper dead, though?'

'Maybe they were being paid by another gang. Why bother paying someone to do it, when you've got a couple of tame coppers who can get it organised for you?'

Thorne nodded. 'What if it was the Black Dogs they were working for?'

Holland considered it. 'Someone in Tipper's own gang wanted shot of him?'

'Possibly,' Thorne said. 'Or these two coppers just wanted rid of him themselves. Maybe Tipper was getting greedy. Not paying them enough, threatening to expose them or whatever.'

The idea struck a chord with Holland, who turned to face Thorne. 'The crime report said the place was completely trashed, and Brooks always said that the two coppers had told him to take "paperwork". If they *were* on Tipper's payroll, maybe there were records of bribes, or photos or something. Stuff they needed back.' He nodded as though telling himself that he'd had worse ideas.

Thorne saw that it made good sense and said as much to Holland. He pushed the car on past Wormwood Scrubs, brooding on their left, then across the flyover at White City. He veered slightly, to avoid taking the wheels over something wet and flattened in the middle lane. A fox or a cat . . .

'What if Skinner was *still* working for the Black Dogs?' Holland said.

It was something Thorne had started to wonder himself. If Skinner and his partner *had* killed Tipper, they might have struck up a new and improved deal with his successor – Martin Cowans. If that was the case, had they known about the plan to exact a terrible revenge on Marcus Brooks? It had been hard to tell much from talking to Skinner because he'd been too busy lying about knowing Marcus Brooks at all.

All the same, Thorne had sensed when they had spoken that Skinner was scared. That Brooks' name was one he hadn't thought about in a long time.

When Thorne dropped Holland off, the DS mumbled something about what he'd said in the Burger King at lunchtime; about how he hadn't meant it to sound so aggressive. Thorne mumbled something back about how it didn't matter.

It was after three when Thorne arrived at the flat in Pimlico. Louise was dead to the world, but Thorne, despite the hour and the day he'd had, felt strangely wide awake. Louise's laptop was sitting open on a desk in the corner of the sitting room. He toyed with logging on and playing some poker, but settled in the end for tea and some low-volume Hank Williams. He had brought a selection of CDs across a few weeks before. Williams, Cash and a couple of newer bands. Had lined them up on a separate shelf as a small, alphabetically arranged alternative to the David Gray and Diana Krall in Louise's collection.

While Hank complained about a world he would never get out of alive, Thorne sat flicking through one of Louise's magazines. He ran over their conversation in bed the night before. The nervous whispering. He thought about Kitson leaving the pub so that she could say goodnight to her kids, and Brigstocke trying to get three of them ready for school before work every morning, and decided that he was probably not cut out to be a father.

It had been Thorne's mum who had done the shouting when he'd been a kid. Who'd thrown a hairbrush with painful accuracy when he'd grown too big to chase. As far as he could remember, his father had always been patient, and though he was turning into his old man in all sorts of ways he wasn't grateful for, Thorne didn't think he'd inherited the tolerance.

He saw young white boys with bum-fluff, in hoodies and bling, talking like rap stars and swearing at shop assistants. He saw pre-pubescent girls scowling in belly tops. He saw kids dropping litter, and barging onto buses, and talking on their phones in the cinema. And he felt like grabbing the nearest hairbrush.

Definitely not cut out for it . . .

When his prepay started to beep and buzz on the table, Thorne jumped up and rushed across to grab it before the noise woke Louise.

It was a text message from Marcus Brooks:

if u r awake, maybe u r as messed up as me. or maybe I'm just keeping u busy, in which case, sorry. just think about the overtime though.

Thorne clicked on REPLY. Typed in: *I'm here.*

Sent the message, and waited.

NINETEEN

Thorne knew that, as far as public perception went, it was all horribly simple. Certainly, for the victims of crime, and for the relatives of the dead, it was cut and dried. If police caught a killer they'd done a good job. If they didn't, they'd fucked up. But few understood or appreciated the importance of luck.

Good and bad. Blind . . .

The bad luck you lived with, but the good you grabbed with both hands and tried to hold on to. It had played a major part in putting Sutcliffe away, and Shipman. And when beaming chief constables stood before the cameras and talked about a 'job well done', there was every chance they were inwardly thanking God, or whatever came closest, for a healthy portion of good fortune. Were praying for more of the same next time.

Following the discovery of Skinner's body, the press office had released a story for inclusion in the late edition of Monday's *Standard*. It had been deliberately low key: no mad, staring eyes or lurid 'Cop-killer Sought' headlines. Just a couple of columns on an inside page: a picture of Marcus Brooks; a few lines explaining that this man, whom police were looking for in connection with an 'ongoing inquiry', may well have changed his appearance since the photograph had been taken; the assertion, *italicised*, that he was considered to be dangerous and must not be approached.

The calls had trickled in over the next two days: names; sightings; at least two people claiming that *they* were Marcus Brooks. All reports were followed up, with particular attention paid to any sightings in the west London area, and overnight a call had come in that looked very much like a solid lead.

Something to be grabbed with both hands.

The caller worked as a night-shift security guard at the London Ark – the spectacular copper and glass office complex in the centre of Hammersmith. He'd reported that on two separate occasions, coming home from work at just before 6 a.m., he'd seen an individual who might have been the man he'd read about in the *Standard* article. The man had been going into a house opposite his own. They had even nodded to one another the second time their paths had crossed.

The security guard lived three streets away from one of the confirmed cell-sites.

The house he identified was divided into three flats, and while it was being watched, front and back, the landlord was traced and questioned at his home by Andy Stone and another officer. It quickly emerged that the man who may have been Marcus Brooks was the tenant of the one-bedroom flat on the top floor. He had moved into the flat two weeks before, giving the name Robert Georgiou, and had paid three months' rent in advance, in cash. When questioned, the landlord told Stone that, yes, thinking about it, he had thought his new tenant was a little odd. 'Quiet, you know? Intense.' But the man had said something about being separated from his wife, so the landlord had put it down to that and left him alone.

'We all need privacy sometimes,' he had said to Stone.

Not to mention cash, Thorne had thought, when Stone had reported back to him.

They'd set up an observation post in a house opposite at 7 a.m., and watched the flat for four hours. An armed unit had been put on standby near by. Adjacent houses had been evacuated as quickly and discreetly as possible.

With no sign of movement, and reliable intelligence that the man had been seen entering the building just before 6 a.m., the assumption that the target was inside, and probably asleep, became official just before midday.

Brigstocke conferred with his commander, then gave the order to go in.

Kitson leaned a little closer to the twin-CD recorder that was built into the wall of the interview room. There was no need, as the microphones were highly sensitive, but it was an automatic movement; like ducking beneath the blades of a helicopter.

'Miss Kemal has once again declined the offer of legal representation.'

The young woman sitting in the chair opposite frowned and tugged at her hair. 'I don't need anyone, do I? I'm not in any trouble.' Her voice was soft, with no more than a hint of a London accent.

'I don't think so,' Kitson said.

'So . . .' She shrugged.

'It's just procedure, Harika. Not a problem.'

The girl was in her early twenties, an accountancy student at North London University. Kitson could see how attractive she was; could see it in Stone's reaction when they'd collected her from the foyer of Colindale station. He had not seen her before; had not been present when Harika Kemal had initially been questioned, on the night Deniz Sedat had been stabbed to death. She had not been at her best then, anyway.

She had green eyes with absurdly long lashes, and brown hair streaked with honey-coloured highlights. Kitson guessed these were probably not the features Stone had noticed first.

'We need to know why you called,' Kitson said.

The girl said nothing.

'*Twice*,' Stone said.

'Look, we know you're scared.' As she spoke, Kitson realised that she was using the same tone she used with her kids when they didn't want to go to the dentist or revise for an exam. 'I could hear it in your voice, and I swear we'll do everything we can to make sure you have nothing to be scared about.'

'I didn't call anybody.'

'Harika, you said you knew who had killed Deniz. We have recordings of those phone calls.'

'Not from me.'

'I recognised your voice.'

'You've made a mistake.'

'We can trace the call,' Stone said.

Kitson could see the dilemma in the girl's eyes. Could see she wanted to tell Stone that he was talking rubbish, but was unable to. She had withheld her number on both occasions but dare not admit it. Instead, she dropped her gaze to the tabletop; picked at its edge with a plum-coloured fingernail.

'We can, if we need to,' Kitson said. 'It's a pain in the arse when a number's been withheld, and obviously we'd like you to save us the trouble, but we *can* do it.'

Stone turned on the charm, such as it was. 'Come on, help us out, Harika. If you know something, if you know who was responsible for killing Deniz, don't you owe it to him to tell us?'

'It's a big deal, I know,' Kitson said. 'But there's no need to be scared. We'll take care of everything.'

When she finally looked up, the girl's eyes were wide and wet. 'I thought I knew something, but I didn't.' She managed to produce a wobbly smile. 'That's all. Stupid . . .'

'Fine, but why don't you let us check it out?' Kitson said. 'If you're wrong, there's no harm done, is there?'

Harika shook her head: twisted fingers into her hair.

'There are two types of people who make these kinds of calls,' Stone said, suddenly harder. 'Some people really want to help. They tell us what they know, and if we follow it up and it comes to nothing, it doesn't

204

matter, because that's part of the job.' The girl shook her head, held up a hand. 'But then there's always a few who like to mess us about. Who send us in the wrong direction, or make out they know stuff when they don't, and when you're trying to catch a murderer that can cost lives. So, I really hope you're not wasting our time.'

Stone's aggression did nothing but bring out something similar in the girl. She blinked away the tears and stared back at him. 'Well, why don't we all stop wasting time, then? I'm under no obligation to stay here, am I?'

She pushed back her chair, but Kitson leaned across and took hold of her arm. 'It was easier on the end of a phone,' she said. 'I can understand that, the anonymity. But this is every bit as confidential, Harika, *really*. If you know, even if you *think* you know, just tell us.' Kitson looked hard, trying to reach whatever it was that had prompted the young woman to pick up the phone in the first place. 'Just give us a name . . .'

The only sound for fifteen seconds was the faint hum of the recording equipment, and the creak of the girl's short leather jacket as she twisted in her chair. She shook her head, kept shaking it. Whispered: 'I can't.'

They sat in silence for a minute more, but it was clear they would get nothing else out of the girl for the time being. Stone looked as though he could happily have stared at Harika Kemal for a good deal longer, but Kitson had better things to do.

Cheap flats anywhere in central London were hard to come by, but all the same, Thorne could see why the owner of this particular property would not have been snowed under with prospective tenants. Why he'd have been happy enough to pocket the cash and not ask too many questions.

Within shouting distance of the Talgarth flyover, the house stood at the grimmer end of an undistinguished terrace. The top-floor flat – one room and a toilet wedged into the eaves – looked out over the roof of Charing Cross Hospital from the front, with the green and grey of

Hammersmith Cemetery the marginally more appealing view from the Velux window at the back.

'No wonder Brooks is in a bad mood,' Holland said.

Pretty much every expense had been spared to create a uniquely desperate atmosphere: three different patterns of carpet in one room; a two-bar electric death-trap mounted on one wall; a shit-streaked lavatory bowl, and a pink plastic shower tray that appeared to match.

'Jesus.'

'I'm surprised he didn't top *himself.*'

'When we've got a minute, can we come back and nick the thieving fucker that rented this place out . . .?'

Thorne walked very slowly from the bed to a chest of drawers. He wasn't in any hurry, of course, was keen to miss nothing, but he could-n't have moved much quicker if his life depended on it. He'd had no more than three hours' sleep the night before. Three hours between drifting away on the sofa with one handset clutched to his chest and being woken by the ringing of the other, with news of the sighting in Hammersmith.

Louise had wandered into her living room just before he'd left, bewildered to see him fully dressed. He'd told her about the body being found the night before. About having to rush off again.

'I'm really not trying to avoid you,' he'd said, laughing.

She hadn't seen the funny side. 'Nobody said you were.'

As Thorne reached for the handle on the top drawer, he was called across to the far end of the room. A Trainee DC whose name he could never remember had discovered a Tupperware box stuffed with cash underneath a table. As Thorne took the box, he could feel its worn edges through the thin gloves. He flicked through the bundle of notes, then passed it across to the exhibits officer. While he was there, the officer carefully bagged up ballpoint pens, scraps of paper and a wrap of rolling tobacco from the cracked Formica surface of the table. It looked to Thorne as though it had been borrowed from a greasy spoon.

'There's a decent amount there,' the TDC said. 'All fifties and twen-ties, by the look of it.'

Thorne called Brigstocke in from the bathroom. They had found clothes scattered about, and personal items on a shelf above the sink. Seeing the cash, though, Brigstocke nodded, as though its discovery had confirmed what he was already thinking. 'Well, either he left in a hell of a hurry or he's coming back,' he said. 'We should get what we can as quickly as possible and get out. Put some surveillance at either end of the street, just in case.'

A crime scene unit never got out of anywhere quite as quickly as they went in, but Thorne suspected that they would be wasting their time anyway. 'Yeah, worth a try,' he said. He walked back to the chest of drawers, took a step past it and spent a few seconds at the dirty window. Remembering what had happened, how he'd felt in the garden at Skinner's place, he instinctively glanced down at the street and across to the houses opposite, as though Marcus Brooks might be watching them from somewhere.

The drawer refused to slide out easily, and Thorne had to kneel down and wrench it an inch or so at a time. The TDC offered a helping hand and snorted when he looked down and saw what was inside. 'Bugger me, he could open his own shop.'

There were perhaps a dozen assorted handsets. Spare batteries and chargers. SIM cards lying loose, in blister packs or mounted, unused, on plastic cards.

'He doesn't have anything else,' Thorne said. 'What he's doing is everything to him.' He nudged some of the hardware to one side with a gloved finger. 'He's spent time putting it all together.'

'I hope there isn't one of those for each message he's planning to send.'

Thorne knew the young TDC was joking, but caught his breath nonetheless; poking around among the Nokias and Samsungs, as if they were knives or handguns. He remembered what Kitson had said in the pub.

'*How much revenge can anyone want?*'

He reached for something at the back of the drawer and pulled out a sheaf of papers, bound with several elastic bands. He read the first page, then gently turned back the corner to look at the second.

207

The TDC was trying his best to read over Thorne's shoulder. 'What you got, old love letters?'

'Not old,' Thorne said, eventually. Now he knew for certain that Brooks hadn't gone anywhere; that if they had missed him, it could not have been by very much. He beckoned the exhibits officer over and handed the letters across. 'I want copies of those as soon as,' he said.

'You want what?'

Thorne repeated the request, his words lost the first time beneath those of Russell Brigstocke, who was walking up and down the room, clapping his hands and urging everyone to get a move on.

Brooks stood with half a dozen others at the end of the road, watching the comings and goings.

As soon as he'd seen the copper waving cars on, seen the tape strung between lamp-posts and the 'Diversion' sign, he'd known that something was up. He'd parked a few roads down and walked back to see what was happening.

'There's enough of them,' the man next to him said. 'Must be pretty serious.'

A woman behind him leaned forward. 'Someone told me they saw coppers with machine-guns.'

He'd got back to the flat around six that morning, shaved and got changed, then headed out again straight away. There had been no point trying to sleep, he knew that, and with business on the other side of the river, he'd wanted to beat the traffic.

How had they found him? How close had they come to ending it all? He looked up at the window to the flat and found himself wondering if Tom Thorne was in there.

Thought about the text messages the night before.

Losing the flat was annoying, but it wasn't the end of the world.

There were people he could count on to find him somewhere to crash until all this was over. That wouldn't be a problem. Same thing with the cash: he was still owed plenty of favours. He could get himself some new clothes, a few new phones, whatever else he needed.

This wasn't going to hold anything up.

He turned and walked back towards the car. Left the woman moaning about getting back into her house, needing to cook the kids' tea.

The letters were the only thing that really mattered, of course. But all he'd lost were the bits of paper. Ink and scraps.

Every word was in his head.

TWENTY

It was like being stone-cold sober when everyone around you was three sheets to the wind.

The breakthrough in finding Brooks' flat had lifted everyone's mood, and back at Becke House Brigstocke and the rest of the team went about their business with a new enthusiasm, as though an imminent arrest were now a foregone conclusion. But Thorne felt as though he were watching it all from the outside, unable to share in the excitement, knowing that the isolation was of nobody's making but his own.

It wasn't as though he hadn't fucked up before, but he couldn't remember ever being this far out of his depth, with no other option than to keep kicking away from the shore.

Brigstocke led a briefing at four o'clock.

While most of the team had been busy in Hammersmith, others had followed up on the discovery of Cowans' body the night before. Interviews with residents of the canal-side flats had so far proved unproductive, and the CCTV cameras had contained nothing but footage of a late-night drinker reeling around on the bank. The conclusion was that Cowans had been dumped in another part of the canal, near to where they'd found his van shortly after finding him. That his body had drifted and remained trapped behind the narrow-boat for more than twenty-four hours until it had been discovered. A preliminary PM report indicated that Cowans had been killed by several blows to the head, in the same way as Tucker and Skinner.

The lack of progress on this front made the discovery in Hammersmith all the more important.

'Obviously, we've yet to examine all the evidence taken from the house,' Brigstocke said. 'But by tomorrow morning, I reckon we're going to have a decent number of leads to chase. We took a lot of stuff out of there.'

Thorne stood off to one side. It was possible that Brigstocke was right to be as bullish as he was. That they might get to Marcus Brooks quickly, before Thorne received any more messages. Thorne might still have some awkward questions to answer, but it would probably be the best outcome for everyone, himself included.

Whether the second copper – the man indirectly responsible for the deaths of Angela Georgiou and her son; the man who had probably killed both Tipper and Skinner – would ever be caught was another matter.

One that troubled Thorne deeply.

'We took a notebook away which we're hoping will be significant,' Brigstocke said. 'There are a couple of phone numbers scribbled in there which we'll be chasing up.'

Thorne's stomach clenched. He wondered if the number he'd texted to Brooks was one of them; if he'd be answering those awkward questions sooner rather than later. He stared out at the ranks gathered in the briefing room and hoped the worry wasn't showing on his face.

Whatever Brigstocke's problems were, he was showing no signs of them. In fact, he seemed newly focused; up for it. 'You've all got copies of the E-fit which our helpful security guard came up with, and which has gone out to the press overnight. This is what Brooks looks like now.'

Thorne stared at the picture. Marcus Brooks had cut his hair very short and his face was thinner than it had been when he went into prison. A very different man, in every sense.

Brigstocke continued: 'The security guard also reckons that Brooks might be driving a dark blue or black Ford Mondeo. An old one. It was parked outside the house several times and we certainly can't trace it to anyone living in the street. It's only a vague description, but it's something we need to be aware of.'

Holland stuck a hand up. 'Presuming it was bought for cash, we could start looking at the local used-car dealers.'

'Got to be worth a shot,' Brigstocke said. 'Let's check out the back copies of *Loot* and *Auto Trader* while we're at it. We need a registration number.' He turned to Thorne. 'Anything to add, Tom?'

All sorts of things, Thorne thought, but instead he just echoed the DCI's positive message. Said that they were getting close, and that they wouldn't have a better chance of a result than they did at that moment. He assured them that the man they were after would try to kill again; reminded them that it didn't matter who he was targeting. Whether it was a copper or a biker or a little old lady, they needed to catch Marcus Brooks before there was another victim.

Brigstocke stepped forward again. 'We've worked a lot of hours over the last few days and most of you are fucked, I know. So anyone who isn't on a late one tonight, stay out of the pub, OK? Go home, get eight hours, then get yourselves in here first thing and put this to bed. Then we can all go back to a few nice easy domestics and drug shootings.'

With the briefing over, the assembled officers scattered fast, moving back to phones and computers. There was a good deal of upbeat hubbub. Someone shouted, 'Come on, let's fucking have it.'

Thorne watched the inquiry shifting up a gear.

Stone-cold sober . . .

Later, Brigstocke called Thorne and Kitson into his office.

'We need to get something out of today,' he said. 'There was no message before he killed Cowans, so it looks like he's decided to stop making things so easy for us.'

Kitson nudged Thorne. 'Or maybe he's just gone off Tom.'

Thorne summoned a smile, or something close to it.

'Maybe he thinks he's cleared his debt,' she said. 'The whole message thing was just for Nicklin's benefit, right? Doesn't mean Brooks has to keep doing it.'

Brigstocke agreed that it made sense. 'Any luck with Sedat's girlfriend earlier?'

'I was just writing it up,' Kitson said. 'A big, fat "fuck all", I'm afraid.'

'Could be there's fuck all to get.'

'She might just want some attention,' Thorne suggested.

'I'm going to have another crack at her tomorrow.' Kitson looked as determined as Brigstocke had done at the briefing. 'She's scared, that's all. Maybe she's scared of whoever killed Sedat, because I think she knows who that is.'

'Get it out of her then,' Brigstocke said. 'See if we can get both these jobs off the books by the end of the week.'

Kitson and Thorne walked slowly back down the corridor towards their office.

'He seems happier,' Thorne said.

'*Seems* . . .'

'Maybe whatever it was has gone away.'

'Since when do the DPS "go away"?'

'Serious, you reckon?'

'That's the thing with them,' Kitson said. 'You never know. He might have lost it and battered someone in an interview room or he might have nicked some paper clips. They still have the same look on their faces.'

They stopped at the door and Thorne offered to go and get them both coffee.

'You OK?' Kitson asked.

'Like he said at the briefing. Fucked.'

'Well, go and have a night in with Louise. Get your end away and forget about it until tomorrow.'

Thorne seriously doubted he would be doing both. 'Listen, if Sedat's girlfriend *does* know something, I'm sure you'll get it.'

'I'm going to give it a go.'

'Take it easy with her, though. Talk to her somewhere she's more relaxed. Everyone's scared in the bin, even if they've got no reason to be.' Kitson just nodded. 'Sorry,' Thorne said. 'I'm not trying to tell you how to handle it.'

'That's fine,' Kitson said. 'I'll take any advice you've got. As long as you remember to take mine.'

Thorne went to fetch the coffees, thinking about how easy it was to stick your oar in, to be objective, when it wasn't your own case. Not that he felt like the Brooks case was his any more. Not his to *work*, at any rate.

Walking across to the kettle, he glanced at the whiteboard; at the job mapped out in numbers, names and black lines; times of death and photographs of wounds. He almost expected to see his own name right next to those of the dead and the prime suspect. In the middle of the board, among the list of those central to the inquiry, instead of scribbled in capitals at the top.

When Thorne had called Louise to say that he wouldn't be back late, and to ask what time she was likely to get away, they'd talked about going to see a movie. She'd seemed in a good mood, certainly relative to the one she'd been in at half past six that morning. They'd argued good-naturedly for a few minutes about what to see before deciding not to bother.

When Thorne got home he suggested trying a new Thai place that had opened on Kentish Town Road, but Louise had other ideas. She had brought stuff round and seemed determined to cook. While she was sorting dinner, Thorne nipped out to fetch a bottle of wine.

Louise looked at the bottle when Thorne got back. Asked how much it had cost, and seemed pleased when he told her.

'Cheap beer and expensive wine,' she said. 'That's one of the things I liked about you first off.'

'*One* of the things?'

'OK, the only thing,' she said. 'Now I come to think about it.'

They ate pasta at the small table in Thorne's living room. Got through the wine, and listened to a June Carter Cash compilation Thorne had picked up for next to nothing on eBay.

'That stuff the other night.' Louise reached across for an empty plate.

'What stuff?' Thorne said, knowing perfectly well.

'It didn't mean that I wanted anything, you know? That I want to have a baby, now, this minute. But I don't think there's anything wrong in talking about it.'

'It's fine . . .'

'It isn't fine, because it obviously freaked you out. So, I just want to make sure we understand each other.'

'Does this mean we need to get into the cheap beer?'

'I'm serious.'

Louise explained that despite what had happened in bed that night, she really did not want to get pregnant. That wasn't to say she wouldn't want to have a child one day, but she had a career to put first for a few more years.

'I look at someone like Yvonne Kitson,' she said, 'see her trying to juggle work around three kids, and I'm not sure I'd ever be able to do it.'

Thorne thought about Louise's reaction when they'd talked about Kitson and he'd accused her of being jealous. He wondered if he'd touched even more of a nerve than he'd realised.

'I'd be stupid to have a kid now.'

'It's fine,' Thorne repeated.

'You keep saying that, but I don't think it is. I'm worried that you think I'm desperate for you to knock me up or something. That I'm some sort of nutter who's going to stick pins in all your condoms or nick a pram from outside Tesco's. Really, I'm happy with the way things are.'

'Good. So am I,' Thorne said.

215

'Great. So that's fine then.'

They moved from the table to the sofa, and when the album had finished they put the TV on and tried to lose themselves in something mindless. After fifteen minutes of saying nothing, though, Thorne wasn't convinced that Louise was succeeding any more than he was.

She hit the mute button on the remote and was about to say something when the phone rang.

Thorne recognised the voice immediately.

'How did you get my home number?' he said. He pictured a glorified cupboard stuffed with recording equipment. A bored technician wearing headphones, ears pricking up on hearing his question.

'Come on,' Rawlings said. 'If you wanted to get mine, how long would it take you?'

'What do you want?' Next to him, Louise was mouthing, *Who is it*? 'I'm in the middle of something.'

'I could do with a chat. Just five minutes.'

'Fine, but not *this* five.'

There was a pause. Thorne could hear Rawlings blowing out smoke; knew that he was swearing silently.

'What about tomorrow?'

'Fine. Call me then.'

'Can we meet up?'

Louise was still asking. Thorne shook his head; he'd tell her in a minute. 'I don't know what I'm doing tomorrow. A lot of stuff happened today, and—'

'What stuff?'

'Right, you've had your chat . . .'

'Come on. We can meet wherever's easiest for you, all right? Five fucking minutes . . .'

Later, when Thorne was in the kitchen making tea, Louise shouted through from the living room: 'What about you? Did you never think about kids?'

Thorne almost scalded himself. 'Thought about it, yeah. Not for a while, though.'

'Why did you and Jan never have them?'

Thorne had split from his ex-wife twelve years before, after ten years of marriage. They hadn't spoken in a long while, and as far as he knew she was still living with the teacher she'd left him for. 'We didn't decide not to. It just never happened.'

There was a pause from the living room.

'Did you try to find out why it wasn't happening?'

Thorne took his time stirring the tea. 'No, we didn't talk about it.' He shrugged as he said it, asking himself, as he had when Jan had left, if it might have been one of the reasons why she'd gone. The not having kids. The not talking about not having kids. Both.

'It's crazy how some couples bottle shit up,' Louise said.

Thorne carried the drinks through, settled down next to her. 'Stupid,' he said.

She looked at him. 'It's important we don't do that. That we talk about things.'

'We *are* talking about things.'

'Right.' She flicked the TV on again. 'It's just a conversation, that's all. I don't see any reason why we shouldn't be able to talk about it. Isn't it part of getting to know the other person?'

'I think we know each other pretty well,' Thorne said.

'I'm just saying it should be like finding out all the other stuff, likes and dislikes, whatever. Where did you go to school? Where do you like to go on holiday? Do you think you might want to have kids one day?'

'The first two are easier to answer.'

'*One day.*' She squeezed his arm and said it nice and slow, making sure he got the point. 'At some point in the future, *maybe*, so don't panic, OK? I don't even mean with me, necessarily. I'll almost certainly have got pissed off with you and buggered off with someone else by then. It's hypothetical, that's all.'

'OK.'

'We're just talking about the *idea* of kids, Tom. Why should that be scary?'

217

Thorne knew that she was right, in theory, but also knew it was not quite as simple as she was making out.

He wasn't scared of vampires or zombies, *in theory*, but a well-made horror movie could still scare the shit out of him.

TWENTY-ONE

Davey Tindall looked up from his paper and eyed the two men at his window above off-the-shelf reading glasses.

'Eight quid,' he said, tearing off two tickets. He sighed when he saw the warrant cards; tossed the tickets into the bin and nodded towards the door that led through to the auditorium. 'In you go then. Film's already started, mind you.'

'Does that really matter?' Thorne asked. He peered at the poster taped below the box-office window. 'I wouldn't have thought *Shy and Shaven* has too much in the way of plot.'

Holland thanked Tindall for the offer, explaining that they weren't from Clubs and Vice, looking for a freebie. Thorne told him where they *were* from and that they needed a word.

'I was in with your lot the other day,' Tindall said. 'DC Stone and the other bloke, Asian . . .'

'That was the other day. With two other officers. And before you spoke to Marcus Brooks.'

Tindall puffed out his cheeks, folded his paper.

'Let's go through to the back and put the kettle on,' Thorne said.

The cinema was one of a string in Soho, all managed by a south

London family who also owned clubs and massage parlours and ran a network of girls in and out of several of the city's top hotels. Tindall had been on the payroll for years, doing a variety of jobs. He worked the box office, ferried girls around, collected the takings. He also passed a tip or two on to DCI Keith Bannard every once in a while, in exchange for cash and a Get Out of Jail Free card.

Tindall locked up the ticket booth and led Thorne and Holland to a small office that doubled as a storeroom. His skin looked as grey as it had on the tape Karim had shown to Thorne, although the eyes were blacker, darting around behind his glasses, as if desperately looking for a friend, or an exit. He had to be pushing sixty; short and whippet-thin, with hair that was silver, yellowing at the temples. He wore new-looking jeans with a sharp crease ironed down the legs, his top half lost inside a thin green cardigan.

'No tea,' he said.

'It was just an expression,' Thorne said. 'We're not stopping.'

There were newspapers and magazines scattered across what passed for a desk and piles of videotapes on the floor. A Jenna Jameson poster was stuck to the back of the door, and a calendar with a picture of a golden retriever was pinned to a cork board, surrounded by cards for cab firms and call girls. The place smelled of booze and bleach.

'When did you talk to Brooks?' Holland asked.

'Who says I did?'

'We got some of his stuff. We found your phone number.'

'So? I've got lots of people's numbers. Doesn't mean I ring them all up every day.'

The Scottish accent was stronger than Thorne remembered from the tape. He wondered if Tindall thickened it when he didn't feel like communicating; when it might be costly.

'We can go through your phone records easily enough,' Holland said. 'We can go through all sorts of stuff; dredge up all manner of crap you'd rather we didn't know about. That you'd rather the bloke you work for didn't know about.'

Thorne flicked through the calendar. 'He's not talking about DCI Bannard, either.' There was a different breed of dog for every month.

'I hadn't spoken to him when I came in on Sunday, I swear.'

'So, when *did* you speak to him?' Thorne said.

Tindall thought about it. 'He called up the next day. I was here.'

'And you never thought to tell us?'

'Slipped my mind,' Tindall said. He began digging around in drawers and cupboards. He asked Thorne and Holland if either of them had a cigarette. Holland had a packet of ten for emergencies, but kept his mouth shut.

'Have you seen him?' Holland asked.

Tindall shook his head. 'I have not.'

'You sure?' Thorne shoved some papers aside and leaned back against the edge of the table. 'Think *really* hard.'

'He wanted a car, OK? Asked if I knew someone who could get him something quickly, for cash.'

Thorne and Holland exchanged a glance. Tindall was talking about the day before Cowans was killed. Thorne wondered if that was why Brooks had wanted the car. He would certainly have needed it to follow Cowans, if the biker had driven around in search of a hooker and headed down to the canal once he'd found one he liked the look of.

'Did you help him?'

'I had a few contacts in the motor trade years ago,' Tindall said. 'Back when I got to know the lad, when we were hanging about with some of the same people. But not any more. I told him he'd have to try someone else.'

'And that was it?'

'That was it, aye. Just a couple of minutes. A cough and a spit.'

'You didn't suggest anyone in particular?' Holland said.

'Told you, I've been out of that game a long time.'

'No offence, Davey,' Thorne said, 'but you're full of it.'

'I swear—'

'Swear all you like. I reckon you helped "the lad" out; for old time's sake, because you feel sorry for him, who knows? Maybe you've been helping him ever since he came out of prison. Fixing him up with the right people . . .'

'Have I *fuck*.'

'None of your friends on the force can help you with this one. Not if you've been aiding and abetting a murderer, mate. Especially one who's taken to killing coppers.'

'Look, he called again yesterday, all right?' Tindall looked quickly from one to the other; checking to see he'd provoked a reaction. 'Late last night. Got me out of fucking bed, matter of fact.'

'What did he want?'

'He needs somewhere to stay,' Tindall said. Thorne looked across at Holland again. Tindall had to be telling the truth. There was no way he could have known about the raid in Hammersmith. 'Wanted to know if I could think of anywhere he could crash for a few days. Someone who'd put him up and leave him alone.'

'And?'

'We talked about one or two people he could try.'

'Such as?' Thorne asked.

Tindall looked pained. 'Come on, you know the sort of people I'm talking about . . .'

Thorne grabbed a ballpoint from the table, tore a strip of newspaper off and passed them both across. 'Write the names down.'

Tindall was starting to look like he needed that cigarette very badly. He cursed under his breath as he scribbled down a few names, pretending to dredge them up. From the cinema on the other side of the wall, the soundtrack of the main feature was all too audible.

'Someone sounds out of breath,' Holland said. He listened for a few more seconds. 'That's top-quality grunting.'

'How many's in there?' Thorne asked.

Tindall sniffed. 'Half a dozen . . .'

Thorne was amazed there were even that many enjoying *Shy and Shaven* at eleven o'clock in the morning. Why hadn't they just stayed at home and watched something on DVD? With whatever kind of stuff you were into now available on disc or download, Thorne couldn't understand why anyone went to porno cinemas any more, or picked magazines off the top shelf while pretending they were looking at *What Hi-Fi?* He could only presume they enjoyed the sleazy thrill of it; like movie stars getting caught with fifty-dollar whores when they could sleep with any woman they wanted.

Thorne took the piece of paper that Tindall thrust gracelessly at him. 'Thanks, Davey,' he said. 'We'd best let you get back to work. Now, you will let us know if he calls again, won't you?'

Tindall scoffed: 'You think I need more of this shite?'

Thorne walked slowly past him towards the door. 'Seriously,' he said, 'I hope nothing else slips your mind. You know what Bannard's like when you try to take him for an idiot?' Thorne guessed that the S&O man could get fairly heavy, and the look on Davey Tindall's face confirmed it. 'Well, I'm a lot worse.'

Tindall blocked their way as they tried to leave. 'Am I not getting something for this?'

Thorne just stared at him, waited for him to move.

'I'm serious.' The voice was thin and desperate. 'Fifty notes, say, just for my time.'

Thorne took one more second of Tindall's time, to tell him to fuck off.

Over the years, there had been periodic attempts to gentrify the Holloway Road. Delicatessens had come and gone. Idiots had opened antiquarian bookshops and sold their stock on a year later. As a hugely busy main road – the major route north out of the city – it was never going to be Highgate Hill or Hampstead High Street. But Yvonne Kitson thought it was the better for it: brash and unpretentious, with lively bars and restaurants, a few decent places to dance and hear music if you could be bothered to look. Certainly a place she wouldn't have minded going to college.

She watched Harika Kemal coming out through the doors of the student union with two friends and digging into her bag for a scarf. Kitson saw the girl's face fall when she caught sight of her approaching.

'Can I just have five minutes, Harika?'

She shook her head. 'Please . . .'

The man and the woman who had come out with Kemal were clearly a couple. The man took a step towards Kitson. 'Is there a problem?' Kitson thought he might be Turkish. Greek, maybe. He wore a shiny anorak with a fur-trimmed hood and glasses with thin, rectangular lenses.

Kitson reached into her bag for her warrant card.

'Can't you just leave her in peace for a bit?' the student said.

His girlfriend was Asian; plump, with short hair and a nose-stud. 'Maybe do something useful,' she said. 'Like trying to catch the animal that murdered her boyfriend?' She spoke with the same mid-Atlantic sarcasm Kitson was already hearing from her nine-year-old daughter.

'It's OK,' Kemal said to her friends. 'I'll catch you up.'

'Is there somewhere we could go and grab a sandwich or something?' Kitson asked.

The girl patted the bag that was slung across her shoulder. 'I've got my lunch.'

They crossed the road and walked just a little way up the side street opposite. Found a bench on a small patch of muddied grass next to an Irish pub. Looking back, Kitson could see that the two students hadn't moved; were staring from the doorway of the union building. Turning back to Kemal, she watched the girl take a plastic box from her bag. 'What your friend said. That's exactly what we're trying to do.'

'I know.' Kemal peeled back tinfoil from her sandwiches.

'And there's no point bullshitting you: we're getting nowhere. We've done all the things we're supposed to do, you know? Everything we can think of. Spoken to everyone we could, put out an appeal on TV. I *know* you saw that.'

The girl said nothing. A cement lorry rumbled slowly past them, waited to turn left on to the main road.

'The only lead we've got is you,' Kitson said.

Kemal shook her head, but to Kitson it seemed more about resignation than denial. 'It's so hard,' she said.

'Of course it is.' It was a knee-jerk response, but Kitson truly believed that it *was* difficult for the girl. Dealing with the loss of her boyfriend. With whatever knowledge she had, much as she might wish to be ignorant.

'How can I face the family?'

Kitson leaned forward on the bench so she could look at the girl square on. 'Whose family? Deniz's?'

Another shake of the head, its meaning even more ambiguous than the last.

'It's OK, Harika. Really.' Kitson watched the girl turning the sandwich over and over in her hand without taking a bite. Looking at her, Kitson found it hard to imagine how she'd become involved with a man like Deniz Sedat. She did not seem the type to be impressed by money and flash cars, and she was certainly sharp enough to have known where that money had come from. Kitson wondered if she was reading Harika Kemal all wrong. Or perhaps there had simply been a physical attraction between her and Sedat that had transcended everything else.

'I would have nobody.'

Kitson nodded back towards the university. 'You've got good friends, that's obvious. People who care about you a lot. And I told you before, we'll make sure that you're protected. You and the people close to you.'

Kemal raised her head suddenly. 'What if it's the people I'm close to who I need to be protected from?' There was anger and impatience in her face, but her voice had broken before she'd finished speaking.

Kitson reached for a tissue. She passed it across, but the girl had already found one of her own. Had been keeping them handy.

'Whatever you need.'

'I need Deniz to be alive.'

'And I need to find the man who killed him,' Kitson said. She thought about taking the girl's hand but decided that would be too much. 'Tell me who it was, Harika.'

The girl sniffed and wiped her eyes, then stuffed the tissue back into her pocket. 'Hakan Kemal,' she said.

'Kemal?'

'My older brother. My brother killed Deniz.'

Kitson nodded, as though she understood, but her mind was starting to race. She had many more questions. She wanted to tear back to the office and get things moving. But she knew that, for a few minutes at least, she needed to stay on the bench with Harika Kemal.

Kitson glanced back across at the two students, who were still watching from the other side of the Holloway Road. They both looked as though they would happily rip her head off.

. . . I was sitting in the park in the middle of the night, getting rained on, and thinking what a soft piece of shite I am. That I can get rid of everyone I blame for what happened, and feel next to nothing, but that I don't have enough bottle to kill myself. It was my first thought back inside, when I got the news. Taking a blade to myself, I mean, and I'll admit that it was a relief when I started to think about making other people pay instead. Once I had that, I didn't have to think too hard about topping myself any more; facing up to the fact that I didn't have the bottle to go through with it.

It might help if I believed in something, I suppose. In fucking anything. If I thought there was even a chance I might see you both again afterwards. I know this much, if I believed in God or whatever else to begin with, I certainly wouldn't any more . . .

And look, I know this is never going to happen, not now anyway, but I've started to imagine what it might be like to be with someone else one day. To have another kid, even. Christ, I'm so sorry, baby, I can't stop those stupid things popping into my head. I think about the sex, and going on holidays and Christ knows what, and the rows me and this woman would have. How she'd always be jealous of you, feel like she was competing with a dead woman, whatever. I imagine her flying off the handle big time, and saying something about you or cutting up an old picture, stuff like that. And then I'd just fucking lose it and want to hurt her. End up boozing, probably, messing up everybody's life.

See? I've got far too much time to think about this sort of shit. All the time when I'm not writing letters to a ghost.

I was thinking, though. If it ever did happen, if someone else came along, I mean. Would you leave me then? Would that be when I lost you and Robbie for good? Thing is, I know you'd want me to be happy, to move on, but it's really not on the cards.

Happy means forgetting . . .

Thorne stared at the last line for a few seconds, then slipped the photocopy of the letter back into his desk drawer with the others. He nodded to Sam Karim as the DS passed his office door, then sat back and slurped his tea, and thought about the terrible power of grief.

He understood what drove Marcus Brooks. The impulse. Looking again at the newest picture of the man, the one based on the description given by the security guard, he was starting to see behind it. To connect with someone anaesthetised by loss; aloof from the basic pain and pleasure of everyday life. Someone astonished all the time by their own capacity to walk, or to dress themselves, and functioning for no other reason than to hunt down those who had smashed their life into pieces and scattered them.

When that trainee DC had eventually grasped the nature of the letters Thorne had discovered in Hammersmith, he had rolled his eyes and said something about Brooks 'losing it'. It was an understandable reaction, and Thorne had smiled and nodded. Had suppressed an urge to give the bumptious little prick a slap.

When I'm not writing letters to a ghost . . .

Thorne had done something similar; had spoken to his father for a while after the old man had died. Actually, his father had been the one doing the talking, but Thorne knew well enough that it amounted to the same thing.

It took a second to say 'good-bye', and a lifetime.

He looked up as Kitson bustled in, tossing her coat across the back of a chair, rattling on about how students looked even younger than policemen nowadays.

'You should chuck the job in,' Thorne said. 'Go back to college as a mature student. Don't you fancy three years of drinking and sleeping with eighteen-year-olds? Thinking about it, I'll come with you . . .'

Kitson told him about her meeting with Harika Kemal. The name of the man she'd identified as her boyfriend's killer.

'How does she know for sure?' Thorne asked. 'She said before she didn't see it happen.'

'I'm not sure about that any more.'

'Going to be iffy without a witness.'

'I'll worry about that later.'

'Did she say *why* her brother did it?'

'I wasn't getting that out of her without thumbscrews,' Kitson said.

'There must be some knocking around somewhere.'

Kitson rummaged in her bag and took out a small jar. 'Hakan runs a dry cleaner's on Green Lanes.' She pursed her lips, ran a dab of balm across each. 'Up near Finsbury Park . . .'

Thorne knew that many businesses in that area paid local drug gangs for protection; that some operated as fronts for the dealers and heroin traffickers. Restaurants, minicab firms, supermarkets. He wondered if Hakan Kemal might be laundering more than shirts and blouses.

Kitson had obviously been thinking along the same lines. 'Maybe S&O had it right all along, and it *was* gang-related.'

'Not the smoothest hitman I've ever come across,' Thorne said, 'but what do I know?'

Kitson was happy to agree on both counts.

Thorne looked across at her, deadpan: 'Have you ever seen a film called *Shy and Shaven* . . .?'

He was trying to give an accurate description of the smell in Davey Tindall's office when his mobile rang. He looked at the caller display, thought about dropping the call, but felt immediately guilty. Sighing, he hit the green button.

'Tom?'

'Hello, Auntie Eileen, I was going to call you tonight.'

'Sorry if you're busy, love. I don't like to phone when you're at work.'

'It's OK . . .'

'Only I'm trying to get numbers organised for Christmas, you know?'

'Right.' It was the conversation Thorne knew had been coming. He winced inwardly at the thought of that technician listening in his cupboard; pissing himself.

'Obviously it'd be smashing to see you, love. We've asked Victor if he'd like to come over for Christmas lunch.'

'That's good of you,' Thorne said. Eileen, his father's sister, had semi-adopted the old man who had been her brother's only friend in the last year of his life. 'I'm sure he'll like that.'

There was a long sigh. 'Poor old bugger . . .'

Thorne wasn't certain if she was talking about Victor or his father.

'So, anyway, you have a think about it,' Eileen said. 'Only I'd hate to think you were sitting on your own, like you were last year.'

In fact, Thorne had spent the previous Christmas – the first since his father had died – with Hendricks and his then boyfriend, Brendan. Now that the boot was on the other foot, and Hendricks was the single one, Thorne had been wondering if he should offer to return the favour.

'The first few Christmases are always the worst, love. That's why I thought you might want family around.'

'OK, thanks.'

'You're welcome to bring your new girlfriend, of course . . .'

Louise had already raised the idea of spending Christmas with her parents, which was problematic in itself. At the time, Thorne had attempted that trickiest of manoeuvres – appearing keen while hedging his bets – and he knew it hadn't gone down too well. They'd agreed to talk about it properly later, which was another conversation he wasn't much looking forward to. He'd never met Louise's parents, but her father had been in the army and Thorne had already formed a daunting mental image of the man. He wasn't sure he fancied a Christmas

Day spent listening to war stories, or a long walk with the family dog after lunch. Much as he wanted to spend the time with Louise, he was starting to think that getting pissed with Hendricks and watching *The Great Escape* sounded pretty good. He needed to check and see who Spurs were playing on Boxing Day, come to that.

'Everything's up in the air, to be honest,' he said. 'They don't sort the work rotas out until the last minute and even then, you know, if we catch a big job . . .'

'That doesn't matter. You turn up on the day and we'll cope.'

'I don't want to mess you about.'

'Don't be silly, love. You know I always get too much in anyway.'

'I can't hear you very well, Eileen.'

'Tom?'

'Sorry . . . the signal's terrible in here . . .'

'Don't worry, love. I'll try you again next week—'

When Thorne put the phone away and looked up, Kitson was staring at him. She shook her head, and he couldn't tell if she was shocked or impressed.

'You are a *frighteningly* good liar,' she said.

TWENTY-TWO

'It's better than digging a ditch.'

In his more lucid moments, Thorne's father had been fond of trotting that old saw out, whenever Thorne had moaned about his particular lot being a far from happy one. There had been plenty of occasions when Thorne would have swapped places with any ditch-digger alive, but he knew what the old man had meant.

It was usually just a question of perspective.

On the Victoria Line rumbling south, Thorne had kept his head buried in the paper. He'd stared at the same page for twenty minutes, the story and the pictures becoming meaningless, and decided that he *was* better off than some. Even allowing for the situation he'd got himself into – 'sticky' or 'career-threatening' depending on his mood – he knew that life could be a damn sight worse.

And was for a great many people.

Russell Brigstocke, slowly collapsing beneath the weight of whatever he was keeping to himself; Harika Kemal, who was paying for giving it up; the families of Raymond Tucker, Ricky Hodson and Martin Cowans; Anne Skinner and her daughter . . .

And Marcus Brooks. Whether or not he spent it in a prison cell,

231

Thorne guessed that the man responsible for most of the misery would probably suffer the most wretched Christmas of all.

It was a thin line, Thorne knew that; between counting your blessings and using the distress of others as a sticking plaster. But whichever side of the line he was on, he wasn't alone in being *altered*. He knew that the things they saw and did every day affected how those he worked with behaved when they clocked off.

There were nights when Dave Holland got in and held his daughter that little bit tighter. When Phil Hendricks couldn't get his hands clean enough. Hours when Louise had clung to Thorne, sweating and near to tears, after the only way she'd been able to get a traumatic day out of her system had been to come home and fuck his brains out. Drink, sex, jokes . . .

Coping mechanisms.

Thorne also knew very well that whatever you used to change the way you felt, it was only temporary. That you'd be back again the next day, moving through it and trying to keep clean; picking up dark bits on the soles of your shoes.

Digging in the shittiest ditch of all.

He stepped off the train smiling, thinking that, towards the end, his old man would not have bothered with homilies at all and would just have called him a moaning little fucker. He walked up and on to the street, checked his watch. It was a little after six-thirty, but in a city where the 'rush hour' was nearer three, the pavement was still thick with people hurrying to get home.

Thorne joined them.

There was someone he had to see first, just for a few minutes, but he would be keen to get back to Louise's place as quickly as he could after that.

Part of him was hoping she'd had a traumatic day.

He'd arranged the meeting in an upmarket coffee bar behind Pimlico station. The sort of place with a loyal clientele of locals that clung on in one of the few streets in the city that didn't have a Starbucks every twenty yards.

Thorne was a little taken aback to see Rawlings stand up when he walked in; almost as though they were on a date and he were trying to appear gentlemanly. Rawlings had an empty cup in front of him, so Thorne asked if he wanted another. Rawlings said he'd been hoping they might be going on to the pub opposite. Thorne told him he was pushed for time, and went to fetch his drink.

'Why here?' Rawlings asked when Thorne came back to the table.

Thorne spooned up the froth from his coffee. 'You said anywhere that suited me.'

'I just wondered. It's not a problem.'

'I'm stopping with a friend round the corner,' Thorne said. Rawlings waited, but Thorne wasn't about to say any more.

He was cagey enough when it came to discussing his private life with those he worked with every day. Kitson knew what was happening, more or less, and Holland, but Thorne wasn't comfortable with the idea of too many people knowing his business. It was why he hated the thought of someone listening in on his phone conversations, whether he was talking dirty on chat lines or ordering pizza.

There were still gags and gossip, of course, however much he tried to keep a lid on it. Andy Stone had cut out a magazine article and put it on Thorne's desk: a company that specialised in 'unusual' gifts and 'once in a lifetime' events was offering a service whereby women paid to be 'kidnapped'. Anyone who fancied it, and was willing to cough up several hundred pounds, would be snatched from the street and bundled into a van. Their partner, who was tipped off as to their whereabouts, would then get to play the hero and rescue them. According to the company responsible, the excitement of this 'uniquely thrilling' scenario could reinvigorate the most mundane of love lives.

Stone had waited until he was sure Thorne had seen it. 'Thought you might be interested. You and your missus, a bit of role-play, whatever.'

'Why don't you try playing the role of someone doing his job?' Thorne had said.

He'd taken the article home that night and shown it to Louise. She hadn't seen the funny side and was all for tracking down whoever ran the company and explaining exactly what kidnap was like. Giving them a uniquely thrilling experience of their own . . .

'What's so urgent?' Thorne asked.

Rawlings was edgy. 'I've got your mate Adrian Nunn on my fucking case.'

'He's not my mate.'

'I saw you talking to him at Paul's place, the night they found the body.'

'I talked to a lot of people.'

'Come on, I know he's been cosying up to you. It's how those fuckers work, isn't it?'

'Shit. I thought he really wanted to be my friend.'

'I'm serious.'

'What do you *want*?'

Rawlings waved to get a waitress's attention, asked her for an ashtray. She told him there was no smoking and he shook his head as though the world had gone mad. 'I want to make sure I know whose side you're on,' he said.

Thorne gave it a second. 'I'm Spurs, you're Millwall, I would have thought.'

Rawlings tensed and pointed a finger, angry at Thorne's refusal to take him seriously. But then he softened, sat back, as though he'd realised that aggression wasn't going to get him anywhere. 'Come on, you know the game, same as I do. It's us and them, always has been.'

'It's all about which is which though, right?' Thorne said. 'That's the whole point.'

Rawlings grimaced; close enough to an acknowledgement. He looked around, glared at the waitress. 'There's hardly any fucker in here,' he said. 'Why can't I smoke?'

'What's Nunn been saying?'

Rawlings pulled the face most coppers reserved for paedophiles. 'He's slick as fuck.'

'Slicker.'

'He's giving it, "Is there anything you'd like to tell me, DS Rawlings?" Which you know as well as I do means, "We've got you by the knackers, so tell us what we already know and save us a lot of pissing about."'

'So, what do they know?'

'Fuck all. He's fishing. Whatever they *think* they've got is obviously not enough to do anything about, so he's trying it on.'

'Fine, so what's your problem?' Thorne asked.

'He is. Nunn. I just want him to fuck off out of my face. I've got half a dozen jobs on the go, a twat of a guvnor who wants them sorted yes-terday, and I've still got Paul's widow calling me every half an hour in pieces. Fair enough? I really don't need that smarmy strip of piss on top of everything else.'

If Rawlings was half as stressed out as he appeared, Thorne thought he needed a lot more than a cigarette. 'What makes you think I can do anything about it?'

'You've been working with him, haven't you?'

'That's putting it a bit strong.'

Rawlings waved his hands, impatient. 'Whatever. You've got some sort of a relationship with the bloke; as much as you can have with their sort.'

'And?'

'And maybe you can get him to ease off or something.'

'Now who's not being serious?'

'I don't know . . . find out what the fuck he's after.'

'Nunn wouldn't tell me what he'd had for breakfast,' Thorne said.

Rawlings just sat there, looking gutted, waiting for Thorne to stop laughing. When Thorne caught his eye, he saw a man trying hard to work something out. Trying to work *him* out, certainly.

'Sounds to me like you're stuck with it,' Thorne said. 'Sod all I can do, I know that much . . .'

The waitress stopped on her way past the table, asked if there was anything else they wanted. Rawlings said nothing, waved his cigarette packet at her. She reddened and walked away.

'She's just doing her job,' Thorne said. 'She doesn't need wankers like you any more than you need wankers like Adrian Nunn.'

Rawlings nodded; muttered something. When he saw Thorne downing what was left of his coffee, he leaned forward. 'Look, here it is. I'm starting to think that Paul . . . might have been into a few things.'

Thorne slid the empty cup to one side. 'What sort of things?'

Rawlings looked down at the table, took a few seconds, then looked up. Lowered his voice, said it slowly: '*All* sorts.'

'And you reckon Nunn wants you to help him build the DPS's case?'

Rawlings nodded; solemn, but pleased to see that Thorne was finally getting it.

Thorne wasn't certain *what* he was getting, but it was all useful. He hadn't exactly dragged this information from the man sitting opposite him and wondered what Rawlings was up to. If he was up to anything. He knew that people reacted oddly when they were threatened, and Rawlings obviously felt under threat.

Thorne glanced at his watch.

'You sure you don't fancy nipping over the road?' Rawlings asked.

Thorne was certainly warming to the idea of continuing their conversation. Not so much for what else he might glean about Paul Skinner – he already knew enough – but rather for what half an hour's more chat might tell him about a man who was suddenly willing to grass up his dead friend.

He looked at his watch again.

Said: 'Just the one.'

The nature of kidnap investigations meant that when Louise Porter caught a big case, it tended to be full on. There were no such things as ordinary working hours, and leaving the job in the office was never really an option. Simply leaving the office at all was hard enough. Happily, the case involving the drug dealer who had kidnapped himself had been judged unlikely to make it past the CPS and scaled down. The wife of the Albanian gangster had turned up with no more than cuts and bruises and with no one willing to press charges. With little else coming in, things had been mercifully quiet for the past few days, and she was feeling pretty relaxed.

She couldn't say the same for the case Thorne was investigating. For Thorne himself, come to that.

There were some inquiries that drew you in further than others. They'd been working on one together when they'd first met and Porter knew the signs. The series of killings, the messages that had been sent directly to him; this was never going to be the kind of job that Thorne could do on autopilot, even if he had one.

She poured herself a glass of wine and looked at the TV for a while. It was almost eight-thirty and Thorne had called three hours before to say he was on his way.

He was a moody sod at the best of times, but then again so was she; so were most of the coppers she knew, even those who drifted through the day with smiles on their faces, then went home and whacked their kids or got shit-faced. She'd thought about it, and put his reaction to the baby discussion down to the case; to an involvement in it that, even by his standards, had become a little extreme. She hoped that was the reason, anyway. Decided that if she were the one being sent pictures of the dead and the soon-to-be-dead, she'd probably be behaving in exactly the same way.

When Hendricks called, she topped up her glass and carried the phone across to the sofa; glad of the chance to talk to someone who knew Tom Thorne even better than she did.

'He's probably off with some slapper,' Hendricks said.

'That's OK, then.'

'Can't blame him though, can you? Poor old bugger just wants to shag someone who isn't desperate to be heavy with his child.'

Porter almost spat her wine out. She'd spoken to Hendricks earlier and they'd laughed about the conversation she'd had with Thorne. She hadn't told him about the incident that had sparked it off; those few seconds she couldn't really explain. When she'd wanted so badly to hold on to him, to feel him come inside her, knowing full well what it could mean.

237

'Honestly though, Phil. You should have seen his face.'

'He always looks like that.'

'I've got a good mind to buy a pregnancy testing kit,' she said. 'Hide it in the bathroom. Just to see the look on his face when he opens the cabinet looking for his Rennies.'

Hendricks spluttered out a laugh. Porter could hear that he was smoking; knew that a spliff was his particular way of winding down at the end of the day. Knew too that Thorne didn't approve.

'Do you fancy coming out clubbing tomorrow night?' Hendricks asked.

'God, I don't know . . .'

She'd enjoyed the nights out she'd had with Hendricks; dancing and drinking in a variety of gay clubs and bars, watching Hendricks make his moves, or more often, get hit on. She was starting to worry, though, that she didn't have more female friends. Any real ones, if she thought about it. There was the odd drink after work with a couple of the women in her squad, but it never went beyond that, and she'd lost touch with all the girls she'd known when she joined the force.

'Come on,' Hendricks said. 'Saturday night, we'll have a laugh. If you're cramping my style, I'll put you in a taxi, OK?'

Not that she had that many close friends who were men, either. Hendricks was about the closest, which was perhaps what was bothering her most. There was Jason, who she'd gone through Hendon with, but she hadn't seen much of him since he'd been posted south. She was still matey with Jon, her ex-boyfriend, but hadn't spoken to him lately; Thorne getting decidedly frosty whenever his name had come up in conversation.

'Let me talk to Tom first,' Porter said.

'Well, *he* won't mind, will he? It's not as if you're going to pull.'

She giggled. 'I just want to find out if he's likely to be working.'

'You'll have more fun with me.'

'Definitely. But, you know, it might be a good idea for the two of us to spend some time together, if we can. We were talking about going to see a film or something.' She reached across for *Time Out*, began flicking through the film section.

'Just don't go freaking him out again,' Hendricks said. 'Daft old bastard's probably got a weak heart.'

'I'll try not to.'

'*I'm* the one who's supposed to be broody.'

Porter said nothing. Listened to Hendricks taking another drag, moaning with pleasure as he let it out.

'Give me a shout if you're up for it,' he said. 'OK, Lou . . .?'

Porter heard the outer door slam shut as she was saying her goodbyes. She waited, recognising the sounds of him – the shuffles and the sighs – as he rooted around for his key.

'Sorry,' he said, before he was halfway through the door. He stepped inside and watched her carrying the phone back to its cradle on top of a low pine chest. 'Been talking to your boyfriend?'

'No, yours,' she said.

He was grinning as he took off his jacket. It was good to see; even if she knew, before she was close enough to smell it, that a couple of pints had helped.

TWENTY-THREE

There may have been more direct routes from Deptford back to his new place, but Marcus Brooks had fancied following the line of the river. It wouldn't take him much more than an hour, hour and a half, and although it was cold, the sky looked clear enough. He'd walked up around the U-shape, the one off the *EastEnders* credits, with Docklands opposite; trying to stay as close as he could to the water, weaving his way around the dark, oily docks and wharves towards Wapping. The tower at Canary Wharf filled the sky ahead of him. The beacon on its roof was blinking away to his right, then eventually behind him as he moved on, where the river straightened at the Rotherhithe Tunnel.

He put one foot in front of the other time and again. Watching the river creep and sloosh alongside, and wanting nothing more than to drop where he was and curl up. Desperate for just a few hours' sleep, but knowing it would be a waste of time to try.

Instead, he looked down and watched his shoes eat up the pavement. Hands in his pockets, humming any song that went with the rhythm of his footsteps. And he saw Angie's face, and Robbie's, as they must have been at the last minute; just before the car hit. Then he saw other faces, how they had been when they'd clapped eyes on the hammer. The plastic bag.

Tucker. Hodson. Cowans.

Their faces were as clear as anything now: frozen with their mouths open and eyes wide. But he hadn't known all of them by sight; not at first, anyway.

Skinner, who'd called himself Jennings the last time they'd met, had been all-too familiar, of course; just older from a distance, and dead by the time Marcus had got close. Killed by somebody else before he'd had the chance.

And some of the bikers had been there at his trial; screaming and swearing at him from the balcony, until the judge had had them chucked out. They'd looked near enough the same when he'd come out of prison and tracked them down.

Ray Tucker had *definitely* been in court six years before, and Ricky Hodson. Although he hadn't known their names back then. He wasn't certain about Martin Cowans – they'd all had long hair and leathers and shit . . . but it didn't matter either way. He'd been one of the gang – the leader, as far as he could work out – when Angie had been killed, and that was all that counted.

He had decided back in Long Lartin, when he and Nicklin were going over it, that everyone had to be treated the same. That they all had to share the responsibility equally. It would have been stupid to do it any other way; to say that the one who'd been driving the car had to die, or suffer before he died, while some of the others should just be crippled or whatever.

It was cleaner to blame them all.

He didn't know this latest one from Adam, but he'd played his part, same as everyone else who'd fucked his life up. First time or second. Second wouldn't have happened without the first, after all . . .

He didn't know him, but now he'd had his first good look. Waited in the cold at the address he'd been given until he'd got back from work. He'd taken out the phone and grabbed his few seconds of video while the bloke was getting out of his car.

Done his bit for Nicklin.

He'd do his own bit tomorrow night.

It was busy coming around the big island at the end of Waterloo Bridge; cars and people. He stopped for a few seconds and watched figures moving north and south, leaning into the wind, lining up and chatting at bus stops on either side of the road, like fuck all mattered. He thought about where they might have been; knew there were cinemas and theatres under the bridge. Then he began to move his feet again; speeding up, because he couldn't care less.

He walked around the back of Waterloo station and up past St Thomas's Hospital. He'd spent a couple of hours in casualty there one Saturday, years back, when some idiot had nutted him outside a club. He remembered Angie having a right go when she caught up with him. Shouting at him, saying he probably asked for it. Kissing his stitches later on . . .

Just a few minutes away now; he'd do it in a little over an hour. Right above the river until the last possible moment, then cutting back and across four lanes of the Albert Embankment. Not running, not worrying about the lights and horns. Making the traffic slow down for him.

Imagining Angie's face when she realised too late what was going to happen. And knowing she'd have been thinking about Robbie. That she would have done anything to save him.

Thinking about his boy; about what might have gone through Robbie's mind at the end.

Hoping he had been in there, somewhere.

Louise had fallen asleep on the sofa, halfway through a documentary neither of them had been particularly interested in. Thorne had plugged in the headphones to Louise's laptop and logged on; settled down to a few hands, playing as a glamorous blonde in a low-cut blouse. Fancying himself, in every sense.

An hour into it, he/she had been heads-up with PokerMom, a shifty-looking character in a cowboy hat. He had just raised sixty dollars when he saw the screen on his prepay come to life; watched the handset buzzing across the tabletop next to the computer. He had switched the phone to silent, so that any call or warning tone wouldn't wake Louise up.

He scrolled down and looked at Brooks' message.

Then he crept past Louise and took the phone with him into the bathroom, while, back at the virtual table, his bet was called and his kings and sixes lost out to three sevens.

were u at the flat?

It had been sent from another new number. Brooks was still using SIM cards once, then disposing of them. He could have no way of knowing that his messages were not being monitored; that Thorne was the only one seeing them and that no effort was being made to trace their source.

Thorne lowered the lid of the toilet seat. Sat down and typed into the reply screen.

Yes. Your letters are safe.

He waited. Watched as he was told that his message had been sent. And, more importantly, received.

His hands felt sticky, something between his fingers. His father's wedding ring, which Thorne wore on his right hand, would not move smoothly when he tried to spin it. He got up and used the sink while he waited to see if Marcus Brooks had anything else to say; was drying his hands when he got his answer:

doesn't matter

Thorne was trying to work out how to respond when another message arrived.

got another vid to send
When?
tomorrow

Thorne did not know what Brooks meant. Would he be sending the video the next day, or killing whoever was on it?

Alive or dead? Thorne waited.

tomorrow

He listened to water moving through the pipes. One of his old dressing-gowns was hanging on the back of the door, faded and pulled to pieces by the cat. He'd brought it over when Louise had treated him to a new one for his birthday. She had also taken a good deal of her stuff over to his place. His bathroom was starting to smell almost as nice as this one.

who killed skinner?

Thorne saw no reason to hesitate. Thinking it was ironic, as he typed, that he should be sharing his theory with the man everyone thought was guilty of the policeman's murder.

Has to be the other copper.

It took a minute for Brooks to come back.

not really surprised

Who is he?

Thorne had got nothing useful from his hour and a half in the pub with Richard Rawlings. The DS had given a good performance, or at least that's how it had seemed to Thorne. Maybe more so, thinking back . . .

'It's looking like Paul was into some nasty stuff.' Rawlings had looked close to devastated, putting away a pint in three visits to his glass. '*Seriously* fucking nasty.'

'That what Nunn told you?'

'As good as.'

'And you knew nothing about it?'

'Maybe . . . I don't know. I had suspicions, now and again, but you keep them to yourself, don't you? We were mates, and I was probably kidding myself, but I never thought it was anything too heavy. Not in a million years. Fuck, you think you know people . . .'

The phone buzzed again in Thorne's hand.

squire

Thorne kicked at the side of the bath in frustration. His hand was clammy again; sticky against the plastic of the phone.

What's his real name?

i'll send u a message

So, Skinner had been Jennings. It was obvious that Brooks thought both men were equally guilty, but Thorne hoped one day it might matter to a court which of them had been responsible for what.

Did he kill Tipper?

one of them did

Thorne was typing too fast now, making mistakes, not bothering to go back and correct them.

Tell me who sow e can findhim

no point Then: *i've already found him*

Thorne's excitement was giving way to irritation, and anger at himself. The exchange with Brooks that he'd been hoping for, that he'd pinned so much on, was going nowhere. The other night he'd felt as though everything he and Louise had said to each other was loaded with meaning, but this was just words on a screen, and none of them were telling him anything he needed.

Contact was not the same thing as connection.

He typed: *I meant it about the letters.*

Thorne knew as soon as half a minute had come and gone that Brooks had nothing else to say. He imagined him on a dark street corner, cracking open the shell of a phone, tossing the tiny SIM into a drain.

He gave it another five minutes, then stood up and washed his hands again; drying them until they were sore, until he could spin the ring freely around his finger. He put the phone away and trudged into the living room to wake Louise.

Davey Tindall hopped off the night bus at Vauxhall Cross and started walking. Spitting feathers. A youngster stepped in front of him, some junkie with his hood up, and was told to fuck off before he'd even opened his mouth.

Tindall's employer had a business to run; had overheads and profit margins and whatnot. Tindall understood that. So it wasn't him he was pissed off with; it was that pair of shite-hawks with warrant cards.

A half-price minicab at the end of a night was one of the perks that

Tindall's boss put his way. He'd rather have had another tenner in the pay packet come the end of the week, but the bloke who paid his wages had interests in a cab firm, so that was that. There'd been no lift home tonight, though. Forty-five minutes on a bus full of nutters and winos. He'd be lucky enough to hang on to his job, he reckoned . . .

The Filth never took that kind of thing into account, did they?

Someone in one of those bargain bookshops opposite the cinema, the ones with wank-mags in the basement, had spotted that the ticket office was closed for fifteen fucking minutes. Nosey cunt mentions it to someone, and word gets passed same as it always does. Next thing, one of the cousins is popping in with his smart suit on, swaggering about and wanting to know what's been happening.

'It was ten minutes, no more.'

'Yeah, ten minutes when our customers went somewhere else. Ten fucking minutes too long, Davey.'

He'd told the cocky little sod he'd had the shits: an iffy vindaloo the night before; had to shut up shop and get to a chemist's. The cousin fucks off, then an hour later the boss calls up, so he has to tell him the same story.

'I don't give a toss. Your dodgy guts have cost me money. Next time use a fucking bucket whatever, just don't stop taking the tickets.'

He'd laughed and said he was sorry. Thought he'd got away with it.

Then: 'How you getting home tonight, Davey?'

Tindall walked back along the Embankment, then crossed underneath the railway line and took out his key. He was starving; started thinking about cheese on toast when he got indoors. He'd normally have nipped across the road for a sandwich at dinnertime, but he'd been scared to leave the booth for so much as a few minutes after the boss had rung. There'd only been kebab shops open by the time he knocked off and that crap really *did* give him the runs.

He shouted a 'hello' when he walked through the door; made a fuss of his Jack Russell, who came skittering across the lino to meet him. He followed her back into the kitchen and slopped some food into a bowl. Then he turned the grill on and wandered upstairs to the spare room.

There was no answer when he knocked, so he stuck his head round the door.

'Sorry, son, I thought you were out.'

'Why d'you come in, then?'

Brooks had spoken without looking up. He was sitting on the edge of the bed, staring at the phone in his hand, pressing buttons. His training shoes were scuffed and dirty. There were papers scattered about on the bed, and more phones. Plastic bags against the wall containing all his clothes, a dirty mug and plate on the carpet.

Tindall stepped in and picked up the empties. 'I'm making a bit of cheese on toast if you want some.'

Brooks said nothing for a few seconds, then looked up and stared, as if the Scotsman's voice had just reached him.

'Anyway, there'll be some downstairs if you fancy it, you know? And tea.'

Tindall looked away, glancing around the room as if checking that everything were to his guest's satisfaction, or that nothing had been damaged. The door caught as he started to pull it to; hissing against the pile of the carpet. 'Need to get an inch shaved off this fucking door,' he said.

Brooks was looking at his phone again, studying the screen.

'You need to get some sleep, son . . .'

Tindall closed the door without waiting for a reaction, and went back downstairs to his supper and his dog.

Thorne woke with his arm stretched across the cold side of the bed where Louise should have been. He walked naked and half asleep into the kitchen. Found Louise leaning back against the worktop in a dressing-gown, hands wrapped around her favourite mug.

'You all right?'

'I just wanted some tea,' she said.

Thorne peered at the digital clock on the front of the cooker. 'At half past four?'

'Why do you never tell me anything?'

That woke him up fast enough. Fuck, was there any way she could have found out about the contact with Marcus Brooks? He tried to hide his alarm beneath confusion and lack of sleep. He breathed hard and blinked slowly. 'Sorry . . . what? Is there some conversation I'm forgetting here?'

Louise shook her head. 'That's the point.'

It wasn't about Brooks. It was something more general; something she'd been saving up. He felt relieved, then irritated, then cold. His hand drifted down to cup his shrinking tackle as he turned to head for the bathroom to fetch the ratty dressing-gown.

'Night then,' she said.

His shoulders dropped, and he took a second. 'What don't I tell you?'

Her eyes rolled up, as though she had plenty to choose from. 'All sorts.' Then, like she'd plucked one out of the air. 'Your father . . .'

'I've told you.'

'I know what happened. More or less. The fire, the fact that it might not have been an accident.'

Thorne sighed. Said it as though she might be stupid, and he was saying it for the last time. 'There was a fire, and he died, and I don't know, will never fucking know if the stupid fucker left the stove on, or if someone came into the house and gave him a helping hand. Is that OK?'

She nodded, meaning that it wasn't.

'I don't see what else you want to know.'

'How you feel about it.' She put down her tea. 'Christ, I—'

'How do you think I feel?'

'I'm asking.'

'I'd've thought it would be fucking obvious.'

'It isn't.'

Thorne raised his arms in a gesture of helplessness; like maybe it was more her fault than his.

'What about the man you think might have done it?'

Thorne shook his head, would not even say the name.

248

'How do you feel about him?'

He studied his bare feet against the tiles; spoke to them. 'I'm stark-bollock naked and I'm half asleep. I can't even think straight. This is stupid . . .'

She took a step towards him, thrust her hands into the pockets of her dressing-gown. 'We've been together five months and sometimes it feels like I've barely known you ten minutes. Five months, and the other night in bed I did something really fucking stupid. I've thought about it and, whatever I said, there must have been some small part of me that wanted it. Even if it was only for a few seconds.' Her right hand came out of the dressing-gown pocket, clutched at a handful of material around her belly. 'Some part of me wanted it, which is why I'm making tea in the middle of the night, because if I'm honest, I don't feel like you tell me any more, *really* tell me any more, than you tell Phil, or Dave Holland, or the bloke you buy the fucking newspaper off in the morning.' She stopped, and waited for Thorne to raise his head; looked for something in his face. 'You're right,' she said, moving towards the door. 'This is stupid.'

'Can we talk about it tomorrow?'

Pushing past him, she said, 'I'm sorry I woke you.'

TWENTY-FOUR

'This job's a fucking joke.'

'You only just worked that out?' Thorne asked.

Kitson walked past Thorne, who was waiting for toast, and dropped a herbal teabag into one of the small, metal teapots-for-one, which invariably dribbled your tea all over the table when you tried to use it. 'A good-news, bad-news joke,' she said. 'A whole fucking series of them.'

Thorne reached for a foil-wrapped rectangle of butter and a sachet of jam, thinking that when Kitson was in a bad mood, she swore almost as much as Richard Rawlings did. His own language was industrial by any standards much of the time, but he'd started to notice it in others. Another hangover from his father's final months, perhaps.

'I take it you've got a joke for me, then . . .'

They carried their trays to a table; sat next to a group of detectives from another team who'd just come off the overnight shift. These officers ate their breakfasts in virtual silence; worn out, but relieved at having put a Friday all-nighter behind them. Thorne had worked that shift enough to know that one or two would be having mixed feelings about a day ahead with their families; potentially tense and stressful after what was invariably the toughest eight hours of the week.

'Good news: we've got the name of a man identified as our killer by the victim's girlfriend.' Kitson poured her tea. Used a paper serviette to mop up the spills. 'Bad news: he's disappeared.'

'Kemal?'

'The dry cleaner's has been closed for a week and the neighbours haven't clapped eyes on him. Done a bunk, by the look of it.'

Thorne spoke through a mouthful of toast. 'Well, it's certainly not great news if you need a shirt pressed, but it sounds like he's your man.'

'Right. Which is why it's fucking bad news.'

One of the other detectives looked across, as though foul language from a woman this early in the day was putting him off his full English. Kitson stared back, leaving him in no doubt that there was plenty more where that came from.

'He'll turn up,' Thorne said.

'If he's still in the country. Probably hiding out in some Turkish fishing village by now.'

'You got people on the ports?'

'It's being "organised".' She put the word in inverted commas, as though to question the efficiency of those doing the organising. 'But I reckon it's too bloody late.'

'Do you think he got wind that his sister knew? That she was likely to grass him up?'

'Who knows?'

'It would explain why she was so scared.'

'Maybe she wasn't the only one who was scared,' Kitson said. 'Deniz Sedat had some seriously unpleasant friends. If I was Hakan Kemal, it wouldn't be the police I was most worried about.'

Thorne nodded, chewed his toast. Thinking that Kitson's theory was all well and good, but that she hadn't come across a certain sort of policeman as yet.

On his way to his office, Thorne walked past as Stone was running over his 'women and bin-bags' routine for an attractive admin officer. It seemed to be working for him.

251

This job's a fucking joke . . .

Plenty of them flying around, and an unusually good atmosphere in the Incident Room. This in spite of the fact that most of those working would rather have been doing something else on a Saturday morning: having sex; watching *Football Focus*; having sex *while* watching *Football Focus*.

Just after breakfast, he'd received a text on his old mobile.

You were SO hot last night. You're the best xxx

Hendricks. Thorne was smiling as he deleted the message. Thinking that a short stay in prison didn't sound too bad as things stood, he'd told Hendricks about the live listening. He knew the cheeky bastard was doing it for the benefit of those intercepting the texts on that line; imagined the comments once they had traced the number.

Mid-morning, Thorne's mood was taken down a notch or two by a call from Keith Bannard.

'Been upsetting my snout?'

Tindall: a covert human information source, or CHIS, according to a thousand memos and expenses claims. But anyone wishing not to sound wholly ridiculous used the well-worn slang, beloved of every fictional cop from Jack Regan onwards.

'Obviously he's easily upset.'

'Yeah, well, it's me that gets the earache . . .'

Listening to him, Thorne imagined the man from S&O as a TV policeman: a no-nonsense country copper running amok in the big city; red face and big flapping hands, constantly outraged by the way people did things and by the price of everything. Sorting things out his way.

Thorne explained why he and Holland had made the trip to Soho. That though Mr Tindall was clearly a very sensitive individual, he was also a lying toerag.

'Get anything?' Bannard asked.

'What, you mean apart from the grief and the offer of free tickets to a dirty film?'

'Yeah, well, we all get those.'

'I got a list of names.' Thorne told Bannard about the conversation

Tindall claimed to have had with Marcus Brooks; about the people he'd advised Brooks to go and speak to about accommodation. He read out the names.

'You talked to any of them yet?' Bannard asked.

'Some are getting visits later today.'

'Good luck.'

Thorne was hardly surprised that Bannard was pessimistic. 'What the fuck is it with these people when it comes to talking to the police? I don't mean incriminating themselves, or grassing someone up. I mean just saying *anything*. With the Black Dogs it's like a badge of honour or something. With the boys in the suits it's right up there with pie and mash, and boxing, and loving their mums.'

'Maybe it's just you,' Bannard said. 'They all talk to me.'

'Only when you've got something on them.'

'It helps.'

'How did you get Tindall to start talking?'

'Money, mate.' Bannard was matter-of-fact. 'Easiest way of all. His wife was ill, about to croak, I think. He needed money to help look after her.'

Thorne felt a twinge of guilt at his appraisal of Tindall. At the same time he thought that Bannard's character would perhaps be too steely for even the most jaded of television viewers. 'Anything you can put our way?' he asked. 'On any of these names?'

'Not really.'

'Thought you might have some . . . leverage.'

'Listen, mate, if I had anything on any of those bastards, I'd have used it by now.'

'Just a thought.'

'No harm in asking.'

'Haven't you got anybody on the inside with any of these firms?'

Bannard sucked in a breath; answered like a taxi-driver being asked to drive south of the river at 4 a.m. 'Can't really go there, mate.' He said he'd ask around, see if anyone else on his team had any bright ideas. Everyone had different contacts.

Thorne said that he'd be grateful. 'What we were talking about the other night,' he added. 'Under the bridge. I was wondering if the Black Dogs had got themselves a new leader yet.' He was thinking about who else Marcus Brooks might be planning on getting rid of. The message he was expecting some time that day.

Bannard sniffed. 'Well, if they have, I don't know who it is. I'll get word eventually. It'll be some long-haired fucker with tattoos, though, I can promise you that.'

Thorne knew what Bannard meant. He'd already been getting the three dead bikers mixed up in his head: a mass of dead white flesh and coloured ink.

'I reckon that's why they've got the nicknames,' Bannard said. 'So they can tell each other apart.'

'Makes sense,' Thorne said. Bannard had been joking, but it was what his old man had done when everything had started to short-circuit. Names had been the first things to go, replaced by simple – and usually unflattering – physical descriptions. Everyone from the man who ran the newsagent's to Tom Thorne himself.

'So, is that your best bet?' Bannard asked. 'The names you got from Tindall.'

'Best bet?'

'Trying to trace Brooks, I mean.'

Well, apart from the cosy text messages we send each other in the early hours, thought Thorne.

'We're chasing up a few other things,' he said.

Actually, there were more than a few.

The so-called golden twenty-four hours after Martin Cowans' corpse was hauled out of the canal had yielded nothing remotely precious, but there were still plenty of active leads to follow up: the property taken from the address in Hammersmith; the latest description of Marcus Brooks; the information provided by Davey Tindall. Though officers had been dispatched to question those on Tindall's list, most of the inquiry team – which had now swelled to fifty-plus police and civilian staff – were busy where most modern detective work was done: at a desk, with phone, fax and computer keyboard all within easy reach.

These days, the majority of medical claims filed by Met employees were for bad backs or repetitive strain injury. Not even patrol officers – teamed up as often as not with CSO part-timers – suffered with their feet any more. Although Thorne thought he probably wore out a little more shoe-leather than most; certainly for someone of his rank.

'Yeah, but that's not because you're chasing stuff up, is it? It's because you're usually running away from something.' Holland, or Hendricks . . . *someone* taking the piss, had said that.

Once Thorne had got off the phone, still with no real idea why Bannard had called, he caught up with Holland.

'Still haven't learned to keep my big mouth shut, have I?' the DS said. At Thursday's briefing, he'd suggested that they might be able to find out where Brooks had bought his car. Aside from his trip into Soho with Thorne, he'd spent most of the time since regretting it.

He pushed a stack of papers across his desk, towards Thorne. 'Used-car dealers in Acton, Brentford, Chiswick and Shepherd's Bush. Hundreds of the buggers, and that's without the dodgy ones.' He reached for a Post-It on which he'd scribbled some notes. 'Found a couple of decent second-hand BMWs you might be interested in. You know, whenever you fancy trading in the puke-mobile.'

'Not listening,' Thorne said.

Holland rolled back his chair, pointed at a thick pile of old newspapers and car magazines. 'That's been a treat, too. Calling up every low-life who might've flogged a dark Mondeo for cash a few days ago. You should hear the intake of breath when I tell them where I'm calling from. Like someone's been killed because they've sold some poor sod a death-trap . . .'

'Sounds like you've had fun,' Thorne said. Holland had been joking, but as far as the cases they normally picked up went, the car was the murder weapon more often than the gun or the knife. Thorne handed the sheaf of papers back across, suddenly reminded that paperwork of his own was tucked away in his desk drawer.

Letters from a man to his dead wife and child.

'The DCI was looking for you,' Karim said, behind him.

Thorne turned. 'Well, he wasn't looking very hard. I've only been here and in the office.'

Karim pulled a *what do I know?* face, and followed it with one that suggested they continue the conversation somewhere else.

They walked into the corridor.

'Brigstocke's got some *appointment* or other.'

Karim had emphasised the word enough for Thorne to know that the DCI had not gone to see his dentist. Thorne asked the question with a look.

'Solicitor,' Karim said. 'Sounds like this DPS business, whatever it is, has moved up a gear.'

Same as everything else, Thorne thought.

'So, you're acting DCI.'

'*What?*'

'Only until he gets back. Shouldn't be more than a few hours.'

'Why me? It isn't usually me.'

'You're not usually around. Anyway, that's what he said, and personally I reckon you could do with more responsibility.'

Karim was laughing as he wandered away, but Thorne's mind was already elsewhere: thinking of something Sharon Lilley had said that night in the pub, when she'd told him that her DCI had stepped back to let her run the Tipper inquiry.

Had she mentioned a name?

She'd said that the idea had been for her to 'try the shoes on for size', get used to heading up a major investigation. But Thorne was thinking of less altruistic reasons why an officer might not want to be involved.

If he knew the prime suspect personally, for example. If he'd been one of the two men responsible for making him the prime suspect.

Thorne walked along the corridor towards his office. Lilley had said she was unsure where her DCI had ended up; something about him being the sort to land on his feet. Thorne made a mental note to try and find out where he had landed.

As he turned into the office, he almost bumped into Kitson coming out.

'We've found Kemal,' she said. 'He's in Bristol, or at least he was two days ago.'

'Aren't you even a *bit* disappointed?'

'Sorry?'

'I know you were angling for a trip to that Turkish fishing village.'

'I'll settle for a day out in Bristol,' Kitson said. 'It's got good shops.'

They stood in the narrow corridor. There were posters behind glass promoting new initiatives: a crackdown on bail absconders; a campaign to keep hate crime out of sport. A bar-chart proudly trumpeting an increase in the clear-up rate of murders Met-wide to 87 per cent.

If they didn't catch Marcus Brooks, Thorne thought, they'd need to redraw the chart.

'There was a parking ticket issued two days ago in Bristol city centre. A Renault registered to Hakan Kemal.'

'Has he paid it yet?'

'I think he's got bigger things to worry about.'

'So what's in Bristol?'

'I've no idea. Somewhere to hide, I suppose.'

'Are you going to talk to the sister again?'

From the office, Thorne became aware of a muffled beeping – the tone from his prepay, sounding in the pocket of his jacket. The sound of a message arriving. He walked casually past Kitson and across to the chair, trying to keep at least one ear on what she was saying.

'. . . called earlier, and got her answering machine . . .'

Nodding, saying, 'Go on,' Thorne took out the phone and automatically angled his body away from Kitson, who had followed him inside, still talking.

'I was thinking about having a word with the parents.'

A small envelope was flashing on the screen. Another number Thorne didn't recognise.

'But I think we should give Harika a chance to get back to me first.'

He clicked SHOW then scrolled down; pressed PLAY to begin the video clip.

At that moment everything they'd been talking about, everything that Thorne had been thinking, went out of his head in an instant. Kemal, the follow-up on Sharon Lilley's DCI . . . *everything*. Kitson's words faded, as though huge hands had been clamped hard across Thorne's ears.

Like she was talking to him underwater.

The fifteen-second clip ended. Froze. A silver estate car; a man walking away from it.

Thorne was looking at a picture of Phil Hendricks.

TWENTY-FIVE

Hendricks laughed when Thorne told him. Nervous laughter perhaps, but he certainly *sounded* unconcerned. 'He's trying to wind you up, mate.'

'Well, he's fucking succeeded.'

'That's been the point all along, hasn't it? Trying to get a reaction.'

Thorne could not remember what he'd blurted out at Kitson as he'd rushed from their office, carrying the prepay phone down to the far end of the corridor. He'd stepped into the stairwell, taken a large, unwelcome breath of apprehension from that new carpet, and dialled Hendricks' mobile.

'What are you doing today?' Thorne asked.

'Getting smashed over the head with a hammer, apparently.'

'Don't joke about it.'

'It *is* a fucking joke.'

'Listen, you should probably stay inside. And get somebody to stay with you—'

'Just calm down . . .'

Thorne was trying his best, but it wasn't easy. Hendricks' refusal to be alarmed was only increasing his own agitation; his own panic. 'For fuck's sake, Phil. Have you not seen what's been happening for the last couple of weeks? How many bodies have you worked on?'

'Bikers and bent coppers, the lot of them. All people Brooks blamed for his girlfriend's death. That's the pattern, right?'

'All people I got sent pictures of.'

'It's a wind-up, I'm telling you.'

'Sorry, but you're not the one who gets to make that decision.'

Hendricks laughed again, but to Thorne it felt like a finger jabbed into his chest. 'Before you start playing the by-the-book copper, you should remember who you're talking to, mate.'

'Who gets to do *your* PM, Phil? Do you have to nominate some-one?'

'Now you're being ridiculous.'

'Seriously,' Thorne said, 'I'm interested.'

'And I'm the one that's supposed to be the drama queen. Christ . . .'

Thorne stared down over the narrow banister, listening to his friend breathe. This was how they argued. Politics or the Premiership, Thorne would be the one to lose it, to do most of the shouting, while Hendricks mocked him; blasé or sarcastic, then often seething for hours, even days afterwards.

'What have I got to do with any of this?' Hendricks said, eventually. 'Just think about it for one minute, and you'll see how ridiculous it is.'

'You're connected to me. That might be enough.'

'Come on, this bloke doesn't kill for kicks, does he? He's doing it to settle scores.'

Thorne's initial panic began to subside a little as he saw the sense in what his friend was saying. There was no good reason for Brooks to want Hendricks dead; certainly not the Brooks Thorne thought he'd been starting to understand. 'I know that, and you're probably right, but I'm just asking you to be careful. Stay where you are and watch TV or something. Get a pizza delivered. It won't kill you.'

'Do you want to rephrase that?'

'Not really,' Thorne said. 'Where are you? At home?'

'No . . .'

'That's good, now stay put.' Thorne had not only recognised Hendricks' car in the video clip. He had watched it pull up outside Hendricks' home address. 'Is there anybody with you?'

'It's not a problem,' Hendricks said. 'I've got a nice, tough police officer to look after me. Well, she's in the shower at the minute, but I don't think she was planning on going anywhere.'

He was at Louise's place.

'She's got strange taste in blokes, but I think she can take care of herself.'

Thorne couldn't argue with that, and he was growing more certain by the second that Hendricks was right – that there was no real cause for concern – but he couldn't help asking himself, bearing in mind where Brooks had probably got his information from, if he knew where Louise lived as well.

He tried to put the thought out of his mind.

'What does Brigstocke say?'

Suddenly, Thorne had an even tougher question to answer. 'He doesn't know.'

'Because . . .?'

Because I'm a fucking idiot, Thorne thought.

He told Hendricks about the night he'd received the first text from Brooks, in the garden of Paul Skinner's house. The moment when he'd realised there was a police officer at the centre of the case who had probably killed twice already and was responsible for many more deaths. When Thorne had realised that was not information he wanted to share. He told him that he'd been in contact with Brooks several times since, on a line that was not being monitored; that he'd known Cowans was dead before his body was ever discovered.

That he knew Brooks was planning to kill again.

'You've got a nerve,' Hendricks said, when Thorne had finished. 'Lecturing me.'

'Warning you.'

'Well, thanks very much, I'll consider myself warned.'

261

'This doesn't change what I said, Phil.'

'Doesn't it?'

'Don't be a twat.' Thorne was shouting; losing it again. But deep down, he knew it was because he'd also lost any authority. 'So, I've fucked up. It isn't the first time.'

'Might well be the last, though.'

'It can't hurt to be careful. All right?'

'Why don't you just ask your friend Brooks if he's planning on doing me in? Might save us all a lot of trouble.'

'It doesn't work like that.'

Thorne could hear the anger in his friend's silence. Imagined an expression he'd seen only once or twice and felt a flutter of relief that they were not talking face to face.

'I'd better go and lock the doors,' Hendricks said. 'Like a good boy.'

'Listen, Phil . . . don't tell Louise.'

'What? That someone might be trying to kill me? Or that you've been getting matey with him on the quiet?'

Thorne didn't have a quick answer.

'If you really wanted to play God, mate, you should have become a fucking doctor . . .'

Whatever his face was saying to the contrary, Thorne spent much of his lunch hour in the Royal Oak telling people that nothing was the matter. He found it hard to share Kitson's excitement at the possibility of tracking down Hakan Kemal in Bristol. Or to react to news that, of those on Tindall's list thus far interviewed, none had cooperated when questioned about helping Marcus Brooks find somewhere to stay.

'Struck dumb as soon as they see a warrant card, those fuckers,' Karim said.

Laughter and jeers when Stone added: 'I wish it worked with some of the women I know.'

Thorne pushed lukewarm shepherd's pie around his plate and thought about what Hendricks had said before hanging up on him.

262

Home truths and hard questions.

Had he chosen to go his own sweet and stupid way because it was his best chance of nailing Brooks *and* the corrupt officer who'd sparked off the killing spree? Because he'd begun to doubt which side anyone was on? Or was it really because he thought that his own judgement was sounder than anyone else's? That a snap decision was smarter than the combined wisdom of a hard-working squad, every bit as experienced as he was?

God wasn't part of a team, after all.

Hendricks had been trying to score a point, but Thorne was starting to think his friend had hit the bull's-eye. His was one of the few opinions that Thorne respected. Which was, he concluded miserably, precisely the problem.

Depressing as these moments of self-realisation were, he was at least feeling more confident that Hendricks was in no immediate danger. But there had still been that nauseating jolt of alarm, when he'd wondered if Louse's flat was any safer than Hendrick's own.

Bearing in mind where Brooks had probably got his information from . . .

Hendricks had been right; it was almost certainly a wind-up. But it hadn't been Marcus Brooks ratcheting up the torment. Thorne decided that he'd be paying another visit to Long Lartin as soon as the opportunity presented itself.

Walking out of the pub, Kitson put a hand on his arm, clearly less convinced than others by his assurances that all was well.

'You're going to get a result,' she said. 'We both are.'

Thorne thought about that bar-chart outside their office and did his best to smile.

'Come on, Guv, it's your job to motivate the rest of us.'

'*Guv?*'

'Acting DCI.'

Thorne pulled on his jacket. I've been acting for days, he thought.

The day was cold; a wind roaring into their faces as they stepped out into the car park. A horn sounded behind them and Thorne turned to look at a black Volvo parked alongside a row of wheelie-bins. He recognised the back of the driver's head and told Kitson and the others he'd catch up.

The Volvo's driver leaned across to push open the passenger door and Thorne climbed gingerly in; backing on to the leather seat first, then swinging his legs around and into the footwell before pulling the door to.

'You OK?' Nunn asked.

Thorne nodded. He'd had back surgery a few months previously and though the pain had gone, he was still cautious. A small part of him still fantasised about stepping in next time Spurs were going through a goal drought, but the more practical side told him not to get out of bed too quickly.

'Nice car,' Thorne said. The Volvo's interior was immaculate; smelled new.

'Thought you were more of a vintage bloke.'

'Have you got Dave Holland working undercover?'

Nunn stared, not getting it. Thorne told him it didn't matter.

It was warm in the car, and Nunn had been listening to the radio. He nudged down the volume. 'How was your chat with Richard Rawlings?'

Thorne saw that the radio was tuned into Magic FM; an old Petula Clark song. 'Was it me you were watching, or Rawlings?'

'Maybe we were watching the pub and got lucky,' Nunn said. 'What did Rawlings want?'

So, Nunn knew that Rawlings had requested the meeting. It was the most likely scenario, but Thorne still wondered if the DPS were privy to the intercept on his home phone. He was past being surprised by anything.

'He reckons you lot have got it in for him. Wanted me to use my "influence" to get you to ease off. Or something.'

'What did you tell him?'

'That I don't have any influence.'

'That took you an hour and a half, did it?'

'Mostly it was him, swearing.' Nunn smiled. 'I *don't* have any influence, do I?'

'It's not the word I would use, but we're working on cases that are hopefully going to cross over at some point. What you do will probably be influential.'

At some point. The moment when the identity of the man they were both after – although Thorne could still not be sure if they were chasing him for the same reason – was brought out into the open. Then it would be down to clout, pure and simple, and Thorne knew who was carrying the most.

'Rawlings is an aggressive little bastard though, isn't he?' Nunn sucked his teeth. 'I wouldn't like to be around when he loses his temper.'

'He's scared.'

'No point being scared if you haven't done anything.'

'That's bollocks,' Thorne said. 'You know very well that you lot are there to scare people.'

'To remind them, maybe.'

'They give you special training, don't they?'

'You're not scared, are you?'

'Constantly.'

Nunn nodded. 'Makes sense. We've got a good-sized file on you, so you'd be stupid not to worry a little.'

Thorne stared straight ahead. Petula had cross-faded into Glen Campbell singing 'Rhinestone Cowboy'.

Three years before, Thorne had been indirectly responsible for the death of a prominent north London gangster. Few had mourned, but Thorne lived with the knowledge that the day might come when he would have to answer for it. He could not know if this event, or others that came close, was in a DPS file; but more worrying were the reasons why Nunn had chosen to tell him such a file existed at all. Thorne could sense that an offer of some kind was being made, but there had also been a threat thrown in for good measure.

He looked across, but Nunn had turned to peer out of his window at nothing in particular.

You'd be stupid not to worry a little . . .

Thorne didn't like Richard Rawlings, and trusted him even less, but he'd been happy enough to remain non-committal in an effort to get Nunn's take on it. Suddenly, it seemed like there was no further point in going round the houses. Not when he was up against an expert. 'When Skinner was killed, I asked if you felt disappointed, that you'd missed out on nicking him, remember?'

'"Robbed" was the word you used,' Nunn said. 'And I told you that yes, I did.'

Thorne wondered if Nunn had a good memory or a tape recorder. Decided he was getting seriously paranoid. '"Robbed" because you'd lost the chance to put one bent copper away? Or two?'

'Two's always better than one. *Always.*'

'Well, either you know who the other copper is and you were hoping Skinner would give you the evidence. Or you were banking on Skinner telling you who his partner was.'

'Doesn't really matter now he's dead.'

'Which is it?'

The advantage of playing virtual poker, especially when your face gave away as much as Thorne's usually did, was that you could dance around with glee when your hole cards were revealed and only someone in the room with you would know you'd been dealt aces. Thorne looked at Nunn, hoping to see some sort of 'tell'. Saw him nodding along with the song on the radio and decided that the DPS man was probably a far better poker player than he was.

'Look, we both know what this man's done,' Thorne said. '"Squire".' That got a reaction. It was the first time the name had been mentioned between them. 'We both want him put away, but it seems to me like one of us thinks it's some sort of competition.'

'You're wrong.'

'Am I? Way it's going, we'll only find out who this fucker is when he turns up with his skull smashed in.'

Nunn looked frightened suddenly. 'That's not going to happen.' It certainly sounded as though he knew something.

'So, is it Rawlings?' Nothing. 'Does Rawlings know?'

Thorne let out a long sigh, sucked it back in hard when Nunn turned in his seat to stare at him.

'So, one of us thinks it's a competition,' Nunn said. 'And I suppose only one of us is being totally honest. Gobbing off like he's the only one playing straight, not keeping anything to himself . . .'

Try as he might, Thorne knew he was reddening. If Nunn knew that he'd been communicating secretly with Marcus Brooks, then Thorne was fucked, file or no file. He felt as cornered as Rawlings had claimed to feel; as he knew Brigstocke felt, whatever he had been accused of doing. 'It's not hard to see why you fuckers are so unpopular.'

Nunn smiled, as though it was a predictable response from someone on the back foot. Like it was something he'd heard plenty of times before. 'You don't think it's worth doing? Making sure the shit gets flushed away?'

'It's not just the shit though, is it?'

'I don't do this because I enjoy the looks when people know which department you're working for. I don't love being called a scab and a fuck of a lot worse, hearing the conversation stop when you walk into the canteen. Do you honestly reckon I'd be doing it if I didn't think it was important?'

On the train a few days before, Thorne had thought he'd sensed a vulnerability; something not quite hidden by the long coat and shaved head. He thought he caught another glimpse of weakness now, in the vehemence, but it had gone before he had even finished the thought.

'We're well aware what people think,' Nunn said. '*Most* people . . .'

Neil Diamond, now: 'Beautiful Noise'. A song Thorne loved, in spite of himself. 'Well, if you've got the faintest idea what *I* think,' he said, 'I'd be happy to hear it. Because at the minute, I haven't got a fucking clue.'

Nunn leaned forward and turned up the volume. Apparently, their conversation was over.

★

The Neil Diamond song was still in his head, becoming less of a favourite all the time, when Thorne called Louise, mid-afternoon. He could barely hear her when she picked up.

'What the hell's that?'

Louise had to raise her voice over some very *un*easy listening in the background. 'Some piece of thrash-metal Phil brought over with him.'

'OK . . .'

Hendricks was still there.

Thorne heard Louise shouting at Hendricks to turn the music down; heard it stop completely a few seconds later. When Louise came back to the phone, she was almost whispering.

'He's in a seriously strange mood, by the way.'

So, Hendricks hadn't mentioned their earlier conversation to Louise. That was probably no bad thing. Thorne toyed with telling her about the message, about Hendricks' refusal to take it seriously, but decided against it. She was bound to ask the same question Hendricks had, about what Brigstocke thought, and Thorne did not want to get into any of *that*. He could always have told her that he was acting DCI, of course, but keeping his mouth shut felt slightly better than such near deceit. So he said nothing.

Enough people were thinking badly of him as it was.

'How's it been?' Louise asked, flat.

'Same as ever. However you feel at the start of the day, it's downhill from breakfast.'

'You must be knackered,' she said. 'Sorry . . .'

'It's fine.' He could hear something being shouted in the background. Told her about the text he'd received from Hendricks that morning.

'Did he? He never said anything.'

It was hardly a surprise. Even as Thorne recounted Hendricks' *you're the best* message, he couldn't help but think it would be the last joke coming from that direction in a while.

'That's funny,' she said. 'Inaccurate, but funny.'

Thorne was relieved to hear a smile in her voice.

'When can you get over?'

'Shouldn't be too late. Eight, half eight.'

'Maybe we can finally get to see this movie. There's usually late shows on a Saturday.'

'Or the three of us could do something together,' Thorne said. 'Might be easier to just get a DVD out.'

'OK,' Louise said, frosty again.

'I'm booked out for the whole day tomorrow.'

'Yeah, fine. Whatever.'

Thorne guessed that the 'whatever' meant anything but; that Louise had been banking on the two of them spending some time alone. But he hadn't quite been able to forget about that video clip. Perhaps he should simply have told her, because by the time he'd hung up, after half a minute more of fuck all, he knew that Louise was thinking badly of him anyway.

He was on his way out of the door when the panic took hold . . .

Hurrying across the Incident Room, thinking about ways to get back in Louise's good books. Pulling on his jacket and cheerfully telling those he wouldn't see until Monday to enjoy their Sundays at work. Walking past the whiteboard, and glancing at the photographs; the bodies of the first two victims. Tucker and Hodson.

Dead white flesh and coloured ink.

Two thoughts, fragments of conversations, came together – *smashed* together – in his mind and started the wheels racing.

The feeble joke Bannard had cracked about all bikers looking the same: all long hair and tattoos. And something Hendricks had said at Tucker's post-mortem, the one they'd watched together . . .

Thorne walked back to his office, pressed his body against the door after he'd closed it. Wondering, *hoping* that this was no more than cabin-fever. He used his prepay to call Louise's flat, then Hendricks' mobile.

Got no reply from either.

He thought hard, *breathed* hard for a minute or more, then dialled another number.

TWENTY-SIX

By the time he got off the phone, it was as sorted as it was ever going to be, but Brooks wasn't happy. It didn't feel right having to involve other people; having to rely on anybody. Each one should have been his alone, by rights.

This wasn't the way he did things.

He sat up on the soft bed in Tindall's spare room, looked at himself in the mirror on the dressing-table opposite.

It was almost beyond belief, this shit-house he'd become.

The way he did things.

Christ . . .

And it wasn't like he was talking about the way he packed a suitcase or drove a car. These weren't things he'd ever thought about, not seriously; even at the darkest moments, just after he'd gone inside. But everything changed you, big or small, didn't it? Turned you into someone else. Every single thing you saw or thought, so that you were never the same person from one second to the next. How the fuck could you be? Maybe, eventually, good and bad, that made you into the person you were always meant to become.

Murder was now something he did, simple as that. And he was a damn sight happier doing it on his own.

Nobody made him take the advice, or accept the offer of help, on this one, but it made sense under the circumstances. It squared things. And this fucker clearly deserved it as much as anyone else.

He pulled faces at himself . . .

It wasn't like he couldn't work with other people. He'd really enjoyed those couple of years when him and Angie were doing the houses together; loved them. But you had to be working for the same thing, doing it for the same reasons. The two of them had nicked shit and sold it to put food on the table. To pay for clothes and holidays and stuff for Robbie. End of story. They both had the same attitude to the work, so they thought the same way when it came to whether a risk was worth taking, whether the payoff was worth it, whatever. They had the same boundaries.

Nobody else involved in what he was doing could feel the same way he did. Not when he was bringing the hammer down. There'd have to be a moment, some point, when any other person would think they'd had enough, and walk away. He couldn't imagine what it would be like to reach that point.

Nobody else could feel as much, or as little, as he did.

He shuffled forward and off the bed; moved across to the mirror on his knees and pressed his face up close to it. Fuck, he looked like he was pushing fifty. Like his dad had looked those couple of times in the visitors' room.

Sorry, baby, he thought. I swear I was looking good right before it all happened; looking better than this, anyway. I'd even been working out for a few months, watching what I ate and all that. I didn't want to come back to you flabby and fucked, like Nicklin and the rest of them, you know?

Everything changes you, big or small; changes your plans. Course, I didn't know that when I was leaving my spuds at dinnertime and doing circuits in the gym at Long Lartin. Didn't think you were going anywhere, did I?

That I'd be walking out of one prison and into another.

★

'Mr Yashere? DI Thorne.'

A pause. 'I left a message with you three days ago.'

'The missing training shoe.'

'Correct. The shoe that has gone walkabout. Do you have it?'

'No . . .'

'Losing such an important piece of evidence is causing something of a problem, to put it mildly.' Yashere spoke slowly, with precision. A Nigerian accent.

'I promise that I will find it,' Thorne said. 'And when I do, I will personally deliver it to you, in a box, with a fuck-off red ribbon round it. But right now I need a favour.'

'I was just about to go home.'

The Crown Prosecution Service had a small office round the corner at Colindale station, but via the out-of-hours service Thorne had been put through to their Criminal Justice Unit at the main station in Edmonton. This was where Anthony Yashere and his fellow-caseworkers were based: collating exhibits; ensuring the integrity of evidence chains; firing off snippy emails and phone calls when blood-stained training shoes disappeared.

Thorne explained what he needed.

Yashere took details, dates and names. Told Thorne that he could probably get him the trial transcript in a few days.

'Not quick enough,' Thorne said. 'Sorry.'

Yashere began to think out loud, guiding Thorne through the process as he logged into his IT system. It provided a summary of all ongoing cases, but was not yet fully up to date with trials whose details had been on the system it had replaced three years before.

Thorne listened to the click of computer keys. To grunts and sighs of frustration.

'We are going back quite a long way,' Yashere said. 'Perhaps I should ask a colleague who knows his way around the system better than I do.'

Thorne had a better idea. 'Who was the prosecutor? You must have that on record.'

'I think so.'

'Do you have a number?'

Yashere logged out of one system and into another. More clicking, more waiting.

'I think you will need a home number,' Yashere said. 'There are not too many fools like you and I still working at this time on a Saturday.' He said that he'd try to get hold of Stuart Emery and have him call Thorne back.

Thorne gave Yashere his prepay phone number. 'Can you tell him that it's very urgent?' he said.

'Please don't forget my missing training shoe, Inspector . . .'

Thorne tried Hendricks' mobile again, and got no answer. He paced the office; told Kitson he'd see her on Monday when she stuck her head in to say goodnight; checked his watch every couple of minutes.

Ten minutes after Thorne had spoken to Yashere, Stuart Emery called.

Brooks climbed back up the bare wooden stairs from Tindall's cellar. There was no electricity down there and he'd had to use a shitty little torch he'd dug out of a kitchen drawer. A kid's thing with a thin, milky beam. He'd managed to find a couple of hammers, in a dusty canvas tool-bag, among the piles of damp magazines and boxes of videos, and he carried them both up to get a good look in the light.

He chose the smaller of the two: a claw hammer with green paint on the handle. Dropped it into a plastic bag which he carried down the hall and left by the front door.

There was plenty of time yet.

He wandered back into the kitchen and knelt to peer into the fridge. Tindall's dog immediately climbed from her basket in the corner and scampered across to see what might be going. Milk, beer, onions. There were some tinned tomatoes in a dish, and Brooks thought about making some toast to go with them. In the end he settled for the plate of cooked sausages, set in fat under greasy cling-film.

He carried the plate to the small table against the wall and dropped half a sausage to the floor for the dog. It was chucking it down outside. He could see the rain bouncing off the felt on the shed roof.

He remembered Angie screaming at him one Sunday after he had taken Robbie over the field for a kick-about and they had both come home soaked, bouncing a muddy ball. Robbie thought it was funny, and shook his wet hair all over the kitchen before Angie could fetch a towel, which made her even angrier. The two of them pissing themselves. Angie shouting while she stripped off Robbie's tiny West Ham shirt.

The dog was on its hind legs, pawing at his shins, so he lifted her up on to his lap. Let her lick the grease off the plate. He rubbed the dog's bristly belly, and tried to stretch the memory out. In the end, he wasn't sure if there were bits he was only imagining, but he had a clear enough picture of his son's face; Robbie shaking his wet head, his two front teeth still coming through.

That would be the picture he'd try to hold on to when he was reaching into the plastic bag later on.

Stuart Emery was brisk, just the right side of surly, asking Thorne what he wanted the information for. Thorne tried to keep it quick and simple.

I want to be proved wrong, he thought.

For the second time, Thorne listened as someone at the end of a phone tried to call up the information that would confirm or assuage his worst fears.

'Got twelve years of review notes on here somewhere,' Emery said.

Thorne tried to stay calm while the wind threw rain against the window like tin-tacks.

'Regina versus Brooks, yes?'

'September 2000. Middlesex Crown Court.' Thorne waited, willing each tap of a computer key to be the last.

'Good job I'm organised,' Emery said. '"Anal", according to my wife.'

For pity's sake . . .

'Here we go . . . right. "Sentencing remarks", "witness statements", "pathology reports", "grounds for appeal" . . . These are just my notes, you understand?'

Thorne stopped him, asked him to go back. Emery read, gave him a name. Then another.

His worst fears.

He spluttered out a 'thank you', then jerked the phone back to his mouth as he was about to hang up. He needed to move fast, but there was one more question he needed to ask: 'Can anybody get hold of this stuff? Is it online?'

'Well, by and large, it's just specialist rulings,' Emery said. 'Judgements that pass into case law, that kind of thing. Mind you, I suppose most things are on the bloody Internet somewhere, if you can be bothered to look hard enough.'

If you've got the time, Thorne thought . . .

The panic fizzed in him, and anger tightened every muscle, every thought. Anger at Brooks, at the man Thorne knew was putting him up to this, and above all at himself. The procedure in this kind of emergency, this kind of *nightmare*, should have been straightforward. But Thorne knew too bloody well that he'd left himself no easy options.

He punched in Brigstocke's mobile number.

Russell, I've been fucking stupid and I don't care what happens when this is finished, but we've got a serious situation . . .

He changed his mind and tried Louise one more time.

'Where've you been? I've been calling.'

'I nipped out to the supermarket.'

'Is Phil with you?'

'No, he left about an hour ago. You OK?'

'I've tried calling him. Shit . . .'

'Tom, what's the matter?'

So, Thorne told her what he'd discovered: about the message that was far from being a wind-up. And in a rush, garbled and guilty, he told her everything else. The evidence he'd kept to himself; the conversations that had gone unreported; the cracked and rotten limb he'd gone out on.

There wasn't even a pause. 'You're a fucking idiot.'

'I know, and I don't have time,' Thorne shouted. 'You can call me everything under the sun later on. Now, I need to get hold of people. To find Phil.'

'You said you'd tried to call him . . .'

'His phone just kept ringing. He hasn't got it with him, or he can't hear it.'

'I know where he is,' Louise said. 'There's three or four places in town, could be any one of them. He asked me to go with him.'

'Three or four?'

'Some nights he calls in on all of them. Depends who he meets.'

'Christ . . .'

'Listen, I've been to these places. I know where they are.'

Thorne was finding it hard to concentrate. He was dizzy with the panic; with the increasing odds against everything turning out the right way.

Who gets to do your PM, Phil?

'Tom . . .?'

'I should call Brigstocke. Tell him everything.'

'Wait.' Louise's voice was quiet, steel in it, suddenly. 'You don't have to call anyone.'

'We need to get officers out there.'

'You willing to fuck your career up?'

'It doesn't seem very important now.'

'We can do this.'

Thorne leaned against his desk, thinking for a moment that he might be sick. There were pinpricks of sweat across his shoulders, in the small of his back. He felt murderous. Helpless. 'How?'

'Who do you trust?' Louise asked.

'I don't know. Holland . . . Kitson . . .'

'Just get Holland.'

Thorne felt the urge to argue, but said nothing. Louise had given him orders before, when they'd worked together. She was better at it than he was. 'Right.'

She told him to stay calm and listen; gave him the addresses of two gay clubs in the West End. 'You and Holland get to those. I'll round a couple of my boys up and we'll take the other two. They'll do it for me if I tell them it's important. No questions asked.'

'It's Saturday night.'

'There are plenty of people *I* can trust, OK?'

Thorne hung up and flew along the corridor. He found Holland at his desk, his nose in a copy of *Auto Trader*.

'Remember what I said about leading you into trouble?'

Holland took one look at Thorne's face and stood up. Thorne began to talk, explaining and apologising, as he all but dragged Holland towards the exit; filling him in as best he could as they took the stairs two at a time and crashed out through the doors, into the rain.

TWENTY-SEVEN

They hit the top end of Tottenham Court Road inside fifteen minutes.

Holland had helped himself to a magnetic blue strobe-lamp and Thorne had stuck it to the roof of the car, running the cable in through the window and plugging it into the cigarette lighter. Neither had said much on the drive, and it wasn't just a matter of necessary concentration, or Thorne's use of the horn, or alarm at their speed on the wet roads, that had kept the conversation to a minimum.

There wasn't really too much to say.

Holland had plenty of questions for Thorne, but he knew they would have to wait. In silence, braced against the dashboard, he asked himself a few questions that *he* didn't have any answers for. Some of the ones Sophie would ask, if she knew.

Thorne had to pull over hard as an ambulance screamed up the wrong side of the road. He waited, revving the BMW's engine and smacking his hand against the wheel.

'Think about it,' Holland said. 'Brooks isn't going to do anything in the middle of a club, is he? He's probably followed him, same as he did with Cowans.'

Thorne nodded, yanked the wheel across and accelerated out in front of a bus. The driver flashed his lights and leaned on the horn.

'Presuming Hendricks is still . . .' Another nod. *Alive*. Holland didn't need to say it. 'We've probably got until the end of the night.'

Thorne looked at his watch: it wasn't even nine o'clock.

'There's time,' Holland said.

What Holland was saying made sense, but Thorne took precious little comfort from it. Driving like a maniac, *thinking* like one, he struggled to focus, to order this thoughts.

He didn't have a picture of Hendricks; nothing to show to bouncers or bar-staff. He'd just have to use his eyes. He thought about the few times he'd been to places like these in the past. There was little enough light to read the label on your beer bottle.

He wondered if he could use the video clip that Brooks had sent . . .

What have I got to do with any of this?

You're connected to me. That might be enough.

Thorne knew now that it was more than that, but he was also certain that he was the primary reason why Hendricks had been targeted. Chosen ahead of another biker, a police officer, anyone.

They crossed Oxford Street on a red light; slowed to weave through the traffic in front of them.

'These two clubs are a couple of minutes' walk from each other,' Thorne said. 'Which one do you want?'

Holland shook his head. 'We do both of them together.'

'No.'

'Come on, aren't we being stupid enough? Whatever you might think about Brooks, about why he's been doing this . . .'

'Fine. Together then.'

'I'm shitting myself,' Holland said, half smiling. 'Don't know about you.'

Thorne knew Holland was right and the last thing he needed was to put anybody else in danger. 'We split up but try to stay in sight of each other.' He knew that he should be afraid of a man who had killed three times, that it ought to make him careful, but it wasn't the thought of confronting Marcus Brooks that was making his stomach jump.

Thorne turned right at Cambridge Circus and stopped the car on yellow lines outside the Spice of Life. They got out.

'So, if I see Hendricks?'

Thorne's fists clenched, and he felt something like relief that he was as angry at Phil Hendricks as he was at anybody else.

'Jump on him,' he said. 'Jump on the fucker hard.'

It had only taken Porter ten minutes to find three officers willing to do as she asked without getting overly curious. She would have liked to put it down to respect, or even affection, but in a couple of cases she thought simple arse-licking was closer to the truth.

It didn't much matter.

On Thorne's insistence she'd sent a DC to Hendrick's place in Deptford, in case he decided to call it a night early. Another officer who lived south of the river was heading for New Cross – to a local place Hendricks used when he couldn't be bothered to go all the way into town. Of all the venues Porter had mentioned to Thorne, she thought that one was the least likely. It was rather more sedate, less 'scene' than the others, and when Thorne had told her that Hendricks had not been answering his phone, she'd felt sure it was because he was somewhere noisy. She thought back to the mood he'd been in earlier, listening to the thrash-metal; guessed that he'd want to be somewhere he could dance, get off his face. Maybe fuck someone until he felt better.

More than anything, she wished she'd said 'yes' the day before, when he'd asked her to go out with him.

Of course, she knew now that Hendricks' mood had been due to his conversation with Thorne. There hadn't been time to get into that when Thorne had finally come clean, but once this was over, *however* it finished, she'd want to know why he hadn't told her earlier; why he'd asked Hendricks not to tell her.

'Guv . . .?'

Detective Sergeant Kenny Parsons pointed towards a small queue running back from a pair of high glass doors, along the front windows of a Pizza Express. Most of those waiting stood under umbrellas, but a few, like Porter and Parsons, didn't seem awfully bothered by the rain.

The Adam was a members-only place, tucked away behind Charing Cross station. It was more bar than club most of the time, but once the dancing kicked off on a Friday or Saturday night, it could get pretty lively. Porter had been here a couple of times with Hendricks and she remembered that this was where he'd met his ex-boyfriend Brendan.

Parsons led the way to the front of the queue and flashed a warrant card at an immaculately dressed female bouncer. She leaned on the door and let them in.

It sounded like the club was in full swing.

Hurrying down the steep staircase, Porter checked her phone. The signal could get iffy below ground, and with Airwave units out of the question for obvious reasons, she and Thorne had agreed to keep in touch via their mobiles.

The music grew louder, and the thought smacked her in the face: if, wherever he was, Hendricks couldn't hear his phone, what guarantee was there that she, Thorne or anyone else would hear theirs? If there was a signal, they'd need to keep the phones on vibrate.

She caught the look from the cloakroom girl as she and Parsons walked past, then pulled Parsons back as he was heading inside and raised her voice above the music. 'Up for this, Kenny?'

Parsons said he was.

Porter had given him a pretty good description of Phil Hendricks, and a somewhat less detailed one of Marcus Brooks. 'Don't worry, he's never used a gun or a knife,' she said, looking through the doorway. 'And look, it's heaving in there. There isn't *room* to swing a hammer.' She leaned in close to his ear. 'Seriously. If I tell you to take someone out, don't fucking think about it twice.'

The club was called Crush, and it lived up to its name, though the place itself wasn't huge, and Thorne didn't think there were more than a hundred people in there. But it was tight and sweaty. The speakers pumped out hardcore soul and Motown, and the small dance floor was heaving with people, most of whom seemed to be dancing *at* each other.

It looked like a serious business.

Thorne took the left-hand side and, as he moved from one end of the main room to the other, he tried to keep Holland in view. The problem wasn't so much the absence of light as the fact that it kept moving. The reds and greens swooped, the circles of white light span and jumped, and none of it stayed in the same place long enough to get a good look at anyone.

Thorne knew he wouldn't need a good look to recognise Hendricks, but Brooks was a different matter.

There was a narrow corridor running off from either side at the far end of the room. To Thorne's left, men were sprawled across chairs, smoking and chatting; some just recovering. He took a long look, then walked back the other way and joined the steady stream of people heading into the toilets.

He put his head around the door; was checked out by several men at the mirror and ignored. He shouted, 'Phil,' and waited. Somebody muttered something and someone else laughed, and the metal hand-dryer rattled against the wall to the bass-beat from the dance floor.

Outside, he caught sight of Holland, who shook his head, and the two of them moved back down the centre of the room to the L-shaped bar by the entrance.

There was a cheer from the dance floor at the opening notes of 'Band of Gold' by Freda Payne. Some kind of remix.

The barman wore a tight black T-shirt with 'Crush' across the chest. 'Yes, guys?' Australian.

'I'm looking for someone,' Thorne said. He realised instantly that it was a foolish thing to say and was grateful that the barman didn't bother with a waspish comeback. He launched into a description of Hendricks.

There was a smile this time. 'Loads of people in here look like that.'

Thorne had seen all sorts since he'd walked through the door. There were soul boys and mods in Fred Perrys. Combats and leathers and expensive jeans with barely any arse in them. No more piercings and tattoos than you'd see in any other club on a Saturday night.

'Not that fucking many,' Thorne said.

The barman swallowed. 'Sorry, mate.'

'So?'

A nod towards bar-staff further down. 'Ask some of the other boys.'

Thorne slid along the bar, and got luckier.

'He got an Arsenal tattoo on his neck?'

Thorne said yes; held his breath.

'Right, I know the guy you mean. Not seen him tonight, though. You want to leave a message in case he comes in later?'

Thorne was already on his way out.

The DJ in The Adam was trying and failing to be Fatboy Slim, but though the music wasn't to Porter's taste, she could see that the clientele were enjoying themselves. She noticed that Parsons was nodding his head in time as he moved among the crowd, clocking everyone. She also saw some of the looks Parsons was getting in return. He was a tall, good-looking black man, and though to Porter he looked every inch a copper, none of the men eyeing him up seemed to notice. Or perhaps they did, she thought. Maybe that was part of the attraction.

The club was spread over two floors and they took one each. It was less crowded than it had first appeared and they managed to sweep the place in fifteen minutes. They spotted a few people who matched the most recent description of Brooks, but no Phil Hendricks.

They began to question the staff, and, after only a few minutes, Porter glanced up to see Parsons beckoning her across to a corner. He continued to wave as she pushed her way across the dance floor. Next to him, a waitress was perched on a small leather cube. Porter wasn't sure if it was a stool or a foot-rest. The girl's ridiculously long legs were emphasised by stockings and a pink tutu. She had dark spiky hair and huge breasts.

Parsons nodded towards Porter. 'Tell her what you told me.'

It was reasonably quiet where they'd gathered and the girl had no need to shout. Her voice was hoarse, though, as if she had been doing a good deal of shouting earlier. 'The bloke he was asking about? He was in here a while ago. He comes in here a lot.'

'Tonight?'

'I didn't see him leave, but, yeah, he was here an hour or so ago. Northern bloke, right?'

'Was he with anyone?' Porter asked.

She ran a hand through her hair; teased up the spikes. 'He was talking to a couple of people, I think. A few of them left at the same time, so maybe he was with them.' She looked harder at Porter. 'I've seen you with him, haven't I?'

'Any idea where he might have gone?'

'Sorry, love, not a clue.' She pushed herself up, grabbed a silver tray which she'd dropped by the side of the chair. She had heels on, but even without them she'd have had a foot on Porter. 'Right, tits and tips . . .'

'Thanks,' Porter said.

The girl's image was as camp as Christmas, but Porter guessed that the tits were probably wasted on the majority of the club's punters. She took a few steps, then came back. 'I heard some people talking about this new place across the bridge,' she said. 'He could have gone there, I suppose.'

'Where?'

'Waterloo, just along from the Old Vic, I think. I don't know, ten minutes' walk?'

When they came back up on to the Strand, Porter checked her mobile for messages. Hendricks hadn't shown up at home, and the second officer had struck out at the club in New Cross. He wanted to know if there was anywhere else she wanted him to visit. Porter called back as she walked, asked him to get across to Brixton. Hendricks had mentioned going to a gay night at The Fridge once, and, unlikely as it was, it seemed a shame to send any of her team home when he was still out there.

Saturday night, we'll have a laugh, he'd said.

When they reached the car, Parsons suggested that it might be quicker to walk. 'There's no right turn on to the bridge. I'll need to go round the Aldwych.'

Porter yanked at the door handle. 'So, go round it *fast.*'

TWENTY-EIGHT

One of the things prison did was change the way you waited.

However long you were inside, and whatever you did while you got through your sentence, you were killing time. Which meant that you never did anything for its own sake. A game of pool was fun or it wasn't, but it was always half an hour's time done. Which meant that you looked forward to things in a different way, or at least *he* had. Being impatient, getting pissed off because a class got cancelled or whatever, was pointless because always, while you were waiting for something to pass the time, it was passing anyway.

Obviously, it depended on what you had on the outside. Some people were pretty calm as it went, but there were always blokes likely to kick off if you looked at them the wrong way. They were usually the ones who didn't care how quick it went, because they had sod all waiting . . .

He waited differently now.

It made him irritable, same as everyone else, and the tiredness didn't help. He'd snapped at Tindall the day before, which he knew was out of order, all things considered.

He'd never bothered with a watch inside; there were always plenty of bells and smells to tell you what time it was. Now he had one, he looked at the thing every few minutes. Feeling every second stagger by on its knees.

Rolling his neck, and swinging the plastic bag.

There were bigger clubs than Beware, Thorne knew that. G-A-Y and Heaven, with thousands of people and four or five different dance areas in the same club. But this was big enough as far as he was concerned. Big enough for Hendricks too, who had told him that the huge places freaked him out. 'The music's better in the smaller clubs,' he'd said. '*Plus*, there's not so much competition when it comes to eligible men.'

'Not so much to choose from, either.' Thorne had grinned. 'Slimmer pickings.'

'I only need to find one good one,' Hendricks had said.

There were three, maybe four hundred people in the club, the strobe lighting making it hard to be any more precise. The sound level made the place he and Holland had just left seem intimate. He had no idea what it was called, and couldn't have cared less, but it was not the sort of music you needed when you were as tense – as scared – as he was.

'Not going to be easy,' Holland said.

Thorne shook his head. He looked up at the lighting rig, at the huge mirrors and the rough sea of reflected heads, and for a few disconcerting seconds he lost a sense of where he was and why he was there. It was as though the noise, the *pressure* of it, was starting to squeeze out the simple thoughts; fuck around with the functions.

He wondered if he'd even know Hendricks if he saw him.

He lost sight of Holland within seconds, as he began to push through the crowd. Ignoring the elbows, and the shoes that scraped his ankles, as he looked at faces and studied the backs of necks.

Christ, it was loud. And hot.

He struggled between two tall men, turned to get a good look at the one with the shaved head. Got glared at by both of them.

287

The sound pulsed up through his feet and pounded in his head like a hammer wrapped in cotton wool.

Hitting and pressing and sucking away the air.

Shtoompshtoompshtoomp . . .

Getting smashed over the head, with a hammer, apparently.

Don't joke about it . . .

Thorne took off his jacket. Craned his head to look for Holland. Caught light gleaming off the metal in a face, and on a jacket, and stared until the man danced away again.

Shtoompshtoompshtoomp . . .

Eyes open, eyes closed as they danced. Putting on a show or lost in it. Face after face and body after body; the shape usually more than enough.

Fuck, Phil . . .

A big man wheeled into the side of him, grinned and mouthed a 'sorry'.

Fuckfuckfuckfuck . . .

He could taste his own sweat and other people's. At the corner of his mouth; diluting the tang of adrenaline.

Salt and metal.

Pushing into warm, wet air and sweaty backs; shoes searching for space on the polished floor; ugly and dull among the Adidas and Nike. What would Phil be wearing?

Trainers, surely; those flashy white and silver ones.

You couldn't dance in biker boots.

Shtoomp . . .

A voice behind, a man he'd just struggled past, telling him to watch where he was fucking going. Thorne stopped and sucked in a hot breath; squinting as a beam of light moved back and forth across his face. Fighting the urge to swing round and lay the twat out.

Saving it up.

Instead, he turned and walked quickly past, pushed back through the crowd towards the raised platform at the far end of the room. Plenty of people mouthing off at him now as he barged across the floor. Leading with his head, sending drinks flying and lurching up to the DJ booth.

Reaching up to slap his warrant card against the glass.

'Turn it off . . .'

The DJ peered down at him as though he were mad. Thorne moved round swiftly and climbed up the short staircase. Realising that this was no ordinary request, the DJ was already pulling off his headphones as Thorne leaned across the decks to grab a handful of his shirt.

'TURN. IT. OFF!'

It was odd, that second or more before the dancing stopped. The lights still swooped and wheeled around the floor as all heads turned towards the platform. A few shouts above the hubbub; arms raised as clubbers demanded to know what was happening.

Thorne leaned into the microphone. 'Phil?'

There was a torrent of abuse from the dance floor. Demands that he be thrown out.

The microphone distorted as he pressed his mouth against it. 'Phil Hendricks?'

Thorne stared into the light, waiting, his warrant card held out for the benefit of two enormous bouncers who were barrelling towards the platform. Five long seconds had almost become ten when his phone rang.

'Maybe that's him,' someone shouted.

With the phone still buzzing in his fist, Thorne dropped down to the dance floor. He shook off grabbing hands, pushed the heels of his own into somebody's chest as he rushed to get out. He caught sight of Holland fighting his way towards him, while the music started up again and he drove his shoulder into the door, hurrying outside to take Louise's call.

'I'm on my way to Waterloo,' she said.

'What's in Waterloo?' Thorne crossed over Wardour Street and took shelter in a shop doorway.

While Louise was telling him about the sighting at The Adam, he saw

Holland come out and scan the street for him. He raised an arm and Holland jogged across through the downpour.

'I'll get to you as quick as I can,' Thorne said.

'No point. Anyway, I've got Kenny with me. Where are you?'

When Thorne told her, Louise suggested that he and Holland check out every bar and small club on Old Compton Street. None of them were regular haunts, as far as she knew, but she guessed that Hendricks had been into most of them at one time or another. 'It can't hurt,' she said.

Thorne smacked his hand against the shop window then started walking. 'Waste of fucking time.'

At his shoulder, Holland pushed back his wet hair and asked what was going on. Thorne grimaced, shook his head.

'What else are you going to do?' Louise asked.

Porter wasn't paying, obviously, but she clocked the fifteen-pound entrance fee as she went in. The other places had been cheaper, but not by much. Three or four different clubs, and four quid a pop for drinks, she couldn't help wondering how much cash Phil Hendricks got through during a typical Saturday night on the razzle.

She and Parsons might have waltzed to the front of the queue and past the ticket office, but there was still an awkward moment when a security guard – with the obligatory long black coat and earpiece – put out a hand to stop them at the door to the club itself.

Porter just stared. Parsons told the man to move.

The bouncer looked awkward, reddened when he spoke to Porter. 'I'm not sure if I should search your bag or not.' He stepped back when Parsons put a hand on his arm. 'I don't know, you might be carrying weapons.'

'Several,' Porter said.

It might just have been the newness, but Vada seemed classier than The Adam. The music was less insistent, and there was more space to move; the dance floor itself took up only a small area of the main room. The atmosphere was not as frenzied, and Porter imagined the place would fill up later, as clubbers looked for somewhere to talk or wind down.

Men danced close, to synthesised voices and a soft beat, as she and Parsons made their way across the room towards the bar. The designers had tried for something louche and late-sixties in the black and red velvet of the furnishings, fibre-optic table lamps, and blown-up portraits of Caine and Jagger on the walls.

Porter got nothing useful from the bar-staff, so she and Parsons split up to explore the rest of the club.

Unfortunately, the lighting was just as moody and atmospheric as the sound. Plenty of dark corners and pools of shadow, as Porter searched; looking for a black, maybe a silver shirt; a cropped hairline, softer at the back of the neck, where a tattoo began. Listening for a familiar, filthy laugh as she moved close to the tables and banquettes, in the areas where the music was deadened by walls of glass bricks.

Trying to stay optimistic.

There was a quieter bar at the top of a small staircase. Porter stalked from corner to corner, aware from some of the looks she received that her expression of frustration was perhaps being mistaken for disapproval. It couldn't be helped.

The barman here was no more help than the one downstairs, suggesting to Porter that her friend probably hadn't come in yet.

She felt another rush of anger at Thorne. He would say he hadn't lied, of course, that he'd been protecting her, but she knew that was bollocks. The anger subsided when a man who matched the description of Marcus Brooks walked past her and smiled; as she found herself wondering how many coppers there might be in the place, aside from herself and Kenny Parsons.

On cue, the DS appeared at the doorway of the bar and shook his head. A look that suggested he'd done enough arse-licking for one Saturday night and was ready for home.

They walked out of the bar and down the stairs, with Porter checking a series of small lounges as they went, determined to cover every inch of the place before she gave up. She was on the verge of doing exactly that – wondering what the fuck was going to happen now with Thorne, what she could say to comfort him, should anything happen – when she finally saw a face she recognised.

The man was sitting in the third of the chill-out rooms, near the door, with two other men and a woman. There was a fair selection of bottles and glasses on the table between them.

Porter had no time for introductions, so let her warrant card make them for her. 'I've met you before,' she said. 'With Phil Hendricks.'

'Almost certainly,' the man said. He ground out a cigarette, blew a thin stream of smoke across the table, then looked up; over Porter's shoulder and beyond. 'He's knocking around somewhere.'

Porter felt something give in her stomach. '*Where?*'

The man's eyes were still searching. 'He was with some skinhead type. Getting very cosy.'

Porter turned, looked out through the doorway for any sign of Hendricks.

'They were here ten minutes ago . . .'

Porter bolted for the door, with the man and his friends still discussing things behind her. She was scrabbling for her phone as she caught sight of Parsons at the other end of the corridor; dialled as he came running towards her.

'Tom, he's here, or he *was*, and maybe Brooks. You should probably get over.' She left the address and hung up.

'Where the fuck haven't we been?'

'Offices?' Parsons suggested. 'Toilets?'

Parsons rushed towards the gents' and Porter made for the ladies' at the other end of the carpeted corridor. Inside, one woman stood at the marbled sink and stared as Porter slammed back cubicle doors. Nothing.

Before the door had swung shut behind her, Porter was moving down to the far end of the corridor. She took a left and found herself in the kitchens; stared past the two waitresses sitting on the counter and backed quickly out again.

There was nowhere else to go.

She saw no sign of Parsons; could hear the music bleeding through the walls, and the rain on the other side of the door ahead of her. She leaned on the metal bar, pushed and stepped outside.

It was a narrow back alley, running forty or fifty yards to a side street that curled around the back of the club from the main road. The water ran from steeply pitched roofs on either side. It fell in sheets, lit in several places by the light from windows or the wall-mounted sodium lamps in doorways.

In one of those doorways halfway down, Porter could see two figures.

She edged slowly along the wall; could hear feet on the floor as someone adjusted their position. She heard something bang against a door. Something like a groan.

'Phil?'

She took three or four more steps along, then away from the wall, and saw the head that turned towards her, the features in shadow.

Hendricks being pressed back hard against the door.

Hands raised around his neck . . .

Porter was running then, reaching into her bag, and when the bag hit the puddle her hands were tight around her telescopic baton. She was shouting something as she swung it hard into the back of the man's legs; pulling and turning him as he fell, then dropping down on top of him.

'*Fuck . . . Louise . . .*'

She drove her knee down beneath the man's shoulder blades, grunting with the effort as she gripped the baton at either end and pressed it down on to the back of his neck . . . as other hands clawed at her own neck and grabbed at her hair.

Then she could hear Phil Hendricks screaming and swearing, his voice jagged, above the drumming of the rain and the roar of her own blood.

TWENTY-NINE

Thorne and Holland were on their way back to the car when the call came.

'It's Kenny Parsons, sir . . .'

Whatever Parsons said next was lost beneath the shouting in the background. Thorne recognised Hendricks' voice; felt relief scald through him. Then another male voice; threatening.

'What the fuck's happening?' Thorne shouted.

There was a pause before he heard the phone being handed over: Louise clearing her throat.

'I got it wrong. He's fine.' She was buzzing, breathless. 'I fucked up.'

'Tell me.'

'I thought it was Brooks, OK? That Phil was being attacked. I saw it and just thought—'

'Slow down.' Thorne could hear Parsons now, telling people to be quiet, raising his voice over theirs.

'He was getting his end away, for Christ's sake. Some kid he met.'

'You sure?'

Louise started to describe how Hendricks had dragged her off the man on the ground; then hesitated, like she didn't want to say too

294

much else. What else she'd seen. 'It looked like this bloke was . . . *on* him, you know?'

Thorne was walking faster now. 'Is anybody hurt?' he asked.

The phone was snatched again, before Louise could answer.

'Right now, all I want to do is fuck you up,' Hendricks said. 'Go straight to Brigstocke and drop you as deep in the shit as I can.'

Thorne knew he had every right to be as angry as Hendricks, and he was. But he fought the urge to sound it. 'You'd best shut up and listen,' he said.

Hendricks got the message.

'It wasn't a wind-up, OK? You're a legitimate target, because you gave evidence at Marcus Brooks' trial six years ago.'

'Fuck off,' Hendricks said. 'I'd barely finished training six years ago. I hadn't set foot in a fucking courtroom.'

'The senior pathologist was Allan Macdonald.'

'So?'

'Ring any bells?'

'I assisted him for six months or something . . .' Hendricks trailed off, and in the pause Thorne could hear the confidence evaporate. 'He died a couple of years ago, I think.'

'Right. Which puts you next in line. Very fucking handy.'

'I still don't know what you're on about. I had nothing to do with that trial. Don't you think I'd remember?'

'The prosecution submitted a written statement confirming that Simon Tipper could have been killed during the time that Brooks was in his house. Time of death was the key element of Brooks' defence. The *only* element, more or less. Once that medical evidence was put in front of a jury, along with the prints on the glass and everything else, the verdict was only ever going to go one way.'

'I was just laying equipment out back then. Cleaning out the sluices, doing the paperwork . . .'

'You countersigned that statement, Phil.'

Just rain for a few seconds, and muffled voices. 'Fuck.'

'Yeah. *Fuck.*'

Thorne jumped slightly at the touch of the hand on his arm. He followed Holland's gaze towards the car, still parked outside the Spice of Life. Saw the sticker on the windscreen, then the dirty orange clamp wrapped around the front wheel.

'Wait there,' Thorne told Hendricks. 'I'll be with you as soon as I can.'

The drink Thorne had promised Holland for his help that night had turned into something more substantial by the time he'd persuaded him to stay with the car and wait for the clamping truck. He stepped into the road, telling Holland to keep an eye on the BMW's dodgy clutch. Shouted back that he'd pick up the car some time tomorrow as he waved down a passing taxi.

The cab was halfway through a U-turn, and Thorne was watching Holland climb into his car, muttering, when the mobile went again.

'I would have let him have some fun,' Brooks said. 'Before the kid delivered him.'

It took Thorne a few seconds to understand. Whoever Louise had found Hendricks with in the alley had been bait. Had been working with Brooks. A quick fumble to get Hendricks interested, then back to the kid's place, where Brooks would have been waiting.

'The poor little fucker came back with his tail between his legs. Some woman had beaten the shit out of him.'

Thorne fell back in his seat as the taxi accelerated away down Charing Cross Road. 'Hendricks is off limits,' he said.

'Because he's your friend?'

'He had nothing to do with what happened to you.' Thorne could feel his chest leaping against the seat belt. Water was running from his hair, dripping down between his ear and the handset.

'Angie and Robbie weren't off limits.'

Thorne quickly wiped the phone against his shirt. He thought about saying that he was sorry. Instead said: 'I know about loss.'

There were brown smears across the window between Thorne and the cabbie, but he could still make out the spots on the back of the man's neck.

Brooks grunted. 'Nicklin said.'

Thorne's hand tightened around the phone. He wondered if there was anything Nicklin *didn't* know about him.

'So?'

'It's not the same.'

There wasn't time for Thorne to argue, though Christ knew he'd been over it in his head enough times. 'Why put other people through it?'

'It isn't—'

'Other *families*?'

The meter ticked over twice, and when Brooks finally came back there was still no answer. 'Look, I'm sorry that he's your friend, the bloke in the club. It's weird how things turn out, isn't it?'

Thorne knew there was nothing weird about it. He knew exactly how the connection had been made. Who had done the necessary research and then passed the information on to Marcus Brooks.

He'd sort that one out himself later on.

'Listen to what I'm saying, OK? Things will go very badly for you unless you forget about Phil Hendricks. You need to know that.'

Ten seconds passed before Brooks spoke again. 'There's other people I'm more interested in,' he said.

It sounded close enough to an understanding for Thorne. 'So, where does it end, Marcus?'

'Fuck knows.'

'You going after the judge next? The people on the jury?' The taxi drove fast around the western edge of Trafalgar Square. Swung left through amber on to the Strand. 'Don't forget the shorthand typist and the bloke who drove the prison van.'

'How long d'you need these days?' Brooks asked. 'To get a trace?'

'Nobody's tracing this call.'

'It's been five minutes already, hasn't it?'

'There's no one listening in, I swear to God.'

'Right.'

'It's why I gave you this number.'

Thorne could hear the fatigue in the pause, and in Brooks' words when they came. In the short time they'd been talking, his voice had been getting slower, thicker; as though an anaesthetic were kicking in.

'I think I actually believe you,' he said.

'That's good.'

'And . . . I don't know.'

'What?'

'Where it's going to end . . .'

'Marcus?'

But Brooks had already gone.

The rain had eased off, and they were waiting at the front of the club when Thorne's taxi pulled up. He had thrust a tenner into the driver's hand when they were halfway across Waterloo Bridge, and was out of the vehicle the second it pulled up at the kerb.

Louise, Parsons and Hendricks moved away from the queue that was waiting to go inside, with Parsons hanging back from the other two a little as Thorne came towards them, his arms outstretched, questioning.

'Why did you let the kid go?'

Louise shook her head, angry. 'What?'

Thorne clocked the glare from Hendricks as he wheeled away in frustration.

'Christ, I was lucky he didn't want to do me for assault.'

'He was put up to it.' Thorne glanced across at Parsons and took a step closer to Louise.

'Kenny's OK,' she snapped.

Thorne nodded, lowered his voice anyway. 'It was all set up. He was going to hand Phil over to Brooks later on.'

Hendricks was studying the floor; scraping a training shoe back and forth across the wet pavement. He wore a thin black shirt over jeans, and Thorne supposed that he'd left his jacket in the club. That the fact he was soaked was probably not the only reason he was trembling.

'Where did you get all this from?' Louise asked.

Thorne could see from the cold smile that she already knew. His voice dropped lower still. 'Brooks called when I was on the way over.' He was about to say more but was silenced by the scream of a siren. They all turned to see an ambulance belting down from the bridge; watched it jump the lights and race south.

'Does he know where I live?' Hendricks asked.

Thorne hadn't given Hendricks too many details when they'd spoken earlier, but there seemed little point now in keeping anything back. 'The video on the message was taken outside your flat.'

'Well, that's fucking dandy.'

'It's all right, Phil . . .'

'Am I coming to yours then tonight, or what?'

'He certainly knows where *I* live,' Thorne said. 'I think we should all go back to Lou's.' He looked across. 'If that's OK?'

Louise was nodding to Parsons, who took off his jacket and passed it to her. When she turned back, the smile had got frostier still. 'Fine with me.' She moved across and wrapped the jacket around Hendricks' shoulders. 'I presume your mate didn't happen to mention if I was in his address book, did he?'

Thorne felt sure that Brooks had been given all such information, but was almost as certain that he would not be using it. 'I think it'll be all right now.' He looked at Hendricks. 'I told him to back off.' Hendricks returned the stare. 'When he called, you know? I think he got the message.'

'You *think*?' Louise said.

'I think we understand each other.'

'Have you any idea how fucking ridiculous that sounds?'

'Louise—'

'How ridiculous *you* sound?'

Thorne stood there, wishing he hadn't left Holland back at the car. For all the self-righteous anger that had coursed through him earlier, he felt isolated suddenly, and apprehensive. Every bit as ridiculous as Louise said he was. When the dust had settled he knew there would be questions to answer and he didn't know how he was going to face them.

The wet pavement smelled like new carpet.

'Right, we should get back to Pimlico,' he said. 'Kenny, you can get yourself off home, and we'll take a taxi.'

Parsons looked to Louise for approval.

'I've got stuff inside,' Hendricks said. 'And anyway, I'm not going anywhere until I've had a seriously large drink.' He began to head back towards the club and, after a few seconds, Louise turned to follow, taking Parsons with her.

Thorne watched them walk away, listening to the fading siren, a mile or more distant. Each hand clutched at the warm lining of a jacket pocket, and he realised that Hendricks wasn't the only one who was shaking.

PART THREE

'FORWARD'

THIRTY

He'd enjoyed more relaxing Sunday mornings.

Up before anyone else, Thorne had watched TV for a while, then decided he might as well head over to Holland's place to pick up his car. He took a paper with him for the Tube ride across to Elephant and Castle. Flicked through it, hoping that gossip or goals or suicide bombs might take his mind off the mess he was in.

The professional frying pan and the domestic fire.

While he had been charging around gay clubs, there had been a double shooting in Tottenham. The estate on which two young black men had died had long been considered a no-go area, and, reading the story, Thorne decided that these latest events were hardly likely to turn it into a tourist hot-spot.

The train from Pimlico had been almost empty, but he'd changed on to a packed Northern Line train at Stockwell, and he could barely read the paper without elbowing his neighbour in the ribs.

He looked at the front-page story again.

A brutal event, and simple; drugs-related almost certainly. Reading, he realised just how much he yearned for something bog-standard, where there were no difficult choices to make. He wanted this one done with. There were cases, just a few, that had marked him, inside and out, but he couldn't remember one that had left him feeling so out of control.

He had no idea where it – where *he* – was heading.

Looking up from the paper, he caught the man opposite staring; watched his eyes flick quickly up to the adverts above his head, then drop to the paperback on his knees.

On Tube trains, everyone was looking at someone else. It didn't matter where you were sitting, on which side. You would never be able to see what was coming.

Holland's girlfriend, Sophie, didn't quite throw Thorne's car keys at him when she opened the door, but she looked as though she'd have liked to. Thorne said hello, then sorry, and stepped inside. It was the warmest greeting he was likely to receive that day.

'I was just going to nip to the shops,' Sophie said when she and Thorne walked into the living room. 'Do you want anything?'

Holland glanced up from the sofa. He looked as though he'd had about as much sleep as Thorne had managed. He shook his head; he and Thorne both well aware that Sophie would just be killing time until she was sure that Thorne had left. A while back, Thorne had contemplated calling her, maybe coming round one day when Holland wasn't there, to try to sort out whatever was between them. But he'd done nothing, and now things were pretty much set in stone.

'You could pick up some kidney beans if you want. I might do us a chilli later on,' Holland said.

When she'd gone, Holland made tea.

'Thanks for last night,' Thorne said.

'I should think so, too. That car's a nightmare to drive.'

'I didn't mean the car.'

Holland looked at him through the steam from his tea. 'What happened?'

Thorne filled him in: everything from when he'd left him in the rain with the BMW, up to, but not including, the point when he had got

304

back to Louise's flat and faced the music. Holland smirked, reminded Thorne of the moment when he'd taken control of the microphone in Beware and started shouting. 'I reckon you're a natural,' he said. 'Just need to get you a baseball cap or something . . .'

Thorne laughed, feeling like he hadn't done so for a while.

'You could still go to Brigstocke,' Holland said.

'No . . .'

'I've been thinking about it.' Thorne was already shaking his head, but Holland ploughed on. 'You could set up another divert, from the prepay phone you're using to talk to Brooks, back to your original mobile. Dump the prepay, and nobody need ever know about the calls. Your word against Brooks', if it ever comes to it.'

'Not going to happen.'

'So just come clean. The guvnor's a mate of yours, isn't he?'

'He's in enough shit of his own already. Whatever it is, *if* he comes out of it, he'll be trying to keep his nose as clean as possible.' Thorne could see that Holland was trying to think of another way out. 'Don't worry about it, Dave.'

Holland's daughter Chloe wandered in from the next room with a fist full of coloured pens. She looked like a little version of Sophie. Thorne had bought birthday presents for the first couple of years, but had missed the last one, a few months before.

'What's your name?' she asked.

'This is Tom,' Holland said. 'He's been here before.'

Chloe had already moved on. She sat down on the floor and pulled a colouring book from a low table. Thorne and Holland drank their tea and watched her work, her lips pursed in concentration. Thorne asked her what she was drawing.

'Sky,' she said.

Nice and simple.

'Still thinking about leaving London?' Thorne asked.

Holland raised his arms, inviting Thorne to look around. 'We'll have to go somewhere,' he said.

The first-floor flat had always been cramped, but with toys scattered

305

about the floor and a pushchair in the hall, Thorne could see how badly Holland and his family needed more space. Still, he wondered if the move might be a step towards Holland getting out of the Job altogether. He knew that his girlfriend was encouraging him to look at other options.

'I think Sophie fancies going back to work,' Holland said. He shrugged. 'Nothing's really been decided at the moment.'

Thorne couldn't remember what it was that Sophie had done before she'd had Chloe. He didn't bother to ask. 'Be good if you didn't go too far,' he said.

Chloe brought the colouring book across to show her father. Thorne enjoyed the way Holland's hand drifted to his daughter's head, how the little girl's arm slid easily around his neck as they looked at the picture together.

He felt envious.

'Now I'm going to draw a shark,' she said. 'And me killing it.' She scrawled for another few minutes, then dragged a small plastic chair across to the television and sat with the remote on her knees.

When Holland got up to fetch the keys to the BMW, he said: 'What did Brooks sound like when you spoke to him?'

Thorne remembered the tiredness in the man's voice, but knew that wasn't what Holland was asking. 'Like he didn't care.'

'About getting caught?'

'About anything.'

'That's bad news.'

'For someone,' Thorne said.

Louise had still not got out of bed by the time Thorne got back, and they'd exchanged no more than a handful of words when she'd finally emerged just before eleven. Had the sofa been OK for his back? Fine. Did he fancy a cooked breakfast? That sounded great, if it wasn't too much trouble. She'd taken tea back to the bedroom, come out dressed fifteen minutes later, and announced that she was going to the shop to get a few things.

'I could have picked some stuff up when I went over to Dave's,' Thorne said, as she was heading out.

Louise closed the door. He didn't know whether she'd heard him.

When Hendricks came out of the spare room a little later, he was wearing Thorne's old dressing-gown and muttering about how good the bacon smelled. Thorne was relieved to see that he looked a little sheepish. Hendricks picked up one of the tabloid magazines, seeming content to hide behind it for a while, but instead he carried it through to the kitchen when Louise called him.

Thorne could hear them talking in whispers as he sat trying, and failing, to read the report of Spurs' goalless draw at Manchester City. After ten minutes, he shouted through, asking Louise if she needed any help.

'We're fine,' she said.

Bacon, sausage, eggs and beans; toast and fresh coffee. Sunlight washing the table and something innocuous on the radio in the kitchen. Thorne finished first and sat watching Louise and Hendricks eat; listened to them making small talk.

Try as he might, he couldn't hold his tongue for very long. 'Obviously, you both think you've got some right to be pissed off with me.'

They looked up as if they'd only just noticed he was there. 'What do *you* think?' Louise asked.

Thorne had lain awake most of the night, pondering how near he'd come to losing his closest friend. Had realised that he might have lost him anyway; that he might lose a good deal more. 'I think we were lucky last night,' he said. 'I think we should be . . . thankful.'

'I am,' Louise said. 'There's a few other things I'm not so sure about.' She met his stare, flicked her eyes to Hendricks and back again. 'I'm guessing you'd rather talk about that later.'

Thorne shook his head, pushed his knife and fork closer together. 'None of this is exactly straightforward, you know. This case.'

'Never is with you.'

'Sorry?'

'You can never take the easy road, can you? Everything has to be a fucking struggle. Like nothing's worth doing unless it hurts. If you want to suffer, that's fine, just don't drag the rest of us down with you.'

Thorne pointed at Hendricks. 'Christ, if it wasn't for me . . .'

Hendricks looked at him, up for it. 'What?'

'If it wasn't for you playing silly buggers, they might have caught this fucker by now,' Louise said. 'Last night would never have happened. How easy would that have been to live with?' She stabbed at something in front of her, the fork squealing against the plate. 'Would *that* have hurt enough for you?'

'You think it was my fault?' Hendricks asked.

'I never said that,' Thorne said.

'You think I should have remembered?'

'I was surprised, that's all . . .'

'It was a body I saw *six* years ago, OK? A PM I assisted on. Have you got any idea how many bodies I work on every week? If I ever did know the name, then I'd certainly forgotten it and I *never* knew the name of the bloke who was accused of killing him.' Hendricks was getting worked up and Louise reached over to put a hand on his arm. 'As it happens, when you're elbows deep in somebody's guts, it helps most of the time if you *don't* think of them as a person, all right? If you forget that they're called John or Anne or whatever. It makes it that much easier when you're scrubbing them from under your nails afterwards and they're wheeling the next one in . . .'

Thorne held up his hands. 'Phil . . .'

'Can *you* remember them all?' Hendricks had tears in his eyes, and pushed at them, furious. 'Every single body, and the name of every fucker responsible for them?'

Thorne thought about what Louise had said. Forgetting those things would have meant taking the easy road. He picked up his plate and carried it out to the kitchen.

Later, with Hendricks crashed out in front of the television, Thorne and Louise talked in the bedroom. There were no more histrionics.

Louise's tone was measured, reasonable. Thorne found it harder to deal with than the shouting.

'You really think Phil's got nothing to worry about?'

'He'll worry no matter what,' Thorne said. 'But Brooks told me he was moving on.'

'Nice that you trust him so much.'

'I never said that.'

'OK, then. Let's just say more than you trusted me.' She smiled sarcastically at Thorne's reaction; counted off on her fingers. 'You thought it was for the best, you didn't want to get me involved and you were trying to protect me. I thought I'd get those out of the way early, save you the trouble.'

'All those things are true.'

'Course they are.'

'It's not like I actually *lied*.'

Louise slapped the edge of the bed in mock frustration. 'Fuck, I *knew* there was one I'd forgotten.'

Thorne felt cornered, because he was. He knew he had nowhere to hide. 'I wanted to go to Brigstocke yesterday,' he said. 'You talked me out of it.'

'When I saved your job, you mean? Yeah, that was very selfish of me.'

'What do you want me to say?'

'Say whatever you like.'

'"Sorry"? "Thank you"? *What?*'

Louise turned away and sat on the edge of the bed. She took a jar of hand-cream from the bedside table, began to rub it in. Thorne leaned back against the wall. He could hear the television from next door; classical music from the flat upstairs. He thought about how much he'd been looking forward to a day off.

'Brooks say who he'd be moving on *to?*'

Thorne seized on the question greedily. Oh fuck, yes, he thought, let's talk like coppers. 'Whoever helped Paul Skinner set him up, I suppose. "Squire".'

'That's what it's all been about for you, hasn't it? Trying to get the other one.'

The professional conversation hadn't lasted very long. 'He's not your average bent copper,' Thorne said. Reaching for the right words, he tried to explain that there had been no grand plan, as such, that there never was with him. Just a series of stupid decisions. But he could see from the look on her face that she knew she'd nailed him.

'And how bent does what you've been doing make you?' she asked. 'Or what I did last night make me?'

'We haven't murdered anyone.'

'What if Cowans had been killed later than he was? Or if we hadn't got to Phil in time? Do you think any of your stupid decisions might have been just a little bit responsible?'

Thorne knew they would have been.

Louise put away the hand-cream and stood up. She was still rubbing her hands. 'You need to learn from this. I mean it, Tom. About how you do things. About *me . . .*'

As Louise moved past him to the door, Thorne thought about reaching out, pulling her to him. At that moment, though, he couldn't read her at all. 'Is Phil going to hang around here?' he asked.

She shook her head. 'Brendan's coming round to pick him up. Phil called him earlier.'

'Wouldn't he rather stay with you?'

'Not if you're here, no.'

'Sunday morning? I wished I'd studied that hard,' Kitson said. Harika Kemal had said she had got a lot of reading to do; that she didn't have time to talk. 'I promise it won't take very long . . .'

'I've told you everything.'

'I know, and I also know how hard it was.'

'I don't think you do.'

Kitson could hear voices in the background. She wondered if it was the pair she'd seen with Harika that day outside the university. 'It's a simple enough question, really. We think Hakan may have gone to

Bristol.' She waited for a reaction; didn't get one. 'I wondered if you had any idea why?'

'I don't know where he is.'

'That's not what I asked.'

'Yes it is.'

Kitson was getting impatient. If Kemal had been in Bristol, he might have already moved on. He may well have realised that the parking ticket he'd received might give away his location. 'I'm starting to wonder if you want us to find your brother at all.'

'I called you, didn't I?'

'And maybe you're wishing you hadn't. Have you been speaking to your family?'

The answer was quick and earnest. 'No.'

'Well, one of us might have to.' Kitson paused; waited to see if Harika's sniffs were the prelude to tears. 'We're going to catch up with your brother sooner or later, you know. Your parents will have to find out. So, why prolong the agony?'

'That will only be the start of it,' Harika said.

'I'm sorry, but I can't help that.' Kitson could hear music in the background now. She took her voice up a notch. 'Look, I'm not going to pretend that Deniz was whiter than white and I'm bloody sure you knew that as well as anybody. But he had a family too, and I have to think about them. *You* should be thinking about them.'

She was starting to wonder if Harika Kemal was still there when the girl said quietly, 'Cousin.'

'What?'

'We've got a cousin who lives in Bristol.'

He was halfway back to Kentish Town when the clock on the dashboard moved round to two o'clock; cutting through King's Cross to escape the hell of Sunday traffic in Camden. He parked up as soon as he had the chance and made the call.

'You must have influential friends in here,' Nicklin said.

'Not really. Just a lot of people who like you about as much as I do.'

311

'Well, be quick, will you? I don't want to miss the *EastEnders* omnibus.'

'This won't take long.'

Nicklin knew, of course, that it was unorthodox for inmates to receive private phone calls, even from police officers. Thorne had spent fifteen minutes earlier in the day on the phone to Long Lartin, crawling as far up the arse of the police liaison officer as he could manage. Eventually, the man had agreed to find a nice quiet office and bring the prisoner down at a prearranged time.

'Sorry about your friend,' Nicklin said.

Thorne had already decided not to tell Nicklin that his scheme had come to nothing; that Hendricks was alive and well. He'd find out eventually. For now, even though Brooks had agreed to leave Hendricks alone, Thorne thought it best to take no chances, to let Nicklin think he was raging and grief-stricken. Nicklin was every bit as stubborn, as *persistent*, as Thorne himself.

The rage was certainly genuine enough. 'You will be,' he said.

Thorne had been struck immediately by how different the attack on Hendricks had been from the others Brooks had perpetrated. He knew that the information had been passed on to him, and had quickly recognised the fingerprints all over it. Knowing something of Stuart Nicklin's past, he guessed who had done the planning; imagined that Nicklin had used contacts from a previous life to find the boy who had picked up Hendricks in the club.

'You wouldn't be calling if you had a single piece of evidence.' Nicklin's tone was that of a man who felt himself to be bullet-proof whatever happened, certainly as far as the law was concerned. Two life sentences were much the same as one, after all. 'Still, whatever you think is best. I'd quite enjoy another few weeks in court.'

'There are better ways,' Thorne said. 'Cheaper ways.' He could hear the smile.

'Your friend will have gone out with a bang at any rate.'

'How would *you* like to go out?'

'This the "long arm of the law" routine, is it?'

312

'If you like.'

'So, what's at the end of it, then?' Nicklin asked. 'An iron bar? A sharpened spoon?'

'I warned you. When we were sitting in the Seg Unit.'

'Careful what you say, Tom. You should know that all my phone calls are routinely monitored. This is probably being recorded.'

'I'm getting used to it,' Thorne said. 'I really don't give a fuck.'

THIRTY-ONE

It might well have been a good film; Thorne had no idea. After nearly two hours he couldn't even have told anyone what it was about. George Clooney, some stolen money, a decent sex scene halfway through with that fit woman who used to be in *CSI*.

He guessed that Louise wouldn't have been able to do much better. The pair of them sitting and thinking about other things; getting on with it, like everything was going to be fine. Trying to put the previous twenty-four hours behind them, when time together felt like something they were wading through.

'I thought it was pretty good,' Louise said, as they pushed through the doors on to Camden Parkway. They'd chosen an early showing. It wasn't quite nine o'clock.

Thorne shrugged. 'I couldn't really follow it.'

They decided to walk back to Thorne's place in Kentish Town. It was a cold, clear evening, and they were both bundled up in scarves and heavy coats.

As the High Street turned into Chalk Farm Road, they just avoided colliding with a group of women coming out of a restaurant. Thorne moved to step around, but one of the women reached for his arm.

'Tom . . .'

Thorne stared at his ex-wife.

Jan had called when his father had died, but they hadn't seen each other in eight or nine years. It wasn't that she'd changed that much – less than he had, almost certainly – but that he simply hadn't expected to see her here. It didn't make sense.

He said her name as he reached for Louise's hand.

'I was just having a meal with a couple of mates,' Jan said. She looked around to the two other women, who were walking slowly away towards Camden Tube station. She turned back, reddened as she saw Thorne staring at her belly; the bump clearly visible, even through an overcoat. 'I was going to call you, matter of fact . . .'

She'd changed rather more than Thorne had first thought.

Thorne was aware that he was nodding like an idiot, so stopped and tried to smile. 'Right. Bloody hell.'

'Don't know what the hell I'm doing, to be honest. My time of life.'

It took Thorne a second or two to work out how old she was. Forty. No, forty-one. He was nodding again. 'Is it . . .?'

She tucked a pale pashmina into the collar of her coat. 'Patrick's.' She faked a laugh, as though Thorne had been joking. 'Of course it is.'

'Great.' The teacher she'd buggered off with.

'He's at home, getting stuck into essays.'

Thorne wondered why she'd felt the need to explain where her boyfriend was. If he was still her boyfriend; maybe she'd married him. He pictured a scrawny, gingerish article; pigeon-chested with curly hair and bum-fluff. Remembered him flying out of bed like a scalded cat when Thorne had caught the pair of them at it one afternoon.

For the third or fourth time, Jan's eyes flicked across to Louise; the glance as fleeting as the smile that went with it.

'Sorry, this is Louise,' Thorne said. 'Jan . . .'

Louise leaned in to shake hands. 'So, when's it due?'

'Six weeks.' She took a step forward. 'Can't bloody wait. Look at the size of me already. I'll be waddling around right through Christmas.'

'Better then than summer though, I suppose.'

'That's true.'

'Be a nice way to start the new year,' Louise said.

The three of them took a few steps towards the kerb as another group came out of the restaurant.

Jan turned back to Thorne. 'So, you well?'

'Yeah, I'm good.'

'Still in the same place?'

'We were just . . . heading back.' Thorne looked at Louise, who nodded to confirm the simple fact.

Jan looked past them to her friends, who had now stopped a hundred yards away and were looking at something in a shop window.

'You said you were going to call,' Thorne said. He nodded towards Jan's stomach. 'Was that to tell me, you know . . .?'

'Well . . . just to catch up, really. So, this has been good, actually.'

'OK.'

Just as the pause was becoming horribly awkward, Louise leaned against Thorne and said, 'I'm cold.' She smiled at Jan. 'I'm sure you don't want to be standing around.'

Then it was just a few noises of goodbye, and Jan saying once again how good it had been that they'd run into each other. How weird, and what a small world it was. She kissed Thorne on the cheek, did the same to Louise and walked away to join her friends.

Thorne and Louise carried on up Chalk Farm Road and cut beneath the railway line towards Kentish Town. They walked quickly, not saying a great deal, with such conversation as there was initiated by Louise. She told Thorne that his ex-wife hadn't looked the way she'd imagined. That Jan looked well and had seemed friendly enough. Thorne did little but grunt his agreement; tried to think of something to say about the movie.

Having switched her phone to silent in the cinema, Louise checked it for messages. She listened, then called Hendricks. As she and Thorne walked, a few feet apart, she told Hendricks that the movie had been decent enough, asked him what he'd been doing. She laughed at something and said she'd call him again in the morning.

'He's doing OK,' was all she said as she put the phone away.

When they reached Thorne's street, Louise announced that she was going to carry on up to the Tube station and head home. She said that she was tired and had an early start the next day.

'That makes two of us,' Thorne said.

'OK, then.'

'No, I meant so you might as well stay.'

She hoisted her bag a little higher on her shoulder, looked at Thorne as though she wanted to say something. She stepped up to kiss him, in much the same way as Jan had done.

Said: 'Let's talk tomorrow.'

For the third or fourth time, a car slowed, then blared its horn when the driver saw that the man waiting at the side of the road had no intention of using the zebra crossing.

Brooks didn't even look up.

He'd thought about bringing some flowers, but knew they wouldn't have lasted long. That was something else that had changed since he'd been inside: bouquets and teddies tied to lamp posts and benches, right, left and centre. He'd seen several of them walking about the last few weeks. He wondered if anyone had left tributes to Tucker or Hodson. A nice wreath in the shape of a motorbike by the side of the canal for Martin Cowans.

It occurred to him that he didn't know what time it had happened. As Angie and Robbie were together, they were probably walking back from school. Heading to the sweetshop on the way home, maybe. It would still have been light then. Nice and easy for the driver to see them both; and for them to see that the car wasn't going to stop.

He wondered if there'd been any skid marks on the road. Bloodstains to scrub off the crossing. 'Joy-riders', that copper had said, when they'd come to give him the news. He remembered the male one with the dirty collar breathing heavily, saying, 'We were able to get a paint sample.'

He hadn't seen their bodies.

317

At the time he'd felt relieved; uncertain he'd have been able to cope with seeing them like that. Now, standing in the cold, a few feet from where it had happened, he wished he'd had the chance. He would have closed his eyes and kissed them. Said something.

A woman arrived next to him and pressed the button. Told him they reckoned there might be snow on the way. When the lights changed she ambled across, turning to look back at him when she reached the other side of the road.

The funeral hadn't given him the chance to say goodbye, not really. He'd stood sweating in a borrowed suit, avoiding people's eyes and moving away whenever the whispering had started. Sitting in one of the cars with cousins and uncles; relatives Angie had had no time for. The priest had said, 'May you have an abundant life' when he'd stepped dutifully up to kiss the icon in front of their coffins. Placed a manicured hand on each ornate casket and said, 'May their memory be eternal.'

A few minutes later, he'd watched the coffins disappear, like props in some dark magic trick, still unable to believe that Angie and Robbie could possibly be in there.

Angie's parents had refused to speak to him the whole time.

Another car sounded its horn, and this time Brooks reacted. He stepped quickly out on to the crossing, then stopped; turned and stared at the driver like a mad person. He watched the woman raise a hand, saw her check to see that her door was locked.

Brooks walked the rest of the way across, and kept going without looking back. There was nothing for him there.

Nothing of them.

He turned into the side street where the Mondeo was parked. Thought about the quickest way to go. With any luck he'd be able to get another picture tonight, maybe a video.

Then he could put Tom Thorne out of his misery.

. . . And tell Robbie that he's going to have to prove it! I want to see that he's just as good as he tells me he is when he visits. We'll get

straight over the park as soon as I'm back and I'll put him through his paces. Both feet, tell him. I want to see him shooting with both feet. He'll have to, if he's ever going to get that trial at West Ham he's always on about. And I'll start taking him to see a few games as well, tell him that.

Christ, I can't wait . . .

When I say 'as soon as I'm back', obviously there's one or two other things I'd like to do first, if you get my drift! Actually, between bed and home cooking, I can't see Rob dragging me out of the house for at least a week.

Fifteen fucking days, angel, that's all. Thirteen probably, by the time this gets to you. That's nothing. It's less than the average holiday, but the stupid thing is it's going to feel like ten times as long. It's the hardest part, the end of it, everyone knows that. When a lot of blokes inside start to go mental . . .

Talking of holidays, though, we should get away, soon as we can. Where d'you fancy? Somewhere hot with a fuck-off big pool. Why don't you look into it, and see what's around? Only thing is, I'm not sure when Rob's on holiday from school.

I don't care where we go to be honest, so you decide. It's all going to feel like a holiday from now on . . .

Thorne laid the photocopied sheet down on the table. The letter that had never been sent; that had been written the day before Marcus Brooks had received the death message.

He walked across to the computer. The game was running, but he'd sat out half an hour earlier. He'd logged on when he had arrived back at the flat, hoping that a few hands might take his mind off things a little, but it would have taken a damn sight more than poker. He watched for five minutes, then sat down again.

Unusually, Johnny Cash wasn't helping: 'I See a Darkness' torn from him; that ragged voice imploring his friend to pull the smiles inside and save him from death.

Thorne reached across to rub a finger under the cat's chin and thought about the look on his friend's face when Hendricks had walked away from him outside the club the night before. Louise's face, too, pale and tight, across the breakfast table.

Christ, and seeing Jan . . .

Would she really have called him to tell him about the baby? It must at least have crossed her mind that he deserved to know. Or maybe just that he would *think* he deserved it. Now he did know, he felt all sorts of emotions, and he felt bad because pleasure wasn't among them.

He looked back at the letter on the table. He imagined Marcus Brooks walking back to his cell, having been told about his girlfriend and son; putting the envelope away in a drawer. It must have felt like he'd been hit by that car. He probably wished he had been.

It wasn't as though Thorne usually had any problem with hate, and it should have been easy to hate Marcus Brooks for what he'd been about to do to Hendricks. But pity came easier.

The same went for himself, this time of night, with a can of beer in his hand and Cash on the stereo.

So much easier to feel got-at and ganged-up-on than ashamed.

He moved quickly when the doorbell went, Elvis half a second behind him, jumping down and tearing under the TV, like she thought there was nothing good coming.

Louise walked in without a word, without looking at Thorne, and stopped in the middle of the living room.

Thorne closed the door and followed. 'What?'

She dropped her bag and started to take off her coat.

'Is everything OK?'

'I had a question,' she said.

'I don't understand. Did you get all the way home?'

'You squeezed my hand.' Now she looked at him. 'When you were talking to Jan. When we were standing around on the pavement.'

'Did I?'

Louise nodded, tossed her coat on to the sofa.

'OK . . .' Thorne just stood, no idea where this might be going.

'Did you think I might be upset?' she said. 'Because it was your

320

ex-wife; because I might feel embarrassed, or awkward, or what-ever?' She took a breath. Tried to smile, or tried not to, Thorne couldn't tell. 'Or because she was pregnant?'

Thorne stepped across and turned down the stereo. He was flus-tered; felt instinctively that a lot depended on his answer. He pushed fingers through his hair, laced them together on top of his head. 'I don't know. I just . . . squeezed your hand.'

When Louise finally looked up at him, the smile was there. Shaky and uncertain of itself. Pushed out of shape by the tremble in her bottom lip.

'It was nice,' she said.

Afterwards, Thorne went to the bathroom to flush away the condom, and brought back some toilet paper so that Louise could wipe herself.

'*That* was nice,' he said.

They talked for a while about Brooks and the letters. Louise said she was always amazed that more people who had lost loved ones violently didn't wreak violence in return; those who had lost children especially. Said she couldn't imagine . . .

Thorne told her about his trip to Holland's place. That Holland was thinking about getting out of the city. 'Maybe even the Job,' he said.

'You ever thought about it?' Louise asked. It was something they'd joked about before; that every copper joked about. She stopped him before he could come back with a flippant remark. 'Really, I mean.'

'I've wished that there was something else I could do,' Thorne said. '*Anything* else.'

'We all hate what we do from time to time.'

'It's what we *can't* do.'

Louise raised her head, eased herself on to her belly and looked down at him. 'Was it one case?'

There were a few; names and cases that prompted something more than a wink or a war story. That pressed ice against his skin still, and fluttered in the gut. A list of dangerous men and women; and of dead ones. He guessed that Marcus Brooks would take his place on one list or another.

Names, cases.

But it was none of them . . .

'Twenty-odd years ago,' Thorne said. 'I was a baby copper working out of Brixton nick. We got called out to a council flat in Thornton Heath, one of those crappy sixties blocks on three or four levels; an old guy, in his mid-seventies. He'd come back one afternoon and found a couple of kids turning the place over. They were never going to find anything worth having, so they were just making a mess of the place, and when this old man turned up, they started taking it out on him.'

'Did you find them?'

Thorne shook his head slowly; frowning with concentration, trying to remember. 'There were dogs on his wallpaper . . . brown on green. And he had a collection of cards out of packets of tea. Hundreds of the things, with old footballers and cricketers on them. Tom Finney and W.G. Grace. Me and this other copper were picking them off the carpet while we waited for the ambulance.' He pulled up his legs, arranged the duvet around the two of them. 'They smashed his face up pretty badly, broke his arm and two or three ribs. Could have been worse, I suppose, but he was in hospital for a couple of weeks.'

He turned his eyes to Louise's. She was waiting; knowing there had to be more.

'Anyway, we got called back, a month after the break-in. I remember seeing that the address was the same and presuming the poor old sod had been done again, you know? As it was, his neighbours had phoned, and when we got there we had to pull him down off the balcony. He was just stood up there, terrified. Trying to summon up the courage to jump.

'We got him down and made him a cup of tea, what have you, but he was all over the place. He hadn't been able to sleep since the attack, wasn't eating properly. The place stank. There was dog-shit all over the kitchen floor . . .

'He was like a different bloke, Lou. Skinny and scared to death, and without a clue how he was supposed to carry on. What the point was in carrying on. He just stood there in his front room, clutching this old box with his cards in them, and he was ranting at me. Trying to shout, but his voice was . . . cracked, you know?'

Thorne summoned half a smile. By now his own voice was no more than a whisper. 'Wanted me to know that when he was younger he'd have sorted the little bastards out, no problem. "No fucking problem," he said. He'd have defended himself, done what he had to, protected his home. Now he couldn't do anything. Told me he was pathetic, because he wasn't even man enough to top himself. On and on about how useless he was, how he wished they'd killed him. And all the time he was talking, he was smacking his walking stick against a tatty old armchair. Dust flying up each time he did it. Standing there, whacking this stick against the chair and crying like a baby.'

'What happened to him?' Louise asked.

'He was put into a care home afterwards, as far as I know.' He let out a long, slow breath. 'Wouldn't have thought he'd have lasted too long.'

Louise inched closer. Pushed her head against Thorne's shoulder.

'I can't even remember his fucking name,' Thorne said.

THIRTY-TWO

'Anything come up on Saturday I should know about?' Brigstocke asked.

'Not that I can think of,' Thorne said.

'Good.'

'Just the Kemal stuff, really.'

'Nice to come back to some good news,' Brigstocke said.

Hakan Kemal had been arrested at his cousin's house in the St Paul's area of Bristol in the early hours of the morning and driven back to London overnight. While Thorne and Brigstocke were busy catching up, Yvonne Kitson was having first crack at her prime suspect in an interview room at Colindale station.

'And how was your day off?'

The questions weren't getting any easier. 'Typical bloody Sunday,' Thorne said.

He couldn't recall a Monday morning when he'd been so pleased to get back to work, and even the grey sky that bore down on the city did little to dampen his enthusiasm. It was good to see Brigstocke back, too. It wasn't clear if his problems had disappeared completely, but if they were still around, he seemed to be rising above them.

The DCI was clumsily multitasking: breaking off from the conversation to sign memos; scribbling on assorted bits of paper; then firing off more questions and comments while he tried to remember what he was supposed to be doing. 'Be even better if we got a break on the Brooks inquiry. Tell you the truth, that was the one I was expecting the result on.'

'I still think you'll get it.'

'I sincerely bloody hope so. I'm just grateful he seems to have gone quiet for the time being. Maybe you've done something to upset him.'

Thorne swallowed hard. 'God knows,' he said. 'We've got a lot more than those messages to go on, though.'

Brigstocke scribbled again, sucked his teeth. 'Nothing we took out of that flat is helping very much. Not helping us find him, at any rate. We've got plenty to put him *away* with if the time comes, but bugger all that's telling us where he is.'

'If we do put him away, where d'you think he'll end up?' Thorne wandered across to the small window. Brigstocke had a view only marginally less depressing than his own. 'He's got to have a decent case for diminished responsibility.'

'It's not going to be clear cut. He planned everything over a period of months, you know? It wasn't like he just lost it suddenly.'

'What happened to his family, though. *When* it happened . . .'

'He killed a copper, don't forget that.'

'Oh, I'm not.'

'Never goes down well with a jury.'

'Skinner wasn't exactly one of our brightest and best.'

'Yes, well. The powers-that-be might be keen to play down that aspect of things ever so slightly.'

'Jesus . . .'

They talked for a few more minutes about other cases. The trial of the man accused of caving in his wife's head with a Smirnoff bottle was well under way, and his defence team were pushing for manslaughter on the grounds of diminished responsibility. The prosecution argued that such grounds were not constituted merely by discovering your wife was shagging her best friend's husband seven ways from Sunday.

Apparently, the smart money – Karim was running a book, and usually managed to turn a profit – was on the bloke getting away with murder and going down for the lesser charge.

Makes sense, Thorne thought. He guessed that Marcus Brooks would not get quite such an easy ride when the time came.

Nobody liked a slag, did they? Or a cop-killer.

As Thorne was about to leave, Brigstocke said, 'How did you enjoy the stint as DCI?'

'Don't get me wrong,' Thorne said. 'The power gives me a stiffy, and I'd like a bigger office. It's just the responsibility and having to make decisions I'm not so keen on.'

'Since when have you worried about making decisions?'

'OK then, having to make *good* ones.'

'You're right about the responsibility, though . . .'

Thorne hovered in the doorway, sensing there was more to come.

'I should have told you what was going on with the DPS,' Brigstocke said.

'No problem. And you don't have to tell me now.'

'It's fine, it's sorted, more or less.' Brigstocke took off his glasses and pushed his paperwork away from him. 'Basically, another officer had one too many in The Oak a few months back and made "inappropriate remarks" to a female member of staff.'

Thorne nodded. He didn't need to be told who they were talking about.

'I was there when these remarks were made, sitting at the same table. I'd probably had one too many myself, if I'm honest, but the fact remains that because I didn't say anything to this other officer at the time, because I was *negligent*, I'm equally responsible, apparently.'

'But now they've decided to drop it?'

'Thank fuck. Stays on my record, though.'

'What about Andy Stone?'

Brigstocke smiled. 'We don't know yet.'

Thorne leaned back against the door jamb, marvelling at the different ways people found to waste time and money. Such incidents raised

326

profound questions about where the energy and resources of the capital's police service should be focused, and Thorne knew he should be seriously questioning an ethos which pilloried good men like Russell Brigstocke for no good reason.

In the meantime, though, there were more important questions to be asked. 'Come on then, spill the beans,' he said. 'What exactly did Stone say?'

It wasn't that Hakan Kemal was saying nothing; but he might just as well have been.

Kitson had seen plenty of suspects struck dumb on the advice of a solicitor, but less so since the law had changed. These days, interviewees were advised that, later on, judge and jury could draw adverse influence from their silence during questioning. Could presume that they had something to hide. That tended to loosen people's tongues a little, but Hakan Kemal was anything but chatty.

'We will have your fingerprint results back by tomorrow,' Kitson said. 'And we both know they're going to match the prints we took off the knife.'

'Let's wait and see.'

Kemal was perhaps ten years older than his sister. A small man, with thinning dark hair and glasses. The voice was high-pitched, with just the trace of a Turkish accent.

Kitson looked across at the young black woman sitting next to Kemal. Gina Bridges, the duty solicitor, wore a beautifully tailored grey jacket and trousers and was perfectly made-up. She made Kitson feel like a badly dressed bag of shit.

'You should tell your client that he isn't going anywhere,' Kitson said. 'He can sit there being monosyllabic for twenty-four hours if he wants. Then I'll happily get an extension and we can start all over again.'

Bridges smiled. Her teeth were perfect as well. 'Until these prints of yours come back, presuming they're of any use to you, I really don't see that you have enough to hold him. Mr Kemal is cooperating fully, as far as I'm concerned.'

327

Kitson turned back to Kemal. 'I don't think you thought this murder through, Hakan. I think you panicked, which is why you dumped the knife in a litter bin. Nobody's got you pegged as a master criminal, OK? Maybe you and Deniz had some kind of argument which got out of hand. Maybe he said something you didn't like. You probably didn't mean to kill him.' She tried to make eye contact. 'Is that what happened?'

Kemal was staring at a point somewhere to the left of her. He shook his head.

'If you didn't kill Deniz Sedat, why did you run? Why close up the shop and try to hide in Bristol?'

'There is no evidence that Mr Kemal was hiding from anybody,' the solicitor said. 'He informed me that he was staying with his cousin.'

Kitson took a deep breath, glanced up at the camera in the corner of the interview room. At the digital clock that told her she'd been banging her head against a wall for nearly forty minutes. 'Did you know Deniz Sedat?'

Kemal wiped his mouth, nodded.

'For the benefit of the recording, please.'

'Yes. I knew him.'

'And did you see him on Saturday, November the sixth?'

He dropped his eyes to the tabletop. The grunt sounded positive.

'Did you see Deniz Sedat at the Black Horse public house in Finsbury Park on the evening of November the sixth?'

'I saw him.'

Kitson tried to keep the excitement from her voice. 'What happened, Hakan?'

Kemal placed his hands against his head; pressing as though he were trying to push through the skull. After half a minute he looked up, and directly at Kitson for the first time.

She repeated the question, although Kemal's gaze was making her bristle with discomfort. She'd felt sized-up plenty of times, and stared right back at men whose darker thoughts were all but dripping down their faces, but she couldn't remember feeling quite so . . . disapproved of.

Kemal refused to say another word.

Later, having terminated the interview, Kitson blew off a little steam with the custody sergeant, then wandered across to the small waiting area, where Gina Bridges was sitting, a bundle of papers balanced on her knees.

Off duty, the woman was friendly enough for Kitson to forgive her appearance. They chatted for a few minutes about schedules and kids, and Kitson moaned about interviewing people who were determined to say as little as possible.

The solicitor laughed, and even though she was looking at things from the other side of the fence, she was happy to admit that Hakan Kemal was a particularly difficult customer. She told Kitson that she'd barely been able to get two words out of him herself.

'Hi, it's me again. Just ringing to see how you're doing. Give us a call when you get this.'

For the third time that day, Thorne left a message on Hendricks' answering machine. For the third time, Hendricks' mobile had rung and the machine had cut in when the call had been dropped. Thorne thought about ringing Louise. He knew she would have spoken to Phil by now. In the end he decided he wasn't going to chase him.

He was getting more than slightly annoyed at Hendricks' attitude to what had happened. What right did he have to be so angry; so self-righteous? Thorne thought that it had more than a little to do with the fact that his friend – if he was still his friend? – had been caught with his pants down.

Stupid fucker.

It could have been an awful lot worse . . .

Outside Thorne's office window, the sky was brooding as much as he was. It was dense and darkening; there was rain coming.

He thought about what Brigstocke had told him. It was ridiculous, no question, but it also made him angry that the DPS could go after someone for something like that while Skinner and his partner had got away with so much worse for so long. Not for the first time, he wondered just how many like 'Jennings' and 'Squire' there were out there.

When Yvonne Kitson came in carrying coffees for both of them, Thorne guessed that she probably wanted something.

'How's it going with Kemal?' he asked.

'I was going to talk to you about that.'

Thorne was relieved that his powers of detection hadn't completely deserted him. 'Not got a result then?'

She talked him through the session at Colindale. 'It's not like he's denying anything, you know? I just don't think he wants to talk to me.'

'Have you tried bribing him with coffee?'

'I think he has a problem with women.'

'You say that like it's a bad thing.'

'Shut up.' She pressed her chin against the lip of her mug. 'I don't know if he's that way all the time, or if he just doesn't want to talk to a woman about *this*. Either way . . .'

'You want me to have a go.'

'We could have a crack together,' Kitson said. 'After lunch, if you've got half an hour.'

Thorne held up his coffee. 'A biscuit would have done the trick.'

'All gone, mate. Have you not seen how much weight Karim is putting on?'

Thorne was more than happy to get involved in something where he would be sure of his ground. Where there was a chance of making some progress. He told Kitson he'd think about it, and walked down to the toilets, where he found himself standing next to Andy Stone at the urinal.

'This is where the big knobs hang out,' Stone said.

Thorne said nothing. He'd heard it before anyway. When he'd finished, he zipped up and turned away towards the sinks. 'Keeping out of trouble, Andy?'

'Trying my best.' A little of the confidence had given way to caution.

Thorne banged at the soap dispenser to no avail. Stuck his hands under the tap. 'Good lad.'

'What about you?'

'Oh, you know what it's like. Some of us need to watch what we're doing a bit more than others.'

Stone laughed and nodded.

'And some of us need to watch what we're *saying.*' Thorne let the water run until it was red hot. 'Do you know what I mean?'

In the mirror, Thorne watched as Stone zipped himself up and walked out without a word. He wondered if he always left without bothering to wash his hands. Guessed he just wasn't feeling quite as talkative as he did when beer and tasty barmaids were involved.

When he felt the phone buzz in his pocket, Thorne moved quickly across to the hand-dryer. There was precious little power and the air was cold. He wiped his hands on the back of his trousers and reached into his jacket.

The message from Marcus Brooks he'd known was coming.

Thorne leaned against the sink and played the video clip. He watched as a man walked a small, black dog along a dimly lit street; tossed a cigarette butt into the gutter; waited while the dog sniffed around the base of a tree.

Thorne recognised the man straight away. He'd had bigger shocks.

The police officer who had once called himself 'Squire' would not be getting away with anything for very much longer.

THIRTY-THREE

Thorne sat in a quiet corner of the canteen with a phone pressed to his ear. The meal in front of him was hardly making his mouth water, but the conversation was one he was certainly looking forward to. One he'd been anticipating since his conversation with Sharon Lilley a week and a half before. That was when things had begun to get difficult; when the case had started to smell as bad as his chicken curry.

It was time to wash the stink off.

'I got sent another message,' he said, when the call was answered. 'What kind of dog is that you've got?'

'Sorry?'

'Marcus Brooks knows where you are.'

Thorne had expected a pause, but he'd hoped it might be longer.

'That's nice for him.'

'Actually, I wasn't sure you'd be around to answer the phone. I mean, he didn't waste much time with Paul Skinner, did he? With "Jennings".'

'Who's Jennings?'

'Oh, for fuck's sake, don't bother.'

There was silence for a few seconds. Thorne could hear a door being closed. 'Well, it's good of you to call, but some of us are working, so . . .'

'Every time we talked, you were just trying to find out what I knew, where the case was going.'

'Doing my job, that's all.'

'I can't believe I didn't see it earlier.'

'You were hardly being honest yourself though, were you, Tom? I knew you were up to something.'

A sergeant who Thorne had worked with for a few months walked past the table. They exchanged smiles. 'Why "Squire"? Did you pick it at random? What's the first name, just out of interest? Seeing as we're mates and everything.'

'Is there a point to any of this?'

'I thought I should let you know, that's all,' Thorne said. 'Forewarned is forearmed, right?'

'I'll consider myself warned, then.'

'You should consider yourself in very deep shit, one way or the other.'

Now there was a longer pause. 'So, why is it *you* calling me, then? Why don't I see the heavy mob kicking my door in?'

'You should hope that's who it is when it happens.'

'Not flying solo on this one, are you?'

'I'm giving you a chance.'

A laugh. 'Go on . . .'

'Strikes me you might want to think about getting yourself some protection. Taking a walk – no, *running* – to the nearest station; and maybe, while you're there, telling them exactly why you need protecting. What you've done to deserve the undivided attention of Marcus Brooks.'

'Or . . .?'

'Or somebody else is going to tell them.'

The man on the other end of the phone sucked in his breath fast. It was meant to sound sarcastic; an indication that he wasn't remotely threatened. But Thorne could hear that he was rattled.

'Why the fuck should I do anything at all?'

'Well, why don't we start with the fact that this conversation is being recorded?'

Thorne hung up, and laid his old mobile phone down on the table. He picked up a fork, then put it down again when it began to rattle against his plate. Pushed the tray away.

He'd pop into The Oak on his way to meet Kitson at Colindale; pick up a cheese and tomato roll.

Maybe get a stiff drink to go with it.

Kitson had explained to Hakan Kemal and Gina Bridges that another officer would be sitting in on the interview. She made the introductions informally, then again for the tape. She asked Kemal if he was feeling OK; if there was anything that he needed before they started. He just shrugged.

'He's fine,' Bridges said. 'But until such time as you have any hard evidence, we really are doing you a favour here.'

'We appreciate that,' Kitson said. 'Mr Kemal wouldn't be here at all had his name not been passed on to us by someone intimately acquainted with this offence.'

Kemal looked up.

'How well did you know Deniz Sedat?' Thorne asked. Kemal stared back, weighing him up. Thorne had no problem with that. He had the man's attention at any rate. 'Perhaps you did business with him?'

'No,' Kemal said quickly.

'But you knew him.'

Kemal looked away again. He was chewing at the inside of his mouth.

'This is not about drugs, or money-laundering,' Thorne said. 'The way things stand, we're not particularly interested in your business affairs.'

Another good, long look from Kemal. He seemed to come to a decision. 'Yes, I knew who Deniz Sedat was,' he said. 'And where his money came from.'

A glance from Kitson. It looked as though she'd been right: Kemal appeared to be happier talking to a man. 'So, you weren't friendly with him?'

'He *thought* he was my friend.'

'Why do you say that?'

'He took me to clubs and casinos. Flashing his money around.'

'This was after he started going out with your sister?'

'Made out like we were family, just because he was seeing her.'

'You didn't like him?'

Kemal's expression was answer enough.

'So, I presume you weren't very happy when he started going out with Harika.'

Opposite him, Kemal sat back in his chair, his lips whitening. Thorne wondered if he was turning on the silent act again.

'It's understandable,' Thorne said. 'I've got a younger sister myself. Claire's a year or two older than Harika, and no man's good enough for her. Doesn't matter who he is, what he does . . . I don't think I'm ever going to like it.' Thorne was aware of Gina Bridges sighing; scribbling something. 'I *do* know that if she ever got involved with someone like Sedat, I'd be on him like shit on a blanket.' He saw the tension ease a little around Kemal's mouth. 'She hates it that I get so worked up, but I can't help it. Our father's not around any more, so . . .'

Thorne stared ahead, trying to avoid catching Kitson's eye. She knew very well he had no siblings.

'Sedat was not so unpopular with our parents,' Kemal said. 'He was Turkish, which is important to them, and he had money. They wanted Harika to settle down and give them grandchildren. They didn't like her college friends very much.'

'So, it was down to you to keep an eye on her.'

Kemal nodded slowly. 'I kept an eye out, yes. Nothing more than that.'

'OK.' Thorne turned to Kitson. The look he got back said *keep going*, but it was obvious that Kemal disapproving of his sister's boyfriend wasn't shaping up to be much of a motive for knifing him to death. It was clear from Gina Bridges' expression that she was thinking the same thing.

'Did you know Sedat was going to be at the Black Horse that night?'

'They went there most Saturdays. Sedat and Harika, and some of Sedat's friends.'

'And did you go because you knew Sedat would be there?'

'I wanted to speak to him.'

'You normally carry a knife when you're going to have a chat with someone?' Kemal looked away. 'We've got your fingerprints on the murder weapon, Hakan.'

Gina Bridges shot forward in her chair. 'You've got *somebody's* fingerprints, Inspector.'

Thorne's eyes hadn't left Kemal's. 'You know whose prints they are, don't you, Hakan?'

Kemal shook his head. Not a denial. A plea.

'What happened in the pub, Hakan? Did Sedat not like whatever it was you had to say to him? Did he threaten you? We know what his sort are like, and I'm sure you didn't mean things to go as far as they did.'

'It was Harika.' Kemal leaned across the table. He was breathing heavily. 'It was Harika.'

Thorne felt the prepay buzzing in his pocket again. A call this time; he recognised the pattern of the vibrations.

He knew who it was going to be.

He lowered his head and whispered to Kitson, told her that he needed to take the call. He apologised quickly to Bridges, and stood up, reaching into his jacket as he pushed back his chair.

Kitson was terminating the interview as he pulled the door closed behind him. From the faces around the table, Thorne could see that Hakan Kemal was the only person in the room not pissed off with him.

It was chaotic in the custody suite: officers queued up, ready to grab a vacant interview room; lunchtime trays were still being ferried to and from the cells; at the platform, two young women screamed at the custody skipper, while the uniformed constable booking them in did his best to calm things down.

The phone was still ringing and Thorne did not want to miss the call. He hit ANSWER while he was negotiating his way through the scrum. Said his name and stepped into the cage – the reinforced entry through which prisoners were brought from the backyard. He'd wanted to take the call outside, but it was tipping down, so he pressed himself into a corner of the cage.

'Thorne . . .?'

The word was stretched and hoarse; the tiredness in the voice even more evident than it had been the last time. Thorne covered his free ear with his right hand. 'I'm here. I got your message.' He turned in a little towards the metal wall. 'I saw "Squire".'

'Looks like he hasn't got a care in the world, doesn't he?'

He's got plenty to think about now, Thorne thought.

'Walking his fucking dog . . .'

'Listen . . . I *know* him,' Thorne said. He waited for a reaction. Watched the rain bouncing off the cars and vans in the backyard.

'Probably not as well as you thought, though, right? He's very good at pretending to be something he's not.'

A WPC jogged around the corner and stepped into the cage. She stood next to Thorne, swearing and shaking off the rain. Thorne grunted a yes into the phone while he waited for her to move inside.

'So, what did you do?' Brooks asked. The simplest question sounded dragged out; desperate. 'Did you tell him?'

'I gave him a choice.'

'That all?'

'So far.'

'You hoping he's going to turn himself in?'

It told him that the man in the video clip was still alive, but Thorne had no easy answer to the question. He knew he wanted to see 'Squire' pay for what he'd done, but that was as far as it went. How he paid was a different matter. 'I don't know what he's going to do.'

337

Brooks released a fractured breath, a short groan. 'I wish I knew what your game was,' he said.

'That makes two of us.'

'You could always just arrest him.'

'I've got no evidence.'

'It's there. You know it is.'

'You going to give me time to find it?'

The pause before Brooks spoke again made it clear that he was eager to get on with the job. That 'Squire' didn't have too long to make his decision. 'So, what's the plan then?'

'There really isn't one,' Thorne said.

'You're watching him, I suppose. Waiting for me to come bowling along like an idiot, so you can nick the two of us at the same time.'

Thorne's ambivalence turned to irritation in a second, and he seized on it hungrily. Staring out at the shitty weather and listening to a murderer telling him what he could be doing. What he knew very well he *should* be doing. 'Why the fuck did you send me this stuff? Any of it? You're not stupid, you know it's going to get you caught sooner or later. Sending the messages wasn't just about doing Stuart Nicklin a favour, was it?'

Thorne had to strain to hear the answer. The rain was getting heavier, and Brooks sounded as though he was drifting away. 'I wouldn't piss Nicklin out,' he said. 'The simple fact is, once this is done, I don't care what happens. I get caught, I don't get caught, it's all the same. Prison isn't going to make the future any worse for me, so it's all just a fucking gamble.' There was another long pause before he spoke again; low and expressionless, like interference from another line. A voice coming through the wall. 'I'm happy just to wait and see what happens.'

Thorne heard the click and three sharp tones; listened to dead air for a few seconds. He wasn't exactly happy to wait and see, but he knew he didn't really have a lot of choice.

Kemal was still talking, but he wasn't saying very much.

He may have taken advice from his solicitor, of course, or perhaps it was just the fact that the interview had been interrupted. Either way, five minutes back into it, Thorne could see that the impetus had gone, and he knew it was down to him to get it back.

'You know how we found you, don't you, Hakan?'

'The parking ticket.'

'No, I mean, how we knew that you were the man we should be looking for in the first place?'

Kemal waited.

'Harika told us.' He nodded, smiled. 'Your sister told us that you had killed Deniz Sedat.'

Next to him, Thorne was aware of Kitson stiffening. He knew that she was not wholly comfortable with this approach, that she'd given Harika Kemal certain assurances. But Thorne felt they had to do whatever was necessary.

They'd spoken briefly before Kemal had been led back into the interview room. When Kitson had urged him to tread carefully, Thorne had reminded her that she'd asked for his help. He told her that Kemal was bound to find out that they'd talked to Harika sooner or later and that getting the truth out of him was surely the most important thing.

Kitson hadn't argued. She had seen that Thorne was fired up. She'd looked at him, said, 'Who the fuck was that on the phone?'

It was warm in the interview room. In the silences, Thorne could hear the sound of water rushing through the hot-water pipes; a counterpoint to the rain clattering on to the flat roof above them. He wondered if the other three were sweating as much as he was.

He stared at Hakan Kemal. 'Does that upset you? Your sister coming to us, telling us that you were the man responsible?'

Kemal crossed his arms. He leaned back in his chair and glanced at Gina Bridges as though he'd only just noticed she was there.

'Come on, that must really hurt. That must really piss you off. Christ, I know how I'd feel if it was my sister. Especially as you were the one who was keeping an eye on her. It seems to me that you were the *only* one looking out for her. That's about right, isn't it?

339

You were the one member of the family who genuinely had her best interests at heart.'

A small nod. Thorne could see that Kemal's fists were clenched beneath his arms; pressed against his ribs.

'Do you think Harika betrayed you?' Thorne saw the reaction; glimpsed a tender spot to dig away at. 'Do you think she's taken Sedat's side against you, against your family?'

Kemal began to rock slightly. He opened and closed his mouth.

'Do you think she's disloyal?'

'Yes . . .'

'Do you think she's let you down?'

'She is ungrateful.'

The word had been all but growled out. Thorne took a beat. 'Why do you—?'

'I did it for her.' Kemal was shouting; his fists out in front of him on the table. 'It was because of what he did to her.'

'You killed Deniz Sedat? That's what you're telling us?' Kemal nodded. 'For the tape . . .'

'I killed him.' Quieter again.

Kitson exchanged a glance with Gina Bridges. The solicitor gave a small shrug, as if to say, 'Well done.' Kitson leaned forward. 'Was Sedat abusive towards your sister, Hakan? Are you saying he raped her?'

Kemal looked awkward, kept his eyes on Thorne. 'He did things to her . . . sexually. Unnatural things.'

'I'm not sure I understand,' Thorne said.

'Sodomy.' Kemal grimaced, lowered his voice. 'He sodomised my sister. Sedat was an animal.'

Thorne looked at Kitson. So this was why Hakan Kemal was uncomfortable talking to a woman. He turned back to Kemal. 'I can understand that you were upset, but what Sedat and your sister did is not illegal . . .'

'What *he* did to *her*.'

'Whatever. It's not a reason to kill someone.'

'He was grinning while he told me about it,' Kemal said. 'Standing at the bar in this nightclub, with all his friends gathered around him. Bragging about what he'd done. Leaning in close, stinking of after-shave, and telling me how he bent my sister over and took her. How it hurt her at first, but how she liked it and begged him to do it again. Laughing while he told me, enjoying himself . . .'

'This isn't about your sister at all,' Kitson said. The blood was rising to her face as she spoke. 'This is about you.'

'No . . .'

'You didn't kill Sedat because of what he did to your sister. You killed him because he told you about it. Because he disrespected you.'

Kemal waved his hand, trying to shut her up. 'No, no. He disres-pected *both* of us.'

'*You're* the animal,' Kitson said.

Then it all came pouring out. How Kemal had gone to the Black Horse that night, intent on confronting Deniz Sedat, with a carving knife taped inside his coat. He told them that he'd been planning to kill him in front of his sister, but that he'd taken the chance when Sedat had come out into the car-park alone at the end of the evening.

By now, Thorne and Kitson were convinced that Harika had seen it happen anyway. That she'd come into the car park a little earlier than she'd first claimed and seen her brother leaving the scene; perhaps even witnessed the murder itself.

'I moved in close and looked at him,' Kemal said. 'When the knife was all the way in. I made sure he could see how much *I* was enjoying myself.'

There was plenty of time to get the rest of the details later, and Kitson was on the point of winding things up when Kemal leaned across and began to confer with his solicitor.

Gina Bridges listened, then grimaced, as though she were only asking the question because she was obliged to do so, and already knew the answer. 'Mr Kemal says that he would like to make a deal.'

'I'm very happy for him,' Kitson said.

'He says he has information.'

Thorne smiled politely. 'Tell him to save it up; use it to entertain his cellmate.'

'I know things,' Kemal said. 'Drug deals, places where money gets lost, all sorts. I hear these things from Sedat, from his friends, different people.'

'Not our department,' Kitson said. 'Write it all down and we'll pass it on.' She verbally terminated the interview and switched off the tape.

Bridges gathered her papers together. Thorne stood up.

'What about a murder? That's your department, yes?'

Kitson rolled her eyes at Thorne. 'You've got thirty seconds.'

'A young woman and her son, killed in June. They were run over in Bethnal Green, but it was not an accident.'

Thorne sat down again. He could feel something prickle at the back of his neck. 'Whatever you think you know, Hakan, your timing's bloody awful.'

'I know who killed them . . .'

Kitson winked at Bridges. 'Unfortunately for your client, that's one we've more or less put to bed.'

'I cannot tell you the names of the men in the car,' Kemal said. 'But I know who gave the order.'

'I told you,' Thorne said, 'you're too late. Not only do we know who the man is; he's dead himself.'

Kitson pushed back her chair.

'No, no.' Kemal was waving his hands again. 'He is certainly not dead. Not the man who organised the murder.'

Thorne looked at Kitson. So, maybe Martin Cowans hadn't given the order. But if not him, then it had to have been Tucker or Hodson. Kitson shrugged.

'Go on then,' Thorne said. 'What's his name?'

When Kemal spoke, Thorne felt as though the breath had been punched out of him; as though the air had been sucked out of the room.

He tried to swallow. Couldn't.

Aware of Kitson's eyes on him, of *everyone's* eyes on him, Thorne slowly asked Hakan Kemal to say the name again.

Kemal could see that something was happening. He hesitated, then said, 'Zarif . . .'

THIRTY-FOUR

The speed camera got him doing fifty-five on the Camberwell Road. He swore and slammed his hands against the wheel; like his mood wasn't bad enough already. He put his foot down again to make it through a set of lights, and left it there. He'd keep an eye out for any more cameras, but he certainly wasn't worried about being pulled over. He could easily sort out any jumped-up fucker on traffic duty; was right up for a ruck, if it came down to it.

He turned left at the Green towards Peckham and New Cross.

He always got himself out of the shit; that was what he *did*. Whenever things had got sticky – and they had, plenty of times – he was the one who sorted it. And until a couple of weeks before, until Marcus Brooks turned up, things had been looking pretty good.

The cash from Martin Cowans and others like him; the pubs he drank in for free; the nods and the favours, and the saunas he could drop into for a late-night freebie at the end of a shitty day.

He always sorted it.

He had made the arrangements all those years before, when Tipper had got greedy and needed dealing with; and he had renegotiated an even more lucrative deal with Cowans afterwards. He had been the one to go into Tipper's place and do the necessary. And he had been the one who had found Marcus Brooks. Lined him up nicely. After that, it was only fair that he'd taken a little more than half of whatever had come their way, and Skinner had known better than to argue.

Skinner could usually be talked into most things . . .

Jesus . . . as fast as he was going up the Peckham Road, there was still some boy-racer up his arse. He slammed on the anchors, two, three times for no good reason, until the tosser backed off. Then he floored it again.

Of course, Skinner had been shitting himself after Thorne had been round. Demanding to know what they were going to do; talking rubbish about leaving the country. Cashing in and fucking off.

He gripped the wheel even tighter, thought about the choice Thorne had given him earlier, when he'd called. The option he'd been offered. It wasn't hard to work out what Skinner would have wanted to do, had he still been around.

A week before, there'd been no way of knowing what Skinner might have done; how silly he was likely to get. In the end, there'd only been one sensible option, and it had been easy enough to go in and sort. He'd known very well it would be another body chalked up to Brooks. That he was only saving him the trouble.

Cowans had been calling even before Skinner had started to panic. Him and the rest of those freaks begging for his help, running around like girls while their mates were dropping like flies.

Did he know what was happening?

Did he know why?

They paid him enough, so couldn't he do something about it?

Yeah, well, once he'd found out who was knocking off the bikers, it was fairly obvious why, but he couldn't do a fat lot, except tell them to keep their hairy fucking heads down.

It didn't do them much good, obviously, and it was almost funny, considering how the Black Dogs never had anything to do with Brooks' girlfriend getting done in the first place. That was certainly funny. Cowans getting irate, screaming about how it wasn't fair;

how when he found out who *had* done it, he was going to fucking kill them.

Brooks coming after himself and Skinner though, that was something he hadn't considered.

He could do without the headache, no question, but he'd get it sorted. He wasn't too worried about Brooks; he'd stitched up the toe-rag once already and this time he'd be waiting for him.

Thorne would be even easier to deal with.

He knew that the cocky fucker didn't have anything concrete on him, and he also had a strong suspicion that he wasn't exactly squeaky clean himself. That would be the way to go at him: he could dig up plenty of shit when he had to and he knew exactly how to make it stick.

Then he would offer Tom Thorne a few fucking options of his own.

He swung the car right towards Peckham Rye, then turned into a side street and eventually found a parking space fifty yards from his front door. He'd leave a note on the windscreen of the car outside his house; make sure the owner knew better than to park there again.

The other car turned into the road as he was stepping out. He'd just slammed his door when he saw the lights; was pressing himself back against the door to let the car past when he saw the headlights flick on to main beam and swing fast towards him.

He tried to move but couldn't; knew that he didn't have time.

The car's engine screamed only a little louder than he did, for those few seconds before he was hit. The bumper squealed against the body-work as it took his legs; spun him up and over the bonnet, into the glass, which smashed him into blackness.

Then, final moments in the air; fierce and crowded.

The dull crack of the screen shattering, and his own bones. The car speeding away.

His ex-wife and the two children he never saw.

His dog . . .

'It's me. Just calling to see how things were going really. Ring me when you get in, and we can see which one of us has had a shittier day.'

'Hello, love, hope you're well. Just wondered if you were any the wiser about Christmas . . .'

'If you want to call me later on, that's fine. It doesn't matter if it's late, OK?'

Messages on Thorne's machine when he got home: Louise; Auntie Eileen; Yvonne Kitson.

Thorne hadn't responded to any of them. He didn't want to have any of those conversations; knew he wouldn't be capable. There was only one person he was eager to speak to.

He could barely remember leaving work, the journey home, or walking through the front door and scattering food into a bowl for the cat. He drifted from room to room like someone waking up. He turned the TV on and turned it off again. He stood and stared at bits of the flat as if he'd never seen them before. The way the ceiling met the wall in one corner. The angle of a door striking him as odd and unfamiliar.

He walked around the flat and thought about Arkan Zarif.

Two and a half years before, Thorne had been working on a series of gangland killings; an inquiry which had then widened to include a search for the man who had set fire to a young girl in a playground in 1984.

It had been a case that had cost many more lives by the time it was over, and although a degree of justice had been meted out, the man responsible for most of those deaths had escaped it.

Had perhaps meted out a little of his own.

The Zarif family owned restaurants and minicab companies, but their main income came from elsewhere: extortion; human trafficking; the importation and distribution of heroin. The business was fronted by Memet, Tan and Hassan Zarif, but the decisions were all taken by their father: 'Baba' Arkan Zarif.

Zarif had seen many of those nearest to him die or go to prison, had seen his business suffer through the actions of Thorne and others. But he had taken care to protect himself and had continued to run his unassuming family restaurant: choosing the meat, carefully preparing the diced lamb and the delicately spiced milk puddings. He had remained untouchable.

347

And life, *business*, had carried on as normal . . .

Thorne had gone to see him just once, when the inquiry had all but run its course. He had tried to make it clear that he was not a man who liked leaving loose ends around. He had fronted the old man out, made empty threats and talked about honour.

Later, he had taken steps that led to a man Zarif had agreed to protect being murdered. Then, a month after that, Thorne's father had died in a fire at his home.

Thorne had gone through that conversation with Arkan Zarif many times since. Recalled every smile, every shift of those powerful shoulders.

'I take my business very seriously,' Zarif had said.

Thorne had failed to protect his father, even though he'd known the old man could not look after himself properly. So he had lived with the terrible knowledge that his father's death had been his fault, whether the fire had been accidental or not.

Just the mention of Zarif's name in the interview room had been enough. His mouth had gone dry in a second, and he could taste the sick rising up into his throat. Not knowing what had happened to his father had been bad enough, but whenever Thorne had fantasised about discovering the truth, he had never been able to decide what it was he hoped to find.

Now, he walked around his furniture and waited for whatever was coming. If Kemal was right, Arkan Zarif had destroyed another family; had indirectly wreaked the havoc of grief among many more people. Thorne felt he might finally have been gifted a chance to tie up at least one loose end.

But it was closer to dread than excitement.

Brooks called just before ten o'clock.

'It's finished,' he said.

Thorne knew at once what Brooks meant. The officer he had spoken to earlier that day had made the wrong decision. Or at least had not made the right one quickly enough. Thorne felt no more than if he'd just been told it was going to rain the next day. 'No,' he said. 'It isn't finished.'

'I'm tired. I don't care.'

'You need to listen,' Thorne said. 'You still believe me when I tell you that nobody is listening to these calls, don't you? That there's no trace.'

Brooks finally sighed, as though it hurt to push out the breath. 'I believe you.'

'Good.' Thorne sat down. 'Because this might take a while . . .'

THIRTY-FIVE

Thorne could have made the journey to Green Lanes in his sleep. He'd sat in his car and watched Zarif's restaurant enough times to be familiar with the routine; to know what times people tended to come and go. He knew where to park so that his car would not be seen, and how to get round to the alleyway that ran along the back of all the businesses in the small parade of shops near Manor House Tube station.

It was just after eleven o'clock.

The service entrance to Zarif's restaurant was no more than a small yard off the dimly lit alleyway. Thorne knew which one it was. He could see the grey plastic wheelie-bins from the end of the alley. He had stood in the same spot several times and watched the old man, or occasionally his wife or daughter, bringing out the leftovers at the end of the night, dumping bottles in the recycling buckets, as the ovens cooled down inside, and the last customers were ushered out of the front door.

Thorne knew that this usually happened before eleven-thirty, or a little later on a Saturday. Within the next half-hour, most of the clearing up would have been done. Zarif's wife and daughter would be on their way back to the grand and gated family home in Woodford, leaving the boss to sit quietly alone, as he did every night, with a glass of wine or a strong Turkish coffee.

Contented and complacent. Thinking about the day's takings from the restaurant. From his other, more profitable businesses.

From the end of the alleyway, Thorne watched a skinny cat creep along the top of one of the gates. The animal probably knew just as well as he did when the bins got filled. It had just begun to clean itself when a car alarm started to scream on the main road, and it jumped down and out of sight.

A minute or so later, Thorne saw another figure emerge from a pool of shadow, a few feet from where the cat had been. He knew that the man could see him; that the street-lamp behind cast enough light to make his small wave visible.

The man raised a hand in return, then disappeared as quickly as the cat had done. Thorne stood for another minute, then walked back round to his car to wait.

Forty-five minutes later, he was listening to drops of water falling on to the roof of the BMW from the trees above as he continued to stare across the road.

Watching as customers left, then the single waitress. Figures still moving around inside.

The restaurant was set back on a wide pavement, between an estate agent's and the minicab office. This was another of the family's firms, run by Arkan's eldest son, but Thorne knew all three sons' habits as well as he did their father's. If Memet or his two younger brothers were in there, Thorne knew that they would be ensconced in the back room by now, deep into a high-stakes card game with associates.

He was fairly sure he could get into the restaurant unseen. If all went well, there would be no reason for anyone other than the two people who mattered to know he'd been there.

At around a quarter to twelve, Thorne watched as a dark Mercedes pulled up. Five minutes later, Sema Zarif and her mother, a woman Thorne had never met, hurried out of the restaurant and were driven away. He watched, and remembered what Louise had

351

said: wondering why more of those who had lost loved ones to violence were not driven to it themselves. He could not recall exactly how many times he'd sat where he was now and come close to it himself. To running across the road, and in, and *at* Arkan Zarif. Taking whatever came to hand: a bottle; a glass; one of those knives of which Zarif was so proud.

'I choose *all* the meat,' he had told Thorne once.

Thorne remembered the smile. The shift of those shoulders.

He waited another ten minutes to be sure, then got out of the car.

The area wasn't one he fancied moving into, so Thorne didn't bother checking out any properties as he moved past the estate agent's; walking quickly, keeping close to the window.

When he reached the restaurant and looked inside, he was alarmed to see that Arkan Zarif was staring straight at him, as though he'd been waiting for Thorne to appear. After a second or two, he realised that it was just a trick of the light. Saw that Zarif was actually staring off into space.

Thorne let his breath settle; put his face to the glass and knocked.

Zarif stood up and moved towards the window, curious. Thorne saw the eyes narrow; then, after five or ten seconds, watched them widen as recognition washed across the old man's face.

Thorne felt anger flare in his chest at not being recognised immediately.

Zarif moved to the door and unlocked it. He was smiling when he beckoned Thorne inside, looking at his watch. 'You must be very hungry,' he said.

It wasn't a big place: half a dozen tables, now with chairs tucked in close, and a couple of booths. The assortment of lanterns that dangled from the polished pine ceiling – glass, metal and ceramic – had all been turned out, and the only light came from a lamp behind the small bar, or drifted up from the bottom of the stairs that curled down to the kitchen in the far corner.

Zarif walked slowly back to one of those booths, where he had a bottle waiting and a drink on the go. He squeezed in behind the table and slid across the brown vinyl seat. There was low-level music coming from speakers above the bar: a woman singing, pipes and tablas. A zither, maybe . . .

Thorne sat opposite. He spread his legs, so that his feet would not come into contact with Zarif's beneath the table.

'No food,' Zarif said. 'We're closed for the night.'

'It's not a problem.'

He'd put on a little weight since Thorne had last seen him, but still seemed bulky rather than fat. He was round-shouldered and had stooped as he'd walked. He wore a white shirt, stretched across his gut and tucked into grey trousers. The sleeves were rolled up, black and grey hairs sprouting above the neck of a white vest where the buttons were open.

There was more grey in the hair, too, but it was still full, and oiled back above heavy brows. The jowls were stubbled in white; the thick moustache going the same way. But the eyes were every bit as bright and green as Thorne remembered. He put a hand on the bottle. 'Raki,' he said. 'Lion's milk. You want some?'

Thorne dug into his pocket. 'Not for nothing, I don't.' He took out his wallet. Pulled out a five-pound note.

Zarif fetched a glass from the bar and poured the drink. 'The till is closed. It will have to be for nothing.'

Thorne shrugged but left his money on the table, folded inside a stainless-steel cruet set.

Zarif touched his glass to Thorne's. Said, '*Serefé.*'

Thorne said nothing, but he remembered the toast. Remembered that it meant 'To our honour'. The drink was clear and tasted like cough medicine, though it didn't much matter.

'You keep popping up at the end of my inquiries,' Thorne said. 'It's like not knowing where a stink is coming from, then suddenly finding the dead thing behind a cupboard.'

Zarif brought the glass to his lips; sipped it fast, like it was espresso. 'Is this police business, or personal?'

'It's a murder case.'

353

'Last time I thought it was both, because you were like a dog tearing at something. You remember when we sat in here and talked about names?' He raised a hand, wrote in the air with a thick finger. 'Thorne. Something spiky and difficult to get rid of.' The accent was thick and Zarif searched for the odd word. But Thorne knew very well that he played up a difficulty with the language when it suited him.

'You told me what your name meant, too,' Thorne said. 'Arkan, which means "noble blood", but also means "arse".' Zarif cocked his head. 'That was back when you were putting on the harmless old grandad act. Before I got to know you better.'

'What do you want?'

'You're a very good businessman, no question. I can see why you've done so well for yourself.'

Zarif spread his arms and looked around.

'I don't mean this,' Thorne snapped. 'Don't take me for a cunt.'

'I will try hard not to.'

'It's all about spotting new business opportunities, isn't it?'

'Of course.'

'Working out how to exploit them.'

'A business must expand.' To anyone sitting on an adjacent table, it would have looked as if the older man were enjoying the company and the conversation. 'There is no point otherwise.'

'The Black Dogs were a perfect opportunity.'

'Dogs? Now, I am lost.'

'Relatively new to the drugs game . . . medium-sized. Easy pickings for a firm like yours.'

Zarif said nothing, but Thorne wasn't expecting him to.

Not just yet.

'Even better if you can keep your hands clean,' Thorne said. 'Farm out the dirty work.'

'What exactly do you think I'm going to say?'

Once Zarif's name had been mentioned, the picture had quickly become clearer; and more horrific. In other circumstances, Thorne

354

might have doubted the conclusion he had come to, but he knew better than most what Arkan Zarif was capable of.

Fully fledged gang wars, such as the one Zarif had been engaged in when he and Thorne had first met, were risky enterprises. Any financial advantage gained was often outweighed by unwanted attention from the authorities; by blood feuds that could linger for years afterwards.

So much better if someone else could wage them for you.

Marcus Brooks had been set up six years before by 'Jennings' and 'Squire', and now he was being used again. All Zarif had had to do was give him a motive. A nice, simple one. Once he had arranged to have Angela Georgiou and her son killed, it had been straightforward to get word into Long Lartin, hinting at who had been responsible. Then he had been able to sit back and watch while Brooks sorted out the Black Dogs for him. Created the space for Zarif and his family to step into.

He had wound up Brooks and let him go.

'How did you find Brooks?' Thorne asked.

Even as Zarif was staring blankly back at him, Thorne figured out that it had probably been through an associate in prison; perhaps the same one Zarif had later used to make sure Brooks knew, or *thought* he knew, who had killed his girlfriend and son. Another possibility was that Zarif had someone working within the Black Dogs themselves. This was less likely, but the thought prompted another.

'Christ, you must have been delighted when Brooks started knocking off the coppers for you as well. Getting rid of any "friends" the bikers might have had in the police. A real bonus that, I would have thought.'

Zarif poured himself another drink, three or four fingers. 'Forgive me if I have trouble following all this. Perhaps you should tell me what it is you think I have done.'

'I *know* what you've done.'

'Good for you.' Zarif gently patted his fingers on the tabletop in mock applause. 'The fact remains that you have come here alone and you have shown me no identification. So, whatever you know, or you think you know, I doubt that I am going to be arrested any time soon.'

It was the second time that day that someone had said as much to Thorne. These fuckers seemed to know instinctively when they were really in trouble and when they weren't. Thorne felt a certain grim satisfaction at the thought that the police officer who had told him to 'bring it on' a few hours before was now a lot less cocky than he had been.

He thought that Zarif, too, despite the confident tone, was looking just a little more strained. Or maybe he was just getting drunker. Jumpier.

'I wanted to give you the chance to tell me.'

'Tell you what?'

'Your last chance . . .'

'Tell you that you're dreaming? Tell you to fuck off?'

'About Brooks. About his wife and child,' Thorne said. 'A car that didn't stop.' *A bottle. A glass. One of Zarif's own knives.* 'Anything else you think I might like to know . . .'

The woman's voice from the speakers above the bar was becoming cheerier, the music a touch more upbeat. 'Now, it's time for you to go,' Zarif said.

Thorne slid along the seat, said, 'I need a piss.'

He took his time walking to the stairs, and when he looked back, Zarif was staring the other way, towards the window. Beneath the table, his foot was tapping in time to the tablas.

Thorne went quickly down the stairs, took a few seconds to get his bearings and pushed open the warped, unvarnished door to the tiny toilet cubicle. He smelled damp and disinfectant; something rank, too, and rising, that was coming from himself.

He leaned back against the door and breathed in the stink.

No, it isn't. It isn't finished.

He reached forward and flushed the toilet. Then, while the cistern was still noisily refilling, he stepped out into the narrow corridor. There were boxes stacked against the breeze-block walls and, through a semi-open doorway, he could see the huge gas burners in the kitchen and an L-shape of well-scrubbed steel surfaces.

He took half a dozen steps down to the far end; to a grey, metal door. Gently drew back the bolts, top and bottom.

Tested the handle.

Then Thorne turned and walked back towards the stairs, stopping just for a few seconds on the way to run his hands under the cold tap.

THIRTY-SIX

Though Zarif was still sitting in the booth, still looking in the same direction he had been, Thorne couldn't help wondering if he'd moved. Had he had time to get up while Thorne was downstairs? Maybe use the phone to let someone know Thorne was there?

'When was the last time Health and Safety had a look at your toilets?' Thorne said, stepping back up.

Zarif turned, nodding his appreciation at what they both knew to be a joke. With the family's money and connections, H&S inspections were hardly anything to worry about. Thorne wondered if 'Baba' Arkan Zarif worried about much at all.

Baba, which simply meant 'father' in Turkish. In an organised-crime context, though, it had an altogether more sinister meaning.

Zarif watched as Thorne walked back to the table, then past it, on his way to the door. He pushed himself out of the booth to follow; to show Thorne out and lock the door behind him. 'I'm sorry I could not be more hospitable,' he said.

'I'll live.'

'I hope you think your visit was worth it.'

Thorne stopped at the door, locked it himself, and turned back into the restaurant. 'Remains to be seen . . .'

Zarif froze, then turned quickly at the noise of footsteps on the stairs. His gut wobbled as he was pulled in two directions at once. As he saw the man appear above the white balustrade, and performed a near-perfect double take; a low noise in his throat.

'Someone else wanted a chat,' Thorne said.

'This is not . . . right,' Zarif said. 'You are very fucking crazy.' He was genuinely searching for the words this time; speaking slowly, trying to order his thoughts.

Talking to Thorne, but staring at Marcus Brooks.

It struck Thorne that, like himself, Zarif would never have seen Brooks in the flesh; may not even have had any idea what the man whose life he had turned upside down looked like. But it was clear from the old man's face that he knew exactly who his visitor was.

Brooks' dark hair was longer than it had been in the most recent E-fit, and he had the makings of a decent beard. But his face was even thinner. He had a large spot, or a sore of some kind, on the edge of his top lip, and above dark semicircles the eyes seemed filmed over and far away.

He wore jeans and a faded sweatshirt under a brown puffa jacket. His training shoes were muddy, and he swung a plastic bag from one hand.

Nothing had been planned – not past this point at any rate – and it may just have been that Brooks was following Thorne's lead, but they began to move towards Zarif at much the same moment. Zarif backed towards the booth at which he'd been sitting; stopped at the edge of the table.

He looked at Thorne. 'You know I have friends close by. My sons . . .'

'I know,' Thorne said. 'Don't you have some sort of panic button? You never struck me as the type to scream for help, but you could give it a go.'

Thorne thought that Zarif looked scared; unnerved, certainly. But there was no mistaking the anger. The olive skin of the old man's face darkened further with blood. He pushed back his shoulders.

'You are trespassing.'

'You invited me in,' Thorne said. 'I seem to remember being offered a drink.'

Zarif turned to look at the man he had most certainly not invited.

'The door was open,' Brooks said.

'Seriously fucking crazy.' Zarif shook his head, swallowed hard. 'Maybe I just go to the phone and call the police.' He pointed at Thorne. 'Talk to someone who will deal with you.'

Brooks took another step forward. 'Tell me about Angie,' he said.

Zarif said nothing. His eyes on the bag; on the weight of it. Thorne knew that even if Zarif did not know what Brooks looked like, he must have known exactly what he'd been doing, and how. Up until this moment, Zarif had probably relished every detail.

'He just wants to know,' Thorne said.

'I want the names of the men you sent,' Brooks said. 'Whoever was driving the car.'

'It's a peace-of-mind thing,' Thorne said.

'Did you know Angie would have my son with her?'

'Or was that another bonus?'

'Was it *planned*?'

Zarif was stock-still, but his eyes flicked rapidly between the two of them.

'I should imagine so,' Thorne said. 'Families have never really been off-limits with you, have they, Baba?'

'Did you plan to kill them both?'

Zarif shook his head.

Thorne leaned back against the bar. 'No, "don't know"? Or no, "won't tell"?'

'Fuck you,' Zarif said, equally casual.

Brooks hefted the bag into his hand. 'Doesn't matter either way.'

'And fuck you, too . . .'

Thorne pushed himself away from the bar and walked behind it. 'If

360

that's as much as you've got to say for yourself, there's no point hanging around, is there?' He looked across at Brooks. The exhaustion was scored in lines across his face; but now Thorne could see hunger there, too. 'I'll leave you to it, then . . .'

'Sounds good,' Brooks said.

Thorne scanned the shelves above him, searching for the CD player. Once he'd found it, he turned up the volume. The woman was laying it on thick; the drummer working overtime.

'Where are you going?' Zarif asked.

Thorne didn't answer, enjoying the fear he'd heard in the question. He nodded his head in time to the music as he walked back around the bar, and away past Zarif, towards the stairs.

'You have to stop now, and think how foolish you are being.'

Trying to look unconcerned, while his heart smashed against his chest . . .

'You are too smart to do this.'

Ignoring the noise as he stepped down: the shouting and the swearing; the sounds of a man losing control. Focusing instead on the voice of the woman; the notes of her song rising to a perfectly pitched scream of joy, or agony, as he walked quickly down the stairs, and out through the grey, metal door.

He took his time walking along the alleyway to the street; then back on to the main drag. It wasn't far short of one in the morning, but there was still plenty of traffic on Green Lanes. Drivers heading north towards Turnpike Lane and beyond, or south towards the City.

Thorne watched the cars, cabs and lorries go past, and wondered how many of their occupants felt part of anything; were really connected to others around them. There were communities in London, tightly knit and isolated pockets, where it was possible to feel as though the people next door gave a shit. But it was also a city in which a copy of the *Evening Standard* could shield you from almost anything.

Where death – violent death, certainly – had become part of the city's fabric, like the extortionate house prices and the impossibility of parking.

361

Where life expectancy in boroughs like Islington, Camden and Haringey could be as much as ten years less in some parts than it was in others.

Where people like Arkan Zarif could make plans and grow fat.

Thorne walked slowly past the front of the estate agent's and stopped for a second time outside the window of the restaurant. He could see the bottle and the glass on the table, hear the music from inside. The place looked empty now. He presumed that Brooks had either moved Zarif into the room at the back or taken him downstairs. He wondered if he had been thinking about the noise.

'Sounds good,' he'd said before Thorne had walked out. He'd looked as though he'd meant it.

Thorne turned from the window, feeling empty, and OK about it. He had decided the first time round that where Zarif and others like him were concerned, his moral compass would have to be . . . adjusted. He had a line, of course, same as everyone else, and there were people who had forced him into stepping over it more than once.

Psychopaths, sadists, users of children.

But Arkan Zarif had fucked with Thorne's view of the world; with his grasp of what was just and decent. Had redefined it . . .

A squad car raced past on blues-and-twos. Thorne blinked and saw Louise's face; flushed as it might be after love-making, or in temper.

He heard her voice, and his own.

And how bent does what you've been doing make you? Or what I did last night make me?

We haven't murdered anyone.

The image dissolved, drifted, and he walked on, happy enough. When it came to Arkan Zarif, getting the right result was the only thing that mattered.

Waiting, Thorne looked at his watch many times. It was seventeen minutes from when he'd left the restaurant, to the moment when his phone rang.

His old mobile phone.

He took it from his pocket but didn't answer. Let it go to voicemail.

Marcus Brooks, calling the number he'd been given. Saying what Thorne had told him to say.

Thorne listened to the message, knowing that he was not the only one that would be doing so, then walked back behind the parade of shops and down towards the service entrance.

He met Brooks at the end of the alleyway.

'What did he say?' Thorne asked.

The light from the streetlamp made Brooks look even more jaundiced. 'He said "please". Not for too long, though.' He carefully handed Thorne his prepay mobile. The one Thorne had left behind on the counter when he had turned up the volume on the CD player. The one which Brooks had then picked up.

Thorne looked at the screen. The phone's voice recorder function was still running, as it had been for the last twenty-odd minutes.

'The names of the men who ran Angela and Robbie over are on there,' Brooks said. He looked down at his training shoes for a second. 'And the men who set fire to your father's house.'

A lurch in the stomach like a spasm of indigestion. Rage and relief cancelling each other out. Nothing more, for now.

'I made sure he knows we've got it,' Brooks said. 'He's not going to be telling anyone we were there.'

Thorne nodded. 'We should get going.'

Brooks swung the plastic bag as they walked back on to Green Lanes and across to where Thorne had left the BMW. Brooks climbed into the back. Thorne pressed a hand into the small of his back to help him inside, then stood, leaning against the car. Stared at the phone for a few seconds before he slipped it into his pocket.

'Thank you' seemed inappropriate. The stuff about being under arrest would come later.

He took the car across the main road and pulled it round; drove at walking pace past the window of the restaurant. Arkan Zarif was shuffling slowly, *painfully*, towards the glass on his backside. It looked as though something had been stuffed into his mouth. Napkins, Thorne guessed.

'You don't know how much I wanted to kill him,' Brooks said.

Thorne flicked his eyes to the rear-view, then back to the figure that was beginning to howl and bang on the restaurant's window.

He knew very well.

It had not been easy to convince Brooks, or himself, but eventually it had been agreed that they should do whatever it took to get the necessary information, but no more. That Zarif would suffer far more behind bars. That they were being anything but merciful.

'You've no . . . fucking idea,' Brooks mumbled.

Thorne eased the car from the kerb and pointed it north, letting the thoughts settle in his mind as he picked up speed. Most of the story was already straight, and would be simple enough to tell. He would put the rest of it together on the way back to Colindale.

Marcus Brooks was asleep on the back seat by the time the car reached the first set of lights.

PART FOUR

'DELETE'

THIRTY-SEVEN

The Kard Kop checked, then raised over the top of the last player left
in the hand. The thirty seconds ticked away, but at the death the other
player folded what were almost certainly the winning cards, and, with
nothing better than a pair of nines, The Kard Kop took down the pot.

'I won,' Louise shouted. 'Forty dollars.'

Thorne walked across, looked at the screen as the next hand was
dealt. Louise got a jack and a four, unsuited. She quickly folded and
sat out of the game.

'How much are you up tonight?' Thorne asked.

'A hundred and eighty-two dollars,' Louise said.

'Fuck . . .'

Not only had Louise picked up the game ridiculously quickly, she
was already a better player than Thorne. Her game was aggressive
without being reckless. And she was better at sussing out the real characters of the players around the table, able to see past their cartoon
images.

She read them quicker than Thorne had read Marcus Brooks.

Better than he had read the police officer who had once called himself Squire.

Most importantly of all, win or lose, Louise knew when to walk away from the table.

'You going to play for a bit?'

Thorne shook his head, so Louise logged off; wandered through to the kitchen to get the food started. Hendricks was bringing a new man for dinner, and Louise was cooking pasta.

Thorne followed and leaned against the kitchen door. 'What do we know about this bloke of Phil's?'

'He's a "cardiologist with a nice arse",' Louise said. 'That was Phil's first description anyway.'

'That it?'

'He seems nice.'

'You've met him?'

'Only the once. Listen, relax.'

'I *am* relaxed.'

'You're friends,' Louise said. 'You'll sort it out. If it's any consolation, Phil's just as nervous about seeing you.'

'I'm fine.'

Shitting himself . . .

Thorne wandered back into the living room and across to the shelves of CDs, Louise's and his own. He was feeling uncomfortable in a brand-new shirt from M&S. He hadn't been bothered to iron out the creases. 'Shall I stick some music on?' he shouted.

There was a clatter of pans from the kitchen. 'What?'

Thorne took out a copy of *Wrecking Ball* by Emmylou Harris, put the disc into the player, and scanned through to the Lucinda Williams song that was his favourite track on the album.

Louise appeared briefly in the doorway. 'I should have started the sauce fifteen minutes ago,' she said. She nodded towards the computer. 'You lose all track of time once you're into the game.' She jabbed scissors into a pack of tortellini and turned back into the kitchen.

Humming along with the song . . .

It was halfway through December. Three weeks since Thorne had made his arrest; since Marcus Brooks had been charged with the murder of Raymond Tucker.

Brooks had made a full confession.

He had detailed the killings of Ricky Hodson and Martin Cowans, and while denying any involvement in the murder of Paul Skinner, he *had* confessed to the attempted murder of another senior police officer. DCI Keith Bannard was on life support in St Thomas's Hospital. Had been since being struck by the car Marcus Brooks had been driving, shortly before Brooks had telephoned DI Tom Thorne, leaving a message to say where he was and expressing a desire to turn himself in.

No mention was made of an attack on the owner of a Turkish restaurant on the same evening as his arrest . . .

Louise carried through a handful of cutlery and dumped it on the small, pine table. Thorne got up from the sofa and began to lay out the place settings.

Through friends on Serious and Organised – all of whom had expressed amazement at the extent of Bannard's criminal activities – Thorne had learned that Arkan Zarif had been discovered in the early hours of the morning by one of his sons, who had quickly called an ambulance. The police had been summoned by hospital staff, but Zarif had insisted that it had all been his own fault. Both of his knees had been smashed in a nasty fall, he said, after having had a little too much to drink.

Hearing this, Thorne had remembered Louise's drug dealer, the one who had kidnapped himself and chopped off his own fingers; had thought about how much damage people seemed capable of doing to themselves in extreme circumstances. It was not an observation he had felt able to share with Louise, of course, however much she might have enjoyed it.

He thought it was for the best. He didn't want to get her involved. And it was not like he had actually lied . . .

The same old shit.

Laying out the knives and forks, Thorne thought about the prepay handset, locked away safely back at his flat; the confession preserved for posterity on its voice recorder. He knew that while it was in his possession, Zarif would not tell anyone what had happened in his restaurant that night, but he also knew it could be a very dangerous piece of insurance. He could never feel completely safe until Zarif was put away for good, and he would use what he'd been given to make sure that happened.

Without revealing his source, he had already begun feeding the information, little by little, through to those he could trust at S&O. Many of those subsequently questioned and arrested would refuse to cooperate, of course, but Thorne knew that eventually one of them would take the deal that was offered. That Arkan Zarif would pay for what he'd done in the proper way, without the evidence extracted by Marcus Brooks ever needing to see the light of day.

That Angela and Robbie Georgiou, and Jim Thorne, and God knows how many others, could rest a little more peacefully.

Thorne poured out wine for himself and Louise; took a decent-sized slurp and topped up his glass.

There had been no date set for Brooks' trial, nor for that of Hakan Kemal, but neither defence nor prosecution in either case seemed in much of a hurry. With both as close to foregone conclusions as you could get, it was unlikely that Sam Karim would be running a book on either.

Two defendants, each on trial for murder, but only one who seemed concerned about the outcome.

Thorne had spent many hours questioning his prime suspect after the arrest, and knew that Marcus Brooks was content to go back to prison. That it was perhaps the only future that made any sort of sense for him. Thorne could recall few cases that had absorbed and disorientated him as much; but equally, he could not think of too many that had been cleared up with so little fuss.

He had settled into the abnormally pleasurable rut of pre-trial preparation; had caught three more murder cases; had got back to work.

He had told Eileen that he and Louise would be coming to her on Boxing Day, if that was OK.

He had not returned the missing training shoe he had promised to Anthony Yashere.

Thorne picked up his glass and walked into the kitchen, while Emmylou's voice soared above a wash of guitar and Neil Young's keening harmonica, telling someone exactly what they'd lost when they left this sweet old world.

He watched Louise at the cooker for a minute, took a swig of wine and said, 'I don't think it's a *completely* stupid idea.'

'I know.'

'I just can't promise to be any good at it.'

She nodded without turning round, kept on stirring.

'Plus, there's the whole age thing,' he said. 'By the time any kid's a teenager, I'll be pushing sixty. I'll be fucked.' Another swig. 'I'm *already* fucked.'

'Nobody's arguing.'

'So long as you know.'

She turned then and laid down the spoon; leaned against the edge of the worktop. 'Look, I know you think you'll be shit, and you don't think you've got any patience and whatever, but I'm really not bothered. And I'm not convinced you'll even *make* sixty, so I wouldn't worry too much about that.' She took a step towards him. 'The side of you that still cares about that old man, that got upset telling me about it, that's the side I'm interested in. That's why I know you'll be fine. Better than fine . . .'

Another step, and he opened his arms as she reached him. It was only for a few seconds, though, before she eased away again, and went back to check the sauce wasn't boiling.

Thorne watched her flick the kettle on. Saw her pour oil then salt into a pan to cook the pasta.

There are other sides, he thought.

EPILOGUE

The Vulnerable Prisoners Wing didn't house too many prisoners, with no more than sixty heading down to the servery come meal-time. It was certainly a more orderly process than that taking place elsewhere in the prison. But whatever the size of the queue at the hot-plate, Nicklin always wanted to be first.

He hated waiting, watching while others were served before him. He imagined that they were getting more than their fair share, that he would get second best when his turn came. He'd always been the same way when it came to food. With any of his appetites, come to that.

Dinner was dished out between six and seven, but Nicklin had been there since a quarter to. Clutching his tray and listening to the kitchen staff making banal conversation behind the metal shutter.

He banged on the shutter at one minute past. There were a dozen more in the queue behind him by now.

'Stop pissing in the soup and open up, will you?'

Laughter from the kitchen, and from behind him. 'It's the meatballs you should be worried about,' someone said.

The shutter was raised and Nicklin moved forward, taking his dinner in silence. Lasagne and chips. A pudding, as usual – apple crumble on a Tuesday – and two slices of bread. Orange juice and bottled water.

'Nice today,' said the fat rapist in chef's whites.

Nicklin moved away from the hot-plate while the ex-magistrate behind him said something sarcastic about Michelin stars, and the chef told him where he could stick them.

He carried the tray up the two flights of metal stairs to his cell, nudged open the door and sat down at his desk to eat. He opened the orange juice, took off the plastic lid that barely kept the food lukewarm.

Fucking lasagne . . .

He wasn't in the best of moods anyway; hadn't been since he'd heard that Marcus Brooks had been caught. Since he'd heard that Tom Thorne's queer friend had not been among those Brooks had been charged with killing.

It had taken the excitement, such as there was, out of his day. Left him with nothing to root for when the cell door clicked open first thing; to smile about come lights-out. There were only basic pleasures left now. Of the flesh and of the belly; limited as they both were.

He poked his fork through the crust of hardened pasta and fished around, then caught movement from the corner of his eye and looked up. A prisoner stood in the doorway, staring.

'What?'

The man shrugged. Askins: a druggie who'd touched up a fifteen-year-old girl. Not someone Nicklin made a habit of passing time with.

'Why don't you just fuck off?' Nicklin said. He took a mouthful of the mince. 'Freak somebody else out—' He stopped suddenly and cried out, spitting a string of blood down on to his plate and reaching into his mouth for the piece of glass.

'It's a message,' Askins said.

Nicklin swore and spat, lifting up the stiff sheet of pasta and pushing his fork through the watery mince. The tines clicked gently against each sauce-coated sliver. He looked up, pale and open-mouthed, at the man in the doorway.

Askins was smiling as he turned away. 'From someone with very long arms . . .'

ACKNOWLEDGEMENTS

Gangs and *Gangland Britain* by Tony Thompson have once again been an invaluable source of information, but on this occasion I am indebted to Tony personally, for his time, good advice and worryingly detailed insights into the workings of biker gangs.

From the Met, I must once again thank Detective Chief Inspector Neil Hibberd, and I am especially grateful to Sergeant Georgina Barnard for her endless patience and the information that got me over a great many brick walls.

Most of the best stories are hers.

I also have to thank Anne Collins from the Crown Prosecution Service, Victoria Jones from HMP Birmingham and, as always, any number of comedians for the liberties I have taken with their names.

If I was as lucky at poker as I have been in more important matters, I wouldn't have to write for a living; no author could wish for an editor or an agent any better than Hilary Hale or Sarah Lutyens. On the subject of poker, I must assure those closest to me that the hours spent playing online were purely in the course of research, and send out a greeting to my real-time friends: The Admiral, The Junkie, Bagels, El

Guapo, The Painter and Special Boy. And yes lads, I know that poker is *very* important . . .

Thanks to Ursula Mackenzie, Alison Lindsay, Nathalie Morse, David Kent, Robert Manser, Tamsin Kitson, Andy Coles, Miles Poynton, Melanee Winder, Richard Kitson, Roger Cazelet, Thalia Proctor, Terry Jackson, Duncan Spilling, Melanie Rogers, Nicola Hill, David Shelley and everyone else at Little, Brown for their support, enthusiasm and hard work.

And to those that are always here: Paul, Alice, Wendy and Michael.